HAVEN

A FANTASY NOVEL

BROKEN WINGS DUET
BOOK 2

S. E. WENDEL

Lady Maddalena Montcaer is the daughter of the two most celebrated knights in the kingdom of Vagora. Following in their footsteps, she trains her whole life to be a knight. Once earning her spurs, she serves under Crown Prince Arion in the newest war against the avian kingdom to the east. On campaign, Lena and Prince Arion become intimate, and it's because of his feelings for her that he sends her home, away from the front.

Lena takes on a street urchin, Alixandre, as a squire and together they go to a southern lord's demesne. Upon discovering abuses by Lord Balderak on women in his demesne, Lena confronts him, and in the fight, cuts off his hand. For this, she is exiled to an isolated mountain castle in the north called Finhöln to guard a single prisoner—Bel.

Prince Arubel Adiiron is a second son of the Adiiron dynasty of avian sovereigns. The often overlooked spare to his much older brother, King Maddok, Bel grows up longing to prove himself. Finally given the chance to go on campaign with his brother, Bel's mistake while scouting ahead allows a human ambush to surprise their party. Maddok is killed in the skirmish and Bel captured. His older cousin Dartegn becomes king.

Bel spends the next ten years in captivity at Finhöln, his right wing kept broken, and is forced to translate avian documents for the human King Artemian. He befriends the deaf cook of Finhöln, Pol, but otherwise leads a lonely existence, avoiding the various wardens of Finhöln who punish the slightest infraction. After learning of the fall of his brother's capital city of Aeriand, Bel decides he must escape and begins training again, waiting for an opportunity.

Neither is what the other expects in a warden or prisoner. Lena tries to make the best of her sentence and help the nearby village, though her efforts are often rebuffed. Dismayed by the state of Finhöln, Lena comes to see both Bel's treatment and her own sentence as unjust. Bel forms a reluctant admiration for his noble new warden, but that doesn't stop him from attempting to run. During his escape, he comes across Lena apprehending a criminal in the woods and helps her after she's wounded. They come to an agreement that Bel will continue training and Lena won't report his escape, and when her sentence is up, she'll turn a blind eye to him trying again.

Within this truce, friendship and then affection grows between Lena and Bel. When Alix intercepts a letter from Prince Arion for Lena, asking her to return to the capital, Alix and Bel decide to burn the letter, believing it's too dangerous for Lena to leave her post. Lena and Bel become lovers, spending the rest of winter together.

When spring arrives, so does Prince Arion, come to retrieve Lena. Feeling she has no choice, she leaves with Arion back to the south. Before she goes, Lena rebreaks Bel's right wing, resetting the original bad break that was left to heal incorrectly.

Back at her parents' academy of Lindenfaire, Lena decides to stay on with her father rather than go with Arion to the capital to plead her case in person, for fear of what King Artemian will do. Her mother soon arrives to berate her for this, insisting she catch up with Arion. Lena learns that her sentence was a plot by the king and others to get her away from Arion and stop his growing attachment to her. Tired of being manipulated, Lena decides to do what she thinks is right. With Alix's encouragement and support, she returns to Finhöln to free Bel.

Meanwhile, Bel is under constant scrutiny from Captain Joran, head of the guard to Prince Arion, who stayed behind to refortify Finhöln. When a message from Bel's old mentor Eamon is intercepted, Bel attempts to escape but his wings aren't healed enough to support flight, and he's recaptured.

Lena sneaks into Finhöln, and with Pol's help, locates Bel in the dungeon. She frees him, and after a fight with Joran, they escape with Alix into the forest and to freedom.

And now...

I

This was Bel's first time lost in a forest. The earth beneath him was rich with dampness and smelled like all the growing things that had come before and were to come. Dew collected at the tips of his hair and the pine needles, the air thick with mist. It was as if a veil stood between each and every tree, leading to new worlds just beyond.

He'd never truly understood how dense and how tall trees could be. There were no straight paths in the forest; the trees decided the path, sometimes even blocking out the sun with their green arms so that all there was to determine direction was luck and a bit of wit.

Between the fog and the forest, pleasure and uncertainty warred inside him. Though he'd spent the last ten years confined to a castle in these very mountains, he hadn't truly felt like he or Castle Finhöln were part of the forest. The trees were always *over there*, away from him, somehow smaller even if they towered above the castle turrets. They were inaccessible when confined as he'd been to the castle grounds, and may as well have been of a different world.

Nothing that reached so far into the sky nor that went on to rival the horizon as the forest did could be anything less than spectacular. But Bel was also avian, a creature of skies, heights, and horizons. It unnerved him a little, being unable to see far in the haziness of the mist, even with his avian eyesight meant for distances further than any human could hope to see.

Any avian worth their feathers also knew what a hazard it was to fly in a forest; he'd proven that truth a fortnight ago in a desperate attempt to escape his prison. His wings hadn't been ready, and the treetops had grabbed him like human hands to pull him back down. He still ached with the aftermath; a broken arm and wing and bruised ribs. All had been reset and were mending, but Bel could still hear the *crack* of branches and bones as he'd fallen.

A shiver pulled him from his waking doze, lulled there by the steady sway of the warhorse he rode and the meandering of his thoughts.

Well, he supposed, the fall hadn't been all bad. He still had the bruises and breaks and scrapes from it, and the beating the humans gave him for trying, but in the end, he couldn't regret it. Falling out of the sky that day meant he was there when Lady Maddalena Montcaer came back for him.

Before him on the horse, Lena shivered and grumbled low in her throat. Small hairs had escaped the ruthless braid she'd plaited earlier that morning, curling in the damp air. The exposed skin of her face wore a sheen from the mist, and her lips had turned red in the cold.

Bel gladly slid his arms into the slits of her cloak to draw her back into his body. Tucked against his chest, his right wing slithered out from under his oilskin cloak to wrap around her shoulders. It fluffed up at suddenly being in the cold air, but Lena sighed happily, releasing a puff of steam.

She tilted her head to the side to rub a cheek on the downy feathers lining the crook of his wing before sinking her face up to her nose in the feathers. Her breath tickled the barbs, and then it was Bel who shivered.

In the days since she'd come for him, saved him from the bowels of the castle and stolen him away in the night, Lena had been on edge. They had no real heading except for east, away from Finhöln and the humans who'd imprison him again until the end of his days. It was by her wits that they'd made it so deep into the thick forest blanketing the northern mountains; when the sun was too weak to follow through the fog, she used moss and lichen to guide their way. She knew which streams to drink from and when it was safe to light a fire.

She knew how to survive out here, how to keep herself and him and Alix alive. And it impressed him no end.

He hugged her closer, as close as he could, and still wished it could be closer. Skin to skin. More. He pressed his lips to the top of her head in a human kiss, feeling the dampness of her hair and breathing in her scent. He lingered, burying his nose in an *ashita*, the sign of deep affection between lovers for his people.

The gratitude he had for this female, this human knight, was beyond measure. It swelled in his chest, aching bittersweetly, almost more than his battered ribs.

He felt when her back eased, accepting the comfort and warmth he offered, and she melted into him. It always felt like something of a triumph, earning a small measure of softness from Lena. He knew what it meant for her to have chosen him, to have stolen him, and to have to keep all three of their little odd band alive—it weighed on her. Dark circles ringed her eyes even though she claimed she slept, and though it was always a point with her to sit up straight, he saw the way her back wanted to bow with weariness.

He could hold her up, wanted to carry that weight.

Her head thumped back onto his shoulder and she let out a long breath. Her eyes closed, long lashes fanning against her cheeks. Bel kissed her temple, her cheek, her neck, and she grinned.

"Where are we going today?" he asked.

"Further east," she teased, eyes unopened.

"You said that yesterday."

"And it's still true today."

"Well *no one* said *anything* about fog!" Alix pulled alongside them, what he could see of her face beneath that massive scarf of hers scrunched and disgruntled. Those jade eyes cut between the two of them, and Lena's back stiffened, putting a few inches between them and forcing him to unwrap his arms from around her middle.

He shot the squire a look, and the girl fired a nastier one right back.

Though small for fifteen—Bel could probably lift her with just his broken arm easily—her spirit was as big as her fluffy black hair. The humans had a word, *spitfire*, he thought it was. Yes, she looked ready to spit fire.

Alix, he'd discovered, wasn't friendly in the morning.

"That's a child of the capital for you," Lena said, though she sounded more tired than teasing now. "Weather doesn't exist there."

"They were smart to put the capital somewhere warm," Alix grumbled. "And it's not really the cold, it's the damp." She pulled the scarf from her head, revealing the frizzy mess of her hair. Usually it hung in shoulder-length curls of inky black, but in the damp of the morning, it frizzed around her in a staticky halo. She looked like a grumpy kitten more than ever.

"The fog will burn off by lunch," said Lena diplomatically. Bel knew she was hoping to distract the squire with the temptation of stopping for food. "And it won't last forever; once spring truly sets in here, and both the air and the mountain warm, it won't fog in the morning."

"We're still going to be lost in the forest by then?"

Lena's mouth drew thin. "We aren't lost."

She ground her heels into Yvain, the great gray beast of a warhorse she and Bel rode, and continued on through the trees at a faster clip.

Why they needed to go faster, Bel couldn't guess. As far as he knew, they still didn't have a heading. Not lost, but directionless.

Perhaps that was why Lena's shoulders remained stiff through the morning. The fog and endless trees made it seem as though they'd gone nowhere despite moving, and not having a path only made it worse.

But Bel couldn't complain. So long as the direction they moved was away from Finhöln, he was content. He was with Lena again and escaping the humans who would send him south, to their capital of Highclere, where he'd rot under the keen eye of the human King Artemian and be forced to sell his people's secrets for survival.

Soon, he'd have to bring up the need to get back to his people. He'd worked as a translator for the human king for most of his imprisonment, copying the stories and histories of avians for humans who wanted to use that very heritage to annihilate them. But Bel had made critical, purposeful errors, hoping to buy the avians time, confuse the humans, but mostly not be the reason for the downfall of his people.

He needed to share what he knew with his cousin, Dartegn. The avian king. The male who hated him most in the world. His guts churned in unease at the thought.

But for now, he was content for Lena to lead them away from immediate danger. They'd find their heading somewhere, somehow. Probably once the fog broke up.

⸺ ◆ ⸺

After stopping to water the horses, Bel switched from sitting with Lena to riding with Alix. It was practically like riding on his own, the girl took up so little room. He'd need to learn this, he suspected. He liked horses, had always looked after those that came with his various wardens, but trying to ride one never occurred to him. He liked riding with Lena, but it was a burden on the horses to bear two riders, even for a beast as big and strong as Yvain.

Mostly, though, he switched to help keep Alix warm. For all that she hated her hair frizzing in the damp, the girl actually hadn't complained much, not about the travel rations, not about sleeping on the damp ground, not about the long hours in the saddle. Bel had certainly hmphed and grumbled about that last one. Lena and Alix had both snorted with giggles watching him walk bow-legged after the first full day of riding.

He'd been touched that not just Lena had come back for him, but Alix too. He doubted Lena wanted to put the girl in danger, so Alix must have insisted she come along. She was his friend, this little scrap of a squire, and it tugged at his heart when he noticed she was cold. She hid it well under that scarf and attitude, but when they'd been long in the saddle, the wet of the mist settling to the roots of their hair, Alix grew cold.

It was the least he could do to make her less miserable. Plus, the less miserable Alix was, the less miserable he and Lena were.

As Lena trotted on ahead on Yvain, Bel drew his wing around Alix. She made a happy noise and stroked one of the feathers.

"I wish I had a pair of these. A down cloak, whenever you want. And to fly!"

Bel grinned. "Well, mine can do one of those."

"Oof," Alix laughed, shooting him a mock wince. "Don't worry, she'll have you on a training regimen once you're healed up. You'll be strong enough in no time. And I'll even help push you off the cliff when you're ready." She winked. "Think of it as a second first flight."

"Thanks," he guffawed. "Nice to know I need to watch my back around steep drop-offs."

Alix arched a cheeky brow at him and pointedly looked around. "We're pretty high up now."

"If I go down, I'm taking you with me, little squirrel."

She huffed in mock-offense. "I'm not nearly vicious enough to be a squirrel. A fox maybe."

"More like a—"

Lena burst from the mist like a wraith, Yvain's hooves throwing up clods of earth. Alix's horse shivered and laid its ears flat, shifting nervously as Alix reined her to a sudden stop.

Bel tightened his wing around Alix, his heart *thump-thumping* in his chest.

"What is it?" he asked as Lena drew alongside them.

She looked over her shoulder, the vein in her neck visibly pulsing and her cheeks flushed bright pink.

"A camp," she gasped, "just ahead, there's a hunter's camp."

2

Lena knew this had been too easy. Yes, getting Bel out of Castle Finhöln hadn't been without its challenges—she still winced to remember the face of Captain Joran, a man she'd once so admired, as she and Bel had held him down until he lost consciousness—but in the days since, they'd come across nothing but birds, foxes, deer, and the occasional badger. No pursuers, no Captain Joran, not even a bear.

Too easy.

Well, that ended now.

The camp was a small one but established. From the number of coals in the fire pit and the way undergrowth had been scraped away or trampled told her the hunters had been here for some time. And in the thickness of this blasted fog, she'd nearly been in it before she realized what she'd found. Thank Matella and all Her Maidens no one was there; the firepit had been cold and the tents and bedrolls all tucked away. She reckoned it was near midday and easily could have interrupted their lunch.

And led Bel right to them.

Goddess, that'd been too close. She clutched the reins tighter to keep her hands from shaking.

She hated this anxiousness knotting inside her, growing and tightening the further into the forest they went. Even though every day they put between them and Finhöln was a good thing, every day they didn't see or hear Joran and his knights in pursuit a win, she couldn't help the growing pit of dread in her stomach.

She was Lady Maddalena Montcaer, daughter of Lady Margot and Sir Warrek, former royal guard to Crown Prince Arion, and knight of the realm to King Artemian IV.

None of that meant anything anymore.

All she had out here was her training, her wits, and a bag of coin she'd taken from her father's estate of Lindenfaire. There were no friends, no allies, no safe harbor. She'd forfeited those things and her very knighthood the morning she rode out of Lindenfaire to save Bel.

But she didn't regret it. She couldn't, especially when she watched his world expanding with every mile they made. He took everything in with wonderment and quiet awe, and his smiles came more and more easily. Outside Finhöln, the world was so different, almost new to him. More than once she'd watched him pick up something from the forest floor—a twig, a pine needle, a broken eggshell—and turn it about in his hands, taking in the textures, the scent, the colors. He'd been delighted when pine sap and oils rubbed off on his fingers as he inspected a handful of pine needles, leaving their scent on his hands for hours. Freedom looked good on him as he relearned all his senses and experienced the world again. She wanted that for him so desperately, wanted to give him all the time he needed and all the experiences he wanted.

She had to protect that chance, had to keep all of them safe. They were fugitives now, without recourse, vulnerable and easy prey for strange men haunting the forest. They needed to—

Alix slithered off the saddle, all fluid limbs as she unwound the bulky scarf from her neck. She replaced it with the thin hood of her cloak, shadowing her face, and all Lena could see when Alix smiled up at her was the white of her teeth.

"What do you think you're doing?" Lena hissed. She flexed her thighs and Yvain stepped Alix's way.

"Gonna go check it out. See what I can...find." She waggled her fingers.

Lena pointed a threatening finger at her. "No. You're not stealing from hunters and you're certainly not skipping into their camp to do it."

"*First*," Alix argued, "I'm not going to skip, I'm going to skulk, there's a difference. Second, they're definitely bandits. Poachers, maybe. No one's all the way out here for a good reason." She waved between the three of them to emphasize her point. "I guarantee they've stolen from other people, so really, this is comeuppance. And *third*—" She held up a finger when Lena began to protest. "No one's in the camp, so no one's going to see me."

Lena worked her jaw, desperate for a reason to counter any of those points. Why did Alix always have to be right about the seedy characters they came across?

She looked to Bel for help, but he just shrugged.

"Figure out which way they went today," she finally relented. "We'll skirt around the opposite way and hope they don't find our tracks fresh."

With an evil little grin, Alix scuttled off into the brush, disappearing through the mist. Lena's heart gave a lurch in her chest.

A hand gripped hers and squeezed. "She'll be fine," Bel whispered. "They aren't nearby, we'd hear them."

She nodded stiffly and turned Yvain south. "Stay here. I'm going to scout that way."

"Just stay here?"

She looked up at his tone. "You'll be fine. Here, just…" She snatched the reins Alix had dropped and showed him how to keep the horse, Miri, in place. "She's not trained for stealth. I'll be back in a minute."

Gently prodding Yvain with a knee, they set out south. From the corner of her eye, she thought she saw Bel open his mouth to argue. She also thought she heard an annoyed huff out of him. But then the mist swallowed him and the horses, unnerving her, and she urged Yvain on so that they could get back quicker.

When they made it due south of camp, Lena tapped Yvain's flanks once, twice, three-four quick. He slowed, hooves softly meeting the giving earth, and Lena slowed her breathing to match his.

She had just enough light to see the ground beneath them if she leaned down, so she trusted Yvain to keep a quiet, easy path while she grasped the saddle pommel and slid down his side. Balanced on one stirrup and holding herself up by the pommel, Lena watched the ground for any sign of the hunters, daring just one footprint to show itself.

Tall ferns brushed her cheek, and Yvain came to a sudden stop.

Righting herself, Lena peered over Yvain's ears into a wide clearing. The mist was thinner here, revealing an open patch of leafy ferns and moss-blanketed boulders. Small blue flowers the color of dusk before a storm peaked out between the feathery leaves, and Lena had the thought this place would be magical at night, with the tree canopy open to the moon.

She almost called for Bel, wanting to show and share this with him, but held her tongue. It was beautiful, but it was too open, too exposed. Though it would only take a minute or two to pass through, the whole time they'd be easily spotted from the trees.

Resigned, Lena took a deep breath, *taking it all in*, as her father called it. She could just smell the sweetness of the flowers and earthy tang of the moss. The forest didn't seem so dark and endless in a place like this, and her skin prickled with wanting to come out from under the trees.

This far north, in the borderlands as they were known, the trees and mountains went on for miles in each direction. Lena didn't quite understand why it was called the borderlands; there was no border really, the Kingdom of Vagora just...ended. The borderlands instead stood as a boundary between known and unknown, claimed and unclaimed, and humans hadn't dared go too deep for fear of what they'd find in the far reaches of the world, past what any map knew or story described. Avians hadn't claimed the land either, so dense it was with trees. Though they liked mountains and other high places, the tall, ancient trees of the northern forests weren't safe for their big bodies and wings.

Castle Finhöln, along with the town of Longbourne and a few other villages, were the northernmost vanguard of Vagora. Lena was sure a few other settlements existed beyond that hazy border that only existed on the maps, but otherwise it was an empty wilderness of trees and crags. Though Finhöln and Longbourne were part of Vagora in name, little was done about or in the north as far as the capital was concerned.

Except for Bel, of course.

But even then, knights in exile sent to be wardens of Finhöln, as Lena had been, were meant to molder away up in the north. To be forgotten. The townsfolk of Longbourne didn't think the capital cared about them much, and the feeling was mutual. They instead took governing and survival into their own hands and didn't rely on or communicate with the south much beyond what was necessary to stay a part of the greater kingdom.

Which was why Lena had decided to stick to these borderless borderlands—she didn't know what was beyond that pretend line on the map and she needed to be close enough to other humans for supplies. She didn't know yet what they needed to do, or what Bel wanted to do, but east felt like the right direction.

She'd been hoping the first humans they came across would be in one of those border towns, full of people willing to trade and not ask questions. Bel could be hidden away outside town, safe with the horses as she and Alix did what was needed. That had been the plan, anyway.

It was her only real one and it'd already gone to shit.

Taking one last breath of the sweet air, Lena turned back the way they'd come.

She found Bel where she'd left him, though his expression had soured considerably. Miri and the packhorses had fallen asleep. He only nodded when she said she hadn't found any signs of the hunters or anyone else.

Alix soon came trotting back, and both Lena and Bel sighed in relief.

Alix held out her hand, and Bel took her forearm to lift her straight off the ground and swing her back into the saddle.

"Pockets." Lena arched a brow expectantly. They didn't need to give these hunters a reason to go out looking for a missing item and then stumble upon their tracks.

The girl rolled her eyes and turned her jacket pockets inside out. "Nothing worth taking anyway," she grumbled. "Must've taken everything with them."

That, or they didn't have much to begin with, which worried Lena more. Desperate people did desperate things.

"They headed east this morning," Alix reported quietly. "Looks like they came up from the southwest initially."

Lena held in her groan. "Then we'll have to head north before going east again. Give them a wide berth."

"More forest," Bel said.

"More forest."

And further north. Exactly where she didn't want to go.

———— •◆•• ————

The ferns blanketing the clearing Lena had seen soon overtook the other undergrowth, their soft fronds a caress against her legs as the horses passed gingerly through. The soft crunch of dried pine needles under their hooves was both a relief, knowing it was solid ground and not a hole that would twist and break an ankle, and a pain as Lena winced at every loud crunch. It slowed their pace, making her skin itch with wanting to go faster and put more distance between them and that camp.

Alix and Bel remained quiet on their shared horse, somber and watchful. Alix's eyes had grown overlarge, darting this way and that; Bel was slower, head on a measured swivel, eyes slightly narrowed as if this helped cut through the fog. She appreciated that they kept their eyes open, but she missed the easy chatter they usually had. Dusk was fast approaching, but Lena wanted to cross over the peak of the ridge they followed before making camp.

The damn mist had mostly broken up after midday, but enough lingered in the late afternoon, casting long blades of saturated light onto the forest floor. Slightly off in color from the mist, the waning sunlight caught on little particles of dust and pollen, turning them into fractals that caught the eye then were gone again.

Something shimmered in her peripheral, and Lena turned to see a delicate spiderweb laced between two branches. The mist had gathered in small droplets along the faint lines of webbing and gleamed and glittered like a crystal chandelier in warm firelight.

Bel saw it too, his head craned around awkwardly to keep looking as the horses passed it by. He looked as long as he could, and Lena watched him, understanding. There could be such beauty in the world, even in this dark, never-ending forest.

He finally turned back around and caught Lena watching him. They shared a smile, and Lena's chest loosened a little at the glitter in his eyes. It was such a small thing, and they'd spent the afternoon in silence hurrying away from potential danger, but still he found joy in such small beauty.

It made her heart glow with warmth, fractals of happiness that gleamed in the light.

She almost blushed at the sticky sweet thought. Lena had felt affection before, had once been half in love with the Crown Prince of Vagora, but this...

His happiness was her happiness. Not out of loyalty or duty or even just affection, but something deeper, wider, vaster. She thought she understood now what all those bards and poets went on and on about in the books that stuffed the shelves of her father's library at Lindenfaire. She wondered what those old, long-winded bards would say about a human knight and an avian prince.

They passed through another slant of light, and the late sun painted Bel in warm tones of bronze and gold. His hair gleamed like golden thread, and the dappled brown tips of his feathers shone as finely as polished bronze. Since escaping Finhöln, his skin had caught a little color, radiating warmth and health though the mist was often thick and the winter sun shone thinly. Gone was the pallor she'd known him to have, once so colorless besides the delicate web of blue veins just beneath.

He shone as brightly as any sun, and she could understand too what humans and avians alike meant when they described Adiirons as golden. The avian royal family had been renowned for their great golden wings —though she still stumbled over the idea of him being an Adiiron himself, she saw it then. With that smile stretched wide across his inhuman face, those turquoise eyes so bright in the sun they burned, of course this male was a prince. How could she have missed it?

Bel's smile turned lopsided, teasing, playful as he held her gaze, and she couldn't stop the blush this time.

"Hey! Up there! Help!"

The bottom fell out of her stomach, and Lena watched her own shock play across Bel's face, his smile dying and his eyes rimming in white. Feathers crackled as he snapped his wings tight to his back, almost muffling another male cry from down the ridge.

"You, up there! Hello!"

The horses didn't stop, kept their slow cut up the ridge, but Yvain's ears swiveled back and forth nervously. Heart hammering in her chest, her head, the roof of her mouth, Lena twisted in the saddle.

Down the ridge, small compared to the towering trees, almost entirely out of sight, stood four men, their faces turned uphill toward Lena. She couldn't tell much of anything about them other than they were all bearded and wore heavy layers of leathers, blending into the brush like shapeless wraiths of the forest, but she felt their gazes, running over her, the horses. Bel.

"We've got a man wounded! Boar attack, he's gored bad!"

A sharp breath caught in her throat.

Her legs twitched, almost enough pressure to bring Yvain to a stop.

"We need help down here!"

She clenched her teeth so she wouldn't chew on her cheek.

"They're lying."

Breaking the spell, her gaze cut to Alix.

Alix looked back at her, a frown shadowing the slits of her eyes. Bel had an arm around her, grasping the saddle pommel, and he'd straightened his shoulders as if to make himself bigger, but Alix somehow looked more ferocious.

"Hey!" Louder now. "We need help!"

"Help us!" A new voice. "He's bleeding bad!"

She looked back down the ridge, saw how the group was circled around another form, perhaps a log or boulder or boar carcass, perhaps a wounded man.

"*Lena*, they're lying," Alix hissed. "They just want to rob us!"

"But..."

"Please! *Help us*!"

The desperation in that voice cut through her, and she twisted the reins in her hands.

"They're just trying to draw us in, see if they can take us."

"Lena," whispered Bel.

The men continued to cry out to them, a third joining now, and she thought she heard the groan of someone in pain, but Bel caught her gaze.

His frown was gone, replaced with an unsure tilt she hated to see. His eyes skittered downhill too, and she wondered what those sharp avian eyes of his saw in the haziness of dusk.

"I can't tell if..."

Alix growled. "They're lying!"

Bel looked back at her, eyes soft but creased. He wouldn't hold it against her, if she wanted to investigate.

She wanted to, or if not wanted than needed, or if not needed than thought she should. They could be...she was a...

She could barely hear the men over her hammering heart. She wasn't a knight anymore, had forsaken those vows to king and country—but she didn't have to be a knight to help someone in need.

Tightness in her chest almost made her wince.

It rent at the very fabric of her to let a call for help go unanswered.

She couldn't do it.

"I'm just going to see how much help they need. Stay at the top of the ridge."

Alix made a grab for her as she turned Yvain with the press of a knee.

Bel kept an arm around her spitting squire, keeping Alix in her own saddle when she would've jumped onto Yvain.

"*Lena*," Alix hissed.

"Keep going," she told them without looking back.

Yvain's ears swiveled back and forth as they picked their way back down the slope. Lena tried to swallow around the knot of worry in her throat and couldn't.

The men continued to cry out, beckoning her closer with their arms.

As she drew nearer, she counted five, with another man laid on a bed of dead leaves. They'd gathered around him protectively, one of them knelt beside the injured man. All of them held a weapon with many more strapped onto their backs and thighs. Months of beard hid their grim mouths, and their clothes and gear were decorated with an array of patches and rough stitches.

Lena pulled Yvain to a stop several paces back from the men.

"What's the trouble, gentlemen?" she asked.

"Boar attack. Just got into ruttin' season, they're all mad with it," said the one nearest her, a tall man with watery blue eyes.

"Two of 'em took us by surprise. Got Malik here bad in the side," said the one knelt by the injured Malik.

"You got any bandages or supplies?" a third asked.

"It'd be appreciated, lady," the first man added. "Supplies ran low a long time ago."

"Of course. Let me check."

Lena leaned back to reach for her saddlebag, not taking her eyes off the men. They watched her carefully, eyes unblinking, though none of them moved or even tensed. She got the saddlebag untied and began rooting around blindly for the roll of gauze she knew to be near the middle of the pack.

Her finger brushed it before the gauze roll wedged deeper in the pack.

She grumbled to herself, eyes flicking down without thinking.

They moved quick, coordinated, one grabbing Yvain's bridle and another her leg. She kicked at the man and tapped Yvain twice.

The warhorse reared with a whinny, front legs striking out. The man who'd grabbed his bridle took a hoof to the chest, falling back with a pained grunt.

But another was there to take his place when Yvain came down again.

They swarmed around her, a hungry pack braying for blood. They ripped at the reins, her packs, her legs, her arms. None drew weapons, none spoke, just moved with a ravenous speed that set Lena's heart thundering.

They wanted her alive. There was only one reason they'd want to take a woman alive.

Lena wrenched the reins back as Yvain danced and circled, battering the men with his flank and chest. She'd nearly gotten him turned back toward the path when a hand grasped her by the jerkin and pulled.

Cursing, she let her foot slip out of the stirrup rather than let her leg be pulled out of its socket. She went down hard on the man pulling her, making him take the brunt of the fall.

Rolling to her feet, she smashed her fist into the first man's face, sending him sprawling. She was ready for the next one too, blocking his strike with her forearm. She pulled him to her and spun, throwing him down and kicking another man in the chest.

Lena kept moving, always moving, always spinning and keeping her hands up. Yvain danced nearby, trying to keep close, even as two men tried to grab and control him.

The men started coming two at a time, realizing she was more of a threat than they'd anticipated. They tried to grab either arm, and one almost got hold of her ankle the next time she kicked. She spun again, backing up toward the sound Yvain, keeping her warhorse at her back.

The hunters ringed her in a semicircle, a few drawing daggers.

Lena pulled out two of her own.

"I suggest you back down and leave, gentlemen. I'm a knight of the realm. Attacking one is a serious offense." She didn't mind lying to vagabonds like these.

"Then we'd better make sure you don't report nothing," hissed Malik, no longer injured.

They advanced as a unit, taking a step forward for every one she took backward.

She'd almost made it to Yvain when the men gasped and drew back.

An arm went round her waist, and huge white-to-bronze wings flared and flapped around her.

"Shit," a man hissed.

"What's one of them doing here?"

Bel bared his teeth at the men, wings drawn up to their full length and height. It was a glorious, terrifying sight, making Lena's heart stop.

"You can't—" she murmured.

He flapped again, threatening, tossing their hair, beards, and hoods.

"*Leave!*" he boomed, nose and lips pulled back in a leonine snarl.

"Not worth it," muttered one of the men, and they all fell back. They backed away from Lena and Bel, not turning their backs until they were out of striking distance. Then they turned and ran, disappearing into the trees.

"Go," Bel urged, pushing her toward Yvain.

Lena threw herself on her warhorse and hauled Bel up behind her.

They pounded up the ridge, not slowing until Alix appeared near the top, holding the reins of both packhorses. Lena pointed, and they all hurried down the other side, following a narrow deer path into the darkening forest.

She didn't escape Alix's "*I fucking told you so!*"

• • ◆ • •

The deer trail followed the curve of the ridge base, and Lena managed to find what she wanted; a little outcropping of rocks that would provide decent enough shelter against the worst of any wind or chill that found its way through the thick trees.

Alix dismounted without a word, not even an appreciative groan, and helped set up camp in silence.

As they stripped the horses of saddles and bits, Lena delivered the bad news.

"No fire tonight, nothing that can be spotted easily."

That did get a *hmph* out of Alix, who started clearing away damp leaves with her boots from the area they'd lay the bedrolls. Their dinner was another simple affair of the last of the salty cheese and brown bread Pol had packed them. Lena wouldn't miss the crumbling castle, but she already missed the quiet cook terribly. Communicating with him through hands, since the man couldn't hear, had been a good way to stop her from fidgeting, and Pol always had a good story to tell. She ate the bread and thought of their friend and hoped Captain Joran didn't suspect Pol had aided their escape.

Thinking of their friend and then Captain Joran brought her thoughts round again to the hunters. She burned with indignation for being duped, for being gullible, for being *wrong*. Alix hadn't spoken to her the rest of the evening, and Bel was quiet too, eyes wary as he looked between her and Alix.

Lena could barely stand to look at him, the guilt churning in her gut.

Those feckless hunters had seen him. She'd promised to get him safely away from humans and instead exposed him.

She'd put others' safety, other humans, before his. And nearly paid the price for it.

Goddess, how could I be so stupid?

Darkness enveloped them quickly without a fire. By the light of one lantern, Alix was the first to bed down. She cooed at Miri, and the amenable mare laid down near Alix and made herself comfortable. Alix scooted closer, into the warmth of Miri's belly, and drew the blankets all around herself with a sigh.

"Guess this'll do," she mumbled before almost immediately dozing off.

Lena had always been jealous of the skill. As a former soldier, she could fall asleep fairly quickly herself, but it was nothing compared to

Alix. She supposed, in the girl's former life as a street urchin on the streets of the capital, you had to snatch sleep and sustenance where you could and do it quickly.

Bel reached out a hand and drew Lena near. She hadn't missed that he'd made a large nest for the both of them, combining bedrolls and blankets. When she was close enough, he wrapped a wing around her, and she shivered in the warmth and slight musk that enveloped her.

She couldn't help running a hand down his feathers, delighting in the softness. They still had a lingering smell of the hair oil he rubbed on them, a nutty, almost sweet smell that always filled her head with memories of evenings in the firelight, working the oil over his wings where he couldn't reach.

His hand ran up and down her back in a soothing rhythm before sliding under her plaited hair. He worked his thumb and fingers on either side of her nape, and she nearly moaned in pleasure as her muscles loosened. She let herself be caught for a moment, taking comfort in resting her head against his strong chest and hearing his heartbeat.

But just a moment. She didn't deserve more. She'd put him in danger today. That wouldn't happen again.

"Come rest," he whispered against the skin of her temple before kissing her there.

"I will. I'll take first watch."

Bel stiffened beside her. They hadn't been keeping watches—mostly because Lena had stayed awake to do it herself. She caught a few hours' sleep each night, mostly in the late, inky hours when nothing was awake, but otherwise kept watch.

"Lena, you need to sleep."

"Those men could come back. They could try and rob us while we sleep."

"Fine. I'll stay up with you."

"No need for both of us to miss sleep."

"Then I'll take the first watch."

"I'm not tired yet, I'll just lie there."

His lips pursed in that way they did sometimes when he knew he'd lost an argument. He sighed and ran his hand up and down her back again.

"Wake me for the second watch, all right? You need to sleep."

"I will."

She felt rather than saw him nod, the curls of his hair catching on the wisps of hers that had escaped her braid. With a small *ashita* along her nose and ear, Bel hunkered down on the big bedroll he'd made and closed his eyes.

Lena wrapped a blanket around herself and listened. There wasn't much to see in this kind of dark, where the moon was hidden and the damp forest floor seemed to absorb any light. As their little band settled, she began to hear the nearby night creatures skittering about, peeking out of their hidey-holes.

She knew Bel didn't sleep for a long while, had slept beside him enough times to recognize the sound of his breath evening out in true sleep. The lines and contours of him, all she could make out in the dark, remained stiff and tense, even as he slowly began to drift off.

Lena sat there through the night with the lantern burning low, picking at her thumb and listening.

She didn't wake Bel for watch.

3

Bel pressed his fist into his stomach to stifle the gurgle so Lena wouldn't hear. He wasn't hungry, not truly; he'd eaten his ration just like Lena and Alix that morning, but the dried apple and lukewarm porridge just hadn't satisfied him. His mouth watered at the memory of all the breakfasts Pol had spoiled him with, and he yearned for even just a bite of the simple brown bread they'd run out of days ago.

Finhöln had been hell. No denying it—he had the scars from years of abuse to prove it. But Pol had always been a bright light, and so had his cooking. Bel wanted for nothing when it came to being fed well in his one-male prison.

When Bel had made a face over his first time eating camp porridge—finely cut oats boiled over a fire—Lena just grinned and said, "*Welcome to the delights of trail rations.*"

He remembered her words distinctly for two reasons; because of how utterly not delightful oats were and because it was one of the last times Bel had seen any sort of smile or grin or even smirk on Lena's face.

Twelve days they'd been traversing the forest, steadily distancing themselves from Finhöln. But from the taut, tired lines of Lena's face, anyone else would think they hurried straight for the human capital and surrender.

He hated the dark circles under her eyes and the grim line of her mouth. She wasn't sleeping.

After that afternoon with the hunters, she'd been evermore vigilant, shoulders tense as her tired eyes searched for an unseen threat.

He didn't blame her for the hunter attack, not the way Alix did with her sullen looks and clipped replies, just wished desperately he'd gotten there sooner, before they'd pulled her off Yvain. Watching her go down had had him leaping from Miri and racing down the slope, forgoing the path to instead slide on damp leaves and debris to get to her faster.

He'd wanted to help. And he did, sort of. It'd felt good to make those men back down, to see the trepidation in their eyes at a full-grown avian protecting his female. His wings had wailed at the use, but he wouldn't back down.

Only, they'd seen him.

The worry niggled in the back of Bel's mind. He suspected it was at the forefront of Lena's.

Each night he tried to coax her into a bedroll and each night she found an excuse to stay awake. Sometimes he stubbornly stayed up with her, calling her bluff, but she outlasted him. Sleep was something he'd done a lot of in captivity; it was an escape, an easy way to fly from the castle and back to a time when he'd been a real avian who could fly and wasn't a disappointment to his people.

Bel figured at least one of them should be getting some rest. It was better than nodding off in the saddle and almost slipping off the horse. She'd done that four times already but refused to acknowledge it. So Bel slept for both of them, just in case someone had to catch someone else when they finally fell off a horse.

He traded a look with Alix as they watched Lena pull Yvain to a stop and dismount. It was time for a midday rest and a small bite of rations. It worried him that their midday rests were getting earlier and Lena's movements were getting slower. Perhaps tonight he'd finally cajole her into sleeping the whole night.

He'd tried more than once to work her shoulders, suspecting she'd fall asleep in mere moments from that, but she shied away from anything more. He wanted to comfort her, to touch her and make her feel safe enough to rest. He knew it was rooted in selfishness, that he wanted comfort for himself, too; Lena was capable and brave and strong and would do her best by all of them, but in the dark, with the cold night air stinging his face, he wanted to be tangled up with her like they'd done before. When it was just him and Lena, Alix, and Pol in that castle and they all lived in an illusion that the world outside didn't matter.

It bothered him almost as much as her not sleeping, that she shied away from him. He wanted her arms around him, wanted to wrap her up in him and not let go until the night had passed. Even when they rode together now, she didn't lean into him, didn't let herself rest against him and trust him and Yvain to keep them going.

She'd closed herself off, so guarded against the trees and the animals and the noises they made that she'd become guarded against him and Alix too, and it stung. And perhaps he wasn't in the best mood himself, the ground an unforgiving bed, but he couldn't help the ache in his chest over it.

Lena rubbed her eyes and stretched as the other horses stopped around Yvain. Bel dismounted ungracefully beside her.

Riding was easy enough, especially since Lena or Alix did all the hard work, but still, it would be nice to know how to maneuver a horse—if not as much as Lena could get Yvain to walk, trot, or even sidestep with different toe taps, then at least enough to start, stop, and hurry up.

"I should learn to ride. Properly, that is," he said, stretching until his back cracked. Perhaps he'd learn how to not ache so much in the saddle, too.

"Yes," Lena sighed, attention on untangling Yvain's reins.

"But you already make it look so easy," Alix teased from atop Miri.

"True, but I'm a firm believer that there's always more to learn."

"Shouldn't be that hard to teach you. I caught on quick enough." Alix dismounted herself with a flourish, hitting the ground without a sound and seamlessly dipping into a curtsey.

Bel rolled his eyes.

"And the horses already like you, that's half the battle. We could add it to training, yeah?" She looked to Lena for confirmation but got no sign Lena had been listening to them. Pouting, Alix said, "That is, if we ever get back to training."

Lena sighed, her eyes rolling to the tree canopy above. Ah, she *had* been listening.

"We will, Alix."

"When? Bel needs to learn to ride right."

"I know."

"And his wings need to get exercised."

"I know that, too."

"He'll never fly if we don't get his wings right. And if he doesn't fly, then I can't fly."

Bel rolled his eyes again, but the look Lena shot her squire was much darker.

"Bel flying isn't about you, Alix."

The girl puffed out a breath, making the curls on her forehead jump. "I know. I'm just saying, we should—"

"We just can't afford the time right now, all right?"

"Sure," Alix said with a shrug, "since we're in such a hurry to get nowhere in particular."

A scoff erupted from Lena, but Bel thought she'd tampered down the screech she really wanted to make. Her face a mask of thunderclouds, she turned away from Alix to untie a pack from Yvain.

"I know where we're going," Lena grumbled.

"Everyone knows how to go nowhere."

The look Lena shot Alix over her shoulder was as sharp as any arrow.

Bel could actually see Lena's jaw working as she ground her teeth, and a vein popped against the skin of her neck. He stepped between them, holding a hand up at Alix, warning her with a look.

The girl crossed her arms over her chest, and he didn't miss the way she quickly blinked away wetness gathering at the corners of her eyes.

"We're getting lost in this forest," she grumbled.

"We aren't lost, Alix," he said gently.

"Sure."

He motioned for her to see to her horse, and she was quick to turn on her heel and busy herself, muttering into Miri's neck.

Bel took a breath to shore up his courage and turned back to Lena. She still worked at the knot of the pack, her nails digging into the leather and making it worse.

"Here," he said, reaching for the pack.

"I've got it."

"I know, but..." He eased her hands away and made short work of the knot. The mangled leather came away from the saddle, and Lena snatched it up and marched a few paces away.

She stood there for a long moment, holding the pack with her back turned to him, and Bel's chest ached fiercely. He'd known this feeling, had let it consume him once when Finhöln had still been as new to him as his broken right wing and the lashes across his back.

Helpless.

She hurt and Alix hurt and he didn't know what to do.

"Lena..."

She threw down the pack unceremoniously and quickly joined it, plunking down on a rock and rubbing her temples.

"She won't like you taking my side."

"Your side?" Bel knelt beside her, but Lena wouldn't look at him. "Lena, there aren't sides. We're in this together. Right?"

Her sigh was long and full of feeling. "Yes," she said finally, and the pause she took before answering only made him grumpy.

"Maybe we should—"

A screech rent the air around them, and Bel's ears throbbed with the vibrations.

Another horrible sound, an animal scream, followed close behind, and then the ground trembled beneath their feet. The bushes and low branches around them quivered and shook, as if the forest itself shuddered with the horrible noise.

A massive blur burst from a berry thicket, a hulking brownish gray creature that lurched to a stop when it saw them. A wild pig stared at them, the tusks pointed low as its gaping mouth drew in great gulps of air. Its sides shivered from running, and for a moment, all of them, pig, horses, humans, and avian, stood in silent shock.

Another terrible scream, and the beast's ears swiveled backwards before flattening on its head. It turned to run, but three more came barreling from the brush, herding the first one closer to Lena on the rock.

The new boars dwarfed the first, and Bel realized that this first one was a female. The newcomers were all males, taller and bulkier, their eyes red-rimmed and tusks curved and wicked, the length of his forearm where the sow's were only finger-long.

"Don't move," Lena said without moving her mouth. She sat stock still on her rock, though her hand had moved to her thigh, where a dagger sat cozily in its sheath.

The boars didn't seem worried about them, not with the sow so close, and a chorus of screeching squeals pierced the air, making Bel wince. The boars pranced and pawed at the earth, at once trying to push the others away and move closer to the female. It was like an awful dance, the four of them pushing their way round and round in a circle as the boars vied to get close and the sow tried to get away.

One of the smaller males stumbled, causing the circle to crash in on itself, and the female lunged for the underbrush. The boars cried out in fury, pounding the earth again, spraying dirt and they tried to get turned round to chase her.

The boars pushed and shoved, and the largest male stomped at the smallest boar, still on the ground. He didn't know the sounds could get worse, but the agonized screeching of the smaller male set Bel's teeth on edge, and he wanted to clap his hands over his ears. The two males scuffled, the smaller one trying to squirm away, and the third male took his chance and went after the sow alone.

Caught now in bloodlust, the greater boar reared back, aiming his sharp hooves for his foe's vulnerable belly. The smaller boar rolled, escaping the worst of it, but blood oozed from a wound and he scrambled to his feet, squealing in pain.

The high screaming bray of the horses caught even the fighting boars off guard, and Bel's head snapped around to see Alix fighting to keep hold of all four sets of reins. The two packhorses neighed and bounced on their front legs, trying to pull free and run, and even Yvain shook his head and pawed the ground nervously.

The sound drew the bigger boar, and Bel could see the red of his eyes, glazed and lost in a mating haze. There was nothing there but fight and mate, and he could only do one now with the sow long gone.

With a shriek, the boar charged the horses, tusks low and ready to gore. The smaller male followed him, too lost himself or his herd instincts overriding sense.

"No!" With a shriek of her own, Lena launched herself at the bigger boar, colliding with his flank before he could get to Alix and the horses.

"*Lena!*" Alix screamed, and all the horses screamed with her, high and shrill.

Body cold and numb, Bel dashed in front of the second boar, still aimed at the horses. He drew himself up to full height, hands outstretched and fingers splayed, and then his wings unfurled. The broken bone flexed in agony, but he didn't care, spread his wings wide and flapped, flapped, flapped, the gust hitting the boar before it hit Bel.

The boar skidded to a stop, pebbles and dirt flying from under its hooves and hitting Bel's boots. It shifted its weight from one side to the other, eyes assessing, and Bel waved his wings, reaching as high as he could.

The boar snorted and backed away, eyeing him before breaking for the trees.

"Bel—Lena!" Alix cried.

The bigger boar wasn't so easily scared.

It tumbled and wrestled with Lena on the ground, keeping her pinned with its weight.

He threw himself at the boar, knocking it back. Lena grunted, sucking in a breath, and from the corner of his eye he saw her fling out the arm that had been trapped.

The boar dug in its hooves and tried to buck him off with a violent heave. Bel filled his fists with mane and pebbly flesh and pulled as hard as he could at the neck. They grunted and pushed at each other, and Bel dug his own feet in, desperate now, cold fear at Lena on the ground with sharp tusks bearing down on her making him stronger.

It struggled in his grip, squirming and wriggling, battering his chest with its flank. He tried to keep his wings up, away from those stamping hooves, but the broken wing was unbearable, flagging closer and closer to the ground.

He yelped when the wing finally gave, crumpling to the ground and getting tangled up in the boar's frantic hooves.

The animal squealed, the sound almost bursting his ears, and then gave a horrible shudder. It fought harder, grunting in desperation, foam splattering Bel's arms from its gaping mouth.

He held on tighter, wouldn't let it hurt Lena, willed his arms to hold.

The boar shuddered again, and he didn't think he imagined it growing weaker.

He felt it then, Lena's fist pressing on his forearm, and he managed to catch a glimpse of her bloody hand, gripped tight around the hilt of her dagger. The animal bucked and stomped, one last burst of fight, and Lena drew the dagger back and plunged it in again, deep into the boar's gut, to the hilt.

The boar groaned and its tongue lolled out of its mouth. The fight drained away, and Lena was able to scramble out from under its massive bulk. Once she was clear, Bel dropped the boar and rolled away, bounding to his feet.

But the beast had had enough. With a horrible gasp, it went silent, blood gushing from two red slashes in its belly. The dagger still sat embedded in the third.

He trembled from wings to toes with the rush of it, breath coming in great gusts that sawed in and out of his chest but never felt like enough.

The little clearing fell silent, the screams of the boars gone now and the horses quieted to a nervous titter. A soft wind rustled the leaves, and Bel shivered.

He came back to himself with every relieved breath, finally able to swallow his pounding heart and right it in his chest. His hands still shook, but feeling was returning to his lips and toes. He wished it wouldn't for his wing; he felt the pain pulse from the base all the way down to the feather barbs.

Grimacing, Bel turned toward the horses, only to find Lena still slumped on the ground, torso upright but not standing.

He was there in two steps, falling to his knees beside her.

"Are you hurt? Lena? Let me see."

His hands were everywhere, checking her for injuries. She sat there unmoving, apathetic, as he wiped dirt away from her eyebrows and straightened the collar of her jerkin.

He hissed through his teeth when he found a slashing cut running from the side of her arm up to heel of her palm. The gore had cut through the leather ties of her bracer and slashed the wool of her tunic, leaving the angry red of the wound exposed to the cold air. It'd missed the big artery in her wrist by a fingernail.

"What were you thinking, throwing yourself at it like that?" He wanted to shake her but instead untied the remaining straps of her bracer.

She said nothing still, eyes glazed and unseeing.

Bel groaned at the sight of her hurt. The wound wasn't deep, thank the gods and the human's goddess too, but it was wide and oozed blood. He hated it, hated the wound and that she was hurt and that she'd thrown herself at an angry boar and that he hadn't been fast enough to stop it.

He drew the edges of her ripped shirtsleeve around her arm, pulling the wound together. "Hold that," he said, picking up her hand and putting it over the sleeve when she didn't move.

Unease thrummed through him, keeping time with the painful pulsing of his abused wing. He watched her for another moment before standing and looking for Alix.

She was still with the horses, valiantly trying to calm them down. She hummed nonsense to them in a soothing voice, and Bel approached slowly, hands outstretched.

Yvain let him near, and he quickly dove into a pack, searching for bandages.

"You all right?" he asked Alix as he moved extra linens around.

"Yeah. You?"

He glanced over at her and saw the girl was deathly pale, her eyes eerily wide in her small face. The grip she kept on the reins was so tight her knuckles had gone white.

Finding what he wanted, he closed the pack and laid a gentle hand on Alix's shoulder.

"I'm sure I'll feel it later. You all right to watch the horses a little longer?"

She nodded bravely.

Bel turned back to Lena and with a mix of relief and shock found her up finally. As he returned to her, she crouched down and pulled the dagger out of the boar's belly. A fresh gush of blood came with it, pooling around her boots.

He pulled her up from her crouch, but the words died on his tongue to see that deadened look in her eyes. Face blank, she wiped the dagger on her ruined shirtsleeve and replaced it in its sheath.

"Don't!" Bel growled, grabbing at her arm. He tugged at the shirtsleeve until her wound was fully bared. "Hold still."

But she shook her head, tried to pull her arm away. "We need to butcher it," she said, nodding at the boar.

"I need to bandage this." He unscrewed the top of a small bottle of ointment that would soothe the split edges of her skin and help ward off infection.

Lena turned away to assess the boar and went to draw her dagger out again.

With a huff, Bel pulled her back.

She squirmed in his hold. "It can wait. We need to dress the meat quickly."

"Leave it. Your arm needs seeing to."

"I can manage. Let me—"

She pulled away from him again, walking around the boar.

He met her at the other side. "We don't have the time. The wolves will be hungry after this long winter. I'm sure they smell it already."

She shook her head, refusing to look at him. "It's food, we need it. Otherwise, it's a waste."

Bel saw how she trembled, her hand a fist around the dagger hilt if only for something to hold onto. Her eyes still gleamed in that dull way, though they darted around, not quite landing on any one thing and never drawing near him.

"It doesn't matter."

He crowded her and ignored when she shied away. He arched his good wing around her, stopping her retreat, and drew his free arm around her, caging her in, making her stop.

"I'm fine," she protested, though the reedy warble in her voice told him otherwise.

"Lena." He grasped her at the elbow to hold her steady. "I'm going to dress that wound and then we're riding out of here."

She stopped trying to draw away, but she wouldn't meet his gaze. Still, he saw it when a tear slipped over the rim of her eyes.

"I had to do it."

"I know you did. He wasn't in his right mind. Now let me see to your arm."

"But it's a waste."

"We don't have the time to do right by all that meat."

"We could—"

"The wolves will be desperate, not even a big fire will keep them away. We'll let them feed on him rather than us."

She shivered against him, and it made his stomach roll, remembering how the boar had felt in its death throes.

Sensing whatever fight she'd had was gone, and the thought of that making his tongue slick like he was going to be sick, Bel made quick work of bandaging her arm. He kept her in the circle of his wing and arm, his movements fast and jerky as he cleansed the wound, keeping her steady when she hissed through the pain, lathered on a layer of ointment, and bandaged her arm tight, drawing the broken edges together.

He wanted to be gentler, hated how she grimaced and winced, but unease and a growing panic made him quick. Her gaze hadn't lost that shiftiness, as if she wanted to barrel into the forest and join that sow on her desperate run. The sooner they got away from the carcass the better. He didn't want her looking upon it anymore, didn't want to see the haunted, downturned line of her mouth and colorless swath of her skin.

With the bandage as good as he could make it, he herded her to the horses.

Without inflection, Lena told Yvain to kneel. He bent his front legs, making it easy for Bel to mount up behind Lena.

Alix scrambled up onto her mare wordlessly, eyes darting between him and Lena.

When they didn't move, Bel covered Lena's hands on the reins with his. He tapped Yvain's flanks lightly, as he'd felt and seen Lena do many times, and the warhorse started into a trot.

He took the reins of one of the skittish packhorses from Alix so she only had to handle one and held them with Yvain's reins and Lena's hands.

Her hands were cold, and he didn't have much warmth in his own to offer. Bel had to settle for getting them away from that clearing and back into the forest as swiftly as they could.

4

S he'd failed.

Those boars had crashed into them, nearly trampled Alix and Bel before she could stop it. Lena hadn't heard them coming, hadn't been able to warn anyone. So she'd done the only thing she could, threw herself in the way to slow it down. There were stories and long epics about the ferocity of boars in their mating haze, how whole hunting parties had been decimated by a single male driven mad with need.

She'd seen the truth of those legends yesterday.

And every moment since, the screams of the boars and the cry of the hunters reverberated in her head. *"Boar attack, he's gored bad!"* Those men had been lying, but it'd almost been true for Bel and Alix.

The sounds of their easy chatter filled her ears, Bel's capable hands covered hers on the reins, and his strong bulk sat straight in the saddle behind her, but it didn't ease the panic that hadn't left her since yesterday.

It'd almost gotten to Alix and the horses. Alix always looked tiny because she was, but never more so than with an angry boar bearing down on her. The sight replayed in her mind over and over. Alix could have been hurt. Bel *had* been hurt; he didn't say as much, but she knew his wing had nearly been broken again.

His wings had been *seen*.

She really needed to see to his wing, too. She needed to make sure it was healing properly and start him on exercises. In the plethora of supplies Pol had sent them away with, he'd managed to squirrel away a book with drawings of avian anatomy, and from that, Lena hoped she'd be able to help Bel heal fully, from the most recent break but most importantly from the old wounds inflicted on his right wing.

She needed to look the book over again, get an idea of how to do this. And she needed to get Alix back on training. Knighthood was a distant memory now, but the routine centered Lena and Alix, too. She had so much to teach Alix, not just about being a knight but about surviving.

And Alix had been right yesterday, Bel needed to learn how to ride a horse. And he needed a horse of his own. If those boars had gotten to one of the horses, all the gear would have had to be redistributed to unburden it. It wore on Yvain and Alix's mare to carry two riders, and they wouldn't be as quick if they ran into more hunters and needed to escape.

They'd need a town in order to get another horse.

Even if she hadn't been avoiding them, towns weren't plentiful here deep in the northern forest.

So they continued with four horses and their dwindling supplies and no heading...

Goddess, what a mess she'd made of things.

At every turn, she was reminded of how vulnerable they were out here. If not human hunters, then the other beasts that roamed the forest. And where could they go for a safe harbor? Where could she possibly take Bel and Alix where they'd be safe, even for a night?

A homestead came to mind, something hidden and defensible. Somewhere she knew the layout and terrain, knew every animal that crossed the boundary, every tree that rooted in its ground. A turf house, perhaps, for warmth and cover. Just the thought of it, cozy, *safe*, gave her a little comfort.

All the things she needed to do and all the things that got in the way of them had buzzed in her head all night and now all morning, too. The shock of killing the boar had made her easily managed last night, so dazed was she. Bel had no trouble getting her into a bedroll and staying up late himself, guarding their huge fire. It'd been bigger than necessary, but he'd only said he wanted to ward away any other animals, especially those that'd missed out on the boar carcass. Body leaden and sluggish, Lena had still only dozed through the night, mind cycling through the worries that kept accumulating like rust on a blade.

That fog of sluggishness still clung to her late into the morning, so much that she didn't notice they'd stopped until Bel said, "Looks like a creek."

Blinking as if awakened, Lena took in their surroundings. Sure enough, a clear stream burbled across their path a few feet ahead, gently curving around an outcropping of boulders and the exposed roots of an ancient cedar. Moss blanketed the rocks and dipped down into the lazily winding water, and dragonflies danced across the surface, iridescent wings gleaming in the light.

They'd come across many streams, just breaking free of their winter shells of ice and frost, but this one stretched wider and seemed deeper than the others. Not quite a tributary but not just a creek either.

"Let's water the horses," she said, swinging a leg over Yvain.

Alix and Bel quickly joined her, and they made happy noises splashing their faces with cold mountain water and washing away some of the grime of travel while Lena wandered downstream a few paces.

The stream kept its size as far as she could see, wending further into the forest without any dramatic bends. She peered down at the water, surprised to see how dark it was. With the current, she couldn't make out any of the river rocks at the bottom, meaning it was deep, perhaps even up to her waist.

Making her way back to Alix and Bel, she followed the water's path with her eyes again before deciding.

"We should follow this," she told them. "It's pretty big and deep. It probably leads to a bigger river or lake." And streams didn't run further into the mountains but followed the slope down with the snowmelt. Maybe if they followed it to a bigger body of water, they'd be led out of the mountains to...somewhere.

Somewhere nice enough for that homestead, maybe?

"Might as well," quipped Alix.

Souring, Lena spared the girl an irritated glance before marching back to the horses. She didn't wait to parse out how Alix had meant it; she was tired of the jabs, even if they weren't really jabs. Or that they were probably true.

She rummaged through a saddlebag, thinking that book on avian anatomy seemed like something that would migrate to the bottom of the pack.

Before she could get up to her elbows in the less important supplies, Bel's big hand closed on her shoulder, and she turned to look at him at his gentle insistence.

He grinned softly down at her, just enough to reveal one of the dimples in his cheeks. Goddess, she resented that dimple—it made her far too amenable to anything he suggested. Even now, she felt the tiredness and worry lessen, that easy grin of his doing things to her heart.

Producing a fresh roll of bandage, Bel picked up her wounded arm and nodded sideways at the creek. "Let's clean this up properly."

She let herself be led to the water's edge. She really shouldn't let herself be so easily led, they had too much to do, *she* had too much to do, but...

The water here ran clear and bluish-gray, the scattered sunlight reflected on the surface like fish scales, glittering silver with the current. Bel unknotted the previous day's bandage, and Lena sighed with how good it felt to sit and sink her hand into the cold water. The sting felt good, but she turned her knuckles to the current so it wasn't too much, just a soothing wash around the angry broken skin.

Only when she'd begun to lose feeling from the cold did she pull her hand out and offer it back to Bel. Her fingers had gone white, but it helped dull the sting as he dabbed her skin dry and applied generous swipes of ointment to the gash. She was pleased to see it wasn't serious and thought it'd heal nicely.

Lena quietly watched as Bel bent his golden head over her arm, so careful in his ministrations. With her forearm balanced on his knee and her palm up and open, he smoothed out the last of the ointment and began wrapping her back up.

He looked so serious, so determined that she didn't interrupt him. She liked watching him like this, poring over his task. He'd always been intense in his attention, whatever he did. Too often, she'd seen that look poised over the translations he did for King Artemian, the one who'd captured him and kept him imprisoned and broken, but then it had almost been a brooding intensity, his brow marred with a frown.

No such expression darkened his face now, but he gave her arm the same rapt attention that she thought so defined Bel. She'd had that attention trained on her before, in other places, and she fought the blush that wanted to conquer her face.

Not here, not now. Everything's changing for him...

She didn't want to push, so she took comfort in his gentle but assured touch.

Too soon he finished, but he didn't release her hand, instead drew it up and to his mouth where he kissed her knuckles. He took her other hand too, gathered them together in his, and ran his thumbs over the hills and valleys of her knuckles. The silence around them changed, deepened somehow, but again Lena didn't interrupt, not sure she wanted to know what he'd say.

"You scared me yesterday," was what he finally said.

"We were all scared by those boars," she agreed.

He shook his head slowly, gaze on where their hands twined together but unfocused.

She watched quietly as he continued to think, disliking when a small frown did start to darken his eyes. But soon he decided something, she could see it in the way his face cleared and his gaze flicked up to search hers. She didn't know what he saw, but all he did was sigh himself.

"So," he said with false levity, fingers running along her knuckles again, "we follow the creek."

All she could do was shrug. "Creeks lead to rivers, and rivers always go somewhere."

One side of his mouth kicked up, but it wasn't quite a grin. "Where are you taking me?"

The tiredness and worry rushed back through her so quickly, she could almost hear it crashing against her ears. Shoulders slumping, she pulled a hand free of his grip so she could rub her eyes with thumb and finger. She pushed the tears that leaked out back into her skin.

"Lena," he hurried to say, "I didn't mean..."

"I don't know," she groaned. "I don't know."

They said voicing one's fears often helped make them better, but her admittance, her bitter truth that she didn't know, hung above her like old stalactites ready to fall from the cave ceiling. She wanted to shrink away from it, crawl in on herself and not come back out until she knew, had a plan.

Bel's hands were warm, placating, but she could only shake her head and keep rubbing her eyes.

"Lena." He bent to crouch before her, trying to catch her eyes.

"I hadn't planned that far ahead." She lifted her head to laugh humorlessly. And avoid his gaze. "Goddess, it sounds so stupid. I didn't plan for what we'd do now. I just had to get you out."

"I'm not complaining at all," he insisted. "If you hadn't come...that would've been the end of me."

"I couldn't let them take you south. I just...I had to do something. I didn't think much beyond how to get you out. I ran through every danger, every problem, everything that could go wrong in getting you out in the days it took to ride back to Finhöln."

"And it worked." He caught her face in one of his palms, thumb running along the curve of her cheekbone. "You got me out. You got us here."

She nodded slowly. "I had to. It was the right thing to do."

A beat lengthened into silence between them, and she watched the skin around his eyes go tight. She searched his face, looking for a clue to what he must be thinking.

Nothing she'd said was untrue—the opposite, she felt the rightness of it with all her conviction, even down to not planning beyond getting him out of Finhöln. But as his silence stretched, a growing dread had her thinking whatever she'd said, it'd been the wrong thing.

"What about Aeriand," he finally said, barely more than a whisper. And not really a question.

She blinked at him, startled. *But it's a ruin.*

She had enough sense to not say that.

"Aeriand?" she choked out. "Why…?"

Her head spun with all the memories crowding in, the sounds of human war machines breaking stone walls, the crush of armored bodies suffocating one another as formations dissolved into chaos, the whistle of avian arrows and the *thunk* of them driving home through flesh.

She pulled both hands free of him but had to fold her arms across her chest so she wouldn't pick at her nailbeds. Instead, she stood up and started to pace.

"It was my home once," Bel said. "I want to see it again. And maybe there, we can get a better idea of…where we need to go."

Lena could only shake her head at everything that implied. He made it sound like they should really be headed to Hadria, the last avian stronghold. As if it was smarter to turn themselves over to the avian King Dartegn than the human king.

Both would have their heads.

Panic gripped her heart in a cold vice and she struggled to get enough air. She turned away before he could see it in her face that she didn't want to go to Aeriand. The humans had prevailed in the end, taking what had once been thought an impossible prize—but at immeasurable cost. She remembered that first day she walked the wide streets in the Crown Prince's guard, the exultation at victory, *finally*, and the heady high of triumph from claiming the heart of their enemy. On the second day, they'd had to begin burying the dead. The thousands and thousands of them. Human soldiers and knights. Avian warriors and families alike. So many bodies, only pits could hold them all. So they'd dug deep trenches and filled them back up again with the dead. And the city had been quiet then, empty of all that had made it alive.

Many soldiers had celebrated for days. The king himself had come to see the spoils and held a feast for over a week. Homes had been ransacked. Statues and monuments had been toppled. Gems had been prized off walls.

Like Lena, Prince Arion hadn't had much of a stomach for it, and so they'd moved out, to scout where the remaining avians headed next. She couldn't wait to leave.

So much bloodshed, so much lost. For what?

A city just as dead as all those souls buried in the pits.

She'd helped do that. She hadn't questioned her orders, had fought alongside Prince Arion to take the city and defeat their enemy. She hadn't been sorry for that. But seeing what was left, the city's skeleton picked over by vultures hunting for war prizes, she'd felt no pride in that.

And Bel wanted to go back there. Wanted her to take him there.

To see it again. To see what the humans—what *she* had done. To *show* him...

"Should I not want to go?"

She finally turned back to him. His expression was carefully neutral, but such hope burned there, like the hottest of blue flames. It nearly radiated from him, this desire to see his home, and Lena knew this wasn't a battle she could fight.

"No, no—I mean, yes, you should want...Never mind." She sighed. "I just—going to avian country has always been dangerous. And I'll need to figure out exactly where we are to decide how to get there. But if you want to go, we'll go."

His gaze was unflinching and serious when he said, "I need to go."

She swallowed the nerves that ran riot in her belly, hoping they didn't show when she nodded. "Then we'll go."

To Aeriand. Goddess, maybe she shouldn't have wished for a heading.

5

As much as Lena hated these briefings, she knew Arion hated them more. It was important to keep apprised of the kingdom, of the important moving pieces and people, even from their entrenched position below Hadria, but, Matella knew, Lord Nandon, King Artemian's personal secretary and purveyor of the briefings to Prince Arion, was perhaps the most boring yet pompous orator in Vagora. Arion had joked with her once that he thought his father sent Nandon himself rather than a deputy to give the briefings as an excuse to get the man out of the capital for a few weeks and give his patience a needed respite.

Lena had to bite her cheek to keep from laughing as she watched the fellow guard opposite her across the tent, Catrin, pinch her lips to keep in a yawn.

Arion's own eyes looked suspiciously unfocused and his lids seemed to grow heavier and stay lower with every blink. Lena didn't envy him having to listen to Lord Nandon; her job was easy enough, securing his safety in the tent. She didn't have to pretend to listen, just keep alert for any threats to the royal person.

He was as safe as he could be at the foot of the avian stronghold. They'd pitched his area of the camp far back in the ranks, a compromise between him and Captain Joran, the head of his guard. If Arion had had his way, he'd be much closer to the front, offering support and morale, but Captain Joran had insisted he could do all that from further back in a safer position.

Sometimes the duty of guarding the prince was more about keeping him safe from his own inclinations.

She tried not to blush at the thought. She'd long given in to one of his inclinations; she'd shared his bed most nights for over a year now. It was the way of a war camp, that some impossibilities became possible with death as a third bedfellow.

She couldn't say the prince was her man and she didn't consider herself his woman. Still, he offered the only comfort, the only happiness in the shadow of this damn mountain, and Lena couldn't bring herself to give it up. She contented herself that she didn't need to protect him from her, she had no intention of wounding him. He had to know what they shared was only for camp tents and the wilds of war, even if they held each other long into the night, whispering to each other as often as they took pleasure in the other. Precious but temporary. Conditional.

Perhaps her heart did yearn sometimes for more, perhaps she didn't like having to always check herself in the daytime that she treat him merely as her duty. Perhaps she'd like someone to call her man, but the only one who'd ever made her feel it worth the trouble of having one was a crown prince. Perhaps, in her deepest daydreams, she wished for a love story like her parents', at least the one the ballads retold; the stars aligning, two forces joining, an unbreakable union between warriors who were strong apart but stronger together.

And perhaps she'd have that one day. But it wouldn't be with Arion. *What depressing thoughts.*

"...and so," Lord Nandon was saying, his impressive mustache twitching in the way it did before he finally delivered the actually important part of the story, "your esteemed father has decided that Lady Margot Montcaer will now lead the campaign in the south."

Lena perked up at her mother's name. Her mother had hinted that she may be headed south in her last letter, but Lena had a hard time keeping up with Margot's many duties. As one of the most celebrated knights in Vagora, her assistance was sought after, and she spent much of her time travelling between demesnes, lending her aid. She hadn't gotten a royal commission in quite a while, though. She'd be pleased.

Arion sighed. "Well, let's hope she has more luck."

Lord Nandon made a few throat-clearing noises and ran a hand over his shaved scalp. His bald head gleamed in the lower light of the tent and juxtaposed the expertly coiffed mustache that curled over his lips. Lena always found it a tad disconcerting, listening to his voice drone on but not able to see his mouth actually moving.

"His Majesty the King thinks a more aggressive approach appropriate. A show of force. Lady Margot's reputation precedes her and should make those barbarians think before they attack again. With any luck, she'll rout them swiftly and bring them to the table for a new treaty, one more favorable to Vagora this time around."

Her mother was known to be a swift and brutal tactician, able to find minute weaknesses and exploit them until all defenses crumbled. Lena knew all too well how capable she was at doing this to people as easily as armies.

She pitied the southern nomads if they did meet Margot in battle.

Yet, she couldn't help but wonder why Lady Margot would be sent for such a strategy. Yes, it was her specialty, but then, hadn't such a tact always been Vagora's strategy? Lena couldn't remember a time when crushing the southern nomads into submission hadn't been the plan. One commander after another had ridden south, retaken territory along the River Dyne, and forced the nomads into a treaty. The peace lasted a year or two, just long enough for the rich farms and demesnes of the south to recover and grow again. Then the conflict started all over again, the nomads crossing the river and raiding the southern villages, the king sending forces to stop it. Sometimes the same commander would go down to righteously reinstate the treaty they'd fought hard for not so long ago. Sometimes they were replaced with a new name.

Well, they hadn't thrown Lady Margot at the problem yet. Perhaps it was the same strategy, but it'd never been carried out by her. Lena had faith that if anyone could make something stick, it would be her mother.

At least, she was sure Margot would get it done faster and more efficiently than her predecessors.

What truly hadn't been attempted was something other than force. A general who negotiated or simply defended the territory and didn't become the aggressor. Someone like Arion.

Force had worked. Sort of. For a while. The king had yet to throw charm and diplomacy at the southern border.

Lena blinked at the thought, regarding Arion.

Yes, he'd likely do well, at least if he was allowed to do it his own way. For all that he loved his father and played a dutiful prince, she knew Arion still liked to do things how he saw fit and wouldn't hesitate to do so even against the king's wishes, though he'd use subterfuge rather than outright insubordination.

No doubt Arion would charm the southerners. He had a way about him, drawing people in, making them feel at ease. She hadn't believed him when she first entered service in his private guard, had thought him too good to be true. Handsome, golden princes who loved their people and sacrificed for them were the stuff of ballads and myths. But it was as if Matella herself, their revered sun goddess, had smiled on Arion and imbued him with a little of her light.

Sometimes she wondered if she'd burn if she got too close to that light.

Such a light wasn't for just one person. It was meant to be spread, to shine on all, and Arion was beloved throughout Vagora for his sincerity and goodness.

And such a light was, perhaps, wasted here in the mountains, buried in the crags beneath an avian fortress. Arion commanded the campaign against the avians, and his presence always lifted spirits, but they'd been here at the foot of this mountain for years now, unable to crack it.

It wasn't Arion's fault, he'd done everything he could think of and everything all of his advisors had thought of, too. She had to repress her shudder remembering the months they'd tried exploring the mountain caverns. Legend held that Hadria had once been a mining colony, and shafts still ran deep into the rock. They'd stumbled and scrabbled their way through the dim, trying to find a way up and in. Sometimes she could still feel the damp cold along her skin, raising the hair on her arms. They'd lost good knights to the dark with nothing to show for it and were no closer to capturing Hadria.

It was a shame Lady Margot hadn't been set upon the mountain. Knowing her, either Hadria's defenses would crack or she would. Her mother lived for such challenges, such triumphs. She could be as hard as the rock that held up the mountain, and Lena had to wonder who would be left standing after such a clash between forces of nature.

That begged the question...why was her mother going south when she'd be best used here? And why keep Arion here when he could do better work against their human enemies?

All she could think was that the king knew more than her and had his reasons. She had to have faith he knew what was best.

"Your father also believes that a show of force would be advisable here, too." From his leather folio, Nandon produced a thin sealed letter with a flourish. He presented it to Arion as if it were a peace treaty, bowing as he backed up to his former place a few paces from Arion's seat.

Arion broke the seal, opening the letter and reading with little aplomb.

"He is also ordering another expedition into the caves, to the north this time. While your knights search, the southern ridge should be retaken. The king is displeased that last year's gains were lost so quickly this spring. He also—"

"Yes, I read it, thank you, Lord Nandon," Arion said. He pinched the bridge of his nose, eyes squeezed tight in a grimace. "My lord father can be as displeased as he likes. It doesn't change the reality of our situation. We had to give up the southern ridge, the loss of life to keep it would've been untenable."

"Surrender is not an option your father entertains, Your Highness."

"Nor do I. But I won't get my soldiers killed for no reason. You may tell my lord father that I'll take his words under advisement."

"Oh, no, Your Highness, it wasn't a—"

"Is that all, Lord Nandon?" Arion asked. To most he sounded

polite, but Lena could hear the tired strain in his voice.

A little thrill of anticipation went through the tent, the knights rousing from their bored stupor at the prospect of the briefing being over.

Nandon cleared his throat again, mustache fluttering. "Not quite. There was one more thing, Your Highness. Not a problem per se, not yet. An anomaly, perhaps. But something to keep abreast of, certainly. If you would just look at these..."

The knights didn't groan, they were too well trained for that, but a collective gust of air did fill the tent with a disappointed sigh. Captain Joran threw a quelling look around the tent, and all of them straightened.

He was a strict commander, Joran was, a knight who adhered to the strictest sense of the knight's code. After years of her mother's witticisms, court etiquette training, and lists of who to befriend and who to avoid, Lena welcomed the strict routine. She'd flourished under Joran, the sensible, straightforward way he led and trained a relief.

For a while she'd thought he might even consider her for a promotion, but whatever favor she might've had with the captain withered away when she began sharing Arion's bed. Joran didn't abide any infractions to the knight's code, including fraternizing with one's charge. More than that, Lena sensed the captain thought she was unworthy of their golden prince.

He was probably right.

But he couldn't do anything when it was Arion she broke the rules with. And after long years of this campaign, Lena had finally decided the comfort Arion offered was more rewarding than the chance of Joran's approval.

Nandon didn't seem to notice the ripple of hope going through the knights as he fished another paper out of his leather folio and presented it to Arion.

"The censuses have come in finally, and—"

A guard really couldn't hold in their groan this time.

"—*and* there are a few things to note. First, you will see that, happily, the stores of grain have remained steady in the midlands despite worries of blight. The resources your esteemed father and Lord Balderak were able to summon seems to have mitigated the worst of it."

"Shouldn't Balderak have been able to take care of something like that himself? He's rich enough."

"Your father is generous and did not want His Lordship to extend himself too far in the process."

"Hm."

"Now, secondly, the capital has grown by approximately three thousand, six hundred, and..."

Arion shifted deeper into his seat, head just resting against the high back.

Lena glanced across at Catrin, and they exchanged long-suffering grimaces.

It took Nandon six points to get to the actual point.

Nandon cleared his throat. "And finally—"

Arion sat up straighter.

"There seem to be several discrepancies in about a dozen villages. Numbers that just can't be accounted for."

Lena's frown matched Arion's, and he quickly looked over the document Nandon had handed him.

"Discrepancies?" he repeated.

"Yes, Highness. It seems that there are quite a few villages with less people in them than recorded two, four, and six years ago. And it is something of a trend, with growing numbers—or, should I say, declining numbers of people in these villages."

"People are allowed to move," Arion noted.

"Of course, Your Highness, but these numbers cannot be accounted for. The additions to the capital and the other seaside cities, those numbers match movement from villages in the east and south. These anomalous villages are in the midlands and to the north. Less and less people every year."

"And there have been no reports of sickness? Or drought?"

"None, Highness. They no longer reside in their home villages but also don't register elsewhere in the kingdom. It is as if they have all simply vanished." And though he'd just reported a troubling conundrum, Nandon seemed to smile a little at his dramatic statement. It was hard to tell under that mustache.

Arion's frown deepened as he pored over the census records. "Villages don't just up and disappear," he said.

No, they didn't, at least not without being destroyed. But all the known avians were holed up in their cavernous fortress, they couldn't be raiding so deep into the Vagoran countryside.

Arion's mouth opened to ask more questions when a horn blared in the distance. It was a sound they all knew well now. Dreaded and familiar.

The knights snapped from inanimate ornamentation to guards again, hurrying from the tent to fall into formation. Captain Joran was at Arion's side in a moment, barking orders in that deep timber that carried across battlefields to ready for imminent attack.

A hive of activity erupted around Nandon, who stood in the middle with bulging eyes that couldn't land on any one thing. Helmets were grabbed, shields taken, gauntlets strapped. The knights moved like dancers keeping time, coordinated and efficient, ready in moments to meet the enemy.

With quick, sure movements, Arion buckled his sword to his hip. Then those golden eyes of his, as intense as the sun itself, trained on her. She knew him, knew his face well enough now to know when he'd made a decision.

"Protect Lord Nandon!" He pointed at Lena, and after a long moment, gestured at Catrin, too.

Lena didn't protest, she was too well trained, but the nod she gave him wasn't enthusiastic. Her duty was to protect *him*, not the king's secretary. He had his own retinue for that.

But then Arion and Captain Joran were gone with the other guards, out to see what new threat the avians had today. Lena could only hope it wasn't the burning cauldrons of oil again.

There was nothing else to do but join Catrin in ushering Lord Nandon and his own guards further into the prince's tent, away from the front and the danger. The lord's hands trembled and he was blessedly silent as they led him away.

They stopped and stood in a dark back room of the tent, as far as they could be without leaving camp. Lena took up position at the entrance and listened, trying to hear what she should be out fighting.

"Sounds like an arrow volley today," Catrin whispered.

Lena nodded. There was nothing quite like the high whine of avian arrows that grew louder and faster the further they flew from the bow. Long and thin with four ridges, they were meant to pound a body into the ground and pin them there. Most never got back up again.

She ground her heel into the floor, wishing to rejoin Arion. Lena didn't know what it would finally take to win this war, but she had to hope that out of his many, many words, Nandon could find the ones to relay to King Artemian that would do their situation justice. Something had to give here at Hadria, and Lena worried that too much longer, it would be them who cracked.

6

I don't like it," Alix grumbled.

Bel didn't like it either. They'd both protested as much, but Lena hadn't listened.

At least she'd taken Alix's advice about her clothes before heading down into the little human village.

They'd followed the creek until it turned into a stream, which turned into a river, which turned into a small lake. From the bluff he, Alix, and three of the horses perched atop, he could spy where the lake broke into three different branches.

A village, or if not a village a hamlet, or if not a hamlet a collection of about a dozen buildings, nestled cozily between the lake and one of the larger branches. They'd come upon it earlier in the morning, the cluster of log cabins shocking Lena. She admitted there wasn't anything on the map about this place. The river they'd followed hadn't been there either.

Bel had taken a look at the map she'd brought and thought they were north of where it ended. He remembered all those tales he'd read of a time before humans and avians vied alone for the world, when it'd been full of other magical creatures. This forest and the humans' ignorance of it had to make him wonder what else the humans didn't know.

His gaze sharpened on movement along the tree line down the slope, a quarter-mile from where the first buildings stood. Lena emerged on Alix's mare, her pace easy, both her hands on the reins and visible.

She'd made it only a few paces from the trees when more humans appeared from their houses, stopping her before she could get too near.

His guts clenched watching her ride alone. His chest burned knowing she'd wanted it that way.

"However much they're looking, they're expecting a knight and squire. Maybe even a big man with them. They won't suspect a lone woman," she'd explained patiently just a few minutes ago.

The tone only made him angrier with her plan.

"If it's so risky, then you shouldn't go either," he'd argued. Again. If it was too much of a danger for him, then he couldn't stand for her to go instead. She may not be an avian in human country, but all of them were wanted, no doubt had prices on their heads. Just because they roamed the fringes of the known human world didn't mean the promise of reward money hadn't reached this far north.

"We need to figure out where we are. And you can't be seen. Not again."

Bel opened his mouth to protest again, but Alix cut in.

"If they're expecting a knight, then don't ride in there looking so much like one." That had made both Lena and Bel pause. Alix nodded when she knew she had their attention. *"Lone woman or not, Yvain is a warhorse. Knights have warhorses. Knights wear bracers and cuirasses and scrape their hair back to look like they've got a stick up their—"*

"Yes, yes, I get your point." Lena had made an unhappy grumble, mouth scrunched to the side in displeasure, but she'd taken Alix's point and divested of her leathers. Her tight, serious braid went next, down into a plain tail at her nape. Somehow, it didn't look like Lena but Lena in disguise just with her shirtsleeves exposed and her hair soft around her face.

Bel had grumbled to himself then, too, acknowledging that Alix was right. There was nothing to do about her ramrod posture, but she threw her winter cloak around her shoulders, hiding the sharp, lean lines of her warrior's body beneath.

She'd unstrapped her sword and largest daggers too, which he'd been less than pleased about. And she'd traded horses with Alix, heading down into the human settlement on Miri and leaving the much bigger and better trained Yvain with them. The warhorse now munched the fresh spring browse poking up from the softening earth, unconcerned about being left behind.

Bel worried enough for both of them, especially watching the small shape of her against a growing number of other humans. The sight of so many, even so far away, had his skin itching. He may have spent the last ten years in human captivity, but within that time, he'd only seen a handful of them. He counted at least seven gathered before her, with more coming. And only with the dagger in her boot and at her back for protection. No leathers, no defenses. Too far away to hear, too far away for Bel to help before...

He let out a snort and cracked his neck to try working off the uneasy prickles in his limbs. He hated the tension building in him almost as much as letting Lena go down there alone.

Gods, she drove him mad sometimes.

"Once a knight, always a knight," said Alix.

Bel turned to see she'd bent forward in Lena's saddle, arms folded on the pommel as she took in the wide view with Yvain down snuffling along the ground for new shoots. A light breeze shifted the inky black curls on her forehead, but those sharp eyes of hers were trained on the lake below.

"How so?" Bel asked, not totally interested in the answer but willing to go along for a distraction. Anything was better than this worry eating at him.

What if they attack strangers? What if someone recognizes her?

Gods, he could drive himself mad, too.

"Always thinking they have to do the noble thing. And that they're always right. And know everything." She huffed an irritated sigh.

Noble. Right. The words churned in his head, making a headache bloom beneath his left temple.

It was the right thing to do, wasn't that what Lena had said. About coming back for him.

Much as it irritated Alix, Lena had been correct, it *was* right.

Why then did the words sit like slag in his stomach? He'd hated them when she'd uttered them and he hated them now, too. Not that he wanted her to have left him to his fate there in Finhöln's dungeon, but was it too much to want...*not* what she'd said?

He scrubbed a hand down his face, irritated with himself, with the day's events, with Lena, too.

"She's doing everything on her own. Refuses help," he ground out. His chest ached like a hot kettle, the frustration bubbling and building inside, his cheeks flushing with it.

"Mm-hmm," Alix hummed in agreement.

He didn't need to tell Alix. He knew that she knew. The girl had been with Lena much longer, had travelled with her many times, so perhaps that was why she responded to Lena's refusal of help with snark and sass rather than the desperate frustration that pooled inside Bel every time she wouldn't take comfort, wouldn't sleep the night, wouldn't let either him or Alix help. He may not have been a true avian warrior, honed on the battlefields, but he wasn't a helpless babe either. Neither was Alix, small as she was, but the thought of Lena thinking he was so helpless, so vulnerable...

His wing bases flexed behind him, as if to ruffle and puff out, make him look bigger, but he winced at the sharp bite of old pain that still lingered in the broken, bruised limbs.

He didn't like admitting it, but he *was* vulnerable with his wings like this. They'd set the wing again after tweaking it fighting off the boar, then tied it to his side for support. It was odd having his left wing splinted, so used to it being his right wing instead. One of the rules of his captivity was keeping his wing broken, something Lena had not only refused but rectified. Oh, she'd broken his wing—at the base, where it'd first been broken and never healed. Broken so it could be remade right.

Another thing she made *right*.

And she'd set his other wing, broken in a desperate attempt at escape before he knew she was coming for him but almost mended, at least before their scuffle with the boar.

He was tired of waiting for his bones to set, impatient to be whole and healed again. He was too reliant on Lena and Alix, out there in a forest that at least in name was human-claimed. His freedom came at their sacrifice, and there was no way to repay them other than help keep them safe, but Lena thwarted him at every turn, taking on the dangers herself. He itched with wanting to be strong again, not just willing but ready to take on more of the burdens.

Gods, is that how Lena saw him? A burden, a thing to be taken care of?

A wrong to be righted?

He hated that most of all.

And he hated that he hated it, for wasn't that who Lena was, down to the core? A righter of wrongs. A fixer. A champion for goodness. It's what he'd always admired about her, even in the early days when he hadn't trusted her, just seen a new warden to guard him through yet another insufferable winter.

Wanting more than that felt selfish.

Well, then, he was selfish. No denying it. He wanted to be a man to Lena, *her* man, who'd be there when she needed him and at her back to defend her. The one who held her in the night and walked with her in the day. The one who kissed her, pleased her, pleasured her in all the ways he could think of. He wanted her to have come back for *him*.

"Is that what this is to her, then? Noble? Righting a wrong?" He blamed it on his dark mood for his words coming out sounding so petulant.

"Always is," Alix said with a roll of her eyes. "You know it's just how she is."

"Yes, but I meant..." When he trailed off, Alix looked to him to see him swirl a finger around, indicating everything but himself. Even though he only meant himself.

She blinked at him, thinking, and Bel wished he could pull

everything back inside, all the sourness and vulnerabilities he'd managed to pack into one question and gesture. Gods, no wonder Lena saw him as something to take care of, if he was this desperate. He felt smaller than a mole with the way Alix perused him and wished he was just as deep under the earth, away from that jade gaze.

"Sort of," she finally said. Supremely unhelpfully.

Bel held in his huff.

Alix looked back down the slope, and they watched in tense silence as Lena was led into town with the other humans. No aggressive moves, and Lena's posture remained the same, but that could easily change. They were all harder to see, to discern when moving among the buildings, and after she dismounted Miri, she easily blended in with the other human bodies without her braid and leathers.

He should be grateful for that, but mostly he disliked losing her. He definitely couldn't help if he couldn't even see her.

They watched for what felt like hours, the only sounds the rustle of the breeze through his wings. The verdant grasses growing along the lake swayed with the wind, tickling his wing tips and calves.

"She was righting a wrong," Alix said thoughtfully, barely louder than the breeze. "But I think it was more...correcting her own mistake. She didn't want to leave you in the first place."

Bel blinked, letting the words sink in.

"It didn't seem like she had much choice."

"No," Alix snorted. "The prince turned everything upside down. And I guess you don't really argue with a prince."

Not a crown prince, at least. Being the heir had its perks. As a spare, Bel had felt about as important as the lichen growing on the north walls of Aeriand.

"I told her about the letter," she said suddenly, louder, hurried. They shared a glance before looking away.

Ah, the letter. It may make him a bad male, but he still wasn't sorry they'd destroyed it. He wasn't proud of it, but even just the name of the human crown prince and Lena's former lover made him burn with jealousy. How different their lives had been, his and Arion's, but both princes, both consumed with the war between their people, and both in love with the same woman. He wasn't proud of the vicious happiness at Lena being with him, here, in the wilderness rather than with *him* in the human capital, but he didn't quell it either.

Alix shifted in the saddle. "I told her I'd destroyed it. I didn't say *we* did it."

Bel nodded slowly. "I'm not sure it matters anymore, if she knows or not. But I appreciate the loyalty."

Alix grinned without feeling.

"I still think we did the right thing," he found himself admitting.

She looked up, startled. "Yeah?"

"Yes. He couldn't truly promise her safety. And...I got more time."

In the time between burning that letter and the prince showing up at Finhöln to fetch Lena himself, Bel had rediscovered what happiness could be, even still stuck as he'd been in that crumbling castle. He'd slept almost every night with Lena beside him, warm and soft, and in the cozy darkness, they'd told each other secrets and learned the other with words, hands, and mouths. He yearned for that again, a tugging pain in his chest that only worsened when she was near but not *near*.

He knew, rationally, that she worried over so many things, always had her head up and searching for threats. She was singlehandedly determined to make sure they made it out of this forest alive, and he couldn't fault her tenacity.

But gods, the woman needed to sleep properly. And he wanted to hold her while she did it. He wanted her smiles and caresses and kisses and anything else she'd give. His soul starved for it, making the desperation in him sharp. Part of him found it pathetic, but he still waited anxiously for anything from her, anything to show that she still felt something for him as a male, not just a cause.

Alix hummed thoughtfully. "That's true. She needed...something good."

That surprised Bel, and he looked up at Alix with arched brows. She and Pol had generally kept out of the budding closeness between Lena and Bel as it grew, had quietly watched as they circled each other and tactfully didn't notice when they spent all their nights and mornings together. He didn't think the girl disliked him or his being with Lena, but something about being considered *good* for Lena by Alix, someone who was possibly even more ferociously devoted to Lena than he, warmed him.

Alix cleared her throat. "If you're worried about *things*, I guess..." She blinked at the sky, searching for a tactful way to say it. "Just talk to her? I know she seems preoccupied right now, because she is, but who knows, maybe you can get through to her. But the important thing is," and she shifted in the saddle when she said this, turning to face him, so Bel figured he should do the same and turned to face what she'd say, "she *chose* to come back."

Bel tried to rein in his frown, unsure quite what to do with that.

"I know she did," was all he could think to say.

Alix grumbled in frustration. With him or herself or perhaps Lena, he didn't know.

"She chose to come back to you. And she chose to defy everyone else to do it."

Alix sighed, a mighty gust, and it almost could've knocked Bel over, he was so stunned by her words.

"I'm not explaining it well..." Alix righted herself in the saddle, blushing.

"No, I...thank you," he said, again not sure what he could say to everything she'd revealed.

For such a surly, snarky young human, there was an equal measure of wisdom packed in that little body.

"I'll speak to her," Bel confirmed, to Alix and to himself. "And perhaps talk her into sharing the load."

"I wish you the best of luck in *that* endeavor," Alix joked, holding her nose up in a high Vagoran accent.

They shared a moment of laughter, but it was soon swallowed up by the worry that only grew every moment Lena didn't reappear. They didn't find much else to speak about as the morning waned into afternoon, and Bel strained his eyes, forgetting sometimes to blink as he waited, *waited* to see a glimpse of her.

But she and Alix's mare remained out of sight. Humans milled about before slowly, one by one, retiring to their homes as the shadows lengthened and the afternoon sunk into evening.

He stood rooted to his spot, the helplessness and anger growing with the worry. Alix finally gave in to her rumbling stomach, but Bel couldn't move, convinced the moment he did, she'd appear for a moment, to signal him, needing him. He just had to wait.

And that's what he did. Waited. While the worries clawed at his insides, wanting out. Howling to do something.

7

Thick stew cascaded into her bowl, steaming her face, and Lena had to hold in her hungry sigh of pleasure. The warm savory smell of meat, the tang of herbs and carrots, and the slight saltiness had saliva pooling in her mouth.

Guilt twisted her gut for getting such a meal, but the aromas were too enticing to lose her appetite over it.

All of this must have played out across her face, for her host chuckled and ladled a little more into her bowl.

"I take it it's been a while since your last hot meal," said Sonja, the woman who'd opened her home to Lena for the night.

"If you don't count the oats," Lena quipped, hands itching to sink into the thick slice of fresh bread sitting beside her bowl.

Sonja snorted. "I never count the oats."

The crackling fire then dominated the conversation as she, her hosts, and their three children all focused on their food.

The meal before her was a hearty affair, all homegrown and cooked, full of earthy aromas and the sweet tang of butter. Lena waited for her hostess and the family to begin eating before descending on her own food. Her mother had seen to it that she know how to eat in a mannerly way, with lords and ladies, but Lena had spent most of her meals eating like a soldier, using her cleanest fingers to shove as much food into her mouth as possible.

She tried for a happy medium as Sonja and her husband, Garett, snuck glances at her.

In her time as a knight, she could have expected to be welcomed into homes on her journeys without question. Her position and the oaths she took for it were a guarantee that she meant no harm. She'd sat at other tables in other homes like this one across Vagora, both as a knight and squire.

But that had been under her own name, Lady Maddalena Montcaer. The first and last parts had opened many doors to her.

Now she was Maddie, a stranger from the wilderness.

And Sonja and Garett weren't opening their doors purely out of hospitality, either.

She kept her expression placid as their children took turns blinking owlishly at her over their bowls. She guessed the oldest girl couldn't have been more than twelve, and while she snuck looks at Lena through her dark lashes, the littler girl and boy weren't so shy, watching her with obvious curiosity.

Sonja and Garett themselves were a little more subtle, but Lena wasn't offended. It made sense.

She'd just appeared out of the forest this morning, seemingly by herself, with a tall tale of losing her hunting party and looking for the largest town in the area, where she thought she could rejoin her group. She'd said her name was Maddie, she was a hunter out with her father and brothers, and they'd gotten lost in the forest then separated after a boar attack. Several people had groaned in sympathy at that part of her story.

Though almost the whole little village had confronted her before she could make it into their settlement, they hadn't necessarily been threatening. A show of force, or at least, a show of numbers, to warn her against force.

Lena had told her story, adding as many truths as possible. She just wanted directions and perhaps a few supplies, which she could pay for. She'd told them as much, flashing the few coins she'd brought with her. She didn't like lying to them, felt it beneath a knight to lie her way into aid, but it wasn't just herself she had to think of. Bel's safety was worth more than a few lies.

And, it warranted reminding herself, she wasn't a knight anymore.

When the questions over her story had finally run dry, Sonja stepped forward and offered her a meal and place to stay the night. It hadn't truly been a request; Lena saw in the way the townspeople watched her that she was staying, at least for the night, willing or not. No doubt to lure anyone waiting for her in the woods out and use her as leverage against them if needed. Thankfully, it wouldn't be needed.

She hoped.

Alix sometimes seemed like an army of one, but she had to hope both Alix and Bel kept their heads and trusted her to do this.

"Come on then," Sonja had said, *"you can earn your keep with me spinning yarn. The king's money isn't good for much out here."*

She couldn't fault them their precautions. She'd been as surprised by their little village as they had at her showing up out of the forest. Apparently they didn't get many visitors, at least not ones they didn't know, which interested her. How many other little towns were there like this? Were they all connected by this unnamed river that ran just above the border of Vagoran maps?

So she'd spent her day spinning yarn with Sonja and her oldest girl, trying not to look too often to the west of town. Once, she thought she'd spied the glint of gold hair, but she willed it not to be so and hadn't seen it again. She kept her head down and strove to be good company through the day as Sonja probed her with friendly but pointed questions.

She'd certainly had worse conditions in captivity; at least she'd be fed a warm meal and offered blankets to bed down that night near the main hearth. When locked up in the king's dungeon awaiting his sentence for maiming Lord Balderak, she'd only had cold, weeping stones and rats for comfort.

The thought of that dungeon and her week spent in it never failed to send a chill down her spine, as if she could still feel the damp coolness of its deep shadows. But unlike before, when the memories had been fresher and her sentence still smarting, it didn't cause her pain.

Only a mild anger flickered at the memory of it, no warmer than the stew she ate.

As bellies filled, the family began to chat about the day, and Lena sat quietly, content to listen. Their easy, warm talk reminded her of nights spent in Finhöln, in those later days when Bel hadn't really been a prisoner, Lena hadn't truly been his warden, and Alix and Pol turned a blind eye to the two of them sharing a bed. She, Bel, Alix, and Pol had taken their meals together, enjoying the warmth of the big kitchen fire that banished the worst of the winter cold, and chattered about everything and nothing. They'd gathered together, just like this family, laughing at jokes made only for them and planning what they would do the next day. They'd relied on one another, like this family and this whole village did, to survive the harshness of a mountain winter.

A sudden ache enveloped Lena's heart, and she just stopped herself from rubbing the spot, as if she could soothe it away.

They'd been like a family at Finhöln. She supposed they still were something of one, although missing Pol.

When her food ran out, Lena tidied up her area of the table, wiping crumbs into her hands and then into her empty bowl. She collected all her dishware and mug and sat them neatly together. But with nothing else to occupy her attention, she sat watching Sonja and her family, hoping her curious gaze wasn't too intrusive.

Garett's big laugh wound down from the story he'd been telling the children. His porous nose and round cheeks had gone almost purple in his good humor, and he made a face at his young son for one more giggle.

"Davey was lucky he didn't get caught by that tree," Sonja remarked.

"You know Davey. Walking disaster. We take him along so he can feel useful." Garett and the children chuckled at that, as if this joke about the unfortunate Davey had been told many times.

With an appreciative moan, Garett reached up and stretched his arms and back. "So then," he said, looking to Lena, and she wasn't fooled by his attempted nonchalance. She'd been ready. "Where did you say you were from?"

"Whitewater," Lena answered. She felt Sonja's gaze on her, listening to confirm what Lena had told her earlier that day. She'd tried hard to remember her story, knowing she'd be telling it again and needed to keep her lies straight, which was why she added as many truths as possible. "A mountain town, though not so far north." Not the northernmost town she knew of, that title belonged to Longbourne, over which Finhöln loomed, but she'd been to Whitewater, a fort town close by, enough to make a good lie out of it.

"A place that's still on the map, then, I reckon," said Garett.

"Yes, one of the last ones, though. I don't think anyone really knows about any villages like yours, this far north. I know I couldn't have found it except by accident."

Garett chuckled to himself. "That's the point of coming up here for most of us."

She couldn't help but ask, "It's worth the winter here? It's bad enough in Whitewater."

"The mountains take the brunt of it," Sonja explained, gesturing vaguely to the west.

Lena had been wondering if they'd finally left the mountains behind. The slope of the forest floor had gentled, and she figured they must now be in the eastern foothills.

"Don't get me wrong, it gets awful cold here," Sonja added.

"Snows up to the eaves some years, but we take care of each other," Garett agreed. "It's a hard life, but a good one. A lot of folk are willing to deal with a bit of cold for a good life. It's what brought us all here."

"From the south? You chose to leave Vagora?"

Garett shifted forward, his eyes growing more serious. Lena kept her shoulders relaxed, not sensing a threat from him, but watched carefully as he leaned his elbows on the table and regarded her.

"A lot of folk would say it wasn't a choice, not really. Not with the way things have gone."

"Things?"

"The war."

"Garett..." Sonja shushed, putting her hand on Garett's forearm.

"It's all right," Lena hurried to say. "I don't know much about it, is all. News is so rare in Whitewater."

When Sonja leaned back in her chair and took her hand away, Lena continued playing ignorant. "Is it bad in the south? With the war? I didn't think it'd come so far down."

"It hasn't," grumbled Garett. "If anything, it's further away than ever. They drove the avians out of their city years ago and further east, into those mountains...you know the ones..."

"The Gogona," offered Sonja.

"Right, yes, the Gogona Mountains. They got a fortress there we hear."

Lena frowned. "But if they're so far away, what's wrong in the south?"

"Well, there's always the nomadic tribes making trouble along the River Dyne," Sonja said.

Garret huffed. "Always an excuse to play soldier against them. Every year they say this will be the time they're finally driven back. This will finally be the treaty that sticks. And every year those generals are wrong."

Lena held back her wince. Her mother, Lady Margot, had been the latest in a series of generals to sign a treaty with the nomads, once again carving out imaginary borders along the river. When Lena had been home last, seeking refuge at her father's academy of Lindenfaire while awaiting word of exoneration from Prince Arion in the capital, Margot had come to fetch her, confident the south had finally been dealt with.

"But that's not a war, not really." Garett paused to take a long pull of his ale. "This war with the avians has been dragging on for years at the base of their mountain. And taxes keep going up to pay for it."

"It got too painful," Sonja summed up. "It was coming to eating or paying taxes."

Garett nodded vigorously. "They're hoping to outlast the avians in their fort, squeeze them until they give up. The king's hoping he can do it before he squeezes everyone else dry."

"I'm not sure it's as dramatic as that." Sonja glanced at her, and Lena tipped her head to show she didn't mind Garett's rising volume. She'd heard about rising taxes; with an estate the size of Lindenfaire, she'd listened to her fair share of grumbling from her own father, but never that others were finding it such a burden.

"Oh yes it is. We took that great big city of theirs. Took most of their land, too. And now what? It's still going. There can't be that many of them left, but everyone's paying more now. Where did the riches go the king promised? If it's land we were supposed to want, we didn't have to take theirs. There's plenty here and we're proof of it! Dozens of villages like ours are doing just fine."

Lena tried to muffle her surprise, knowing Garett and Sonja would misunderstand it. It wasn't that they said such things about the king—Lena liked to think she no longer blindly believed whatever King Artemian said was truth. No, it was that Garett was completely right.

Did anyone really know what lay to the north? What was on the other side of this forest? The winters were harsh, but they survived fine in Longbourne and Whitewater. Why fight so hard for avian lands that were often mountainous, craggy, or arid? The avians had never made designs on Vagoran land; really, what would they do with all the flatland that was really only good for vineyards?

It was a good question, though Lena feared she already knew the answer. Avian land and riches had been touted as spoils of the war, but never as the point of it. Instead, the king vowed the annihilation of the avian threat.

With the continued siege at Hadria, their mountain fortress and site of their last stand, she could only conclude the very existence of avians *was* the threat.

The stew didn't sit well in her stomach anymore.

Garett sighed and leaned back in his chair, the fight draining out of him along with the air. He scrubbed a hand through his dark red hair and shook his head slowly, eyes distant.

"A whole lot for nothing at all, if you ask me," he finally said, voice much lower now.

"Nobody wants to fight avians in the homeland," Sonja said, patting Garett's shoulder. "But nobody seems to think that'll happen anyway. So many are moving up here now; we settled here with half of our previous village. We've known most of these people our whole lives."

"Couldn't stay there and pay for a war that never seems to end. Felt like we were dying along with all those avians. And we'd started to hear rumors of drafts. Nobles paying their taxes with commonfolk to send to war." A haunted look crossed his eyes, and he glanced at his children. They'd stayed quiet through the adults talking, watching with mild interest. Perhaps they'd heard all this before.

Garett pulled the half-finished loaf of bread out from under the bread-cloth and cut everyone another big slice. Lena took hers gratefully.

He didn't speak again until the children were down to gnawing the thick crusts.

"It may sound bad, up and leaving our home. But we did what we had to."

Lena blinked. "No, it's...quite smart," she said, and meant it. Many of the king's ministers would find a way to call it treason, dodging taxes, but Lena couldn't argue with Garett and Sonja's decision.

The couple looked at her in surprise, and she nodded.

"The war hasn't gotten to Whitewater, not really, but taxes have gone up. People are having to make do with less. And it's hard to understand why. You did what was best for your family, and no one can fault you that."

Sonja smiled gratefully, and Lena breathed a sigh of relief that that had been the right thing to say. Perhaps it was a lie that taxes were getting higher in Whitewater, but she doubted it. And the rest had been the truth. She'd rarely stopped to think as a soldier what bought, supplied, and transported the human war machine, with its long columns of soldiers, knights, artillery, horses, cooks, camp aides, tents, food, wagons, armor, medics, smiths, and more. It was always just there, provided, and though Lena had little to say for the front lines, rations had never been late and supplies had never been low. It was a small comfort as she lay on her bedroll, waiting for the sound of avian arrows raining down in the night. But knowing that it all had come at a steep price for her own people, that they went without so she and her fellow soldiers could fight another day...it was an uneasy, complicated knowledge that sat heavy in her heart.

"Well, I think that's enough war talk for one night," Sonja said, clapping her hands.

Lena helped her gather the dishes as Garett herded the children upstairs into the loft of the cabin to bed. She and Sonja fell into an easy rhythm of washing and drying, and soon there was nothing left to do but take her bundle of blankets and bed down for the night.

"Thank you for this," Lena said as she took the blankets Sonja offered. "You've been very kind to me."

"I hope you aren't upset at Garett's talk. Or that all of us have been...disloyal."

Lena shook her head, hating Sonja's pained expression. "Too much was asked of you. You're parents who want to feed your children. Not even Matella could condemn you for that, and I certainly won't."

Sonja snorted good-heartedly. "Do all of you speak so formal in Whitewater?"

Lena swallowed, but before she could say anything, Sonja just smiled and patted her forearm. "Goodnight, then, Maddie. We'll see you in the morning." It was a statement, not a wish.

"Goodnight."

Sonja nodded and headed up to the loft on the not quite stairs, not quite a ladder. Garett held out a hand and helped her up the last bit, and they shared a smile.

Left with the fire, Lena made a nest for herself near the hearth and tried to get comfortable. The noises of the family readying and then going to bed soon faded away, and the house fell quiet. In the silence, Lena willed Bel and Alix to know she was all right, to keep themselves warm in the night and be patient.

She'd get back to them as soon as she could.

--------•◆••--------

It was late in the night, when the inky shadows were deepest and the coals at their reddest, that something woke her. It was hard to tell what in an unfamiliar place; she was usually good at keeping mindful while she slept, ready to come awake and move if needed, often dreaming of the very unfamiliar place she slept in—but something must have caught her ears.

The house made house noises, small creaks with the wind and its occupants turning in their beds. All soft, nothing that should've woken her.

Lena blinked blearily, searching the dark, still cabin. Again, nothing. No creeping figure or reflective eyes. No shuffling or breathing.

She shifted a bit, easing her weight from her complaining hip. The blankets Sonja had given her were soft but the timbered floor was not.

Something caught in her peripheral, and Lena trained weary eyes on the far window.

Something gold glinted in the moonlight, washed a pale tone in the colorless night. She blinked, vision foggy, but again something gold teased along the right side of the window frame.

Whatever it was, it shouldn't be in the village.

She put a finger to her lips and shook her head.

The gold glint lingered, hovering just along the periphery like a ghost, but finally disappeared.

--------•◆••--------

So just follow this branch?" Lena asked, tracing the line Garett had drawn.

Garett straightened up from the crude map he'd sketched her of the next few villages. "Yeah, easy enough. A lot of people decided to settle along this river. Doesn't overrun its banks too often."

"And they go this far east?" She'd wrapped her mind around little clusters of Vagoran expatriates going north, but it was a bit more difficult to fathom how far east they'd settled. Any further and they'd be skirting avian country. Or what used to be avian country.

At least she knew there were resources on their way to Aeriand. And she thought she knew how to get there now.

"Yup, preferred the flatter land, I suspect." Garett picked up the paper, blew off the extra charcoal, and folded it carefully to hand to her.

"I appreciate this," Lena said, pocketing the map, "and everything you've done."

"That's what we have to do out here to survive, help each other."

Lena nodded and followed Garett out of the cabin to where Miri stood waiting. Sonja had sent her eldest girl to fetch Miri from the village stable, a large building where everyone's horse was stabled for convenience and warmth, and have her saddled.

Outside, Sonja wrestled with a pack bulging with dried fruit, oats, and the season's first carrots. Lena's stomach gurgled greedily even though it was already full of hot eggs, biscuits, and jam. Her mouth watered thinking of the jam, and she grinned when Sonja saw her, winked, and slipped a small jar of it into the pack.

"You didn't have to go to all this trouble," Lena said, hefting the pack onto Miri.

"It was a pleasure to have a guest," said Sonja. "Don't get many of them all the way out here."

"If your travels ever bring you this way again, you're always welcome here," added Garett.

Lena's eyes burned for a moment, tears threatening, and she had to stop herself from bowing to the couple. Knights did that. So she chewed her lip and stuck out her hand and heartily shook Sonja and Garett's.

"Here." Digging in her pocket, she pulled out the handful of gold coins she'd brought with her.

Sonja protested, but Lena pushed them into her hands.

"Please, take them. They may not have much use out here, but you never know. Use them if taxes ever make their way up here."

Garett snorted a laugh and Sonja nodded, smiling gratefully.

"Take care, my dear," Sonja said.

"Matella watch over and keep you."

Much of the village had come to see her off, and she waved and nodded to a few people as she mounted up and pointed Miri out of town. She turned in the saddle before hitting the tree line and waved. Sonja, Garett, and their children waved back.

"Bye, Maddie!" shouted the younger girl.

The cool dampness of the forest enveloped her, and where her neck had begun to sweat under her loose braid grew chilled. Her eyes took a moment to adjust in the shade, but she kept her eastern path even and easy, just in case one of the villagers followed her.

She rode for almost half an hour before looping back, making for the northwest shore of the lake. As she retraced her way back to Bel and Alix, she noticed how the trees thinned around the lake and village, no doubt for use in their cabins but also as a defense. They'd seen her coming even before she left the forest yesterday.

Lena could only hope that hadn't been true for Bel and Alix.

She stayed in the thicker part of the forest, where the woody columns should conceal her, but tried to pick up the pace, growing nervous now. Plenty of the villagers had left town throughout the day yesterday; Garett himself had spent the day logging. She supposed news of an avian wandering the forest would've gotten back to Garett and Sonja, so she had to hope that meant Bel remained hidden.

She needed that hope when she found where they'd parted yesterday empty. Abandoned.

The grass and low foliage was trampled or bitten off, making a sort of clearing at the top of the berm she'd left Alix and Bel upon.

Panic panged in her chest, and for a horrible moment, nausea swirled in her stomach as she imagined Bel and Alix captured.

Lena sucked in air, assessing the little clearing and trying to order her thoughts. Her movements were jerky as she shifted about in the saddle, looking...looking for what she didn't know...something, at least.

A handful of long, awful moments trickled by, and still neither of them appeared from between the trees. She didn't dare call their names, worried her voice would carry downhill and across the lake.

Finally, finally, there it was, a tuft of uneaten grass bent differently than the others. She moved Miri closer and saw a small trail leading deeper into the woods. The prints they'd left were shallow, the mud firm from several days without rain, but she could tell three horses and an adult male walked this way.

Lena dug her heels into Miri and hurried to follow their path.

The trail wended gently through the trees, not obvious but certainly not hard to find when looking for it. She hoped that meant they'd left it for her.

She followed their path south a ways before turning east, parallel with the lakeshore. For a moment, she lost the path around an outcropping of boulders. Her pulse jumped in her throat, and she urged Miri around the rocks, hoping to find—

Five sets of startled eyes fixed on her as she came barreling around the rocks. She had to rein in Miri, dirt clods flying as they skidded to a stop.

Alix jumped to her feet, and Yvain's ears twisted towards her happily. Beside a packhorse, Bel's wings twitched as he turned.

A sound of pure relief escaped her, and Lena leapt from the saddle. She wanted to embrace both of them, all of them, the horses too, but Bel was faster.

He was there in a moment, but before she could throw her arms around his neck and hold on tight like she wanted, his big hands captured her face. That intense blue of his gaze roved over her even more frantically than his hands, darting between her eyes, ears, mouth, shoulders, legs, hands, but not settling any one place.

"Bel." It felt good to say his name. They'd only been apart a night, and she'd had a pleasant enough time in the village, but the longing for him, to see him and know he was safe, ached almost as much as the relief of getting what she wanted.

"Did they hurt you?" He ran a hand over her head, around the crown and to the back, then down to her nape and behind her ear.

Lena shivered, not from the cold. She wanted him to hold her and to hold him too, fill her arms with him and just *feel* him.

But his eyes and hands moved in short, frantic bursts. So she gripped his wrists in either of her hands and said his name again.

This time she caught his gaze with hers, and she gently squeezed his wrists.

"They were very kind to me. I got what we needed and more."

He took a shaky breath. "I didn't like this at all."

"I know," she soothed. "It wasn't ideal."

His wings shivered before dipping and flapping anxiously. "We're not doing that again. You aren't going in alone again."

"Bel..."

When he shook his head, a frown darkening his face, Lena began to wonder if she'd underestimated just how much he'd worried about her going into the village. She hadn't been scared, not really, figuring the worst that would happen was she'd be run out of town. But as Bel threw his good wing around her and hurried her toward the horses, she realized just how fearful he'd been for her.

"Let's go," he clipped. He'd herded her to Yvain, and left with little choice, she scrambled up into the saddle.

She'd expected at least a quip from Alix, but the girl hurried over and mounted Miri before gathering up the packhorses without question or comment. Her expression was hard to read as she came alongside them, mostly because she wouldn't meet Lena's gaze, but she thought angry tears gathered in Alix's eyes.

Bel pulled himself up behind her and drew her back against his chest, wing around her and arm banding across her middle.

Without preamble, they hurried deeper into the forest. Lena's head spun from the speed of it, and words clogged her throat, all wanting out at once.

She twisted to look up at Bel, wanting to share what she'd learned, but his gaze was ahead, focused, shuttered and his mouth a thin, serious line. He held her close with almost his whole body but somehow felt distant. He held himself rigid, attentive but not to her.

The joy of her relief withered away, and she closed her mouth with a *click* of her teeth. Bel and Alix wanted to be away from there quickly, without the story, without even a word. Fine. The jar of jam would be her little secret.

8

Lena was annoyed with him, that much was clear as the awkward, stiff silences between the three of them stretched into a second day.

Well, that was fine, Bel was annoyed at her right back.

The sounds of stopping for the day rang overloud in the evening shade, buckles unbuckling, blankets rustling, leather creaking, horses snuffling, grasses and twigs cracking underfoot—no chatter or banter muffled their noise as the horses were unsaddled and camp began to take shape.

Despite not having the distraction of talking, Bel's movements were unfocused, and more than once he almost tripped or doubled in half running into Alix, and he kept bumping into Lena trying to fetch supplies off a packhorse. In trying to avoid eye contact and simmering nerves, they somehow managed to all be in each other's way.

It was a relief when he could finally slump onto a pile of folded blankets and just sit still. He gnawed on some jerky as Lena sorted out what they needed to cook for the day's dinner and Alix arranged her own bedding.

Bel watched Lena with tired eyes that stung when he blinked, soothed a bit by the steady motions of her hands. Calloused and scarred, they were a warrior's hands, strong, with a broad palm and tapered fingers with the nail cut to the quick.

The residuals of his worry for her trembled in his chest. The jerky he'd chewed sat like lead in his gut, and he had to remind himself that everything was all right, she hadn't been harmed, those villagers had been kind. He was even now eating the food they'd provided. But the unease that'd consumed him was hard to shake off, and its last vestiges left him jittery.

She'd told them haltingly over the last day what had happened in the village—or really, a lack thereof. She had more to report about these new villages sprouting in the north and how they could follow the river and these villages east, almost to the border of what had once been avian country.

It seemed they finally had their heading, and while some part of Bel looked forward to seeing his city again, no matter its state, most of him remained listless, a vague sort of dread tickling the back of his mind knowing they'd be sticking so close to human settlements. Places Lena would no doubt enter for supplies and information.

Just the thought had Bel's stomach twisting around itself. He knew she was capable, knew this worry was his burden to bear, but the desire to just hold her close and not let go was palpable and hard to subdue.

So was the sickly feeling of uselessness, of being hobbled. Shelved. Here he was, finally able to do something with himself, and he had to wait on the fringes again.

He gnashed the jerky in his mouth to a pulp.

Lena cleared a space for the evening's firepit while saying, "We should discuss the plan for tomorrow. I'm told it's a much bigger town this time."

"That's not saying much," quipped Alix around a big yawn.

Lena made a noncommittal noise. "Still, we know what's coming this time, sort of. We'll need to decide what the plan is."

"Other than you just going in alone and leaving Bel and me behind?" She said it in the lilting way of a joke, but there was a sharpness to Alix's eyes and shoulders that alerted Bel she was looking for a fight.

Lena's lips pursed and her jaw worked, as if she chewed on the words that wanted to come out, but in the end, she only shook her head and stood up.

"I'm getting firewood." And she marched from the new camp into the darkening forest.

She left a gaping silence in her wake, and when Bel glanced to Alix, the girl wouldn't meet his gaze.

A heavy sigh escaped him, his chest deflating as quickly as his mood. "Alix..."

"Don't," she snapped. "You don't have to scold me, too."

"I'm not going to scold you." Not when he'd been thinking the same thing. But that Lena had even brought up a plan, suggested they all should talk about it, and her quick retreat from camp, had him scolding himself. It was easy to be annoyed with her when Alix piled on too, but hadn't he told Lena before that there were no sides?

He rubbed his eyes with thumb and finger, relieving the mild burn of his tired eyes. "Why do you goad her?"

Alix shrugged, still not meeting his gaze. She pulled one of her blankets out from under her and draped it around her shoulders. They sat for long enough that Bel didn't think she was going to say anything, until, finally, "I guess...to get a rise out of her, to try getting her out of her head."

"Hmm." He couldn't fault the argument for getting Lena out of her head and her worry, but..."I think...it only adds to her burden, more than anything."

The realization struck him as the words left his mouth.

Gods, he could be an ass.

For all her stalwart demeanor and unflappable competence, his and Alix's moodiness affected Lena, even if she seemed unfazed. She fed off their moods, their surliness. None of it corrected or helped Lena, all it did was make her retreat further into herself, further into that overactive mind that they so wanted her to break free of.

He sighed again and stood, cracking his back. "I'm going to help her find wood," he said.

Alix just nodded.

Bel hesitated but gently put a hand on Alix's head. Riotous as they were, her black curls were soft to the touch.

"We're all tired," he offered softly. "Let's just get some sleep and see what tomorrow brings."

"Yeah," she said in a small voice.

Bel squeezed her shoulder and trotted off into the trees to find Lena.

The scent of moss and decaying plants was strong, almost heavy in the gloaming hour, but he didn't have trouble tracking Lena. She hadn't gone far, and he picked out her silhouette amongst the graying shapes of dusk.

Her back stiffened and her head cocked to the side, aiming her ear at him, long before he made it to her.

Bel picked up a fallen branch as he went; it was too large for their fire as it was, but he needed something for his hands to do. He made a noise in his throat—not quite clearing it, that felt like too much—and was grateful for the dark haze hiding the worst of his reddening cheeks and ears.

Lena looked over her shoulder at him, blinked, and turned to pick through a pile of twigs.

He'd half expected her to say something along the lines that she could do this herself, but when she remained silent, he forged ahead.

"Alix is just tired."

"We're all tired," she said in a tired, raspy way.

"You'd be less tired if you'd sleep through the night." It was out before he could stop it, delivered in a patronizing tone that even he winced at.

Even in the waning light, he could see the fierce cut of her glare. She frowned at him before turning away and stiffly moving further into the trees.

"I've got a lot on my mind," she said, more to the trees than to him, but he heard.

"I know. I know you do," he said, hurrying after her. He passed up several prime sticks, but they both knew he hadn't really come out here for firewood. "Lena, I'm sorry, wait please."

She huffed, and he could hear the depths of her frustration in that one sound. It made him wince again.

He came alongside her, shoulder to shoulder, not sure she would welcome his touch then. Perhaps it was cowardly, but speaking to the trees, into the dark, made words easier to say and he tried his best to pick the right ones this time.

"I worry about you."

She sighed. Not a huff this time but a weary sound that cut him to the quick.

"Really, I'm fine, it's just travelling—"

"I'm sure that's part of it. You've travelled much more than I have, of course. But, Lena, I can see all the worries you carry. They keep you up in the night, waiting for a threat that may or may not be there."

"We have to stay vigilant."

"Of course we do. But that doesn't mean you have to do all the watching *and* planning *and* protecting. I worry—Alix does, too—that you're running yourself ragged."

She turned her head away, staring out into the gathering dark that he knew her human eyes couldn't penetrate.

"We just...we want to help, is all. We're in this together and I want to do my part. I want..." He dragged in a long breath. "I'd bear your burdens, if you'd let me."

"I know."

It was said so quietly, but her answer stunned him. He turned his head to regard her; her profile was sharp as ever, but he marked the lines that ran under her eyes and around her mouth.

Bel wanted to smooth them away with his thumbs, and the itch to touch her was too great to bear anymore. He hooked a few of her fingers with his, pulling her just a little closer.

The next breath she took was stuttering, but she turned her palm into his and laced their fingers together, each digit easily finding its space beside the other, resting neatly in the valleys between knuckles. As if they were always meant to do this, had been formed just to slide into place between the other.

Just this small intimacy had Bel's chest aching. She held his heart as surely as she gripped his hand, but in their days in the forest, he'd begun to worry that his heart was the only one in danger.

Those days in Finhöln, those *nights*, had had an ease to them he longed for again. The openness, the closeness, breathing each other's air as they shared secrets and smiles in the cozy darkness. He'd known what she liked and wanted because she showed him, allowed him to see where she was vulnerable and how to please her.

He didn't know how to talk to this closed off Lena who would share nothing of her worries, but he knew he had to try. He hadn't tried, not really, not this, and it shamed him that he hadn't been trying for her, fighting for her. Enough people in the world wanted to destroy him and Lena both for what they were and had done; they didn't need to fight each other, too.

"What worries you so?" he asked her softly.

Bel thought he knew, but assumptions had gotten him nowhere. Neither had telling her not to worry.

She shifted her weight and curled the arm bearing a handful of kindling closer to her chest as if she wanted to curl that arm around herself, to protect against his question or to keep all the worries in or something else. But she held onto the wood and he held onto her other hand, needing to know.

"I know I worry too much..."

"They trouble you."

"I just..." She squeezed his hand. "I don't want to fail you. I want to get you somewhere safe and and...and..."

"Out of this damned forest?" he joked weakly.

Lena laughed just as weakly. "Yes. Just...*away*. A house somewhere, a homestead, maybe. But I don't know where or how." Her words died on a groan, and he remembered her anguish when he'd asked where she was taking him. Not knowing ate her up inside.

"Lena, wherever you are is where I want to be."

"But Aeriand…"

"I should go, for my people's sake. And for mine, I think. But if you said it was too dangerous, or that you wouldn't go with me, then to all Seven Hells with it."

She groaned again, but he thought it sounded less frustrated and more humored this time.

"I don't know if that's better," she admitted. "You were the first one to have any idea where to go."

And she hadn't liked the prospect of going to Aeriand, that had been plain enough in her reaction. Yet she'd adjusted their course and promised he'd see his former home again.

Lena let out another one of those stuttering breaths that Bel hated to hear. "No plan, no idea where to go, no aid if we need it. If anything goes wrong—if anything *else* goes wrong, I worry I couldn't fix it. That you or Alix could get hurt and I just…couldn't help you."

Tears garbled the last of her words, and Bel couldn't stand it anymore. He tugged her toward him, and she came easily, dropping the firewood so she could wrap her arms around him. Relief coursed through him, sweet and syrupy, as he drew his wings around them.

He'd already taken off his scarf and hood for the day, and her cheek found an exposed patch of skin just below his throat. Bel shivered at the contact, the heat of her damp cheek burning into him. He tightened his arms and gently rocked them.

"I'm not going to tell you not to brood over possible disasters. We both know I'm quite good at it myself." Her watery chuckle gratified him. "But if you've taught me anything, it's to meet them. And we can, Lena, together. I know there are few friendly places out there for us, but we can make it."

"I don't know what to do," she whispered into his collar.

"You don't have to," he whispered back. He nuzzled the soft hair at her temple, drawing in the earthy-sweet scent of her.

She burrowed her face deep into the warmth of him, down past the cloak and collar and shirt to where his pulse beat fast at his neck. They stayed like that for a long while, the night noises of creatures cautiously venturing from their hidey-holes a soft murmur as the last of the sunlight evaporated.

When she did speak again, it was into his neck and he barely heard her. "This is what I wanted, when I found you the next morning," she murmured.

Bel barely remembered their quick departure from the borders of the lakeside village; the roar of his terror had been loud in his ears, not ameliorated even with her in his sight again. All he'd been able to do and think was to get away, far away, and keep her safe. He hadn't allowed for anything else before grabbing her and getting away. Not even an embrace, a smile, a *thank gods you're all right.*

His whole body grimaced with knowing he'd let her down. Perhaps it was in a small way, perhaps his reaction had had its own merit at the time, but that didn't matter to him now. He dropped his cheek to the top of her head and held on tighter.

"I'm sorry, Lena. I was so worried I couldn't think straight. I didn't mean to add to your burden. You've already done so much, and I don't..."

The next words didn't want to come out, not easily at least.

Bel sensed her attention sharpen on him in the way her shoulders stiffened. He felt the moment she thought about drawing back, away, to look up at him, but he crushed her to him, so close he could feel her heart beating against his, and hooked his chin over her head.

"I don't want to be a burden," he admitted quietly to the night.

She'd gone quiet in the way only trained knights could, her breathing measured, no shifting weight or errant ticks. All that focus was on him now, terrifying and waiting.

"You've done everything for me, sacrificed everything, and I know I can never repay you for it. I owe you everything."

"You don't owe me," she murmured.

He shook his head, her hair rasping under his chin. "I do. I know I do. What you did for me was noble and good and I...all I feel is selfish."

Lena startled in his arms, made a small move as if to look up at him, but he wasn't ready for her searching gaze yet and didn't ease his grip or raise his head.

"Why do you feel selfish?" She sounded baffled.

Bel forced himself to say, "I want it to have been for me. I want you to have come back for *me*. Part of me hopes you'd have done it for any avian imprisoned like that, and I think you would. You're good down to your bones. But another part wants it to have been for me, because you care for me—not just as someone to protect or a wrong to right."

He heard her sharp inhale and knew she thought back to her words, as he so often had since she'd said them. *I had to. It was the right thing to do.*

"I don't want to be a cause or a burden. I just want to be *yours*. Your equal...your man. I'm selfish because even though I'm grateful for you coming for me, I want more. I want everything you have to give."

"Oh, Bel..."

Bel swallowed hard, shoving down his dread.

A stretching silence was his immediate answer, and he fought not to buckle under it.

Her hands moved from where they'd been clenched in his shirt at his sides to his back, caressing up and down in comforting strokes. Her touch was soft but somehow firm, the blunted nails creating just enough of a drag along the underside of his wing bases to make him shudder.

She turned her head, making stray hairs tickle at his nose, and kissed his throat.

"I'd be lying if I said doing right by you wasn't part of why I came back," she said softly. "So much was done to you by humans who were supposed to stand for good and integrity, and I...I couldn't let myself be one of them."

"You could never be one of them," he said with a conviction that rumbled through his chest.

He'd never fully understand her need to fall on the sword to atone for others' sins, but gods did he love her for it. It was almost painful, the amount of good Lena had inside her. He knew how lucky he was, that she'd spared him some of that goodness, and knew how selfish it was to want even more of it. All of it. And not just her goodness but everything that made her Lena. He'd made peace with this selfish need, but it was another thing entirely to stand before her with hands out to receive.

"I can't do nothing if I see an injustice. It's just not how I am. And I've done many stupid things to try fixing them."

He wouldn't call standing up to a cruel lord to defend the women he'd abused stupid. Approaching strange men in the forest hadn't been the smartest, but he'd known the moment they cried out for help she'd answer.

"But, Bel." She snuck a hand between them to trace his cheek and ear. He lifted his head, still not prepared to meet her eyes but knowing he needed to, whatever she said. They were a colorless dark in the burgeoning night, but they caught a little stray starlight, enough for him to see how they shone with her own conviction when she said, "There isn't just one reason I returned to Finhöln. So many of them are all bundled up together. But know, they all led back to you. I came back for *you*."

He couldn't help the grin that stretched his mouth; her words demanded it from him and he vowed to always give her what she wanted.

Her gaze, with pupils blown wide, dropped to his mouth, and in the next breath, Bel captured hers in a kiss that was sloppy, unpracticed, and perfect.

She made a startled noise in her throat, but then she was leaning into him, and he took it, took her weight, her kiss, everything she gave. He relearned the shape of her mouth and how she liked her kisses, how she wanted to be chased before being captured. He banded an arm around her back and lifted her even higher, making her balance on the toes of her boots but taking most of her weight.

Bel cradled her head in his hand, bracing her for the undertow of want that nearly drowned him. His grip was hard, his kisses and *ashitai* fierce; he couldn't be gentle yet, taking her lips in greedy passes that left her gasping. Her hand fisted in his hair, and for a panicked moment he thought she'd push him away, but she tugged him closer, telling him without words how she wanted it.

He consumed her; that's how it felt, like he took great gulps and mouthfuls of her to feed the heart beating hard enough she had to hear. A starving man at a feast, that's what he was, and he couldn't just sample, he needed to gorge himself.

She tasted just as he remembered, a mix of sweetness and spice and warm woman. A taste that was somehow both soothing and enflaming. He licked the inside of her mouth, needing more of it.

Lena scraped her nails across his scalp and nipped at his lower lip, making him want to combust from his own skin.

When they finally had to part for air, he realized he'd almost bent her backwards over his arm. She blinked up at him with owlishly wide eyes and lips swollen and pink. His self-satisfaction was thick and vicious, his smile smug, but he pulled them upright after one last kiss to her forehead.

She cleared her throat and pushed her hair out of her face with a trembling hand. "What a pair we make," she laughed softly.

"If by that you mean fierce, perfect, enviable, then yes."

Her laugh was genuine this time, just as he wanted.

"You didn't leave your vocabulary behind at Finhöln."

He smiled at that and couldn't help himself when he leaned in for an *ashita*. The gentle caress of his face against hers was so different from their frantic kisses before but no less perfect. It filled him up, soothing the raw, tired parts of him that were too quick to grumbling and surliness.

He worried sometimes that what he wanted, what he took was too much, but then, he gave himself in return. The human bards always put these feelings so eloquently yet didn't seem to do them quite enough justice. He couldn't quite describe it—how he needed her, needed her heart and goodness and sweetness but also needed to give himself away, to her, to her care. An exchange seemed too mercantile. A symmetry, perhaps.

Yes, he liked that.

He ended his *ashita* with a small kiss to her temple, where he could feel her pulse beating under his lips, fast and hard.

"I would be your man, if you wanted it," he said into her skin.

Lena drew her arms around his neck and hugged him tight.

"You're enough, Bel. More than enough. Don't ever feel you aren't my equal."

His arms closed tight around her again, and he sank a hand into her thick hair, digging under the day's braid. Her words felt almost as good as her kiss, but they weren't all the words he wanted right then.

Still, as she said, it was enough. For now.

It was full dark when they finally drew apart. He could still see the shapes of the trees and rocks, but Lena blinked blindly in the dark and gripped his hands.

"We should get back," he said, retrieving what sticks she'd found.

Lena nodded but didn't move.

He squeezed her hand and ran his thumb over the delicate skin of her wrist, content to wait.

"I'll try to do better," she finally said.

Bel lifted her hand to his lips and kissed each knuckle.

"The only thing you need to do is trust me. Let me show you what a man I can be to you."

"You don't have to prove yourself, Bel."

"Neither do you."

She went quiet at that, and Bel decided not to push. He tugged on her hand, and they carefully picked their way back to camp.

They were met by a roaring fire with a rabbit roasting on a spit. Alix sat turning the spit and munching on an apple. The girl looked up at them as they emerged from the dark, and a relieved smile creased her face.

"Took you long enough," she grumbled, but only halfheartedly.

Bel added their meager findings to Alix's impressive pile of wood.

"What's all this?" Lena asked, sounding pleased.

"You two were gone..." Alix coughed delicately, "a long time.

Figured I'd get things going."

Perhaps Bel should've felt guilty over Alix having the time to find a night's worth of firewood and dinner too while he and Lena kissed each other senseless, but when he thought about it, a smug grin was all he managed.

Lena sat down by the fire to help Alix begin carving the meat, and Bel set about making up a bed roll. For the two of them. He was more determined than ever to see she slept well tonight.

"Hey, Lena, I'm...I'm sorry. About before."

Bel looked up in surprise. Alix stared determinedly into the fire, avoiding both his and Lena's wide eyes. Noting the hard set of her jaw, Bel turned back around and made himself busy with the bedding.

"I didn't mean to upset you. I just...I'm not a kid, haven't been for a long time now. And don't tell me I'm fifteen, that's still a kid. You don't stay young for long in Cheapside."

"I know, Alix. I wish it were different," said Lena softly.

"Yeah. Me too." Bel thought her voice sounded a little wobbly with tears, but he didn't turn to check, just went on pretending deafness and disinterest.

"But I just mean that, I can help. You don't survive on your own out here, you know?"

Silence, then the creak of leathers. Bel peeked over his shoulder to see Lena embracing Alix. The girl threw her arms around Lena's neck and squeezed.

Bel smiled to himself and returned to rearranging the blankets for a third time.

"I rely on you so much, Alix. I want you to know that. I'll do better to let you and Bel help. We're in this together."

Alix made a watery noise of agreement before grumbling, sniffing, and pawing away her tears.

Clearing her throat, she said, "You can turn around now, Bel."

The females shared a wry smile as he joined them.

A lightness permeated the camp, and conversation flowed easily between them as they devoured Alix's catch, a handful of crabapples, and a spoonful of blackberry jam each. It was a simple meal but sated Bel in a way he hadn't felt in days. They spoke of the big town they'd get to the next day, deciding to find out what they could before entering. Between the three of them, they compiled two lists of provisions, one of necessities and the other of cravings and wishes.

By the time the spit was clean and the fire had been banked, they had a plan and Lena looked untroubled for the first time in weeks.

As Alix made herself comfortable in her blankets, Bel reached for Lena's hand. He pulled her toward the big nest he'd made.

"Come to bed," he whispered.

Her eyes darted between his before she nodded with a shy smile. He took a step away and around to the other side of the blankets, not wanting to crowd or push, in case she changed her mind, and worked to keep the fiercely pleased grin from his face.

He pulled off his outer clothes and tried not to watch her too closely, but his eyes caught on her nimble fingers as they unlaced the ties of her leather cuirass. He had to bite back an offer to help. Instead, he made himself busy getting settled under the blankets and adjusting his wings. It was over too quickly and then there was nothing to do but watch her.

Lena kicked off her boots, down to just knit stockings, undershirt, and socks before crawling into the nest beside him. The motions of bedding down with her were familiar and bittersweet, a memory of how it had been and how it could now be. He grinned when she scooted her back into his front and shoved her socked but shockingly cold feet between his shins.

He hummed in pleasure when she drew his arm around her waist and hugged his hand between her breasts. She settled into the blankets, going still and quiet, and Bel traced his thumb along the smooth skin of her sternum.

The crackle of the fire eased to a soothing cadence, a complement to the soft night noises of the forest. The horses' eyes and heads drooped, and Alix quickly fell quiet, just her head of curls visible above her blanket.

Bel enjoyed the calm and the warm woman in his arms. She hadn't fallen asleep, and he wouldn't until she did. He didn't push, though, just kept stroking his thumb back and forth, back and forth, drawing comfort and giving it in return.

She pulled his hand almost up under her chin. When she drew in a small, fortifying breath, he waited.

"I'd love for you to be my man...if that's what you want."

The words hit him like the crash of an avalanche, leaving his ears ringing. Bel pushed himself up on an elbow so he could lean over and look at Lena. Her pink cheeks didn't seem to be entirely from the heat of the fire. She peered up at him without lifting her head, as if worried what he'd say, as if fearing his answer would be anything other than, "That's what I want."

Her slow smile was incandescent, filling him up with the light of her. He used the hand she had hugged to her to pull her under him and angle her chin up so he had her whole gaze when he said, "I'm going to kiss my woman senseless now."

Lena huffed an embarrassed laugh, her cheeks flushing from pink to red, and he couldn't help the evil chuckle before swooping down to catch her mouth with his. He didn't know how she smiled and kissed at the same time, but he loved learning every curve of it.

Easing some of his weight down, Bel melted into her, the heat of her centering him in a way he hadn't felt in a long while. The night wasn't so dark, the forest not so vast when she smiled, and he drew in a long, mighty breath, taking her in, filling up on her, feeling the tightness in his chest finally fall away.

When her tongue teased his, he groaned and followed her down into the blankets. She cupped his face in her palms and traced the delicate points of his ears with her fingertips. He chased her tongue, chased the sparks of joy and lust bursting inside him. He could kiss her all night, could forget wanting to let her sleep, with how good she felt in his arms.

His wings shivered, and he drew his stronger one over them and planted the crook in the blankets beside her to free his hand. It was she who shivered when his fingers dragged down her throat and breastbone, and he couldn't resist the hot handful of her breast.

He swallowed her small gasp, lost in the petal-soft velvet of her skin. For how strong and calloused she was elsewhere, she'd always been maddeningly soft here, so soft his own calloused hands felt like a rough sacrilege. But her gasps and squirming hips made him think she didn't mind, maybe even liked the contrast of his rough palms against her softness as much as he did.

His thumb found the aching point of her nipple and stroked back and forth, back and forth. A warm sigh of pleasure hummed in her chest, and Bel greedily swallowed that, too. Gods, he'd missed this, the feel of her, the warmth, the chase and capture. What he wouldn't give for a bed and an hour to do this properly, but he was greedy, not choosy. If they could—

A gagging sound from across the fire had Bel and the horses' ears twitching. He and Lena looked sheepishly across the fire to see Alix, hands planted over her ears, making fake retching noises.

Bel heaved a sigh and tried not to pout. Too much.

Lena's quiet laugh puffed against his face, and he was struck again by her sweetness. Color still high from their kisses and Alix's antics, Lena brushed a thumb across his lips and rolled to her other side, into his waiting arms and wings.

Bel eased back down with Lena tucked against him, content as the camp settled again and off into sleep.

He stayed awake with the fire for a while, watching the lines ease from her face, and couldn't help kissing the gentle, unworried curve of her brows. Bel closed his eyes sometime later, arms and heart full, a smile still on his lips.

9

With nowhere else for her nerves to go, Lena settled for wringing her hands. She would've preferred to pick at her cuticles or bite her nails, but she'd kept her gloves on to safeguard them as she and Bel waited atop Yvain for Alix to return.

It was the best plan, she knew, the one they'd all decided on. Alix would go down on her own, on foot, into the sprawling town nestled between the river and two gently sloping hills. Large cabins of dark wood had been built up and down either slope, some even two floors with a whole thicket of chimneys squatting along the peaked, moss-covered rooves. Dozens, possibly hundreds of buildings housed perhaps a thousand people, larger even than the town that surrounded her father's academy at Lindenfaire.

Alix had decided it'd be easy to creep between the back gardens of a few houses and walk into town. She thought she could mix with the townsfolk going about their morning easy enough in a town that size and suss out what all they could find and possibly buy.

Alix could move silently and blend in in a way that Lena hadn't taught her and that Alix couldn't teach her, either. It came from a childhood spent on the streets, creeping down alleyways and into places she shouldn't be, looking for something to fill her stomach. A deadly combination of careful yet determined made her footfalls silent, and her slight frame often made her below notice.

It all made good sense when they discussed it, but now, with Alix out of sight, Lena needed to fidget.

It didn't help that guilt rode her hard; she understood now what it'd been for Alix and Bel to wait and watch her go into town alone. It must've been agony to wait through the afternoon and night without word.

Bel shifted behind her, peering over her shoulder. She felt his small grin as he pressed his lips to her cheek and offered his hand instead. "Here."

She took his big hand between hers and wrung it instead, and more than the fidgeting, his touch and warmth helped calm her a little. After a few moments, she came down from fidgeting to simply playing with his hand and fingers, tracing and caressing and massaging the calloused pads and defined lines crisscrossing the palm.

"She'll be fine," Bel assured her. She welcomed his confidence, but his posture remained stiff in the saddle. They both battled their own worry for Alix.

"I know she will." She sighed, the sound rolling into a groan as she slumped back against him, her head smacking his shoulder. "You're right, though, this waiting is awful."

"Yes." Bel took his turn with her hands, gently rolling his thumbs over the centers of her palms and working the tension out of each finger.

She hummed in pleasure and leaned back fully into him, letting him take some of her weight. She was almost embarrassed at how fast his small massaging had her eyes blinking more languidly, and after a few minutes she was in danger of dozing off. She blinked away the heaviness but was too comfortable to move.

It was as if her body, finally knowing a good night's rest, was all too ready to seek another few hours of sleep. A night spent in Bel's arms, knowing he was at her back, feeling his warmth and weight, had done her a world of good. The fire had lulled her to sleep, and she hadn't opened her eyes again until Bel woke her with more kisses.

Refreshed. That was the word for it. Even though all three of them were caked in the grime of the road and in need of deep, long baths, her heart was lighter for the rest and Bel. She hadn't told him that, of course, didn't think she'd survive his burst of smugness, but he'd watched her as they prepared that morning with a pleased glint to his eye.

They hadn't restarted training that morning, Lena decided they'd leave that for after this larger town, but she had gotten them going with stretches. The ache and pull in her limbs had been delicious, joints popping and bones cracking, relieving more pressure. Alix seemed more focused afterwards, all lithe grace as she climbed onto Miri. Lena had even been sure to work Bel's wings, stretching them out and checking the healing.

It never ceased to amaze her, the avian wingspan. Fully extended, each wing alone had to stretch eight feet. How they folded into such a neat bundle on his back was extraordinary. Both she and Bel had been more than pleased with his range of motion. His right wing, the one that had been broken over and over, still gave him some trouble, and she didn't want to voice her concern that it might never be fully corrected. There was just so much damage...but she made herself cling to hope that perhaps, one day, it could bear his weight.

One day, he'd fly again. She'd make sure of it.

His left wing, broken much more recently, had healed nicely, though she eventually pried out of him that it ached toward the end of the day. "*It's a good ache,*" he'd rushed to assure her, "*the one where you know everything's knitting back together.*"

So, they'd started their day stretched, limber, and well-rested. It'd been a much better start than the dozen or so that had come before.

Still, Lena could feel the tension creeping back into her shoulders as the time trickled by without sign of Alix. She and Bel kept quiet, listening for any commotion in town, any call for help, but nothing came. *That's a good thing*, she kept telling herself. She'd been fine with Sonja and Garett. Alix would be fine too, was perhaps even better suited to such a mission than Lena with her small stature and quick feet.

Lena reckoned a full hour passed before she thought she spotted a little hooded head bobbing between the squash in one of the gardens that bordered the forest.

Bel's grip tightened the slightest bit; he'd seen it too.

Sure enough, Alix came bounding up the slope to them, her breath puffing in the morning chill and her mouth wide in a happy grin. She flicked back her hood, giving her curls freedom, and planted her fists on her hips, triumphant.

Lena and Bel sighed in unison.

"It's perfect!" Alix announced.

Lena threw a leg over Yvain and dismounted. She couldn't help holding Alix's head and turning it this way and that. Just checking.

"Nobody noticed you?"

"Nope," she snorted, though she let Lena fuss a little longer.

Finally satisfied, Lena took a step back and gave Alix a nod. "All right, let's hear it. Layout?"

"A hodgepodge that'd make the king's city planners weep," Alix snickered. "A lot of houses, but there are a few businesses toward the river. Looks like they've got a little harbor going too. And the best part." Alix's eyes twinkled and she leaned in, as if about to deliver earthshattering news. "There's an inn. At least ten rooms, if I counted windows right."

Lena's brows rose in surprise. Perhaps it seemed mundane, but an inn, all the way out here? In a town that shouldn't exist? Perhaps not earthshattering but surely earth-shifting.

She scrubbed a hand down her face, thinking. The twinkle in Alix's eyes speaking of the inn was easy to decipher; Lena's own temptation at the idea of a bed and hot food and water hit hard and strong, her hair feeling lankier, her skin grimier. Her stomach almost worked up a supporting growl.

And there was an inn nearby that could solve all these things.

Lena groaned, linking her hands behind her head and twisting around. Such a temptation, but did they dare bring Bel into a human village? Of course they couldn't.

She hadn't anticipated anything this big, even with Garett's description, but it did present opportunities. They really did need to get Bel his own horse, and much of their supplies had run low. But that didn't mean they could risk Bel just for a hot bath.

She'd give up almost anything right then for a hot bath, but not Bel's safety.

Bel slid off Yvain to join them and asked Alix to point out where about the inn was. Alix enthusiastically gestured to what landmarks she could, describing in detail the roads and the houses and the busy people in them.

When she finished, Lena looked to Bel and asked, "What do you want to do?"

He blinked in surprise before shifting his gaze back to the village.

"I vote inn," said Alix.

"That was a given," replied Lena.

"You saying you *don't* want a bed and bath?"

"Of course, I do. But we can't just ride Bel through town. This might not be Vagora proper, but we don't know what these people think of avians."

Alix hmphed but replied, "Yeah, that's true."

"I think we should go."

They looked at Bel, shock written across their faces.

"Bel, I don't think..."

He shrugged. "I know it's a danger. But I think it's worth the risk. Besides, these people left the kingdom. They aren't sympathizers with King Artemian."

"That may be, but we can't say for sure they'd be friendly to an avian."

"No one's saying he needs to go in there with his wings out," suggested Alix. "With your cloak and hood on, you look human enough."

From a distance, perhaps. Up close, there was no mistaking the hard-cut planes of his face or the slightly inhuman size and color of his irises. And while his wings were hidden from sight under his cloak, they still made a noticeable contour along his back.

"Plus, I guarantee nobody down there's seen an avian," Alix added. "Unless you've gone soldiering, all people know about avians comes from the stories brought back and the old books. Hells, I was honestly a little disappointed you didn't have a beak when I first saw you. And chicken feet."

Lena couldn't help her laugh, and Bel touched his nose, looking offended, but his grin was hard to hide.

"We aren't birds," Bel grumped.

"As far as humans are concerned, avians are monstrous beasts, more animal than anything. They won't expect you to be human-shaped."

"I'm avian-shaped."

Alix huffed, and Lena bit back her grin. Bel could be difficult just to be difficult, and it never failed to rile up Alix.

"You know what I mean," Alix dismissed, rolling her wrist.

One side of his mouth kicked up in a grin, Bel looked to Lena. "I think we can manage it. I'll lay low. And who knows, we may find or hear something important."

Lena's guts churned, and she wanted nothing more than to rip off her glove and chew on a nail, but she made herself pace instead. Alix and Bel watched her quietly walk back and forth, back and forth.

"If we do this—"

Alix whooped. "First! I get the first bath!"

"—then we do it carefully. We think everything out."

They spent the next half-hour deciding on how far up to place Bel's hood. He patiently sat on a rock while Lena and Alix debated, sliding the hood forwards, backwards, and forwards again. Too far back and it might fall off, revealing the sharp point of his very avian ears. Too far up would completely hide his face and make him look nefarious. They'd be going in together and the key would be to not draw suspicion. A hulking male with his hood drawn low would garner looks.

When they'd settled on where to put the hood—not too far back and not too far up—next came the problem of his back. Lena finally decided to strap her broadsword over his shoulder. A hulking male with a big sword strapped to his back would garner looks, but to the sword mostly, not the peculiar profile of his back.

Her churning guts hadn't calmed by the time they were ready to go. Bel scrambled up onto Yvain by himself while she mounted up with Alix on Miri. They needed to resemble a family, at least at a quick glance, and Lena and Alix thought the arrangement would look the most commonplace.

"You going to be all right on him?" Lena asked.

Bel smiled and patted Yvain's neck. "We males take care of each other."

Yvain chuffed and started down the slope at a fast clip, bouncing Bel back into the saddle. Lena urged Miri to follow with the packhorses as Alix snickered.

"I'm buying everything, all right? So get however much food you want," she told Alix. The girl more than deserved it.

"Jam? Preserves?"

"Yes."

"Milk buns? Sticky buns? Teacakes?"

"Yes, yes, and yes. We'll buy out the baker if we have to."

"Candied nuts?"

Lena laughed. "If they have them."

Alix whooped again. "Hope you don't regret it," she laughed, patting her stomach.

Lena hoped she wouldn't either.

———— •◆•• ————

Her insides still clenched with worry, but the further into the village they got, the more cautiously optimistic Lena became. They entered on one of the main paths into and through town, following others making their way from homes on the outskirts further into the village. They weren't the only ones to come out of the forest, either; others on horses or leading mules came in with bundles of furs, firewood, and moss to sell and thick layers of outerwear.

She was most relieved by how many still had their hoods or cowls up in the morning chill.

Of the three of them, she worried she was the one who most stuck out. *Don't ride in like a knight*—that'd been Alix's advice before, but it was harder than it seemed. Even with Alix in front of her, she felt vulnerable, exposed without her cuirass and sword. She couldn't help the straight, stiff way she sat in the saddle and had to hope her expression wasn't too grim.

Hopefully if anyone looked at them, all they saw was Alix, uncovered head twisting this way and that, trying to look at everything at once, and squirming in her seat with excitement.

As for Bel, she needn't have worried about him looking hulking or nefarious. Those big eyes sat wide in his face as he took in the human village. He went slower than Alix, lingering on each new sight before moving on to the next. She watched him for any sign of anxiety or fear, ready to turn them around and back into the relative safety of the forest, but his posture remained tall, if guarded.

A burst of pride swelled in her chest. He may not think so, but riding into a human town like this took so much bravery.

The houses grew thicker the further into town they went. All made of a wood that had darkened into the black-brown of rich earth, the browns were broken up by shocks of greens, reds, and oranges. Moss insulated the steep rooves like fur caps, and here and there new wildflowers burst from the muzzy blankets, adding a pop of purple or yellow to the greenish brown. Almost every house had a garden and vegetable patch with fat squash and tomato vines wending around fence posts and porch columns. Colorful curtains peeked through the small panes of glass on the front windows, giving the houses a look of sleepy peace.

A few townsfolk stood on their porches, sweeping, tending to gardens, or putting on boots. Neither they nor the people already out wandering the packed earth streets gave their little group much mind, and Lena thanked Matella and each Maiden that they didn't seem worth more than a passing glance to passerby.

Lena couldn't quite see the shore through the buildings, but soon the tang of water and mud touched her nose. From their perch in the forest while waiting for Alix, she'd been able to make out that here, the river widened into something of a delta, branching out into many different fingers, some wide, some shallow, some narrow, deep, or sandy. It made her wonder if, when the rains came in spring, this area was more like a lake.

"It's around this next bend," Alix muttered to her.

Lena had guessed from the growing number of people out and about that they approached the town center. The road narrowed as it gently curved to the left, making everyone pack in a little tighter.

She urged Miri forward a little quicker, getting in front of Bel and Yvain to take the lead since Alix was the only one who knew where they were going.

She caught Bel's gaze as they passed, and he gave her a nod, assuring her he was all right.

Lena needed that assurance as they fell into single file; she didn't like Bel being out of sight. It wasn't that she didn't trust him to guard her back—*he* was the one most in danger here, not her, and she had to fight the urge to check on him over her shoulder.

The inn was easy to spot once they'd turned the corner. Easily the largest on a street full of buildings made of wide, bulky timbers and brightly painted doors, it sat like the biggest bird in a line of roosting hens. Three stories tall, the peaked roof had been painted a cheery red rather than covered with moss, with a wide front door to match. Acorns, berries, and various foliage had been carved into the door and thick timber eaves, and an acorn-shaped sign hung from a horizontal pole above the door, proudly proclaiming it the Riverbend Inn.

Miri's ears swung in irritation as Alix squirmed and wriggled, practically vibrating with excitement.

Lena swung a leg over and dismounted, handing Alix back the reins. "I'll go see about rooms," she told them, looking back at Bel.

He didn't look frightened or unsure, but the lines around his eyes were tight, and Lena thought she understood. There were many people about, more than he'd seen in years. Human people.

Lena shouldered the satchel with her money purse inside and hurried through the gleaming red door. It swung open easily, without even a squeak from the hinges, and the warmth of the inn enveloped her like an embrace.

The tang of yeasty bread and beer saturated the place, but not unpleasantly. The dark wood of the town continued inside, but it'd been polished to a high shine, gleaming as finely as metal in candlelight. She walked further into the great room, weaving between neatly placed tables and chairs. A wide bar at the back beckoned her, and she realized this must also serve as a tavern. Kegs that could've easily fit her, Alix, and Bel inside together loomed over the bar, which had been made of a lighter wood than the rest of the building, polished to such a high shine that it could almost be mistaken for amber.

A man and woman stood behind the bar, talking low to each other as they passed plates between them. The woman's riotous red hair had been partially tamed into a messy tail at the top of her head, but a cascade of curls had escaped the confines to hang about her freckled face, neck, and shoulders. Her cheeks glowed pink as she worked elbow-deep in a sink full of suds, scraping dishes that she then handed to the man. He took each dish diligently, working the dishrag over ceramic plates and cups with a delicacy that belied the girth of his meaty hands and fingers. His shaved head gleamed almost as much as the bar, and he peered up at her from below a heavy, bushy brow.

"Customer," he grunted, elbowing the woman.

"Well, what d'you want me to do about it? I'm soaked through."

The man cleared his throat, a blush peeking over the massive beard hiding his lower face.

"What can we do for you, lady?" he asked.

Lena swallowed at the moniker, reminding herself that it was just politeness. Ladies weren't just female knights.

"I was hoping you had a room available."

"How many?" The woman bumped him with her hip. "I-I mean, how many people?"

Lena opened her mouth but had to consider. Did she say two and sneak Bel in somehow? Or did she say three and make him walk through the room to the stairs at the back?

"Three," she said, deciding it would be hard to hide a large avian male.

The innkeeper nodded. "Should be doable."

"We've only got one room left," the redhead said from over the sink. "Everyone's in town for the salmon run."

"Oh, yes, right," Lena played along, "it's that time again. I'd forgotten."

The woman huffed a laugh. "You won't again while you're here—all anyone talks about is fish." She lifted her head to peruse Lena, eyes narrowing infinitesimally. "You come to fish?"

"No, not this year. My family and I are just passing through, headed south after this."

The innkeeper made a sympathetic sound. "Don't envy you that."

"Mm," Lena hummed noncommittally. So this was another place, albeit much larger, that had no love for Vagora—at least a Vagora under King Artemian. A town this size, with so many thriving businesses and families, had to have taken some time to establish, though. Sonja and Garett had only been in their homestead two years, but something like this town would've taken longer, perhaps even a decade. At least Lena assumed—she couldn't exactly ask now.

Lena tried not to grimace when the innkeeper told her how much a few nights, food, horse stabling, an extra cot, and hot baths would be, but they settled on a price that she could stomach. Only one of the bigger rooms was left, many of the travelling fishermen taking smaller rooms or piling into one to save money and maximize their profits from the salmon run. The redhead assured Lena the bed was large and a comfy cot could be provided for another. Lena agreed and added an extra coin for the warmest blankets and coziest cushions for Alix. Perhaps Alix wouldn't be buying out the baker, but there would be plenty of coins she'd taken from Lindenfaire left for the girl's sweet tooth.

"I assume you still take the king's gold?" She fished out the bag with the coins, trying not to make it jingle or give away too much about how much she had.

"Gold is gold," the innkeeper agreed.

Lena counted out the coins, leaving them neatly on the bar for the couple to see. She ignored how the redhead watched her but was ready for her next question.

"Where did you say you were from?"

"Whitewater." And she told them the story she'd spun Sonja and Garett—her name was Maddie and she'd lost her family on a hunting expedition, though this time the family had been her husband and sister. She'd reunited with them yesterday a few miles outside town and they'd decided to regroup and resupply before heading south again.

"Well, time it right and you'll be able to buy your weight in salmon cheap in a few days," said the redhead, returning to her dishes, seemingly satisfied with Lena's answers.

"You'll get sick of the stuff quick enough," added the innkeeper.

"Anything beats boiled oats." The couple nodded agreeably. "We'll stable our horses and head up to our room, if it's ready."

"I'll go open the windows to let some air in," the redhead said, drying her hands on her apron. "But baths will have to be tomorrow, it's lent right now and two other rooms got their names down before you."

"A few buckets of hot water will be fine, if that's doable."

They agreed, and Lena went outside again, dreaming of clean hair and a face scrubbed raw.

Bel and Alix were where she'd left them, though Bel had dismounted and stood between the horses, obscuring him from those passing on the street.

"Room and board," Lena announced, making Alix whoop.

"And baths? Please say baths," Alix pleaded.

"And baths. Tomorrow."

"I'll take it."

She led them around back, where the innkeeper had said they kept a small stable. It was almost full to bursting with the three horses already there plus their four, but Yvain and the others settled in happily. Her trained, expensive warhorse whinnied merrily when the saddle came off and buried his face in a bucket of oats. Lena had to laugh, giving him a quick brush down before gathering with Bel and Alix just outside.

Alix had her fists on her hips, head tilted way back to observe the upper floor windows.

"Do you know which one's ours?"

"No. Why? You going up the hard way?"

"No, but I figured Bel would be."

Bel pouted. "Not my favorite way of getting into a room."

"Speak for yourself," Alix quipped, all arched eyebrows and feline smirk.

"Nobody's scaling walls or sneaking anywhere. I told them there'd be three of us. Just keep the hood up," Lena told Bel.

He seemed more enthusiastic about risking going inside than climbing into their room, and Lena couldn't blame him. They couldn't all be Alix.

Bel readjusted his hood, unstrapped the sword from his back, and grinned at her, wings shivering in excitement under his cloak.

"Let's go."

"You're sure?" She wanted to be absolutely sure he'd considered the risks.

"Nothing's keeping me from a real bed. Lead the way."

10

Bel held his breath passing over the doorstep of the inn. It was an old Bavian superstition to ward off evil spirits when entering a new place, and he couldn't help it, even if the acorn sign and cherry red door exclaimed that anyone was welcome inside.

The noise and smells of the town fell away inside the warmth of the inn. All the woods had been polished to a warm shine, and a healthy fire crackled away in a cavernous hearth on the east wall. A rack of antlers, ceramic vases, dried flowers, wooden balls, pewter mugs, and other trinkets littered the mantel. He couldn't help thinking all of it was carefully deliberate, to give the inn a sense of warmth and welcome.

It worked; he almost felt welcome.

His wings rustled and shivered with the change in temperature, and he clamped them even tighter to his back, ignoring a twinge of pain. At this rate, they'd be stiff and half-asleep when he could let them loose, and he didn't look forward to the pinpricks that'd come with it.

He followed Alix and Lena, who nodded to a bear of a man at the back of the great room. Bald and bearded, the man was even larger than Bel, with wide square hands and a nose that had been broken more than once in a brawl.

The innkeeper nodded at Lena before surveying Alix and then Bel.

Habit almost made him drop his gaze when it met the innkeeper's. Drawing as little attention as possible had kept him alive in Finhöln with his other wardens. They too had all been brawny human men with wide chests and strong hands. Bel had fought at first, rebelled against his captivity with the determination and foolishness of youth. His first warden, Hallan, had beaten and whipped the fight out of him.

The innkeeper took in his face and hood, blinked, and nodded again.

Bel nodded back and finally sucked in a breath. His stomach grumbled from the smell of baking bread.

The warmth and smells reminded him so much of Pol's kitchen, sending a pang through his heart. He'd never be homesick for that dreary castle, but he did miss his friend and the warm illusion of safety Pol managed to create. The memory settled bittersweetly in his mind, making the sensation of being indoors again a little less jarring.

He'd spent so much of the past ten years inside, confined, that sometimes he thought maybe he'd never want to go indoors again. But the roaring fire and promise of a bed was hard to argue with.

A diminutive redheaded woman came marching from further back in the inn, laden down with blankets and cushions. She was the opposite of the innkeeper in almost every way, nearly half his size, but his look and movements were exceedingly gentle as he reached to take her load from her.

The woman smiled, shaking her head. "Grab a few buckets of hot water for them, love."

The innkeeper obliged, and the redhead beckoned the three of them deeper into the inn, near the back, where a staircase followed the west wall before turning further up along the north wall to the upper floors. An uneven door stood open under the stairs, a mountain of cushions stacked neatly inside.

"Here now, have your man take these, and I'll grab a few more."

Bel only had time to hold out his arms before blankets and cushions came crashing onto his forearms. He held in his grunt, shocked such a small woman could carry all these.

Alix giggled, and Lena reached up and adjusted his hood for him, a small smile on her lips.

The woman returned to lead them up the stairs to the second floor, chattering the whole way. They learned her name was Nina and her husband was Lorne and they'd been running the Riverbend for over five years now. They'd had an inn somewhere in southern Vagora before but left it for here, where they got to build an inn they could be proud of. It was a lot of work, especially with so many in town for the salmon run, but Nina enjoyed the bustle and all the new faces coming into town.

"I love hearing everyone's story," Nina said, ushering them into one of the north-facing rooms. "So be ready to tell me something interesting over dinner!"

Bel clasped his wings as tightly to his back as he could as he passed her into the room.

Nina's chatter about the town continued as they laid out all the soft things they'd carried up and she showed them the view of the river. Bel took stock, pleasantly surprised by the room. It was indeed large, larger even than his old room and library in Finhöln, with a plush four-post bed dominating half the room. An empty trunk sat open at the foot, and chairs flanked either side of the headboard. The west wall had a bricked fireplace, which Nina bent over to get going. This mantel too had all manner of trinkets, porcelain animals, wood carvings, decorative bowls, and a vase with dried flowers and twigs. A thick carpet covered the floor from the hearth to the bed, shot through with reds and blues that matched the delicate embroidery of the quilt and pillowcases.

Nina caught him taking it in, and he nodded politely. "This is wonderful. Thank you."

She nearly glowed with pleasure. "This is the best room, if I do say so myself. I hope you'll be comfortable."

Bel had no doubt with the number of cushions, blankets, and pillows they'd managed to fit in the room, not to mention the bed.

Lorne the innkeeper soon arrived carrying two deep, steaming copper buckets in one hand and the frame of a cot in the other. Nina and Lorne insisted on putting the cot together and piling it with some of the cushions and blankets. Bel and Lena exchanged sheepish glances as they stood out of the way, helpless to help.

Nina finally stood at the center of the room, hands on hips, surveying the turned down bed, roaring fire, steaming buckets, and cozy cot. What she saw seemed to pass muster and she nodded.

"Well, we'll leave you alone now. Please let us know if there's anything you need, and we hope to see you for dinner."

"Wouldn't miss it!" Alix called.

Nina smiled fondly, waved, and shut the door behind her. She left the room warm, cozy, and strewn with cushions.

"I hope you paid them well," Alix said, elbow-deep in her pack. "This is great!"

Lena hummed in agreement, peering out the window. "She said earlier we can leave clothes out for laundering; she has a friend who will do the washing for guests."

Alix moaned in happiness. "I think I might love this woman."

Bel seconded that. His skin itched with wanting to get out of the shirt he'd been wearing for too many days. All their clothes were like that, stiff with river washing and days of grime.

He threaded the small chain lock on the door; it wouldn't stop anyone determined to get in, but it gave him enough confidence to start peeling out of his layers. He couldn't help the long moan of pleasure at finally unfurling his wings. The feathers made a slick rasp as they drew apart, and he flexed the long primary feathers out as much as he could, working back some feeling.

All three of them fell on the warm water with gusto, scrubbing hands and faces. When Alix wanted her back and hair washed, Bel turned around to decide what he could ask to get laundered without raising brows, since all of his shirts had been cut to accommodate his wings.

By the time the water had cooled to lukewarm, Bel felt infinitely better with some clean skin. Lena and Alix too seemed lighter, their moods sunny as they organized their packs and locked them in the trunk.

"All right, well, time to see what this town has," Alix announced, shoving her feet back into her boots.

"You want to go back out?" Bel asked in surprise.

"I've been promised sticky buns," Alix replied. "And, sorry, but I'd like to see some faces that aren't the two of yours for a few hours."

Lena laughed and began fishing in her satchel. "Fair enough." She pulled out the coin purse and put the whole thing in Alix's waiting hand.

The girl's eyes went wide and her grin was nothing short of diabolical.

Lena pointed a finger at her. "Remember what we definitely need to get—most importantly, a horse for Bel, dried meat and fruit, thread..." Her list was long, but they'd used so many supplies on their journey here. He didn't know how much longer it would be to Aeriand, but it stood to reason there wouldn't be towns like this one the closer they got to avian country.

"You don't need to get any of that today, but be on the lookout at least."

Alix saluted. "You can count on me."

"And save us each a sticky bun."

"No promises."

Kitted out with money, cloak, and a dagger hidden at her waist, Alix headed for the door. "I'm off. But I'll be back for dinner." She shot a significant look over her shoulder at the two of them, making Lena blush.

"Far be it from you to miss dinner," Bel teased.

"Mmhmm, very out of my character," Alix agreed, and with a wink, she unlocked the door and swept out of the room. They could hear her march merrily back down the stairs and loudly ask Nina which baker was the best in town.

Lena looked to Bel and laughter bubbled between them. Iridescent soap bubbles of happiness and relief had Bel feeling lighter than he had in days. The clean face helped, but mostly it was seeing the tension in Lena's shoulders ease.

They were as safe as they could be now, and for the first time in a while, they'd be comfortable, too.

"Well, did you want to wash anything else?" Lena asked. Her blush deepened and she cleared her throat. "I'd hate to waste the water."

"I'm sure everything could use a wash at this point."

She'd gone almost shy again, her color ranging toward pink. She wouldn't quite meet his gaze as she pulled together a pile of clothes for washing. Then there was nothing left but what they wore.

Bel kicked off his boots and nearly moaned with pleasure at the soft carpet under his toes. He made quick work of his trousers and tunic, and Lena added them to the pile left outside their door. Then she set the chain lock again and it was just the two of them, alone in a room covered in cushions in just their warm underthings.

Then those were gone, too. Bel's wing bases prickled with awareness.

They both blushed before setting to work with their buckets. Bel tried not to stare too blatantly at her breasts as she washed under them and down her stomach. His own strokes with the rag were quick, almost rough, and he couldn't quite pay full attention to his task. His roughness did nothing to stop his obvious want of her.

Her eyes weren't on him, so he took another longing look at her perfect breasts, memorizing how droplets gathered at the tips, and then bent to take care of his legs and feet. He hoped the distraction and cooling water would cool him too, but when he straightened and found her gaze on him, a new flush of heat burned through him.

He didn't miss her eyes flicking down to mark the throbbing evidence of how she affected him, and he wasn't dreaming when a small, playful smile kicked up one side of her mouth. He clenched with wanting to taste that smile.

Her color was still high, shyness still in the slope of her shoulders, but the same hunger reflected in her eyes.

She turned, presenting the elegant line of her spine and generous curves of her backside. Rounded and firm with muscle, he desperately wanted to renew his memories of sinking his fingers into that flesh.

"Will you wash my back?" she said, voice too low and husky to mistake her.

He made an affirmative noise, words beyond him at the moment. Drawing up behind her, he couldn't resist pulling the leather thong from her hair and unwinding her braid. He dug his fingers into the heavy mass, entranced at how the different browns caught the light, some gleaming like honey and others the red of cherrywood. She groaned as he worked his fingers up her neck to the base of her skull, head falling back, creating a waterfall of waves that nearly touched the top curve of her backside.

Bel pulled her hair over her shoulder and skimmed his fingers along the curve from neck to arm, making her shiver. Working the rag over her shoulders, he got distracted as the water sluiced down her back, gathering at the dimples just above her backside before running in small rivulets over the generous globes.

He couldn't keep his eyes from the perfection of it.

He groaned, wanting to follow with his tongue, and Lena chuckled. It turned into a soft gasp when he stepped forward, rag forgotten, and his cock bobbed against her. It was Bel who shuddered then.

"You can ignore it if—"

"Do you want me to ignore it?"

His head slumped to her shoulder and he huffed, "No."

That made her laugh again. She turned to face him, kissing his cheek with his head still hung low, and smiled up at him.

"Should we oil your wings?"

Bel thought he might combust; part of him wanted to throw her on the bed or a cushion, anywhere really, and sink inside, but another, the part that saw her playful smile and the happiness she radiated, wanted more of this.

"I have some left," he said, stealing a kiss.

He pulled himself away before he got lost in her completely, retrieving the bottle of oil he used on his wings. It was a concoction Pol had made him, a combination of hair oils that was light enough for his feathers. Avians produced oil for their wings naturally, but it was stimulated by flight. Bel had been oiling his wings for over ten years.

It was always a pleasure when Lena did it instead.

He returned to find she'd stacked a few cushions to make something of a backless seat. She plucked the bottle from his hand and patted his shoulder. He sat ungracefully while extending his wings, feathers rasping in anticipation of her touch.

Lena hummed in pleasure as she worked the oil between her hands, the fragrant, slightly nutty scent warm in the heat of the fire. She started at his wing bases, her touch gentle, and he had to clench his teeth to keep from losing control. Her hands were soft on his long primary feathers, gliding over the barbs and depositing just a hint of oil before moving on to the next.

When she finished with the backs, he lifted his wing for her to duck under, and she began on the insides. She used her fingertips on the delicate inner secondary feathers, and Bel watched her raptly, every nuance, every dip of her brow and flutter of her lashes. Her fingers took their time, teasing over every barb and shaft. Each delicate touch at the underside of his wing base, on the sensitive spot between inner wing and skin, made him shiver.

Eyes half-mast, she watched the effect her touch had on him, drawing out this agonizing pleasure. It was perfect, over too soon but also not fast enough. She didn't speed up or linger too long in one place, but it seemed like they spun faster and faster in their own momentum, caught between the glowing fire in the hearth and his spread wings, thick with the heady scent of oil.

It was heady too, having a strong human knight do this for him, standing naked before him, vulnerable and open and smiling gently. The fire bathed her warm skin in golden tones, creating shadows in the planes and contours of her stomach and chest. She was so strong, and he couldn't help running his nose up and down the centerline of her in an *ashita*. He held her hips in either hand and kissed the warm skin between her breasts.

Lena carded her fingers through the down and hair at his nape and worked up, spreading the last of the oil into his hair. He leaned into her touch, delighting in the scrape of her nails, and his eyes fell closed in bliss.

Her lips were soft when they touched his, and Bel followed her lead, keeping their kisses slow, gentle. Her mouth didn't leave his, but he felt when she lowered herself down, changing the angle. His eyes slid open to see her knelt between his legs.

She kissed his mouth again, then his chin, his throat, the hollow at the base of his neck, down along the midline of chest, down his abdomen.

Bel's breath stuttered out of him.

He watched her, unmoving, not wanting to break whatever spell this was, not quite believing her mouth hovered so close to his cock. She'd done this for him before, at Finhöln, taken him in her mouth and proved she was a goddess incarnate. He barely believed it those times, either.

She looked up at him through her lashes, green eyes burning like spring and new life, as she took him. Bel grunted, his head almost lolling back at the sheer decadence of it, but no, he had to see, had to watch. Those eyes of hers held him as surely as her mouth and pumping fist did, and Bel sank into the pleasure.

She worked him with mouth and tongue and fist and just the slightest hint of teeth, and he wanted to give in, oh he did, wanted it so badly his back teeth ached with it. But Bel had told her before, he wanted everything. This afternoon, he was determined to have it.

When she drew back for a breath, Bel pulled her up, sliding back a little further on the cushion so she could straddle his hips. Arms settling around his neck, she smiled, rocking just so.

Bel hissed at the heat of her. "You're burning up."

She hummed, hips picking up speed. The wet slide nearly undid him, and he greedily swallowed her gasps of pleasure in a bruising kiss. The haze in her eyes told him she was close, closer even than he'd been with her mouth wrapped around him, and it only made him want to tease her a little longer. He might die of wanting, but he'd already admitted to being a selfish male. He wanted more, all of it.

Bel lifted her by the hips and took himself in hand, teasing her.

"Yes, yes," she moaned. "Bel, *yes!*"

Bel's mouth fell open on a silent gasp as he slid inside her heat. It was tight, tighter than her mouth had been, and tension gathered in his lower back, ready, so, so ready to pump and thrust until they were both lost. He set his teeth against the curve of her neck and made himself go slow, made himself pay attention to every clench and shudder of her against him.

"Look at us," he murmured in awe at the sight of their joining, their chase and capture. "Look at how good you take me."

Lena's head fell back, the ends of her hair tickling his thighs, and she dug her nails into the meat of his shoulder. "Bel!"

He couldn't resist those perfect breasts thrust in his face. He gave each their due, drinking the scent of her where it was strong. She cried out again and bore down, sealing them together.

Bel grunted, just hanging on from the sting of her nails raking his scalp. She snapped her hips, trying to set a brutal pace, but Bel dug his fingers into the plush flesh of her backside. He held her still and guided her up and down, up and down, slow and steady and maddening.

"Bel," she keened, as close to a whine as he'd ever heard Lena make.

He kissed the hollow of her throat. "I've waited weeks for this, you can wait a few more moments," he teased.

She growled, actually *growled* at him. "You think I haven't been waiting? Wanting this? Wanting you?"

Her words broke the last of Bel's control, his ears ringing with lust and fury and need. He flipped them faster than she could react, and she landed on the cushions with a soft, "Oh!" Bel was there, surging inside again, and her mouth popped open in a silent cry.

"This what you wanted?" he rumbled in her ear. "You want to be so full of me you'll break?"

"Yes! Yes, Bel!"

He couldn't stop now, couldn't gentle or slow his pace, but he managed to grit out, "Why then?"

"Everything's new for you," she gasped. "Didn't want to push."

He planted his elbows and fisted a handful of her hair so she'd look at him.

"I'll always want you. Always. Now take what you want from me."

Lena moaned and wrapped her legs around his hips, heels digging into the small of his back. "Harder," she rasped, "give me everything."

He'd promised himself he'd give her anything she wanted, and so he did.

He didn't hold back as he thrust, making her breasts bounce and her stomach shudder. His wings snapped and fluttered around them, a cool brush of down against their heated skin. He crashed against her as surely as a wave along the rocks, framing her face with his forearms and digging fingers into her hair as a wave breaker, a way to ground himself even as the heat inside him boiled and churned. He claimed her mouth and drank down her cry as she came undone.

Bel followed her down, losing himself to the pleasure, to her. The pressure in his lower back exploded, and Bel couldn't contain it anymore. With a fierce flap of his wings, Bel gave her everything.

———— ••◆•• ————

His ears still rang from her cries many moments later, and his body buzzed and hummed in the afterglow. Nothing could compare to taking Lena and being taken by her, losing himself in her and feeling that moment she clenched him tight and lost herself too, but a distant second was this moment, the syrupy sweetness of loose limbs and flushed cheeks and tender smiles. Holding her in the aftermath of their lovemaking was its own kind of intimacy, and Bel wanted all of it, wanted to bask in it like a cat in a good sunbeam and soak up every drop.

She'd blush and fluster if he told her she was his sun. His Matella, bright and golden and warm. The center of his sky.

Bel kissed her panting mouth and then slid onto his side. He brought her along, tucking her against him, and shivered at the hard pebbles of her nipples pressing into his chest. He distracted himself from their lure by playing with the silky strands of her hair.

Lena's eyes nearly fluttered closed, lids heavy with contentment, and she traced little patterns on his skin. They lay like that for Bel didn't know how long, all light fingertips and softness, relearning textures and touches.

Eventually, the room began to darken with the waning afternoon. Shadows crept along the walls, stretching just a little farther each time Bel looked.

Nuzzling close, Bel said against her lips, "I've missed this...missed you."

He could feel her smile. "I've been right here."

"Mm-mmm." He tapped a finger lazily against her temple. "You've been in here."

She said nothing for a long while, letting some of the warmth and ease between them seep away. Bel held perfectly still, fighting the urge to crush her to him. His heartbeat picked up speed waiting for her to say something, a worried thrumming that only grew with the silence.

But then her warm lips kissed his chest, right over his racing heart.

"You're right." Lena tucked her head under his chin and burrowed against him, as if she searched for more warmth, more reassurance.

Bel wrapped arms and wings around her and held tight. He couldn't see her face, but he didn't need to, to feel her anticipation as she searched for the right words.

"I've been so worried, so scared that something might happen."

"Something probably will happen," he said honestly. It was perhaps the biggest difference between them, other than the wings of course— that he'd learned to see the worst in people and expect the worst from them. Something bad would happen eventually, it always did.

Lena didn't see it that way, he'd come to understand. She saw the good in others, but more than that, she *expected* goodness from them, too. She'd been taught by that damned knight's code that if she did right, things would turn out well. Those expectations had been dashed, people she'd once respected failing her, and Bel hated to see that optimism diminished because of it. He didn't want her to be a brooding pessimist like him.

It didn't escape his notice either, the irony that she expected others to do right—held them up to high expectations, standards that she held herself to, too—yet she didn't expect anything from him. In some ways he appreciated no expectations placed on him, that for once in his life he'd been given the room and time and safety to just be Bel—but another, bigger part of him wanted her to expect things of him. She should anticipate things from him—care, loyalty, affection. He wanted her to count on him, expect he'd do anything for her, as her man, as her due.

Lena was *good*, and she deserved everything that was good.

Bel nuzzled her hair again, liking the feel of it sliding against his lips. "But no matter what it is, we'll face it, together."

"Together." She ran a hand up his back to the wing bases, and Bel couldn't help the low rumble of pleasure from deep in his throat. "I've never had to...I've served under and fought alongside many good knights. But I've never had to rely on anyone for...this."

He thought he understood. His life in Finhöln had been a long, lonely stretch that was its own kind of torture. Pol had been the one comfort and probably the only thing that kept him sane. But even then, there were parts of him that had simply withered away, atrophied with disuse or abuse. He survived, relying on no one, never allowing himself to be vulnerable in any way. He'd refused to give the ones who'd kept him captive any more power over him.

How ironic, then, that this human woman who'd been sent to be his warden, his captor, his enemy, now had all the power over him. Power that he'd freely given her, handing over a heart already so broken but needing keeping.

He'd never needed someone the way he needed her. And there was something utterly terrifying about that, but damnit if Bel wasn't desperate to give her everything. He couldn't stop himself even if he'd wanted to. She was the sun in his sky, and he was in freefall.

"I've never felt this deeply for anyone, never so much that it could be the ruin of me," she whispered.

Bel groaned, tilting up her chin and capturing her mouth with his. Gods, this woman. How she cut him to the quick, made his heart squeeze as if it was her very fist wrapped around it. He took her mouth, her kiss, her warmth, sated but always wanting more of her. He kissed her until his lips felt bruised, hoping, needing it to tell her everything words didn't have the power to.

"You're already the ruin of me," he murmured.

Lena's gaze searched his, wide and glassy. The breath in his lungs hitched at the softness, the vulnerability of that look, and he brushed her hair back from her face so she could look her fill and see it, *know* how he was for her.

"I've never had someone who was mine...never belonged to someone."

His nostrils flared at that, and he pulled her closer, crushing her breasts against him. Hearing she belonged with him...it set some primal, male part of him alight.

"I don't know how this is supposed to go. I've never kept a man before, never been someone's woman. I just wanted to give you time, I never meant to spurn you or make you feel like I didn't want you because I do. I *do*." Her fingers were a little firmer this time running along his wing bases, and Bel arched into the touch.

He bumped her nose with his. "Say you want me again."

Lena's smile was small and a little shy but all the more precious for it. "I want you, Bel. Now, today, tomorrow...always."

Bel engulfed her, arms, hands, wings, feathers, legs, all of her he wrapped up with himself. He rolled onto his back so both wings could fully curl around her, cocooning them in feathers.

From inside the canopy of wings, she whispered, "I promise I'll do better."

This woman. His heart couldn't take it.

"You've done nothing wrong. I want your happiness. I want you to come to me with your worries, your needs."

She propped her chin on his chest, showing off a teasing little grin. "My needs, hm?"

"That one especially." He palmed her backside and squeezed, hauling her further up his chest. She gasped at the delicious drag of skin against skin, and her hips rocked along the almost painful length of him that was oh so ready to take her again. "But all the others, too. Every single one."

Hands splayed across his chest, Lena pushed herself up to straddle him. She brought his wings up with her, the crooks balanced on her shoulders so feathers draped and cascaded down her sides, like she had wings of her own. The sight did something to him.

Bel could feel his pupils dilating, an avian ability to take in as many details as possible. The colors of her sharpened, the reds of her flushed cheeks and chest, the dusky pink of her nipples and lips, the greens of her eyes, soft and sultry as she took him in, laid out beneath her.

Running her hands over him, she admitted, "I've never been the affectionate sort."

"Neither have I."

"I'd like to be with you, though."

Excitement had him filling his palms with her thighs as she leaned over him.

"I'll always want your touches," he told her.

"Always?"

"Always."

"Anywhere?"

"Everywhere. We don't have to scar Alix to be affectionate, though. I want all your touches." He took more from her touch than pleasure; just the squeeze of her hand or press of her side to his offered reassurance, comfort, happiness, and Bel was greedy for all of it.

In the long stretch of years alone, he'd thought perhaps he'd be used to not feeling another's touch. That perhaps he'd even come to dislike it, especially when the only thing human hands did was hurt him.

Oh, how wrong she'd proven him to be.

Now, the more she gave, the more he wanted.

She smiled, pleased, and shocked a grunt of pleasure out of him when she ran a gentle hand over his cock that had been aching for her attention.

"We may need to practice."

"I'm *very* amenable to practice." He nearly choked when she slid back, touching her heat to his, before sliding forward again to tease them both.

She eased into her own rhythm, the slow, slick slide of it driving Bel mad, but he'd sooner tear off his wing than rush her. He watched her greedily as she explored and teased and took her own pleasure. He wanted to be what gave her this, wanted to be the one who fulfilled and sated her. He wanted her to take him and use him and claim him.

She'd said she'd never belonged to someone before.

Bel had never belonged to someone, either. He'd been a spare, a charge, a nuisance, a failure, a captive, and many more, but never someone's.

His heart soared as surely as it ever had when he'd skimmed the clouds to be hers.

She played with him until the shadows stretched long and thick and the fire had died away almost to coals. When she finally took him inside, they both yelped with the sharp pleasure of it, almost too sensitive for more. She rocked and bounced on him, staying to her rhythm until neither of them could stand it anymore.

Bel slammed her hips down to meet his, undone by their sounds and the thick smell of their lovemaking hanging in the air.

They probably *would* scar Alix at this rate.

But he couldn't care, couldn't think beyond—

He bucked, nearly unseating her, cresting and lost. But he needed her with him, needed to feel her come apart, and fixed his thumb where she liked it most.

With a final keen, Lena dug her nails into him, marking him, and that primal part of him loved it, hoped the red welts would last forever so anyone who saw them would know he was hers. He held her up as she shivered and shook, finally spent.

Bel groaned when she smiled triumphantly down at him, her hair falling around them in a heavy curtain. "You've slain me, woman."

Her smile and gaze softened as Bel ran his fingertips along her brow and temple before gently tucking a few strands behind her ear. She caught his wrist and pressed a kiss to the center of his palm.

"I love you, Bel," she said, shattering him.

He framed her face in his hands and ran his thumbs under her lower lashes, devastated at the small gathering of wetness there, as if she thought he could feel anything less than, "You're my heart, Lena, and everything else. I love you with all that I am, *c'vana*."

Mate. That's what he called her. *Sweetheart. Beloved. Life-mate. Heart-bonded.* The Vagoran language just couldn't capture everything she was to him. They needed so many words to get close to just one—*c'vana*.

She eased down to him, and Bel cuddled her close. Lena was the first person who truly loved him, *him*, Bel. The vastness of his devotion to her, the fierce need to do anything for her probably should've scared her and him, too—but there was nothing for it now; he'd bound himself to her.

They still had their path to Aeriand; Bel needed to tell his kin what he knew from his translations for King Artemian, and part of him needed to see the city that had been his only other home. He owed his people nothing, but he still bore the scar tissue of his love for his brother, and for him he'd do this one last thing.

Beyond that, if it ever came to choosing his people or Lena, it would never be a choice. She was his people, and he'd choose her every time. Always.

Because that's what it meant to be *c'vana*.

———— •◆•• ————

A quiet chorus of unfamiliar sounds roused Bel. He blinked away the fogginess of sleep, taking in the gray of their room. He still lay on the floor, surrounded by cushions and blankets, with Lena curled against him.

His gaze caught on the perfect vision she made, face unlined in sleep, hand fisted under her chin. It was so perfect, so adorable, he almost didn't cringe at letting them sleep the night on the floor.

Finally, a bed within reach and they didn't even use it. Still, the cushions had beaten the ground, and the blankets Nina gave them were warm and soft.

He vaguely remembered they'd had the sense to rebuild and stoke the fire and wrap up in blankets before getting distracted in each other again. After that, the world had fallen away, his body spent and his heart content.

Bel listened carefully, beyond Lena's soft breaths, to the sounds that'd woken him. Feet padded along the corridor outside their door, and voices made it all the way up to their window from the makeshift harbor outside. He held perfectly still, waiting, but none of the footsteps or voices seemed meant for them.

When no one came bursting in shouting *"Avian!"* Bel shifted to look at the rest of their room.

A modest lump took up the right side of the four-post bed, black curls just visible on the giant pillow. It seemed Alix had managed to get her skinny arm around to unhook the chain lock, confirming that it was for comfort rather than actual security. He flushed a little guiltily at forgetting to leave the door open for her.

Gathering the softest blankets around her, Bel lifted Lena in his arms and carried her to the bed. She didn't wake as he set her down beside Alix, nor when he rearranged the blankets around her, showing just how tired she'd been. It made him all the more determined to see that she rested.

Lena shifted, rolling onto her side and propping her fist under her chin again with a contented little sigh. Bel's chest squeezed.

He checked the chain lock next, even if it was just for show. Pleased it was in place, he went looking for clothes and found the basket of washing just inside the door. Alix must have found it and brought it back in with her. All of their clothes sat neatly folded in the basket, and Bel nearly groaned running his fingers over the clean, sweet-smelling fabric.

Pulling on a clean pair of trousers for the first time in weeks was an excellent way to start his day.

He tugged a blanket around his shoulders on his way back to the bay windows. He stopped to kiss Lena's forehead then plucked one of the chairs and set it gently back from the furthest window.

Settling himself down, Bel was content to watch over them as they slept and more than a little curious to watch a bustling human town. He'd known about Longbourne, so close to Finhöln, but it was hidden away down the slope of the mountain in the trees. Now, he could watch what humans actually did day to day and see for himself what exactly a salmon run was.

II

In the end, the room, beds, and warm food were too good to give up after only one night. "*Happy to have you as long you need,*" Nina had said agreeably, more than pleased when Lena paid for another few days upfront. As Lena had counted out coins, Nina leaned in conspiratorially and whispered, "*With everyone at the run, I'll let you cut the line for the tub.*"

Which was how Lena found herself the next afternoon soaking with Bel in lukewarm water. She'd wasted no time hustling the copper tub to their room and helping Nina fill it, and as promised, Alix got first wash. Bel made himself scarce, feeling safe enough under his cloak and everyone out chasing salmon to go tend the horses. Lena washed up after Alix, sinking with a moan into the warm water.

Alix shook out her wet hair, splattering everything.

"I thought I picked up a kid in Highclere, not a puppy." Lena blinked water out of her eyes, laughing.

"These curls don't get bouncy on their own. I have a regimen."

Lena snorted a laugh under the water, making bubbles.

Just like her drying curls, Alix bounced from the room shortly after, rejuvenated from the bath. She sighed and moaned putting on freshly cleaned clothes, and Lena was pleased with how her cheeks shone pink with health and her ribs weren't prominent in her narrow chest anymore. Alix had been skin and bones when Lena found her, and she'd vowed the girl would never go without again. In the forest, she came close to breaking that promise.

"See if one of the bakers is open and get more of those sticky buns," Lena suggested.

Alix didn't need to be told twice to snag the money purse. Announcing she was off to watch the salmon run, she flounced from the room. She sent Bel back up behind her.

By the time he got his turn, the water was a bit murky and not nearly as hot. He made no complaints, sinking in up to his chin with a happy grumble.

Lena couldn't help smiling at the sight of him, his big body folded in the tub, water lapping at his chin but kneecaps breaking the surface like twin islands. His wings slumped over the sloped back of the tub, spread out across the floor and rustling happily. From point to point, they covered the expanse of the room.

She ate up the sight from near the hearth, squeezing the water from her hair and letting the fire dry the long, heavy waves. Despite being wet, her head felt lighter and her skin cool and content from the scrubbing. Lena sighed; the whole of her was so content in this moment, warm, clean, and fed.

"Lena." Bel held a dripping hand out to her, and Lena went.

When he tugged her to the bath, she blushed. He sat to make room between his legs, which didn't help her blush. She'd never bathed with anyone before—at least, not like this. Not with a lover. Her blush could've reheated the bathwater as Bel gazed up at her lasciviously, a sparkle in his eyes.

Seeing him look at her like that, like she was the most beautiful creature he'd ever seen, decided her.

Pinning up her partially dry hair into a loose knot, Lena stepped into the tub with Bel, his hands guiding her down to him. There was nowhere else in the tub for her body to go but ease back into his.

The solid warmth of him had her sighing again. Even with the cooling water and cramped space, as his arms came around her and his legs cradled her hips, this second bath was even better than the first. She closed her eyes and let her head fall back onto his shoulder as his fingers gently stroked her between her legs.

They spent the afternoon nuzzling, kissing, and wrinkling in the cool water. It was Lena's most favorite afternoon in a long while.

On the second morning, Lena woke before the others and re-learned Bel's sleeping face in the soft morning light. She'd woken to the sight of him for days now, but there was something about lying together in a real bed, limbs tangled together, that made this special. She'd cherished every morning she'd woken to the sight in Finhöln, but on those mornings, there'd been a sadness about it, a sense that she needed to memorize every line, texture, color before it all came to an end.

She enjoyed taking a leisurely perusal of his sleeping face, memorizing the relaxed arches of his brows and inhuman cut of his cheekbones—not because she needed to but because she wanted to. Because everything about him, his golden lashes, the sharp tip of his nose, the little freckles that had begun to dot his face with more time in the sun, everything was so, so dear that her heart hurt with it.

Perhaps she should've been embarrassed by her soppiness, but her love for him was too sweet, too precious to care. She needed these moments to remind herself this was real, to look upon him and think *yes, this is my person. He's mine.*

Bel woke to a silly little grin on her face she couldn't help.

He's mine.

He captured that grin in a kiss that had her toes curling. Sheets and feathers rustled deliciously as they slid closer, their bodies fitting together with an ease that amazed and delighted her.

"Good morning," he murmured against her lips.

"Good—"

They didn't get a warning before a pillow came flying from the cot across the room, hitting them smack in the face.

He's perfect!" Alix announced that afternoon.

Lena suppressed her grimace with sheer will as she watched Alix prance around the horse she'd found for sale.

He was a beautiful thing, yes, bay in coloring with a chestnut mane and muscular flanks. He wasn't too old, and his liquid brown eyes were clear and curious. All in all, a fine horse; the problem was...

"He's a workhorse," she grumbled, trying not to upset the cartwright selling him.

"He's also the only one for sale in town," Alix whispered back.

Rubbing her eyes with thumb and forefinger, Lena tried to see the merit in a twenty-hand workhorse who was bigger than Yvain and no doubt half as fast.

Sensing her hesitancy, the cartwright pulled out an ancient saddle and riding kit. "I can throw this in. Haven't used them much with him, but it'll fit him."

Lena looked over the old leather, taking her due diligence as a buyer, but she saw, just as easily as the cartwright did, Alix playing with the horse's mane and how the gentle giant chuffed her cheeks and nibbled her hair. He smiled wider.

"What's his name?" she asked as she counted out the coin.

"Doesn't have one, haven't really bothered with it. Well, I suppose I call him Beast sometimes and he seems to know I mean him."

Lena sidestepped, blocking the glower Alix shot the cartwright.

"We're not calling him Beast," Alix hissed as they led the horse back to the Riverbend Inn.

"Well, I think that's Bel's choice. It's his horse, after all." Whether or not he'd ever be able to ride him.

———— •••◆•• ————

At Nina's insistence, Lena went with Alix to see the salmon run on the third afternoon. "*There's more to see in town than just those four walls of yours,*" she'd said with a wink. Blushing furiously, Lena had followed a snickering Alix out into a mild afternoon.

Alix led her around the inn to a network of docks that extended out into the wet sands beyond the town. They followed several others farther out, careful of rotted planks, to watch as the first boats returned from deeper waters. She could just spot the masses of boats, a little closer than the horizon, bobbing where the heart of the river ran and a current churned lazily.

"Nina said that in spring, when the snow melts, the waters get pretty high, almost into town, so they had to make these docks to keep the boats where they need them," Alix chatted. She told Lena of how this was the largest town north of Vagora, how it had become a trading center over the years and a hub for fishing. She even knew of the local joke about how nobody could agree on a name for the river that many of the small villages nestled along, so it'd gotten stuck with the name Fish River.

Not for the first time, Lena marveled at how easily Alix got on with people. She thrived in new settings with fresh faces. Lena never knew how to easily start a conversation with someone who hadn't spent most of their lives training for knighthood. Alix, meanwhile, could chat with anyone under Matella's great sun.

Alix had told her before she didn't care about being a knight, didn't think twice about coming with her to save Bel. It would've been a difficult road to achieve a knighthood for the street urchin from the Cheapside of Highclere, but she would've done it, Lena was sure. But now, as she listened to Alix's tidbits, she realized something else entirely.

Alix would make an excellent spy.

She didn't know what to do with the thought, so she stowed it away for later.

Just in time, too; the docks quickly transformed into a frenzy of activity, fishermen scrambling off their boats and hauling in nets full of wriggling fish. Lena and Alix pressed back against the railings, out of the way, and watched in awe. It seemed like chaos, but really, after a few moments, Lena picked out the rhythm of it, watching as fish were transferred from nets to barrels. Boat after boat came in, depositing its load, and more than one shanty kept time to the beat of wet slaps of fish against the dock.

The air grew heavy with the salty smell of fish, and after a while, Lena and Alix retreated back to town. Not emptyhanded, though.

Nina was pleased with the fresh fish they brought back to her, and she promised something special for dinner. "Drag that man of yours down here in an hour and you'll see," she said. Lena fumbled for an excuse, but Alix smoothly explained how Bel had a serious old wound on the back of the head, from the wars, you see, that he didn't like people seeing. "Well, tell him to keep that hood up if he likes, then. But be here in an hour. Lorne's made his famous berry tarts and they go fast."

Alix nearly licked her chops and agreed. Outmaneuvered, Lena explained it to Bel while trying not to wring her hands.

He considered for a long moment, looking between her and Alix, before finally donning his cloak and slipping a sheathed dagger into his belt at his back.

"Not sure I can pass up fresh berry tarts," he said.

Alix whooped, making quick work of washing up.

A sad look passed over Bel's face. Lena crossed to Bel and squeezed his arm.

"I miss Pol, too," she whispered.

A heavy breath expanded his chest, and Lena hated seeing the pain lining his eyes. Bel drew her close, and she wrapped her arms around him to hold him tight. She couldn't stop him from missing Pol or simple things reminding him of his dear friend and only comfort in captivity, but she could do this when the ache got to be too much. He took her comfort, and she was content to hold and be held as long as he needed.

She'd used her body for many things, had fought, hurt and inflicted harm, defended, brought pleasure...but it was new to use it as a safe harbor. And, the remarkable thing was...she took just as much comfort in his closeness.

Bel buried his nose in her hair. "Thank you," he whispered.

She squeezed his hand, trying to shore up both their courage, and pulled him along down into the great room.

Only a handful of other patrons had returned for dinner when they came downstairs, and Nina waved them to one of the tables in the back, where the shadows were thicker, with a knowing smile. Bel settled with his back to the wall, and Lena moved her chair closer to his, blocking an easy view from the side.

They sat in silence, watching the others in the room as if at any moment they'd jump from their chairs and charge, until Nina swooped in with full mugs of cider and fish pies that still steamed from the oven. The smell of herbs, butter, pastry, and fish had Lena's stomach audibly growling, and she thought a drip of drool escaped Alix's mouth.

Nina winked at their wide eyes. "Eat up! There's more where that came from."

"I love her," Alix groaned as Nina swished away to see to the other patrons.

Lena would've agreed, but her mouth was too full of pie. The thick cream and flaky fish nearly scalded her mouth, but she didn't care. Sweetness burst from perfectly crisp peas and carrots, and the pastry melted on her tongue.

Thankfully, Nina hadn't overestimated, and they all ate their second and third pies voraciously. Their host just laughed, beaming at their obvious pleasure, and kept the food coming even as the great room filled with more patrons, in from a long day of fishing. The angles of their shoulders spoke of their weariness, but smiles abounded, and nobody headed upstairs to bed before taking a seat and filling up on food and talk.

The tang of mud and fish came in with the fishermen, not unpleasant, mixing with the sweet woodsmoke of the fires and lavender infused in the candles. The inn glowed with warmth, happy chatter rising to the rafters, and Lena sat quietly with Bel, happy to watch as people enjoyed their dinners and praised Lorne and Nina, who wove with a dancer's grace around the tables, keeping mugs full.

Bel's hand slid to her thigh after finishing their second round of berry tarts, and Lena hugged his arm to her chest. She rested her head on his shoulder, feeling pleasantly drowsy and full in more than just her stomach. A soft smile touched her lips, and she was content to sit with Bel as he avidly watched the other patrons.

Her smile grew once the cider and mead had begun flowing and a song broke loose from across the room. It was an old Vagoran folksong, all about leaving home and a girl behind to find fame and fortune, and soon almost everyone was singing along, even Lorne from behind the bar. Alix raised her mug and began belting the words, too.

Ears ringing with Alix's horrid singing and face sore from smiling so much, Lena could finally put a finger on what it was warming her chest.

Happiness.

A happy glow filled the room, the merriment and sense of community evident as one song rolled into another, and it filled Lena too, full to the brim. She fell asleep that night with that smile still on her lips.

On the fourth day, with the salmon run finishing up for the season and the town full to bursting with fish ready for curing, the inn was quieter than it ever had been. They slept late into the morning, no sounds of patrons shuffling down the hall, no fishermen rushing to their boats, no calls to hoist sails and untie lines.

They slept late enough to have missed the normal breakfast. As the first one fully awake, it was Lena's task to forage for something downstairs and throw herself upon Nina's mercy.

She padded down the stairs, steps quiet out of habit, but mind on the chance of any berry tarts having survived the night.

Voices drifted up the stairwell to her before she reached the landing.

A familiar timber had her pausing on the next step.

"You're sure?" a man said.

A cold rush froze Lena on the steps, memories of that voice, the voice that had led her into battle and advised a crown prince, piercing the safe, warm little dream she'd been living these past days.

"They were spotted by hunters headed east a fortnight ago," said Captain Joran's voice.

Lena's guts twisted in guilty knots.

"The description doesn't sound familiar," said Nina.

"It may not be all three of them—it could just be a woman and girl, or a woman and large man."

A pause. Carefully, so, so carefully, without breathing, she eased down two more steps until she could crouch and peer down into the great room below through the banister.

Dread knifed through her chest.

Flanking the bar stood six figures, all unmistakably knights of the realm with their armor and the suns embossing them. At their center was a sight just as recognizable—the mercilessly shaved head of Joran Farland, Captain of the Guard to Crown Prince Arion.

He towered over the bar and Nina, using his impressive height to stress authority. Lena had seen it many times, had been the recipient of it many times, and knew the weight of such a tall, imposing man looking down his nose at you.

Nina's eyes flicked between the knights before catching sight of Lena between railing posts over one of their shoulders. She blinked but looked away quickly.

Lena's hands went cold.

"No," Nina said slowly, "I don't remember seeing anyone like that around. And a knight would surely stand out. What did you say the name was?"

"Maddalena Montcaer, brown hair, long, though she may have cut it, with green—"

"Montcaer...Montcaer as in...?"

"As in the traitor to king and country."

Any other time, she may have winced with shame from no honorific preceding her name—there was little doubt now she'd been struck from the registers, and she could almost hear her mother's shriek of affront. Any other time, the words *traitor to king and country* may have wounded her on the spot.

But in that moment, with her heart pounding in her throat and panic surging through her veins, all she could do was think of Bel, nestled comfortably in bed, happy, full, with two unbroken wings.

That man down there, a man she'd once respected and thought of as a mentor, meant to undo all of that. Not out of malice or pride but *duty*. Because he thought it was *right* to capture Bel, chain him, hurt him, break him. For *king and country*.

Bile burned the back of her throat. She wouldn't let that happen.

"We'll need accommodations while we conduct further inquiries," Joran told Nina.

"Afraid we're full up. All the rooms are taken for the run."

"Madam, I think you can make room for king's business."

"I'm not putting patrons out on the street just because a couple of you in armor come knocking." Lena watched as Nina banked her temper, perhaps remembering that these were king's knights in a town that wasn't supposed to exist. Straightening her apron, Nina amended, "You're welcome to wait down here until a room becomes available. Some may be leaving town soon with the run finishing up."

Joran nodded. "Acceptable. We'll be stabling our horses for the night as well."

"May be crowded tonight, we've got—"

"Many people in town, yes, I understand. We'll make do. They just need shelter and a good meal."

Joran and his knights, two women and three men, looked like they needed just that, too. Though they wore the king's colors and symbols, their armor wasn't polished to Joran's usual standards, and their cloaks were in desperate need of laundering. Deep lines and dark circles rimmed their eyes, and more than one had peeling sunburns across their noses and cheeks.

"Very well. Make yourselves comfortable and we'll see what comes about this evening," said Nina, not sounding like the welcoming host Lena had grown used to.

Before Joran and his knights turned away from the bar, Lena scrambled back up the steps, careful to keep her footfalls light. She held her breath all the way back to their room, not daring to breathe until their door was between her and Joran, closed and locked.

Alix and Bel had cleared the floor of cushions, stacking them neatly to the side to make room for morning stretches. They both turned smiling faces on her as she entered, and she hated watching them snuff out as they took in her pale face and white-rimmed eyes.

"What's happened?" Bel asked.

"He's here. Joran." Lena's heart stuttered with the words said aloud, and she had to suck in a long draw of air to make sure her chest didn't collapse in on itself. "He followed us. The hun-hunters—we shouldn't have s-stayed here, I-I sh-shouldn't—"

"Lena!" Bel grabbed for her when she went down, catching her up before her knees hit the floorboards.

He carried her to the bed and sat her down while her breaths came in jagged pants. Her lungs burned for air even though she gasped and swallowed great gulps of it. She could barely hear Bel talking, Alix too, over the pounding crash of her heart, and their words sloshed around her head, lost in a vortex of panic and dread. All centered around one thing: she'd failed.

She'd tried to help those hunters. She'd trusted Sonja, Garett, Nina, and other villagers. She'd let her guard down, let them stall and dawdle over little luxuries, and now look. Joran was here. Joran would find them—how could he not? Nina may have lied for them, but—

Oh, goddess, and Nina! She knew! She *knew* it was them Joran asked about. She'd lied for them, but what about tomorrow? What would her price be? How would they get out of the inn now, with the knights' horses stabled alongside Yvain, Miri, and Beast-who-wouldn't-be-called-Beast? How could—

"Lena, Lena, sweetheart, I need you to breathe. Breathe for me."

A hand pried the large fist she'd made out of hers open. It was big and warm, with blunted fingertips, and she grasped at it, let it be her anchor in the maelstrom of her mind. The panic wanted out, wanted her to scream and scream, but she couldn't draw Joran to them, couldn't be the reason Bel was found and taken away and chained and broken and and and—

He told her to breathe, and she tried. She did, in and out, felt her chest rise, up and down.

She came back to herself in increments, though she tried not to fight the panic. It needed out, needed to run its course like any flood, and she fought to stay out of its way and just breathe.

It left her shaky, but finally, the panic passed.

A hot stream of tears scalded her cheeks. She made to wipe them away, but both her hands were clutched tight. Alix had both her small hands wrapped around one, and Bel held tight to the other. When she finally looked from their hands to his face, Bel smiled softly and, making soothing noises, dried her face.

Lena took in a big, wobbly breath. "Joran's downstairs asking about us. They want a room and will stable the horses here."

Bel grimaced. "How many?"

"Six total." She squeezed his hand. "We can't fight them. They may be strangers here, but we don't know how the town would handle an avian and a traitor harming knights of the realm."

"They might join in," Alix muttered.

"We don't know that." They needed a plan. So long as the knights were downstairs waiting for a room, they couldn't leave, at least not through the front door.

A light knock at the door made them all jump.

"Hello?" a woman whispered on the other side. "It's Nina."

Lena clutched at their hands. "She knows. She lied for us but she *knows*."

Nodding, Alix said, "Then I guess we see what she has to say."

"But—"

"Let's see *what* she knows and if she can help us."

Alix stood up and, grabbing a dagger from her things and hiding it behind her back, she opened the door just enough to peer out.

"Can I come in, Alix dear? Please. I mean you no harm, I swear it."

Bel straightened as Alix took the woman's measure. He kept Lena's hand in his, but he put his body between her and the door.

"Bel, your wings—get your cloak," Lena muttered.

But he only stood there, stalwart and resolute, his wings fluffing to make him seem bigger. One curved over her, as if readying to pull her into the safety of his body.

Alix looked over her shoulder at them, and when she got a nod from Bel, quietly undid the chain and ushered Nina into the room. She didn't seem perturbed by Alix standing sentry at the door, but she gasped at the sight of Bel.

"Oh, my," she murmured. "I've never..."

"You've never seen one of my kind?" Bel asked, tone dangerously neutral.

Nina shook her head. "You hear stories, but..." Kneading her apron with her hands, Nina looked to Lena. "So what those knights said was true?"

"That depends on what they said," Alix spat from the door.

"Fair enough. They're saying you freed a dangerous avian captive who was bound for the capital. That you were supposed to oversee him, but you ran off with him instead. You're wanted, the two of you. I'm not sure they know anything about you," she said, nodding at Alix.

Anger chased away the last of her shakiness, and even though Bel grumbled and tried to keep her behind him, Lena stepped forward to meet the accusations.

"He isn't dangerous. And they failed to say that Bel was a captive for over ten years. They kept him locked away with cruel wardens who broke his wing so he couldn't fly. They took him as a youth, a *child*, and let him rot away for ten years. When plans were made to take him to the capital, I couldn't let that happen."

Bel came to stand alongside her and took her hand. Nina marked it, a knowing look in her eyes.

"I was the same male last night, eating your food, sitting at your table, as I am today," Bel said. "I mean you no harm. I mean *nobody* harm."

"We just want to get somewhere safe," Lena added. "We didn't even realize we'd been followed east until today."

Nina looked between them, taking a long moment before saying, "I believe you."

Lena swallowed, wetting her dry throat. "You lied for us down there, to the knights. Why?"

"Well, my dear, that's easy. Good innkeepers know their loyalty is to good patrons who pay upfront. Those knights down there are strangers to me, where you have been wonderful guests. Honest...at least when you could be. Lorne and I, we value that. Those knights may be king's men, but that isn't much of a compliment out here." She looked to Bel when she said, "It isn't avians that drove us off our land."

"So you won't rat us out?" Alix asked sharply.

"Of course not. Everyone in town, we've all run away from something. Who am I to stand in your way?"

Lena blinked in shock, not trusting that it could be true, that this human woman wouldn't turn them in. For days and days they'd had no safe harbor, no help or allies. She'd had to fool Sonja and Garett for their help, but Nina...she offered her aid, even knowing...

"Why should we trust you?" Alix cut to the quick of things.

Nina shrugged easily. "If I wanted to turn you in, I would've by now. You'd be talking with those lovely knights downstairs rather than me right now. And besides..." A blush crept up Nina's neck and cheeks. "They said down there...you're Maddalena Montcaer?"

"Yes."

"The daughter of Margot and Warrek Montcaer? *Those* Montcaers?"

"Yes..." Lena was nearly as baffled by this turn as she was by Nina's almost shy blush.

"Everyone's heard of the Montcaers, everything they've done. If a daughter of theirs did what those knights are saying, then I have to think it was for a good reason."

All Lena could do was blink in shock. Of all the parts of her name, Montcaer had of course always been the most notable, but being knighted, becoming Lady, had always been the important part to Lena. She couldn't quite imagine what her parents would think of their name being used like this.

Perhaps a little pleased. Definitely horrified.

"I was raised on the knight's code," she told Nina, "and I believe in it. It isn't something to throw away when it's inconvenient or king and country demand it. What's been done to him is wrong. But, more than that, he...he's..."

She looked up at Bel to find him watching her, his gaze somehow both tender and fierce. She lost her words under that look, like he'd fight the world for her.

"He's special to you," Nina finished.

"Yes."

A wry grin broke across Nina's face. "Well, far be it from me to ruin this story. You best believe I'll enjoy telling it, too, when those knights are gone. Now, how do we get you out of here and on your way?"

"We can't get to the stables without passing them. They know our faces," said Lena.

"There should be a room or two available for them tonight as people leave," Nina replied. "I'll get them set up the furthest away I can. Maybe give them our strongest stuff with dinner so they can't ask too many questions."

"Thank you," Lena said, meaning it. "If we could, we'll wait in here until nightfall. I'll pay for another night."

Nina clapped her hands and smiled. "You see? Good patrons! It'll get you far, my dear. Now, here's what we'll do..."

12

Lena held still as her mother fussed over her tunic, wiping away non-existent fuzz and tightening her belt. A blush burned her cheek, and she chewed the inside of it as the other squires sniggered. Margot quelled them with one sharp look from her steel-gray eyes.

Lena only blushed hotter.

"Right, that's good," Margot said, more to herself than Lena.

Her blue velvet tunic was freshly brushed, the golden thread of her family's prancing horse crest gleaming in the bright light of the basilica. Lena had pulled the standard-bearer tunic over her head that morning and twirled in front of the mirror, admiring herself and how the deep blue almost made her look...pretty. Then Margot had called from the next room not to crush the velvet or work up a sweat.

Lena was still young to be standard-bearing, the line of squires extending on either side of her all at least a year her senior. Margot thought she was ready, though, and Lena quietly glowed under the roundabout praise.

Yet, she couldn't help feeling every year, month, day, hour of that gap between her and the other squires as she held the polished wood pole of her mother's standard, silently enduring her mother's fussing.

"Let's hope this doesn't take long," Margot muttered as she straightened Lena's tunic. "He can't really be stupid enough to declare war on the avians again. It won't erase losing the River Dyne after another poor choice of commander."

Lena bit down on her curiosity, knowing the comment wasn't really meant for her.

Margot took a step back, looking Lena and the standard over twice before nodding in approval. "Excellent. You do the Montcaers proud." And with that, she turned on her heel, spurs clicking on the stone floor as joined the other esteemed knights and nobles gathering near the dais to await King Artemian and his announcement.

Her mother had been agitated since receiving the summons yesterday morning. The king only issued such summons when the news would affect the whole kingdom and only with such short notice when the decision went against his council's advice, according to Margot.

"*Goddess, what now?*" her mother had sighed when Lena brought her the wax-sealed parchment, delivered by a liveried palace footman on a silver tray.

The basilica had quickly filled that afternoon with the most eminent of Vagora's knights and nobles, all called in to hear the king's news. A little burst of pride warmed Lena to see her mother among all the most important figures of Vagora, and she held her head high in the line of squires, back straight and standard still.

She ignored the looks and scrutiny passed down the line. And the snickers.

She couldn't ignore the whispers.

"Anyone know why we're here?" muttered a squire two down on her right.

"Sir thinks it's another war against the avians," the older girl next to Lena said quietly.

"Thought they'd given up," said the boy to her left over her head.

"They negotiated a 'strategic armistice,'" mocked the older girl.

The boy to her left snorted. "Right. Surrendered is more like."

"Things went bad in the south," said another girl, three down on Lena's left. "Time to distract from that."

"Lady says that he'll never give up the war on the avians, no matter what," said the boy next to her. "Not after what happened to him."

"His sister was killed by avians, right?"

"No, idiot. His nursemaid."

"Who starts wars over their nursemaid?" scoffed the older girl.

"They were on a tour of the kingdom," the boy on her left whispered, pleased to have the attention on him.

Lena stared resolutely forward, pretending she didn't hear, even if she listened just as raptly. Her blush now was for her disloyalty to the king—in her heart, she didn't believe her mother's grumbles or these squires' gossip, the king was a wise man who led their kingdom nobly. It would be such an honor to kneel before him and earn her spurs.

But she couldn't help holding her breath to catch every word.

"Out on the eastern border, near the Grass Sea. They say avians attacked, unprovoked. Started a brush fire that trapped most of the party. When the old king and his knights beat back the flames, they found everyone dead, burned alive. All except Artemian. His nursemaid had hidden him under her own body, protecting him from the flames. His chest was horribly burned, but he was the only one to survive. Since then, he's barely left the capital. Never forgave what happened to him and his nurse, either."

Lena's heart ached for the little boy the king had been. How terrifying it must've been, flames closing in, the air growing thinner as smoke blackened the sky. The hopelessness that little boy must've felt, pressed into the ground by his nurse's own body, listening to the wails of the dying.

She shivered just thinking about it.

A glint of gold appeared from a side door near the dais, making the squires fall silent. Lena stood tall and straight, pulse pounding with excitement.

King Artemian swept into the basilica, as resplendent as the sun shining through the tall west windows. Adorned in gold armor, the consummate warrior, he ascended the dais steps with the grace of a lion, his long cream cape flowing behind him like water, rippling along the steps. It matched the silky cravat tied around the column of his throat, though Lena didn't think it was just her imagination and the older boy's story that had her thinking she saw the ugly red of a burn scar just peeking from the top of the cloth.

His hair hung in soft brown waves over his shoulders, and a trim beard covered his chin and sharp line of his jaw. Eyes the blue of sapphires stared out at the gathered crowd of knights and nobles down the elegant line of his straight nose. Handsome, commanding—that's how he looked.

A sun god come to speak, and she stood dazzled by his brilliance.

Surely her mother and these squires were mistaken. Surely, whatever the king decided, it was for good reason. King Artemian loved his people, had met the avian and southern threats at every turn, had created dozens of foundling homes for the war orphans, had donated vast sums to demesnes in need. It was through Artemian's generosity that the Montcaers even had Lindenfaire.

So when the king's fine nostrils flared, taking in air to enlighten them on why everyone had been summoned, Lena waited with bated breath.

"Lords, ladies, sirs," the king said, voice carrying through the basilica without having to raise it, "the avian threat has grown untenable..."

13

A symphony of wet splatters echoed just above their heads, the heavy rain overloud under their tarpaulin. It protected them from the worst of the rain, but if she laid on her back, Lena's nose would almost graze the fabric.

Beside her, Alix shivered and grumbled, wriggling further into her blankets. Lena put her arm over Alix, resting her hand on Bel's flank. He drew closer too, on Alix's other side, and hitched his wing a little higher so that the crook rested on her shoulder and Alix was covered from head to toe.

Wrapped up in oilskins, blankets, and feathers together was the best they could do that night. A fire would've been hard to keep alive, but they hadn't risked a fire the past two nights either—it might as well have been a beacon for Joran to follow.

A storm had chased them down and caught them first. Hair and skin damp, the warm comfort of the inn was a distant memory now.

Lena couldn't think of the inn without wanting to gnaw off all her fingernails.

She knew better. She'd been seduced by warm food and blankets and a bed and a bath and—

As if he could feel her thoughts spiraling, Bel pressed his forehead into hers. His eyes were closed and the tip of his nose was cold, but Lena focused on that, on the steady rhythm of his breath.

She was glad one of them could get a little sleep. She'd slept enough at the inn, she could stay awake for a little while longer, just in case, just in case...

The steady patter of the rain eventually lulled her eyes closed, but Lena would only let herself doze. Her ears remained alert, just in case. She had to do better, had to make sure they were safe, even if all that meant anymore was *away from Joran.*

All she could do for now was hope he wouldn't follow them all the way to Aeriand. If he did...well, she supposed there were many places to hide in a hollowed-out city.

———•◆•———

The morning brought a stiff neck for Lena, bent feathers for Bel, and a cough for Alix—but, thank Matella, an end to the rain, too. Air crisp with the fresh dampness of recent rain, the forest and hills seemed sharper, as if she could see farther and in more detail with the air so clean. Billowing white clouds with slate-blue bottoms lumbered across the sky, but none unleashed more rain.

Lena was of two minds about it.

As the morning grew and they journeyed on, the horses in their riding blankets and riders all bundled up in their driest layers, Alix's cough grew worse. The wet sound of it rattling in her narrow chest made Lena clench her teeth to keep the tears back. "I'm *fine,*" Alix would insist from under her voluminous scarf every time Lena looked over to check on her. Her nose was hidden under the folds, but Lena knew it was red and runny.

Lena had to hope drier air would help the cough.

Yvain stumbled a half-step but caught himself quickly, grumbling. Lena patted his neck but couldn't help grimacing at the clear hoof slide left in the mud. They'd been leaving easy tracks to follow all morning, the ground wet and ready for footprints, and only more rain would wash away the evidence of their passing.

She couldn't bear Alix coughing, but she couldn't help worrying over the obvious trail they left behind.

All she could hope was that Joran was far enough behind that the previous days' tracks had been washed away the night before.

Between the mud and Alix's cough, they didn't make it as far as Lena wanted that day, but she could only push so hard. They broke at dusk for a meal of dried salmon and the last of the brown bread Nina had packed them.

The innkeeper's generosity still stunned her. Both Nina and Lorne had helped them prepare, getting clothes laundered, fetching any supplies Alix hadn't found yet, and filling their saddlebags to bursting with so much dried salmon that, three days out, they were all sick of the stuff. But still so, so grateful.

Lorne had kept watch as Nina hurried them out of the inn in the small hours. She'd whispered advice about where to head—keep due east, even as the river wended south—as they'd packed, strapped, and buckled. When it came time to go, Nina wished them good fortune and clear skies.

From under his cloak, Bel had pulled out a small, downy secondary feather and given it to Nina. *"For your mantel collection,"* he'd said. *"Thank you. For everything. I won't ever forget your kindness."*

Teary-eyed, Nina had accepted the feather and held it close. *"We won't ever forget the avian who came to town. I hope our paths cross again one day. Now go, be safe."*

The kindness and extra supplies had softened the blow of stealing from town in the dead of night and spending the next days on the run, a sense of urgency driving them on that Lena hadn't felt since those first days after stealing Bel from Finhöln. She'd expected Joran then, had waited and waited for the sounds of pursuit, but...nothing.

She'd begun to think he hadn't come after them. That perhaps they'd be safe to find that homestead in her mind.

How wrong she'd been. Again.

Her dourness was hard to hide, and she noticed the looks Bel and Alix shared. Nobody spoke much as they hunkered down on the damp ground for another night of no fire. Without the light, there was little point to staying up when the sun disappeared, and Alix was quick to bed down.

Bel was quiet as they lay down together, and Lena was grateful. She didn't want to speak her thoughts, didn't want to be told not to worry or that it wasn't her fault. She *did* worry and it *did* feel like her fault. Still, his warm body was a comfort she couldn't turn down, and she curled into him as he carded his fingers through her hair and gently scratched her scalp.

She woke the next morning from a deep sleep, unsure how he knew to do that. She appreciated that he wasn't too smug about it, though.

Alix's cough hadn't improved, but it hadn't worsened, either. Lena tried not to fuss, but from the huff and eye rolls she got from Alix, she didn't succeed.

They broke camp after a cold breakfast. Lena watched Bel mount his new horse with approval. He'd taken to the animal quickly, and the big bay was gentle and friendly, forgiving any jerky tugs on the reins or clumsy mounting. He hadn't even seemed bothered by Bel's wings, which twitched and fluttered and rustled without Bel ever meaning to, making strange, sudden noises that still spooked the packhorses sometimes.

There hadn't been time or a good enough mood to give him a new name, even for Alix, so Bel had taken to calling him *friend*. It was enough for now, and Lena had to hope so were Bel's basic riding skills.

As morning gave way to afternoon, the dense, verdant hills of the forest gentled out into a smoother landscape of pines and scrub. The ferns, mosses, and leafy brush of the forest dwindled, replaced with squat juniper bushes and thickets of purple thistle. Clusters of wildflowers dotted the ground, the orange of poppies and blues of cornflowers breaking up the gray-green of the scrubby ground.

A breeze touched Lena's cheek, the air drier than she'd felt in days. The loamy earth of the forest had given way to a sandy, silty dirt that Lena knew would be soft to the touch.

She'd seen this kind of landscape before, on her march years ago to Aeriand.

Lena twisted in the saddle to find Bel.

The look on his face nearly broke her heart.

Mouth slack, Bel sat still in his saddle, the breeze playing with his golden hair. Pupils blown wide, those inhuman eyes took in everything, all the colors and textures, and wetness gathered along the rims.

They'd reached avian country.

She didn't quite know if he'd welcome it, but she reached for his hand, needing to hold onto some part of him as he took in the sight of his ancestral lands. He clutched her hand back, crushing it in his grip, and brought it to his face to kiss her knuckles.

A tear breached his lashes, running down his cheek and into his wide, shattering smile. A special kind of agony played across his face, a bittersweetness of coming home, of getting where you never thought you'd ever be. It was a joy so great it bordered on pain because it'd taken so much to get there.

Lena couldn't resist the incandescence of his smile, the raw joy and relief so stark in his gaze. She smiled too, felt it cracking across her face, through the crust of worry and shame that had hardened over her.

Then the wind shifted.

Yvain's ears went with it, and he shuffled beneath her.

Bel's smile dimmed, and she *hated* that. He cocked his head, ear pointed behind them.

For a moment there was nothing, only the sound of the wind through the brush.

Then, a hoof pawing at loamy ground. Faint—and not one of their horses.

A strangled puff of air left her as her heart jumped to her throat. Bel grimaced.

There wasn't time to look—she wheeled Yvain to the northeast and drove her heels in.

"*Fuck!*" Alix yelped.

The horses lurched forward, ears pinned to their heads, and weaved through the bristly pines. Lena squeezed her thighs and tapped Yvain twice with her heels for *quicker, faster now.*

It was easier to navigate this terrain, but the trees and scrubs provided no cover and the silty soil kept imprints of each of their footfalls, but Lena couldn't care, couldn't think beyond—

A shrill braying split the air, followed by a chorus of yells. They'd been spotted.

Lena bent over Yvain's neck, making herself a smaller target, and cut to the left. They skirted a shallow hill, weaving between boulders and bushes, but Lena didn't waste time or effort taking the high ground; there were too many to fight.

The land passed in a blur, gently rising as the horses' hooves pounded, kicking up a great plume of dust. Lena's heart kept time as she led them into a creek and kept to the water. They hurried onto the opposite bank when a horse and rider leapt from the trees half a mile downstream. Soaked from the thigh down, they raced through the trees, making patterns with their path.

She played every trick she knew, every switchback, every feint, but still the riders gained. Lena nearly shrieked in frustration—the man who'd taught her almost everything she knew to do was the very one who pursued them.

The sun burned down on their heads when they burst into a wide field of swaying grasses and solitary sunflowers. She set her teeth and led them across as fast as they could, Yvain's great muscles quivering under her.

From the corner of her eye she spotted two horses with riders. She stood halfway up in the stirrups and spied another rider to the north.

Joran was trying to flank them.

They charged into the trees, scattering branches and brambles. One of the packhorses whinnied in fright, but Lena wouldn't stop.

Not yet.

Find a hidden spot first.

The trees offered what cover they could, and Lena led them single file through thick berry bushes. Yvain huffed at the thorny branches littering the path, but Lena pushed on.

The sounds of their pursuers died in the trees, and finally she spotted what she wanted.

She drew on the reins within a dense copse of trees, sending dirt flying. Alix on Miri came next, the horse's neck and flanks shivering and sweat-streaked. Then the packhorses, and finally Bel on his bay. The horse huffed and puffed but seemed determined to stay with the others.

Lena turned her head but couldn't hear much over the panting horses and her own thundering heart.

Alix was sick, her color pallid even with the exertion, and Bel's horse, while strong, just wasn't as fast or well trained. She let her mind run through all the combinations of horse and rider, but she kept coming to one conclusion.

Resolve settled like lead in her stomach.

Bel saw it and shook his head once, sharp and angry.

"Don't," he growled.

"Keep going, single file," she said, handing over the packhorses' reins to Alix.

"Where the hells are you going?" Alix panted.

"Lena." Bel leveled her with a glare that would've made someone lesser cower and submit. In that moment, she saw the Adiiron prince he'd been once, the one he'd been born to be. But she'd faced princes before, and there was no other way, nothing without far more risk than she was willing to take.

She tapped Yvain, heading the way they'd come. Bel made a grab for her arm, but she dodged and slapped his horse's flank.

"Hi-ya!" she yelled. The other horses quivered and chuffed and surged forward again.

With a squeeze, Yvain took off in the opposite direction.

"LENA!"

Her heart clenched, but it was too late now. She hoped she could apologize later.

She followed their tracks back, arrowing straight for the riders until she caught sight of a cloak flapping. Yanking on the reins, she sent them careening over boulders and through another small creek, racing north.

Yvain cantered until she was sure they saw her, sure they turned to pursue. She couldn't count individual horses in the maelstrom of pounding behind her, but it was enough of them.

She picked up the pace, winding around trees, making a show of it, always leading them further north. She cut across an open plain that made her crouch low in the saddle. Her hair buffeted and stung at her face, coming loose from its plait. She waited for the whine of arrows, but they never came.

Joran wanted them alive.

At least wanted Bel alive.

That cooled her resolve into a solid, steel mass in her heart.

It was easier to outmaneuver them when it was just Yvain. He proved worth every coin he cost as they ran, never slowing, always ready to cut left or right, dancing through brambles and leaping over logs. She trusted him to run true as she kept her head swiveling, trying to count riders.

They'd flanked her and would spring their trap soon.

"There's just one!" she heard a knight call to the others.

"She's leading us away!"

"Double back and—"

Lena doubled back and burst from between a pair of trees, close enough to catch the surprise in the knight's eyes. The woman watched her pass with mouth hanging open, and then Lena was gone again.

She needed them to spring that trap on her alone.

The call went up again, hooves pounding, and Lena gave Yvain his head while she looked for what she needed.

She found it in the deep shadow of a massive overturned tree, the mess of exposed roots and dark earth forming a shield wider than a portcullis.

Lena leapt from Yvain's back and arranged his reins.

She gave him the signal to return home. If they'd been staying somewhere, he'd go there, but out here, he'd search out the other horses of their little herd.

But he didn't move.

Lena huffed in exasperation and Yvain matched it with his own chuff, as if he thought her idea stupid.

It probably was, but she was doing it anyway.

"Just trust me," she grumbled at him.

Yvain pinned his ears to his head and bit at her with his lips.

"Bad horse." Dancing around his nipping mouth, she made the signal for return home again and smacked his flank.

He jumped forward, and Lena turned on her heel and ran the other way.

She kept northward, the ground under her feet rumbling with the riders in pursuit—less than before, three maybe. A shout went up as she leapt from an outcropping of rocks, hitting the ground running. She didn't bother feinting and zigzagging anymore, just kept going, drawing them further and further away.

Arms pumping, legs churning, she ignored the burn in her lungs, focused only on the next tree, the next rock, because it was just that little bit further from—

She didn't see the eroded hillside until it was too late.

Loose dirt gave under her left boot, taking Lena down with it. She thrashed, grabbing onto saplings and exposed roots to slow her fall, but the ground came up to meet her. Her hip slammed into the hard earth below, forcing a pained groan from her lips.

She ached, but Lena couldn't stop. She started with hands and knees and picked herself up from there. Her head swam for a horrible moment, trees bending and hanging off the inverted ground like bats. She took a deep, long draught of air before she was running again.

It was more of a limping jog, but it was all she could do.

She heard them before she saw them.

Pine needles and twigs snapped and sprayed as two horses came bursting from the trees. On her left, two more knights on foot tried to flank her.

"Maddalena! Stop now!"

Joran's voice cut through the trees, giving her another burst of speed. She feinted, as if she'd duck around the mounted knights, but cut for the opposite tree line. Her lungs burned and bellowed, and sweat stung the little cuts on her face and dry, cracked lips.

She dodged between the larger trees, trying to lose them in the tall pines. She slid down a shallow slope, dead, brown needles making it a quick slide to the ground below.

She ran, ran past the point of knowing she couldn't run anymore. She ran even when she saw a knight in either periphery, ran even when she could feel the hot cloud of horse breath buffeting the back of her neck. She ran because they followed, and if they were following, they weren't chasing Bel and Alix.

She ran and ran, and would've run right off the cliff face if some part of her mind hadn't registered the wide-open sky just beyond the tree line. Pebbles went flying as her boots scraped and skidded along the rock, and she threw her weight backwards to stop herself.

Lena landed on her backside, one leg dangling off the sheer drop of an escarpment.

Mouth open wide to pull in gulps of air, she rolled to her feet, locking her knees so her shaky legs would hold her up. To her left and right as far she could see, the land simply stopped. At her feet, a vertical drop loomed over five hundred feet above the land below. It was more pines and scrubs down there, as if the ground there and here were a matching set, just broken in half by a few hundred feet.

The scrabbling pound of feet running up behind her had Lena turning. She wiped the sweat from her eyes and pulled a dagger from her belt. She planted her feet and took a solid fighting stance, not willing for an errant breeze to be what brought her down.

The knights had circled her, pinning her a step away from the sheer drop. Those still on horses had drawn arrows, and the other two approached with swords and daggers drawn.

It was only Joran, at their center, who stood without weapons. He didn't need any, his flinty gaze weapon enough.

She met that gaze, sweaty, bleeding, exhausted—but determined. She was still standing, still had breath. That meant she'd fight.

"You've made your point, Maddalena," Joran said, the hint of a stern frown forming on his brow. "This has been quite the merry chase, but it's over. Put down your weapons. In the name of Vagora and King Artemian IV, I'm arresting you for treason, aiding the enemy, assault..."

Lena had almost caught her breath by the time he was done with the list. Surely nothing mattered after treason, but Joran believed in thoroughness.

When Lena didn't surrender after his speech, his mouth drew down even further. She didn't see how she could disappoint him any more, but apparently she'd managed.

"We aren't in Vagora," Lena reminded him. "You've no authority here."

"I've got the authority, if only from superior numbers. Put down your weapons, Maddalena."

"No."

"It isn't you I must bring back alive. I'm giving you the opportunity, though. Be smart and take it."

"It isn't me I'm worried about."

Joran sighed. "I appreciate what you're doing, stalling, hoping they get further away. It's admirable, in its own way." He took a step forward, hands folded behind his back in a posture that was so familiar, as if he was merely coaching her stance or issuing orders for the day. "But how long do you think it will take them to come for you? The avian cares for you. Surrender now and convince them to surrender, too. Nobody needs to be harmed."

Her smile was vicious. "Except when you break Bel's wing, of course."

Joran frowned, his mouth opening to speak, but the knight to his left shoved him down, out of the way of the big body hurtling from the trees. A thunderclap of feathers and golden hair crashed into Joran and his knights, spooking the horses and scattering their formation.

Joran ducked and rolled out of the way, just missing the dagger Bel buried in the dirt where he'd been. Bel jerked the blade out of the ground and swung, catching the sword that came for him from another knight.

Lena watched in awe and horror as he battled his way to her. Her heart clenched painfully in her chest, not knowing whether to sink in dismay or jump into her throat.

It happened so quickly, she couldn't intervene or shout at him; she felt lost in a daze, a slow, viscous dream watching Bel in combat. He struck hard, fast, vicious, a flurry of movement that never stopped. In that moment, he was the avian fighter he'd been training to be, a warrior prince with the fury of his people behind him.

Two knights tried to tackle him, and Lena could only gawk when he deflected their blows, danced back two paces, and then ran at them head on. His wings pumped behind him, and he jumped, legs wheeling, wings kicking off the ground to give him the height to soar over the knights' heads.

He landed in a run, and then he was there, taking up all her vision, all her senses. That glare of his still stark on his face. She didn't know whether to shove him or kiss him.

Glancing over his shoulder at the knights, he sheathed his dagger and said, "Hold on tightly."

"Bel—"

His arms clutched her like vices, and when his wings unfurled to span over a body length in either direction, she instinctively threw her arms around his neck.

He held her just off the ground, the toes of her boots scraping, and then he was running, flapping, gaining speed to—no, surely not, surely they weren't—

The bottom fell away from her stomach and from under their feet.

They fell.

The wind rushing up to meet them stole the screams from her mouth.

Lena threw her legs around his waist and held him in a crushing grip. Bel palmed the back of her head and pushed her face into the crook of his neck.

The air rushed by in a horrid whooshing that pummeled her ear drums and whipped at her skin. Her stomach jumped and lodged in her throat, and her eyes nearly groaned under the pressure.

A noise huffed out of Bel, a curse, and they fell, down, down, down.

His wings gave a great flap, jostling her against him, but still they fell.

He flapped again, fighting the wind that pulled them down like grasping hands, but still they fell.

Tears stung her eyes and Bel's fingers dug painfully into her scalp. Any moment now, any moment and then—impact. She hoped she didn't feel it when she shattered into pieces.

Lena yelped when a gust buffeted them, sending them spinning to the right. He flapped again, again, fighting to gain speed and height—but he was losing; even with her eyes clenched shut, she knew the ground still came at them, that they wouldn't survive impact.

His pulse pounded against her forehead and she could feel the tendons in his neck drawn taut. He clutched her somehow even tighter and flapped, flapped. For a sickening moment, she thought the wind would tear his wings from his back.

He screamed and screamed, a desperate cry as they fell, and Lena screamed too, for how close they'd been, for the life they wouldn't have.

One more great heave of his wings, bowing his back, and…

They jerked midair, as if the bottom had been wrenched out from under them again, and Bel's wings caught enough air to level out.

Lena's eyes popped open, not believing what she'd felt.

They flew.

The ground was close, so close, but they didn't fall. He kept them airborne somehow, with another sharp cry pulled from the depths of his chest. He cast his wings wide, feathers spread like individual fingers to catch as much air as possible. They rippled and sparkled like waves in the blazing sun.

They didn't fall, but the ground came to meet them anyway.

Bel tried to take the brunt of it, tried to get his legs under them, but they came in too fast.

Impact punched the breath from Lena's chest, and they crashed through bushes and shrubs until Bel's wings finally gave out. They tumbled across the ground, and in the violent crash, she lost hold of him. Lena yelped, bouncing along like a flat stone on a lake, branches catching and scratching at her.

She rolled and lurched, aware of every bone in her body and how the next roll, the next rock or branch would be what broke them all.

The rough dirt gave way to the slick of tall grass, and it was just enough to slow her. Throwing a foot out, Lena stopped her tumble, coming to a jarring halt with a mouthful of dirt.

The world spun around her, making her think for a horrible moment that she did too, but she forced herself to look at the sun hanging in the sky, no matter how it burned. When it was more than she could bear, she shut her eyes and breathed through her nose.

After three breaths, her head stopped sloshing, and after six, she got command of her stomach. After ten, she started to believe she truly was alive rather than flattened after falling hundreds of feet.

She didn't want to—oh no, she wanted to lie there on her back forever—but slowly, one muscle at a time, Lena pulled herself up. With the dizziness fading, all the aches and hurts crowded for attention, and the hot sizzle of pain nearly brought her down again. She flexed her wrist and took a step forward, another, until the pain receded just enough to be tolerable, and with every step, bone and tendon and ligament cracked and popped and fell back into place.

A golden gleam drew her eye, and she hobbled as fast as she could through thickets of tall grass to where Bel struggled to his feet.

His chest heaved like a pair of blacksmith bellows, and he vibrated with how violently his limbs shook. He got his feet under him by the time Lena reached him, and he caught her when she nearly stumbled.

Together they held each other up and staggered through the thick undergrowth until they found cover under a line of trees. Hidden from view, she finally got a look at Bel.

A cut streaked red across his forehead and severed the tip of his right brow, and his skin was a patchwork of brown grime and gleaming sweat. It made the wild width of his pupils and the azure of the irises almost painful to look at in their intensity.

They panted open-mouthed together, staring, not quite believing they'd been standing atop that escarpment facing down certain capture just moments ago.

A frantic laugh bubbled up Lena's throat.

The sound snapped something in him—he grabbed her by the shoulders and got in her face, wings taking up any of her vision his scowl didn't.

"What in hell was that?" he shouted in her face.

Teeth bared in a snarl, emotion welled in his eyes and spilled over, tears tracking little lines through the dirt coating his face.

"Bel, I—"

But his words didn't, perhaps couldn't stop, flowing with the tears. "*Stop sacrificing yourself!* You aren't disposable, gods damnit! Why must you always throw yourself in the way?"

She gripped his wrists and gently squeezed. "I'm sorry. I...I thought it was the only way."

"We could've done—we could've planned something. Together, damnit! When will you see—" He clenched his teeth and his hands slid up to hold her face, hot palms pressing into her cheeks. "You don't have to prove or sacrifice yourself—not for me, never for me. You're everything, *c'vana*. Everything. And I—I can't—"

His big body shuddered, and his grip on her head became almost painful.

"I can't lose you," he whispered, just a breath.

She didn't realize she cried until the salt of her tears stung her cracked lips. She stepped into the curve of his body, and something settled in her, deeper than blood or bone or viscera. His head fell onto hers, their slick foreheads sticking together, and she breathed him in.

Her heart hurt for him, for what she'd put him through, but she couldn't apologize. It was in her nature to protect, but more, she'd always, *always* protect him. Her love for him burned in her chest, heart beating sharp and fierce at the thought of Joran or anyone else doing him harm. But there was a sweetness there, too—she'd never been everything to someone before.

They'd both done something rash and honestly rather stupid today, for the other.

She'd never had someone face down opponents and jump from a cliff for her before. Just thinking about it took her breath away, the awe palpable and the shock of it lingering. If she was honest, the memory of how he'd fought then jumped over those knights lit a spark of lust in her.

He'd come back for her.

He said she was everything. He said he loved her. For the first time, in the shadow of that sheer drop, Lena finally believed him.

Every limb ached, every scratch and cut stung, and she could almost feel the colors her hip would turn, but something much stronger kept her standing there, in the lee of Bel's body. Joy, radiant and molten, scorched through her—to be alive, to be with him.

It was more than she knew how to say, more than the words she had. So, Lena canted her lips up to his, taking his mouth in a kiss she hoped said everything she couldn't. They were *alive* and she needed to *feel* it.

Their teeth clacked together, lips scraping and tongues dancing. It was messy and slick, and Lena threw her arms around his neck, fusing the lines of their bodies together.

"Lena," Bel breathed into her mouth. He filled a hand with her backside, pulling her up, aligning them so she could feel the heat of him even through their clothes.

She nipped his lip, kissed his chin.

"Thank you," she whispered.

His pupils blew wide again, but they were full of heat now, taking in every detail of her. Finally, his gaze fixed on her mouth and he swooped down to take it, to take what was his. Bel groaned deep in his throat, a wholly male sound that made her writhe.

Then there were no more words, just mouths and teeth and hands. He bore her to the ground, blighting out the sun as he made her take his weight. She loved it, loved being surrounded, being crushed by him and his heat. It didn't matter how she hurt—she *ached* for him.

Their hands shook and fumbled, and they couldn't wait for clothes or caresses. His mouth fell on hers, tongue invading, sealing them together, as trous got pushed out of the way. He hissed when she took the scalding length of him in her hand and pumped once, twice. Lena planted her bootheels in the dirt and rose to meet him.

She wasn't ready enough for him, wasn't prepared for the brutal thrusts that invaded her, but she welcomed the burn. It was exquisite and savage, rutting in the dirt—he devoured her, taking everything he wanted, and she gave it to him, met him thrust for thrust, hips rolling and crashing together.

He kissed and nipped and sucked, mouth never leaving her skin. Lena raked her nails through his hair, making him growl.

She felt the noise in her very center and gasped.

His mouth closed over hers again. His hands gripped her hips hard enough to bruise, keeping her still, making her take and feel every frantic thrust. A thumb, hot and rough, pressed where she needed it most, unyielding and firm and wonderful. Lena cried out at the brutal pleasure of it, climax ripping through her unbidden, unannounced. She came apart, the pleasure too much, the ache giving way to a humming, mindless pleasure, thick as syrup.

It was too much, painful, and perfect.

She came back to herself slowly, the sound of their gasps and panting loud in the canopy of his wings. Her aches and pains were still there but muted, nothing compared to the heady, ferocious satisfaction thrumming through her.

They lay there in the dirt for a long time. Or, perhaps it wasn't long, but the moment felt timeless to Lena, stretching out in a languid slide of bodies and rasp of feathers. She floated there under the delicious weight of him, savoring his heat, his textures.

Too soon, Bel lifted his head. He pressed warm, lazy kisses to her forehead, cheek, neck, the desperation of before easing into a pleasant languidness that made her teeth ache with the sweetness of it.

They both groaned when he pulled away from her, and Lena shivered from the loss. He stood slowly, finding his balance, and tucked himself away. She smiled up at him, feeling almost drunk on the happiness and relief.

Bel held out a hand and pulled her up. With quiet tenderness and stolen kisses, they cleaned each other up the best they could and righted the other's clothes, buckling and tying and straightening what the pursuit and plummet had undone. When there was nothing left to fix or tie, Bel gathered her close and tucked an errant lock of hair behind her ear. "Everything, *c'vana*," he whispered into her skin.

She smiled against his neck. She needed to ask him what that meant, even if she thought she might know. There would be time. For now, she just held him in her arms. And it was everything.

Lena ran her nails lightly over his wing bases, making them shudder. He held his wings aloft, without any apparent pain, and she had to hope that meant they hadn't been damaged when—

Lena gasped. "Bel!" She grabbed his startled face. "We flew!"

A smile wider than the sky above lit his face. Eyes glittering, he chuckled, "Well, it was more of a glide, if that—"

She threw her arms around his neck and dragged him down for a hard kiss.

"We *flew!* Bel! That was *amazing!*" Heart pounding, giddy excitement and pride fizzed inside her, and she kissed him again. "Just wait until we tell Alix!"

14

They realized at the same moment that in the shock and heat and amazement at surviving, they'd left Alix and all the horses out there on their own.

Lena grimaced. "She's never going to forgive me for this."

"Yes she will. It'll just take some bribery."

She huffed a laugh before casting her gaze around them. Bel joined her, actually taking in their surroundings for the first time. The landscape was much like on the higher ground, but here the trees were less densely packed, making room for thick clusters of tall grasses and colorful horns of larkspurs. To the east, the land eased into grassy flatlands crisscrossed with creeks lined in cattails and reeds.

He remembered such landscapes, had flown above them hundreds of times as a fledgling. Being so close to Aeriand...it was like a dream, one he might startle awake from at any moment. He wanted to see his city, he did, and the anticipation was there, it was, but alongside it, buried deep in that pessimistic heart of his, was a foreboding trepidation. He knew it wouldn't be the city of his youth, knew Maddok and Eamon wouldn't be waiting for him to return—it probably crawled with humans, and it was probably insanity to go there in the first place. He didn't quite know what he would do once he got there, but like a meteor pulled from the sky, it felt inevitable that he'd return, see it with his own eyes. Perhaps it was a morbid curiosity; perhaps it was to finally say goodbye to the boy he'd once been.

"Alix and I spotted a confluence of several streams," Bel told her. "I said I'd meet her there."

"How far do you think?"

It was his turn to grimace. "It's on the south side of the cliffs."

Her face fell, panic stark in her wide eyes, and Bel rushed to add, "She can take care of herself, sweetheart, you know she can. You've taught her well. And she's got all the supplies."

Lena blinked at him, and he watched his words tumble through her mind. Finally, she took a deep, long breath.

"You're right. I know you're right." She pulled in a fortifying breath. "We should have some time. I drew them as far north as I could."

"It'll take days for them to go back around," Bel agreed.

She stepped back to pat her belt and bracers. Bel checked himself, too. Between them, they had a handful of daggers and an empty water-skin with a broken seam.

"I can probably fix it," Lena said, picking at the broken threads.

"If we find water, we can follow it to the confluence."

"And Alix."

Lena nodded, drawing herself up. Bel watched with no small measure of pride as the knight in her came to the fore, determination writ in the set of her brow not to back down from a new challenge.

They started northeast, following the escarpment in a wending path, sticking to tree cover where they could. Though they'd left Joran behind, if the knights lingered along the cliff, they'd have an excellent view of the landscape.

Bel let Lena set the pace, though the longer they went, the more he noticed how she favored her right side. She'd tumbled and fallen more than once today, and he hated that she was hurting.

Had it been rash to leave Alix alone with the horses to go after Lena? Probably, yes. But he'd never regret it. The thrill of fear for her still coursed through him, dampened only by the thrill of their moment of flight. The memories fought for attention in his mind, of feeling the wind in his feathers again, of seeing weapons trained on Lena with nothing at her back.

He hadn't really thought of what he'd do when he got to her, just knew as he'd pumped his legs and run faster than he ever had that he needed to get there *now*. Seeing Lena pinned down, the open horizon behind her, jumping was the first thing that came to him, and he hadn't waited to think about it.

They'd been threatening Lena, his woman, his *c'vana*.

No time for thought or plans. He'd had to trust himself and Lena too, that she'd hold on, that she'd trust him, that her stretches and careful attentions had healed him enough.

He still didn't quite believe it'd worked.

As the afternoon lengthened, Bel subtly adjusted their pace, slowing down incrementally. She'd set a brutal pace, and any other time he would've been fine to match it, but he couldn't ignore the pained twist to her mouth as they pushed on.

She would've walked through the night too, but Bel insisted they stop and rest. Broken ankles wouldn't get them to Alix any sooner, and he didn't want to run into any of the night predators that would soon come looking for a meal.

With the last of the light, they shared the few sips of water that hadn't escaped the skin and chose their hidey-hole for the night. Bel sat in the chosen nook of a tree, hidden on either side by tall walls of grass, and pulled Lena down to join him. She fit her back to his chest and sighed happily when his wings came around them to ward off the worst of the chill.

"Get some sleep," Bel whispered into her hair. "I'll keep watch."

Lena snuggled closer, rolling so her good hip took her weight. Bel shifted his legs, cradling her off the ground.

"Wake me in a few hours," she yawned, settling her cheek on his shoulder.

"Mm."

He'd do no such thing.

———•◆•——

Bel had forgotten the terrifying sound of a coyote pack. The ghastly yowls bounced between the trees, making the down at his neck stand up. They never sounded too close, though, and he wished all the rabbits out there luck. Lena stirred at the haunting sounds but never fully woke. Bel held still, making soothing noises, and drew his wings around her head to muffle the noise.

In the darkness, without a view of the moon, it was impossible to tell time. The night slipped by, giving way to the gray dawn, and Bel drew out of his doze. He hadn't slept, but that was all right; Lena slept safely in his arms, and besides, his mind whirled with the sensory memories of flight.

He could almost feel the wind, the way the air lifted them and took their weight. His wing bases ached with the exertion, sore from the suddenness, and he relished it.

He'd need to restart his *ariant* forms, the base of all avian martial arts. It emphasized strengthening the wings and back. For years, he'd dutifully trained, waiting for his moment to escape Finhöln, but it'd never felt totally right. With a broken and badly healed wing base, the forms could never truly be done correctly. But now...It was only Lena resting in his lap that kept him from jumping up and starting on the forms while the sun started the day.

A touch of color suffused the sky by the time Lena slowly came awake. She stretched against him, shifting about but not opening her eyes.

"You didn't wake me," she said, voice thick with lingering sleep. She curled up, burrowing her face in the side of his neck.

"Mm, I forgot," he lied, cuddling her close.

She snorted but let him hold her like that as the day brightened and all the morning birds struck up their songs.

Eventually, they heaved each other up, stretching sore muscles and popping stiff necks. Bel didn't miss the wince she tried to hide testing her bruised hip and leg. When she realized he'd seen, Lena just shrugged.

"How's your knee?"

The mess of scar tissue lining the side of her left knee had healed well enough but bothered her in the cold. It'd been earned sacking Aeriand, he'd learned one rainy night in Finhöln. Her unit had been overwhelmed, pinned down, and no one escaped unscathed. He'd spent a long time that night kissing away the memories of what his kin had done.

"It'll warm up once we get moving."

Bel made a noncommittal noise and nodded for her to lead the way. Thankfully, she set a reasonable pace this morning.

"How are your wings?" she asked.

Bel flapped and preened for her, holding one wing out, high, and backwards and the other low and forwards then switching, as if he paddled through water with his wings. It hurt like hell, dormant tendons, sinews, and muscles jumping to action for the first time in years, and he loved it.

Lena smiled through her snort of laughter. "Showoff."

He smiled back cheekily. "It's all thanks to you."

The lines around her eyes tightened, just for a moment and it was gone, almost making him think he imagined it.

The forest of scrubby pines slowly changed to great, barky oaks and beeches. Their path wound around expansive junipers and thick berry brambles, and they had to stop at every break in the tree canopy to track the sun and make sure they headed generally in the right direction.

By midday, the burble of a stream finally came within earshot. At first he'd thought it was his grumbling stomach, but Lena picked up her hobbled pace. Around a set of boulders and a juniper, they found a dark-blue stream bordered with cattails, iridescent dragonflies dancing along the surface.

Saliva pooled in Bel's dry mouth at the sight of the cool water. He looked up and then downstream for any dangers, and his gaze snagged on a creature drinking a stone's throw away.

Bel laughed in disbelief.

"What?" asked Lena. "Oh!"

His mane was tangled and he was missing a saddlebag, but otherwise, Yvain looked hale as he guzzled from the stream.

"Yvain!" Lena cried happily, hurrying along the bank.

The big warhorse's ears swiveled in their direction. Seeing them on the opposite bank, the horse huffed and stamped his front hoof.

Bel stopped alongside Lena, watching Yvain toss his mane and throw a horse tantrum.

"I think he's scolding me," Lena said.

"Yes, he's got some choice things to say about that stunt."

She scowled at him, making him laugh, and he retreated across the stream to fetch Yvain before she could swat at him.

Yvain didn't seem overly pleased with him either, bobbing his head and chuffing when Bel drew near, but a few compliments and some twigs pulled out of his mane, and the warhorse eventually deigned to cross the stream with him back to Lena.

The big brute leaned down and snuffled at Lena's hair with his velvet lips, checking her over. Lena threw her arms around his thick neck and buried her nose in his mane.

"I won't do it again, I promise," she whispered to him.

"You didn't make me any such promises," Bel teased.

"That's because the ride is much smoother with him." She arched her brows cheekily, a saucy little grin on her face, and swung up into the saddle.

Bel guffawed in offense, making her laugh as she tapped Yvain with her knees.

"He's better trained, too," she quipped and then trotted off downstream.

He chuckled as he chased them down, eventually sweet-talking his way onto the horse behind her.

⸻ ◆ ⸻

Dusk threatened, but they made good time atop Yvain, who trotted easily beside the stream. It had widened as they went and joined another creek before tumbling over a knee-high waterfall. When they hadn't found any sign of Alix, they decided to keep going, as Bel thought he remembered seeing three streams converging.

It was Yvain who heard it first, the soft chuffs and nickers of other horses. His ears perked up, and an excited, answering whinny burst from him.

Lena reined him in, though, legs tense. Where she'd been reclining against Bel just a moment ago, she held herself alert, eyes darting through the growing gloom.

Bel palmed the hilt of his dagger and fluffed out his wings.

They slowly rounded a copse of trees, ducking under the low branches. Yvain's steps were measured and quiet, though the warhorse didn't seem agitated or worried.

The trees gave way to a little clearing with an outcropping of rocks in the center. Around it stood four familiar horses; each looked up and whinnied hellos as Yvain approached. Ignoring Lena's directions, Yvain trotted over merrily and greeted Miri and the packhorses.

The big bay Bel had been riding the past few days came over to greet them, his head higher than theirs even atop Yvain, he was so tall. Bel patted his velveteen nose and let him snuffle at his hair and feathers.

"Where's Alix?"

Bel looked up at the note of panic in Lena's voice. A little further into the clearing, a neat pile of saddlebags circled a bedroll with the blankets tossed hurriedly aside.

Lena threw herself off Yvain, and Bel was quick to follow. He grabbed for her hand when she would've marched straight to the little nest, worried it could be a trap.

He cocked his ear, listening, but only heard Lena shout, *"Alix!"*

Bel winced.

A tree behind the little camp rustled, limbs shaking off loose leaves, and then a small figure dropped gracefully from a lower branch. Alix shuffled out from under the tree, sheathing her dagger and giving them a limp wave.

"Welcome back," she rasped before unceremoniously flopping onto her bedroll.

Even from a few paces away, Bel saw the puffy redness of her nose and eyes. A closer look confirmed it, she was in the worst of the cold she'd caught a few nights ago. A shiny line leaked from her pink nose, and her voice sounded thick and nasally.

Lena clucked and fussed, hunkering down beside the girl and pressing her hands to Alix's clammy face. "Oh, Alix, look at you. You're burning up."

"I ate all the jam," Alix babbled. "And I'm not sorry about it."

That got a chuckle from both Lena and Bel.

"You deserved it," Lena said.

"Damn right I did. *I* was the only one who did the smart thing. Now, tell me everything."

Bel listened with one ear while Lena recounted her maneuvers, trying to throw Joran and his knights off. He fetched her some rags and the little pot of balm Lena kept for chapped lips. He filled a bowl with cool water from the stream as well as all of their waterskins and got out the small kettle to make a quick soup.

Lena dabbed Alix's forehead and chatted, answering the girl's questions about their exploits over the last day, as Bel went about setting up camp. Alix had done a commendable job for being on her own and sick, but the horses were pleased to have a turn getting to drink and eat, and Yvain was happy to be rid of his saddle.

He smiled and confirmed Lena's story when Alix gasped and exclaimed over their short flight off the escarpment. Alix spent the rest of the evening prodding Lena for more details of what flying had been like, as "*Moderately terrifying*" didn't seem to satisfy her.

The evening passed pleasantly, Lena tending to Alix and Bel tending to everything else. A palpable relief linked the three of them, like silky spider threads cocooning them from outside threats. Though she talked with Lena, Alix kept looking over to check for Bel, and he stopped by her nest frequently to ask how she felt and what she needed. She enjoyed having every whim answered, judging by her feline smile.

Their fire was modest but good enough for a basic stew and to keep Alix warm. She grumbled when hers was just broth and mashed peas.

"We'll try more tomorrow once your stomach has settled," Lena said.

Alix begrudgingly finished off her broth and was quickly asleep in her nest. With the horses lined up with their backs to the stream and heads to the fire, their bodies created a warm wall, keeping the heat near Alix and hopefully blocking some of the light.

Bel held Lena through the night, pleased when she fell asleep almost as easily as Alix. Surrounded by horses and firelight, the night animals left them alone, no haunting calls or creeping paws.

By morning, a fine mist hovered over the stream, adding a damp chill to the air. Bel left Lena snuggled in their nest to rebuild the fire and see to the horses. When he laid a gentle hand on Alix's forehead, he found it still clammy and overwarm. They wouldn't be leaving today.

The day went much like the previous afternoon, Lena sitting with Alix, fussing and apologizing and trying to keep her company. Bel saw to all the little tasks and kept the food and water coming. As he trekked between Alix's nest and the campfire and the stream for water and forest for wood, the big bay trailed behind, content to watch him with softly curious eyes.

He learned not to turn around too quickly or else he'd run smack into a broad horse chest.

He'd never had a horse of his own, and he found the big animal amiably following him around charming.

As he prepared a small lunch, Lena apologized for the sixth time for going off on her own. Alix rolled her wrist, batting away the words.

"Figured you'd both do something like that eventually. You're as bad as those lovers in the epics. Ugh. So sweet and nauseating."

That got Bel smiling as he cut up some dried fruit.

"I think the last bit is just that you're sick," said Lena.

"Pfft," she grumbled into her blankets.

Bel handed over the food and made a show of bending down to kiss Lena's forehead. Alix launched into a fit of fake gagging.

As the females ate, he helped Lena work her sore leg, bending her knee and massaging the sore muscles. She couldn't hold in the moan when he worked down her calf and on to her ankle and foot.

"You never did tell me how to land properly," she teased, putting her other foot in his hands for similar treatment.

"Next time," he promised with a wink.

When her legs were warm and loose, Lena stood to cleanse herself at the stream, using Bel's shoulder to get up. He felt as her fingertips trailed along his wing, and he had to hold in his shiver.

When he met Alix's gaze, she rolled her eyes and stuck her feet out of the blankets, wiggling her toes.

Bel breathed a put-upon sigh. "Only because you're sick."

"Mm-hmm."

He set to work on Alix's small feet, going slow with how tiny they were in his large hands. How miniscule each bone must be shocked him, and he was careful not to apply too much pressure.

After a moment, he felt a telltale wash of hot breath buffet the crown of his head. The bay nuzzled and nipped at Bel's hair with his soft lips, arranging it to his liking.

Alix giggled. "He's been following you around everywhere."

"Yes. That's why I'm going to call him Ruan. *Shadow*."

"Ruan." Alix smiled. "I like it. Much better than Beast."

He hummed in agreement.

They lapsed into a comfortable silence, but soon, Bel felt the weight of unsaid words gathering in Alix. He waited patiently while she put them in order, running a firm thumb down her arch and carefully popping her toes.

"Thank you," she said finally, voice small and slightly muffled by the blankets. "For going after her."

Bel looked up to meet her gaze, understanding how serious this was for Alix. She didn't take looking after Lena lightly.

"I always will. She's...she's my *c'vana*."

Alix's eyes went large, especially white against her feverishly rosy cheeks, but she didn't say anything for a long moment.

"The avian books you let me read used that word. It means...true love?"

"Yes. It means I'll always take care of her. And you, too."

Alix snorted. "I can take care of myself."

"I know that. And I think Lena's starting to understand that, too. But you deserve to be a fledgling for a while. You don't have to bear everything."

When Alix's eyes next lifted to meet his, tears gathered along the rims, her throat working to swallow. He could see the battle of emotions inside her, relief and disbelief evident in the cut of her brow.

That was all right. She didn't have to believe him yet. She'd been taught her whole life she could only rely on herself; it couldn't be forgotten in a few weeks.

She wiped at her eyes with the heel of her palm, a suspiciously wet sniff pulling everything back inside. When she looked up at him again, it was with a silly grin kicking up one side of her mouth.

"Good, then you can stay with the horses next time."

"Even better—next time, I'll take *you* freefalling with me."

15

Lena padded down the stairs, the plush rug her mother had spent a small fortune on softening her steps. The townhome her mother kept in the capital was something of a puzzle to Lena; for all that Lady Margot was a hardened warrior, used to battle and hardship and restless nights under the stars, she filled her Highclere residence with soft luxuries. It always made Lena feel the need to take her boots off the moment she entered.

The lower floor boasted a comfortable sitting room with a deep bay window overlooking the lush back garden, perfect for curling up in with a book to enjoy the afternoon sun. The pillows and paneling and sofas were all a rich jade green, complemented by the creams and golds of the trim. Across the foyer was a dining room, a long table of glossy dark wood dominating the space. Cushioned chairs stood sentry around it, and a monstrous candelabra lay in wait at the center. Mahogany curio cabinets lined the walls, displaying Margot's growing collection of fine porcelain and silver through intricate leaded glass doors.

Then there was Margot's office, nearly as fine as Da's back at Lindenfaire, with its ornately framed portraits and neatly arranged bookshelves. More offices for her staff and whichever squire she currently had sat further back, as did the kitchen, a warm space full of gleaming copper cookware and herbs hung to dry from the rafters. Margot kept a full staff year-round, whether she was in the capital or not.

"I think I've earned a stiff cup of coffee and perfect lemon tart waiting for me when I come home," Margot would say.

In the way that Lindenfaire was a refuge for her father, bedecked and furnished with every color, texture, and style he enjoyed, Margot's townhome was her own little palace, a place to keep and display all the treasures and keepsakes she'd earned and bought throughout her illustrious career.

The upstairs was mostly bedrooms, all sumptuously decorated and wallpapered in silk. Margot spared no expense with the bedding, down duvets dyed in jewel tones spread across beds of fine cotton.

"Are you expecting royalty?" Lena had joked when she first saw the beds.

Margot had just arched a brow at her, steeping her look in significance that made Lena blush.

But with just her mother in residence most of the time, the fine beds went unused. Lena always appreciated the luxury of slipping into the one in the room that was hers when she visited. She'd thought her guest would appreciate it, too, but Lena had opened the door to the first guestroom on the left this morning to find the bed empty, the duvet thrown back in a careless heap.

She looked everywhere on the upper floor for the waif she'd brought home yesterday, desperately hoping to find her merely lost and looking for the water closet.

Dread pulled tight across her chest as she descended to the lower floor.

———— •◆• ————

It'd taken her a little too long to figure out the scam the urchins in Cheapside ran. She'd had to go down there on an errand and made the mistake of bringing a coin purse with her. That part of the city had always been a bit rough, but in her years away on campaign, the streets had eroded and layers of filth painted every building. The salty fish smell of the nearby harbor pervaded the streets, soaking into the wood and clinging to Lena's surcoat.

The people of Cheapside had grown rougher, their clothing threadbare and eyes flinty. Lena had made quick work of her errand, disquiet tugging at her. She'd never seen so many children begging before and hadn't hesitated to drop a gold coin in their hands.

It wasn't until she put a coin in the palm of a child she'd already given to that she realized their game. That's when she'd felt a hand near her hip, going straight for the source of gold. Lena reacted on instinct, grabbing the hand and flipping the body attached over her shoulder.

An absolute slip of a girl landed in the street before her. Dark, dirty curls hung limply over a hollowed face streaked with grime. The hand Lena held was small, fragile, the bones more delicate than chicken bones, turning her stomach.

But for all her smallness, nothing about the pickpocket's eyes was little or afraid. She glared up at Lena, eyes sunk in her head, like a ghoul out for vengeance. She wrenched at the hand Lena held, shouting, "*Fuck off!*"

Lena hadn't known what possessed her; the obvious hunger in the girl, the fierce defiance, or her own distress over the state of this place. Perhaps it was that even in her gaunt face, so much fire and life burned in the girl, the likes of which Lena hadn't seen or felt in years while on campaign in the east. But she'd let go of the pickpocket to offer her a meal, a safe place to sleep, and, if she was amenable after Lena explained the demands, squire training.

She couldn't leave her there. She couldn't send her back out to the streets.

And...the girl impressed her. The defiance, the determined cut of her narrow shoulders, the way she commanded the other urchins, just out of sight and reach, with her eyes...some commanders took years to garner such loyalty and effectiveness.

The pickpocket had looked on suspiciously at Lena's offer, an obvious denial hovering on her lips. Then, with a feline grace, she'd leapt up from the street and bounced a few steps ahead of Lena.

"*All right, then. Let's start with that meal.*"

Lena hadn't gotten to explain much between the girl shoveling a worrying amount of food into her mouth, mildly horrifying Margot's cook, and Margot returning home. Her mother hadn't been pleased with their guest, but Lena insisted they at least let the girl clean up and have a safe place to sleep.

Margot had finally agreed but whispered to the cook, *"Lock up the silver."*

She hadn't said it quietly enough for Lena nor the girl to miss. The pickpocket's cheeks and ears had gone pink at the insult, her fiery gaze shuttering before she dropped it to the massacre of crumbs on her plate.

Lena had hated to see it. So, before bed, she'd promised to explain squire training in the morning. And asked the girl's name, more than a little ashamed she hadn't until then.

"Alix," the girl said. *"Well, Alixandre, but nobody calls me that anymore."*

Lena hadn't asked who'd once called her that and Alix hadn't offered.

—————— •◆•• ——————

Now, with all the upstairs cleared, Lena pressed her ear to the dining room door. Muffled voices and the sound of clinking silver had her heart sinking in dismay.

She thought she knew what she'd find when she opened that door. And she did. Only, it was much more elaborate than she'd ever imagined.

Caught in the act, at least a half-dozen street urchins stood frozen throughout the room. Lena thought she recognized some from yesterday. Another face stared at her through the open window, her hands extended awaiting the porcelain vase Margot had gotten as a wedding gift and started her love of bone china. They'd formed something of a line, like the ones people made from the nearest well to a burning building, passing buckets between them. Except they passed Montcaer valuables out the window.

They blinked at Lena, and she blinked back.

A pack of startled racoons, that's what they reminded her of.

A sharp whistle broke the spell. "Scatter!" Alix yelped, jumping down from a curio she'd busted open.

Some of the children dropped their loot and darted for the window while others hurried to fill their skinny arms with more valuables before beating a retreat.

"Wait, wait!" Lena cried, hurrying in and closing the door behind her.

The flash of a blade had her instincts flaring, but she swallowed them down. She raised her hands in no contest as Alix confronted her, brandishing a wicked dagger almost as long as her arm. It was far too big for her and had a pommel encrusted with jewels, so they'd obviously hit the small armory of pretty blades Margot kept in her office.

Lena could disarm the girl in two moves, it'd be nothing with how little she weighed, but she didn't. Instead, she met Alix's glare with calm.

"How did you manage all this?"

"You think we go alone to rich houses?" the girl spat. "Lost enough of us to learn, you always follow and find out where they're taking us."

Lena's stomach cramped with horror.

"It's not—I'm—"

"Sure. Look, we'll be gone in a minute, all right? You'll be fine." She waved her free hand in a circle, indicating the rest of the house and all the expensive, frivolous things that filled it.

"I'd like you to at least hear me out about squire training."

The girl frowned in confusion. "Thought that was a joke. Just your reason to get me here."

"No, I meant it."

"Don't need your pity."

"It's not pity. I'm—"

"Lena!" Margot called from another room. "Lena, are you down yet?"

The children still in the room shared nervous glances before looking to Alix for what to do. Alix's eyes jumped from Lena to the door, her hands trembling.

"Stay here and stay quiet," Lena told the other children, but she beckoned Alix forward. "Put that down and come with me."

Alix's mouth scrunched unhappily, but after a moment, she laid the dagger silently on the table and stalked toward Lena.

She opened the door, letting the two of them out into the front hall. The door had just clicked shut behind them when Margot came around the corner from the kitchen.

"Ah, there you are. I see our guest is still here."

Lena straightened and folded her hands behind her back. "We were just about to have breakfast, and I thought I'd explain to Alix what to expect from squire training."

Margot's steely gray eyes flicked over the girl at Lena's side. Her face didn't change, at least not perceptibly to someone who didn't know her, but serving as her own mother's squire had taught Lena all about looking for and interpreting the subtle changes in her mother's expressions. Her mouth ticked down just a hair, eyes narrowed infinitesimally. It was the look she had when she deeply disapproved of something but either hadn't decided yet what to say or didn't want to offend who she spoke to.

Alix shuffled her feet.

"Oh," Margot finally said. "I thought you were joking."

"I wasn't."

Margot's expression wasn't small or subtle when she sighed and rolled her eyes. "Lena, I've got a list of better options from good families for your first squire. You'll be in demand, a war hero returned from the front."

"I'm not a war hero. And I didn't ask you to do that," Lena said. She'd only been back in the capital a week, and honestly, she struggled to readjust. She didn't miss waiting for an avian barrage or the gnawing boredom that stalked every soldier. She also hadn't swallowed her anger at Arion for sending her away.

"Well, I did. I figured it would give you something to do while you wait for reassignment. I'd like to get it settled before I head south again to resume my command."

"Mother, I don't—"

"We'll go see some of the candidates today. So make breakfast quick." She looked to Alix then, her face mild. "I'm sorry for the confusion. We'll pay you for your trouble after breakfast."

"No, Mother. Alix and I will discuss matters like she and I talked about. If she decides not to take on training, then I'll look at your list. But I gave her my word." From the corner of her eye, she saw Alix look up at her in surprise.

"Lena, I understand wanting to help. We'll see about making donations to the orphanages and food houses—there are so many now. But you can't solve everything by taking on a street child."

Even Lena winced at the patronizing tone.

"I'm not trying to solve everything. I just want to help. I think..." She glanced down at the girl standing beside her and found Alix gazing up at her—not in a scowl or smirk or glare but in disbelief. "I think she'd make a fine knight."

"Lena," her mother scoffed, "she's had no basic training."

"Making it out on the street seems like plenty of training."

"Don't be smart, you know what I mean."

"I'm going to train Alix, if she wants it. Who I take on is my decision, mother."

Margot leveled her with that iron stare, one that had made bigger warriors and greater names than Lena quiver. But she'd received that stare so many times, the effect had lost a bit of its power.

Finally, Margot threw up her hands in exasperation. "Fine. I try to help, but..." Shaking her head, she turned on her heel, headed back to her office. "I'll leave this list on my desk for you when she disappears at the first sign of trouble."

Margot left an awkward silence in her wake.

Wincing, Lena turned to Alix to apologize.

"I don't scare easy."

Lena's brows arched in surprise. Alix gazed back at her with her own steely look, that defiant fire burning bright again.

"No, I don't think you do."

They considered one another.

"All right," Alix said, "tell me about being a knight."

Lena smiled, nodding to the dining room door. They went back in, finding the little gang of urchins more or less where they'd left them. The children all looked immediately to Alix.

"I'll make you a deal," Lena said quietly once the door was shut.

Alix cocked an eyebrow. "Heard that before."

Lena hid her horror by fishing her coin purse from her pocket. She jangled it, the tinkling of coins catching every waif's attention.

"Give back the silver and everything else. Instead, I'll give you half this purse now and the cook the other."

"Not enough coins in there to make that a good deal," Alix said.

"Fine. I'll give you all this and the cook more. He'll see that you're fed any time you come to the house. Just...try not to come when my mother's home. You'll have a nicer meal."

Alix snorted. "So you do all this if I come with you?"

"No. I do all this to get the silver back. Whether you want to start the training is entirely up to you."

The look in Alix's eyes as she assessed Lena and her offer was unreadable; or at least, Lena didn't know how to read all her expressions yet. But she hoped she'd get the chance. Something about this scrappy girl gave Lena...hope.

Alix snapped her fingers. "Bring it back in!" Children burst into motion, clambering through the window and climbing up the curios. Controlled, coordinated chaos, that's what it looked like.

Alix waggled her fingers in front of Lena's face. She put the purse in the girl's hand, and it quickly disappeared into the gaggle of children.

"All right. Food first, then we'll talk."

16

They were close. Bel could taste it on the wind and feel it with every step Ruan took in the soft earth. It wasn't just that he recognized the general landscape or was able to name the flowers and creatures that flitted through the brush. He *knew* that rock outcropping. He *remembered* the little deer path leading west into the forest.

And soon, it was more than just deer paths crisscrossing the land. Footpaths rose from the dirt, harder packed and darker than that around it. Though they used their wings for most travel, avians were known to walk, especially with heavy loads. They'd found such a path in a web of them, all leading home.

To Aeriand.

"We're close," Bel said, unable to hide the anticipation thrumming through him.

A warm hand clasped his, and he looked over to smile at Lena. Riding beside him, her answering smile was smaller but no less true. He knew what this cost her, to be here again. The lines around her eyes had been tight since they'd left their last camp once Alix was feeling better. For three days as they neared the avian capital, she'd been quiet, present but watchful. And it wasn't just the threat of Joran and his knights bursting from the trees.

Her memories of Aeriand were very different from his.

But she was here, beside him. That's all that mattered.

"So what's the plan here?" asked Alix, trotting up on Miri. Her voice still carried a whistle from the remnants of her cold. "I thought we were all about plans these days."

"There should only be one garrison guarding the city," Lena said. "Last I heard, anyway. That information is...outdated."

"Avoid the guards. Good start. What else? What are we looking for here?"

Both Lena and Alix looked to him, but he didn't have an answer for them. He'd been trying for days to put into words his desire and his dread.

This had been his home, the seat of his family line. His blood had ruled and protected Aeriand for centuries, their names and faces carved into the very rock that formed the city. His mother had birthed him, died for him here. He'd taken his first flight here. He'd lived a life of both anonymity and scrutiny, the spare an important insurance but too young to be of any real use. His time had been his own, mostly filled with wandering the city, exploring all its mysteries and hidey-holes when Eamon wasn't trying to sharpen his mind and strengthen his sword arm.

He didn't know how to tell them this, nor the most important part —this was his brother's city.

Bel knew, from messages secreted to him by Eamon during his captivity, that his cousin Dartegn now ruled, the last known living Adiiron. The son of his father's sister, Dar's wings and eyes were an inky black, so unlike the golden hues of Bel, Maddok, and their Adiiron ancestors. He didn't have the coloring but at least he had the name. After the devastating chaos of that horrible night, when Maddok took the sword aimed for Bel, destined for Bel, in the crush of the human ambush that was Bel's fault, the Adiiron name must have been enough.

But Bel had only ever known Dar as a moody young warrior; quick in temper but fierce in his loyalty to his family and duty. Never, never as king.

Bel had only ever known his father Skandar IV and then his brother Maddok V as king.

In his mind, in his heart, his king had only ever been his older brother.

As king, Maddok had been inextricably tied to Aeriand. They were symbiotic, two halves of a whole. There was no Aeriand without Maddok.

Proven when, just a few years after Maddok's death, Dartegn lost Aeriand. Abandoned their home, their ancestors, and holed up in the mountain stronghold of Hadria to the southeast. A dark, craggy place that had once been a mining colony.

A familiar crackle of anger teased Bel's chest. He tried to soothe it, reasoning that he hadn't been there, didn't know what Dar had gone through or what a burden it must've been to ask their people to abandon their city. He tried to remind himself that the youth he'd been, barely into his adult feathers, broken in body and spirit after that night, wouldn't have been able to give the people what they needed from their Adiiron king. And he tried not to think that, despite all this, *he* wouldn't have lost his brother's city.

Except he did think it.

He couldn't explain all this to Lena and Alix, couldn't convey how he wanted to see the damage and destruction for himself. Imagining it for years now had been its own kind of pain; he needed to know the truth of it. He needed to understand what made Dar abandon Maddok's city.

Perhaps Lena read some of this in his eyes; whatever made her clear her throat and answer Alix, "An idea of what to do next," he was grateful.

He squeezed her hand again.

"All right," Alix said, drawing out the sounds, "and can we just look at the place from afar or do we really have to sneak in?"

Bel cocked an eyebrow at her. "You don't want to sneak in?"

"I mean, of course I do. I've never heard of anything like Aeriand. But if it means more trouble…"

Lena huffed a laugh. "You want to avoid trouble for once, and I want to sneak in somewhere we shouldn't be. Matella has a sense of humor today."

Alix rolled her eyes, but Bel didn't miss the tight set of her mouth. She didn't want to run into trouble, into more humans, and be separated from them again. It struck him then, how truly worried Alix had been for them.

"I don't know exactly what I'm looking for. I'm hoping I'll know when I see it. Something useful. An idea of where to go next."

He didn't voice the next logical place would be Hadria, as something inside him recoiled from the idea of that dark place. He'd visited a handful of times with Maddok and never liked it. Full of twisting passages that led nowhere but down, the shadows stretched as thick as the hewn rock, and a fall from one of the vast drop-offs in the heart of the mountain meant death, even with wings.

He didn't want to go there. He certainly didn't want to take Lena and Alix there.

But that meant they'd need somewhere else to go. Maybe they'd find what they needed here, in the skeleton of his old home, to find their way to a new home. Lena had mentioned a homestead; perhaps here they'd find what they needed for that.

Alix nodded slowly, accepting his answer, before asking, "How do we get in? I'm guessing we can't just knock."

Aeriand had one gate in its great circular outer wall. For a winged people, they only needed the one. All over the city, even places on the defensive walls and battlements, were landing areas and perches. The city was easily accessible and navigable by wing.

The wall was only to keep the earthbound out.

With just one gate for the human occupiers to guard, no, they wouldn't be knocking. But, "There are other ways into the city, ones that don't require wings. Maybe a bit of crawling, but I think we can manage."

A strange noise came out of Lena, a pained sort of garble. Bel looked over to find her avoiding his gaze and color rising in her cheeks.

Lena explained in a small voice, "We won't need to. We could never take the front gate so...we knocked sections of the wall down." Her grimace grew with every word until her whole face contorted in a cringe.

He couldn't help cringing too, mind rebelling against the idea. Surely they couldn't have brought down sections of the wall. It towered so high...had been so thick...

"Oh," was all he managed.

Her gaze snapped to his, suddenly panicked. "Bel, I didn't—"

"I know, sweetheart," he hurried to say, gripping her hand tight.

She chewed on her next words and the inside of her cheek for a moment before she said, "It isn't the place you remember, Bel. It's...we broke it. Took what we could. It's just..."

"A shell."

Her throat bobbed and she nodded.

The dread that dogged the heels of his determination to see Aeriand sunk in his stomach, congealing into a sad resolve. He knew it would be, knew that the sight would break his already broken heart. And more, he knew that no matter how prepared he was, no matter how Lena warned him, the reality of it would still shock and devastate him.

Bel had figured out long ago that if there ever was to be something of a homecoming for him, the return of the younger Adiiron prince to the ancestral lands, it wouldn't be in triumph.

He knew all this, so there was nothing more to do than get it over with.

Still, an hour later, his stomach fluttered when the first spires poked from the treetops and the path gently wended toward a familiar floodplain. Glimpses of the city winked through the branches, rising until it was taller than the trees and blotted out the sky.

They stuck to the shadows of the trees, as if that could hide them from the great face of Aeriand.

Bel's breath caught in his throat.

Across a narrow floodplain, bordered by a lake to the east that reflected its eerie twin, stood Aeriand.

It was everything he remembered and imagined, only worse.

Rising from the floodplain like a mountain, the stone city

dominated the hills behind it, the lake beside it, and the forest at its face. Built from one of those hills many thousands of years ago, the city rose in circles to crest in a peak at the Mount, the topmost point of Aeriand. Great basilicas, halls, homes, and palisades spilled out across the levels, a waterfall of rock cascading down to the great wall that stood sentinel around the city.

In Bel's youth, the wall had ringed the city unbroken except for a great gate, flanked by two watchtowers, latticed in iron, and reinforced by two sets of portcullises. No gate stood guard now; instead, a yawning mouth of an opening stood in the battered face of the wall, the only remnants of the gate a few warped, jagged pieces of iron clinging to the frame.

All along the wall and inside, on the homes and buildings, heavy mats of ivy coiled around stones and into broken windows, as if the forest sought to retake the city for itself. The pale lavender of wisteria painted great swathes of the city; once kept groomed in the many city gardens and decorating the trellises and pergolas of thousands of avian homes, the purple cones warred with the ivy for choice spots in the sun.

An upended cornucopia, that's what it looked like.

The first thing Bel noticed was wrong was the stillness. There should've been flags, banners, and standards flapping in the perpetual breeze, their bright colors and golden threads catching the light to announce which family, guild, or unit it represented. There should've been hundreds of avians navigating the skies in and around the city, the sun glinting off the brilliant golds, whites, bronzes, blacks, browns, and reds of their wings. They should've been winging between the markets, heading in from the lake, taking off on official royal business. Formations of warriors should've been visible as they made deliberate circuits around the perimeter.

And the city itself...it should've shone. Built from quartz-rich granite and white limestone, Aeriand should have sparkled like crystal in the afternoon sun, the polished stone cut so precisely that they held together without mortar. The marble colonnades ringing the royal quarters should have glinted with their veins of quartz and gold.

Instead, even from the forest, Bel could tell Aeriand was...diminished. Nothing shone, covered in layers of dirt and dust that turned the stone a flat beige. The curtains of ivy and wisteria couldn't completely hide the great piles of debris and rubble, and the whole western profile of the city had been destroyed, four middle levels completely collapsed.

"It's beautiful," Alix murmured.

Bel turned to smile at her sadly. "It was."

Lena cleared her throat, but her voice was still thick when she said, "This way."

They kept to the tree line, following one by one to circle the city to the northwest. Lena led, and Bel watched, training his gaze along the battered line of the wall. Nothing. No movement, no patrols that he could see.

It took the better part of an hour, navigating through the trees, to find the spot Lena remembered. He grimaced at the hole punched through the wall, a gaping wound littered with crumbling rock and jagged edges. Rubble lay on either side of the hole, a macabre stairway up into the city.

It must have taken a massive effort to do such damage. And this part of the wall...Bel frowned, searching his memory. Many of the guard barracks lay just beyond; the area would've been populated with warriors and heavily guarded.

"How did you do it?" he asked.

"Battering rams," Lena answered, her voice still off, as if she spoke from a great distance away.

He shifted to regard her and realized she *was* far away, deep down in her memories. Lines creased her forehead, between her brows, and beneath her eyes, telling of all she'd seen at that wall.

"That must've taken a long time," Alix said.

"Days. We'd gotten information that the wall was weaker here, less defended. Our commanders thought we'd surprise them with the rams, knock enough of it down before they could stop us."

Lena shook her head, tears gathering along her lashes. A knife of anguish worked into Bel's chest listening to her story, knowing how hard his people would've fought to save the wall, imagining the utter terror they would've felt when it broke open.

"The information must've been bad. They knew we were there immediately. Fought us all the way, with all they had. But the commanders wouldn't stop, had been ordered by the king himself to take it from there. Every unit had their turn manning the rams. Every unit lost—" She wiped at the tears that escaped, and Bel wanted to comfort her, put his wing around her and shelter her from the memories, but he was frozen in the saddle, a cold fear twisting that knife of despair deeper into his chest.

The information must've been bad.

"We lost many—so, so many. The arrows, they just...never stopped. You just got in a rhythm working the rams, working together to cock them again, release them. Goddess, you could feel it in your bones when it hit the wall, it shook the ground. The shields they'd put on top of them were shredded in a day. We'd have to stop, pull everyone out so we weren't tripping over—" Lena gasped, breath lost in a hiccup as her words rushed out.

Alix gripped her forearm.

Lena startled as if coming awake, blinking back to awareness. Her eyes shone overbright with tears, and she wouldn't look at Bel.

He didn't know if he wanted her gaze just then. Not when he realized why it struck him as strange the humans had attacked here, one of the worst places they could. They'd been misinformed, led astray.

The information *had* been bad.

One of the first projects Bel had worked on for the human king was old poems and stories about Aeriand. He'd held out for the first few months of his captivity, refusing the king's terms, but his first warden at Finhöln had been fond of the whipping post. Bel's shredded back and feathers had become too much to bear, so he'd capitulated. The whippings stopped...mostly, except for when Hallan was feeling particularly malicious.

But Bel had never done what the human king demanded. Not fully. He'd spend years on his translations, figuring out what the king hoped to learn from the documents. He translated the texts and then did it again, only slightly wrong. Small, subtle changes.

It was defiance, a way to keep his tattered honor from completely unraveling. He didn't think anything came of it. He hadn't considered that the human king would rely on the translations of an avian captive to destroy more avians.

He hadn't thought what that misinformation could mean for all the human soldiers and knights who marched at the king's orders.

His gambit had worked spectacularly, it seemed. And perhaps, all those years ago, Bel would've felt a spiteful glee knowing he'd made it difficult for them, bought his people just a little more time.

But today, seeing the horrors that haunted Lena's eyes, Bel carried nothing but sadness—for Aeriand, for avians, and for all the humans he'd gotten killed.

———————— •◆•• ————————

They waited for the longer shadows of late afternoon to make their move. Lena went ahead as a lookout and waved them in when no one came to stop them. They picked their way up the rubble and remaining lip of the wall, carefully leading the horses over. Inside, they remounted and headed carefully into the city.

The old barracks were empty, as was the nearest guard outpost. Thick layers of dirt and dust had worked between the cobblestones, almost making the ground level. Still, the horses' hooves clipped and clopped, echoing down the abandoned lanes.

With every new corner and street found empty, they gained a little more confidence and a little more confusion.

Plopping back down into her saddle after checking the next crossroad, Alix shrugged and nudged Miri forward in a quick trot. Bel and Lena followed, watching as Alix guided Miri around a crumbled fountain at the center of a square with a shallow pool of water choked with green algae.

Quail chittered and hurried out of Alix's way, and Bel saw a feline tail disappear into a dark corner. Overhead, crows, sparrows, and other small birds fluttered between open or broken windows.

As they moved past the square, beginning the gentle climb up the terraces and levels, that's all they saw, the occasional animal scavenging through the empty streets, ducking in and out of abandoned buildings. He thought he spied the reflective eyes of a coyote peering out from the cellar of a house. Hummingbirds zipped between heavy sprigs of wisteria, blue-bellied lizards and wide-toed geckos sunned themselves in the late afternoon, and ringtails weaved along the vines between pergolas. Cats, dogs, deer, chickens, and ducks roamed the streets, the offspring of those left behind when the city was abandoned.

Other than the quiet scrabble of claws on cobblestone and soft tittering of mother quails leading their chicks, there was nothing.

At the next empty square, Alix turned from further up the street and trotted back to them to say as much. "There's nobody here."

Bel didn't quite know what he expected, but it wasn't this. He'd prepared himself for skeletons to litter the street, bones washed white in the sun and feathers moldered down to the shafts. He'd pictured great clots of dried blood staining the rocks red-brown. The streets should've been clogged with rubble, debris, and broken things. There should've been signs, other than the gaping wound in the wall, that the city had been taken, that there had been a fight for it.

Ruins. That's all Aeriand was. The city could've been abandoned fifty, a hundred years ago from the quiet stillness of it. A crumbling shell of a civilization, a people whom time had already forgotten.

Somehow, that grieved him more than seeing humans occupying the city.

They made it to the middling levels of Aeriand by the time the sun began to disappear into the lake. The oranges, pinks, and purples of sunset reflected on the surface, making Aeriand look dowdy in comparison. It should've gleamed like glass; instead, breezes picked up loose dirt and dust, and thick layers of moss padded the northern walls of the buildings.

They chose a larger house to bed down in for the night, one with doors large enough for the horses to enter. Even in the waning light, Bel could see what a fine avian house this had been once. A wide atrium led to a central courtyard, open to the sky, ringed with columns and a gallery on the second level above. Pieces of the mosaic that had once decorated the floor were missing, leaving gaps in the story it illustrated, and dirt had replaced the once colorful mortar.

The house held a few subtle clues that something had happened here. Doors hung crooked on their frames or were missing entirely, and one of the central beams of the second story had collapsed. Scuffs on the walls, drawers and cases upended. Cushions had been pulled off the chairs and chaises, left to mold.

But it was dry and available, no family of coyotes or worse loitering in the kitchen or cellar. The horses were content to browse through the overgrown plants in the courtyard, and Bel followed Lena and Alix into one of the nearby rooms, what had once been a large bedroom or perhaps an office. Nothing was left, not even an empty case, so he couldn't tell which.

They spoke little that night, wanting to hear if anything came creeping close but also not finding any words worth saying.

Lena felt distant as she lay down beside him, as though she'd drawn into herself for safety. Or perhaps it was him who'd retreated inside to the safety of his own mind. Being here...it was almost too much to bear. But it was enough to draw her close, and he took a little heart when she tucked her head under his chin.

Bel buried his nose in her hair, the familiar smell comforting his whirring mind.

None of this made sense. Everything was gone, taken in the flight to Hadria or stripped in the ensuing sack. But Aeriand's value was inherent, the city itself. The cost to take it had been high, and the human king had paid it.

Why abandon the city, then? Why leave Aeriand to the animals?

As he fell into a fitful sleep, Bel thought about his final project, all the documents King Artemian could find on Hadria, and how Dartegn had dug himself in.

It felt too ridiculous to consider, but...was Aeriand abandoned because the humans had no other choice? Or had something worse taken over the city?

If Bel had thought the lower levels of the city were bare, it was nothing to the royal quarters. Sitting like a crown at the peak of Aeriand, the Mount sprawled in terraced colonnades, open gardens, courtyards ringed in statuary, and winding corridors with recessed alcoves for displaying the great figures of avian history. In its own wending way, it all led to the center of the Mount, the basilica.

Their feet echoed on the stone floor, reverberating as if they'd stepped into a cave, not the heart of avian sovereignty. The air in the great room was eerily still, the morning light that filtered in from the stained-glass windows catching on hovering particles. The shafts and fractals of light were the only color breaking up the somber gray.

Bel walked between the great pillars of the basilica, fluted columns that rose to meet the roof and spread like tree branches over the ceiling. Banners and garlands should've been strung between them, the petals sweetening the air. Lapis panels should've adorned the column faces in brilliant patterns. Crystals should've winked down from the high ceiling like stars through the forest canopy. Gold incense burners, candle stands, benches, altars, and shrines should've glinted in the light and created a gilded maze through the hall.

Everything that could be prized from the walls had been, even the more colorful glass tiles in the mosaics and panels of the stained-glass windows. Gilded and jeweled eyes had been popped from what statues remained, and marble casings had been pulled from the wainscoting.

"It's like a crypt," Alix whispered.

She hushed when Lena shot her a look, but Bel honestly agreed. The air carried a chill, making their breath mist. The colorless basilica, stripped of its trappings and artefacts, had been hollowed out, butchered and scraped for every last treasure before being discarded.

The great space was dead, buried in dust and left to rot in ignominy.

He'd run between these columns as a fledgling, sometimes just to make Eamon mad and chase him, sometimes to try getting close to Maddok while he saw to affairs of state. There'd always been places to hide, some furniture or shrine to duck behind. Now the columns stood lonely, ribs protecting a heart that no longer beat.

Bel weaved between them now, running his fingers along the cold stone. Many bore scars from where chisels had pried away their ornamental cases. They marched forward like a funeral procession, leading toward the central apse.

Even as a royal son, Bel had always been impressed by the sight of his brother, the king, standing before the apse. Perfectly centered, the domed semicircle arched above the most elaborate of the mosaics. Tooled with tens of thousands of glass and marble pieces, the mosaic showed the night sky, the constellations spiraling together, but at their center was Halva, the Evenstar, the First Star. Aeriand had been built to honor Halva, aligned so she rose from the top spires in the evening and bade the city good day at dawn.

The avian sovereign stood on this dedication to Halva, as Aeriand's guiding star. From here they ruled and protected the avian people and their great city.

Behind, in the great curve of the apse, frescoes illustrated all the first flocks coming together under the eight-pointed star and single sovereign. It was a moment in avian history every fledgling learned, when, under Halva's guidance, the eight flocks agreed to stop fighting one another and instead became one, growing stronger and working together to build Aeriand.

The gilt had been scraped from the frescoes and the faces of the first flocks scratched out. Hammers had been taken to the mosaic, cracking the marble and glass down the center. Only three of Halva's eight points remained.

It was almost breathtaking how thoroughly the humans had crushed everything avians honored.

Bel's lips went numb in the cold air. He stared at the desecrated apse and truly understood, for the first time, what it was the human king wanted. It wasn't war or treasure or even genocide, though he'd orchestrated all those things. King Artemian would settle for nothing less than the annihilation of the avian race, their lives, their culture, proof of their existence. He wouldn't stop until avians were just a memory, one forgotten in a few generations. Relegated to legend like the dragons and harpies and griffins and centaurs had been, centuries before.

And Bel had helped him.

Oh, he'd done his mistranslations, hadn't given truly useful information. But he'd sat in that castle the human king put him in and he'd stayed and he'd done as he was told and he'd given Artemian the avian stories and legends and poems and he'd *stayed* and—

Lena came alongside him, bumping his shoulder with hers. Her face and body were all grim, downturned lines showing her displeasure at what her kind had done. Her arms crossed over her chest, hands tucked away, as she stared at the damage.

She stood beside him in silence, and Bel was grateful. He didn't think he could bear comfort now; a tender touch might be enough to break him.

Alix drew up on his other side, eyes wide and curious. "There's no throne." She said it quietly, but her voice still echoed down the cavernous aisles of columns.

"Humans use thrones. Avians don't need them. The sovereign stands here," he pointed down at the remains of Halva, "where they're visible to all. Available to anyone."

"Then who guards their back?"

Bel blinked down at her. *What a human thing to ask.* There hadn't been a coup or attack on an avian ruler in hundreds of years. Dynasties, handing down leadership from parent to child, were normal, but if a child was unworthy or a ruler became a danger, there were ways of taking power away. A new ruler would be named for the good of the people. Bel's family had ruled for hundreds of years peacefully—at least amongst their kind. A worthy successor had always been found within the Adiirons.

Until now.

"The ruler doesn't fear their people," Bel answered Alix, "and the people don't fear them." He turned away from the apse, the sight already burned in his mind.

"But isn't there something about watching backs in the mating ritual?" asked Alix, keeping up as he retreated from the apse. He suspected she wanted to distract him.

"Yes, they promise to guard the other's back during the mating ceremony. It's more metaphorical at this point. It's about protection, safety."

She asked more questions as he followed his feet to the east side of the basilica. Lining the wall and looming between columns stood the many dedication shrines to past avian sovereigns.

Hewn from marble, red granite, limestone, and even a few from obsidian, the shrines captured the likenesses of great avian sovereigns and told the story of their rule. Many had carved wings, delicately tooled and so thin they were translucent, arching over the sculpted sarcophagus, an effigy of the sovereign buried inside laying peacefully under a shroud.

As a boy, Bel had strolled down the Path of Sovereigns many times, marveling at the faces of his brother's predecessors. Though cut from stone, the faces had looked out at him with such life, and he liked to imagine they whispered to him, told him secrets about Aeriand and how great a ruler Maddok would be. He always put little offerings on his favorite shrines, the ones that spoke to him most, as well as his father's, out of duty. That stern face he remembered was rendered perfectly in stone.

He hadn't liked to look at it long as a youngling, remembering all the times he'd had that unfeeling gaze turned on him. Bel hadn't understood when he was young why his father hated him, but he knew it to be true regardless. The court whispered how much his father had loved his mother. It'd been one of the strongest mate bonds seen in a long time. And Bel had ended it with his first breath.

He didn't like looking at his father's shrine now, either. The stern face looked out coldly, the same as it always had, except all the offerings had been swept away. All the shrine altars stood bare, their coins and jewels and trinkets and artefacts stolen. King Berwick III's famous helmet with the dent. Queen Cassia I's throwing daggers. Queen Farrah's phoenix-feather hair pins. King Halmir VI's breastplate and bandolier. All gone.

Bel moved along the rows, past his father and grandmother, searching for something he didn't want to find. Both worry and relief threaded through him when he kept not finding it.

He looked twice along the rows before returning to his father, the last avian king before Maddok. Then, finally, he saw a small shrine tucked beside his father's.

Sparsely adorned, hastily carved wings arched above a simple stone plaque.

In Memoriam of King Maddok Adiiron, Fifth of his Reign, Son of Skandar Adiiron, Fourth of his Reign, King of the Avian Kin, Star of Aeriand...

A small stone box sat beneath the plaque, barely big enough for a head to fit.

Rage quick as wildfire through summer grasslands scorched him.

Dartegn had said he loved Maddok, would always be loyal to him. And *this* was all he could do? This scratched rock was all he dedicated to the king he said he loved like a brother?

Hot tears gathered and fell from his eyes, and Bel slumped to his knees before the last, inadequate evidence of his brother.

"I'm sorry," he told it, "I'm so sorry."

17

Lena watched Bel bury his face in his hands and his wings slump across the floor. She felt his agony, palpable as the first sobs racked him, and almost thought she could hear his heart breaking again. It sounded like the crack of glass and crushing of rock, the shattering of what had lived for thousands of years. Her heart broke with his, added to the pile of rubble that Aeriand had become.

Her chest ached with grief and felt hollowed out with shame. She could barely look at the palace, could barely let herself remember what it'd felt like to march at Prince Arion's side as they knocked down the doors of this basilica and entered like the conquerors they were. The humans had filled up Aeriand, first looking for more avians to kill and then for treasure and loot, anything to make the high cost of taking the city a little worthwhile. They'd gorged themselves on the marvels and beauty of Aeriand, stripped her bare and taken everything they considered of value, then destroyed whatever remained that the avians might have. Out of spite. In revenge. To fill the gaping wounds inside themselves at witnessing so much death.

The glory of it had worn off quickly for Lena, and Arion too. They'd left Aeriand soon after King Artemian arrived to take over the desecration, pursuing the remaining avians across the Grass Sea to Hadria. She hadn't seen the final outcome, hadn't guessed how bad...

Alix was right, this place was a crypt, a necropolis for a whole people.

She drew close to Bel, wanting to comfort him. But she held back, kept her hands tucked under her arms, because she didn't know if he would welcome a human knight's touch then.

This shrine he wept before, so much smaller than all the rest and clumsy in its workmanship, could only be his brother's. She couldn't read runic, the avian script, but she didn't need it to know what such a small sarcophagus meant.

Another shudder rippled across his broad back, and she couldn't help it. She knelt behind him, between his wing bases, and threw her arms around him.

She wasn't a knight anymore, she had to remember. And today, that was a good thing because Bel didn't need a knight.

She held him while he wept, gave him the only thing she could—her comfort...and her regret.

When the shaking in his shoulders eased, Bel took great gulping breaths that shuddered wetly in his chest. Lena squeezed, pressing her face into his nape, where hair transitioned to down.

"He saved me," Bel gasped out. Lena felt the words reverberate in his chest. "The attack—we were outnumbered but there was a chance and—there was an out. He should've gotten out!" Bel shook his head viciously, almost throwing Lena off. "He came back for me. I'd fallen behind, gotten myself surrounded. The blow came and I—it should have hit *me*, it was meant for *me*, but he—"

Bel's lips peeled back, mouth open wide to bear his teeth in a silent howl. Lena could only draw her arms tighter, sensing somehow that she held him together, that if she let go or hesitated for even a moment, he'd break apart right there, in the hollow heart of his ancestors.

"I can still hear it, running him through," he said, so quietly Lena almost didn't hear. "He should've let me die. That's what spares are for. I should've been the one—"

His wings shuddered and flapped, nearly unseating her again, but Lena hung on, needing him to feel her.

When the sob passed, Bel let his head fall back onto Lena's shoulder. She kissed his tear-dampened cheek and placed her hand on his chest, over his hammering heart.

"I should've been the one to die," he told the empty basilica. "I'm nothing."

"You're everything," she growled into his ear, giving the words back to him that had touched her deep inside.

Bel squeezed his eyes shut.

"Maddok sacrificed himself for me. And I couldn't even build him the shrine he deserves. How could this be all?"

Lena swallowed on nothing, her mouth and throat dry with the realization that she couldn't tell him. Not now. Not as he knelt at his murdered brother's small shrine in the desecrated hall of his dying people. She needed time to find the words to tell him why the shrine was only big enough for scraps, the courage to explain how the destruction of the avian race started with his brother's very body.

It was before Lena's time as a knight, but the stories had flown fast and wide. How King Maddok V Adiiron had been hacked apart at each joint, his hands thrown into the river, his chest burned on a spit, his legs fed to the dogs and his genitals to the pigs. His head had been mounted on a pike and paraded before all the human troops for days, though there were rumors that it had been recovered. But the wings...

No one knew how King Artemian's chemists and goldsmiths did it, but King Maddok's wings even now hung in Highclere, behind the throne. Anyone who knelt before Artemian on the steps leading up to the dais would see, spread out behind him like a fiery corona, the gold-dipped wings of an Adiiron king.

No, Lena couldn't tell him that.

Instead, she said, "Come away now," and gently pulled him to his feet and away from the stone faces and bitter memories. They left the basilica and all it no longer held behind, venturing further into the Mount, deeper into the life Bel once had.

———— •◆• ————

The chambers beyond the basilica hadn't escaped the debasement; an upended piece of furniture or odd bauble sometimes decorated a room, but otherwise, there was nothing.

The further they got from the basilica, the steadier Bel seemed to be. He walked through the halls and corridors with a somber assurance, knowing where he went. He answered Alix's curious questions but offered nothing else than what was asked of him.

Still, they learned his favorite route down to the kitchens, his favorite hiding spots for when Eamon was determined to drag him to his arithmetic lessons, his favorite places to stroll when he was bored. Which seemed to have been often. As Bel quietly recounted for Alix another story of the busy lives of the workers, clerks, guards, and officials who populated the royal quarters, Lena couldn't help noticing they were all stories of him watching.

These halls had once bustled with activity, but it hadn't included Bel. He'd watched from one of his spots, the lives of others flowing around him. Her father Sir Warrek had told her once that a leader was like that, a rock in a river; it was their duty to be steady, undaunted, ready for whatever came. She didn't think it was that, though.

Instead, as they passed a deep window seat set back along the curve of the corridor, Lena could only imagine a young Bel, sitting on folded legs and wings tight to his back, out of the way.

The vision filled her with sadness for that lonely little prince.

She'd known what that was like as a girl at Lindenfaire, always surrounded by other cadets and squires but apart, the rock that jutted out of the river.

Alix ducked in and out of rooms, determined to find something interesting, but Lena trailed behind Bel.

With the ornamentation stripped away, it was hard to tell when they arrived at actual personal rooms except for the corridors growing wider and the doorways more ornate. Bel paused outside an arched threshold, feathers quivering.

"Were these yours?" Lena asked gently.

He nodded, keeping still for another long moment before cautiously entering rooms that had once been his.

A short hallway led into a foyer, home to a single stone table. The circular top had once held another elaborate mosaic, but many of the pieces had been plucked out and Lena couldn't tell what the scene had once been. The jade color of the walls had faded to the muted green of a still pond.

Beyond the entry, a bay of windows filled a spacious square room with light. Nothing was left here except for a few scratches on the stone walls and the tattered remains of curtains hanging above the windows.

A smaller, darker room, the bedchamber she supposed, waited behind another arched threshold, but Bel didn't go there, instead running his hands along the stones of the east wall.

Lena watched him, unsure what to do or where to stand in this room that had once held Bel's life. That everything was gone, had been stolen away by violent, greedy hands, bothered her. She should've been able to walk into this room and learn things about the boy Bel had been. She should've seen the life that was lived in this room and the things that decorated it. She should've walked into this room and not thought of the trunk in her old chamber at Lindenfaire, the one that held the baubles and decorations of childhood and a former life.

But she did think of it, and that she should be grateful that at least she had a trunk's worth of things, of memories. Not that she'd ever see them again. Not that she thought her life at Lindenfaire had amounted to only a trunk's worth.

Still, what little was left, it was something. And just knowing they existed, the things she'd once held dear in her younger life, was a comfort.

Anger burned in her chest for him, that he was denied this comfort, too.

As she stewed and steamed, Bel picked at one of the stones of the wall, using a fingernail to work it free. Finally, a false stone face fell into his hand, and Bel reached into the hidden cubby it concealed.

From it he pulled a small felt drawstring bag. She heard his breath hitch as he loosened the strings and emptied the bag into his palm.

The first item was a small wooden box, stained a rich red-brown. The second was a flat gold circle; at first Lena thought it was a large coin, but when she looked again, she realized it was a beautifully engraved rondel.

Two things. Two small items had been important enough for him to hide.

Bel looked at the items for a long time, as if he was deciding if he truly wanted to hold them. When he finally moved, it was to bring the trinkets to her, a small, sad smile on his face that cracked any tiny, unbroken part of her heart left.

He held his hand out to her, and she carefully took the wooden box. The little latch had begun to rust, but with a nail, she lifted it and the lid. Inside, on a bed of blue velvet, rested a curl of faded golden-blonde hair, looped and tied together at the ends with a thin white ribbon.

Lena held the box with her fingertips, terrified of disturbing the curl. She knew, somehow, even before he told her, that "It was my mother's. Maddok saved it for me, to have a piece of her."

A few of the ends had frayed at the crest of the loop, as if it had been stroked and touched many times by small, reverent fingers.

Lena's lower lip trembled.

"And this," Bel held out the rondel, letting the light catch on the engraved insignia of wings spread around a sea of stars, "this is a piece from Maddok's first set of armor. He gave it to me to keep, to put on my own one day."

"They're beautiful," she said, because they were, and because what else could she say.

Lena looked at the treasures with Bel for as long as he wanted, though she fought to keep the tears down. When he took back the box, Lena turned her head and wiped at any errant wetness. Her eyes stung with the hot ache of needing to cry, for Bel, for the mother he never knew, for the brother he'd loved above all others.

Bel replaced the box in the felt bag and returned them to the hideyhole. The rondel, though, he slipped into an inner pocket of his jerkin, over his left breast. Lena watched in surprise when he put the false stone over the hidden opening.

His eyes were bright with memories and tears, and Lena knew if she shed hers, he'd be lost to the sorrow.

Instead, she asked him to tell her of his life as a prince, a life she knew so little about.

And Bel told her, the words pouring from him as surely as the tears had before. He spoke of the many books and scrolls that always littered the main room, how some were for lessons but many others had been taken from the library. He liked reading, liked the adventures, and Eamon, his appointed caretaker, had had to coax and cajole him to read anything else.

As a warrior, Eamon kept a strict schedule. Up early in the morning, exercises, lessons, training, and if Bel did all this well, the afternoons were his. He liked to read in the afternoon sun during the winter, usually in front of his bay of windows or his favorite nook in the vast library. In the warmer summers, he'd venture deeper into the palace or, if he could slip past Eamon, go exploring down into Aeriand itself and watch the busy lives of others. He liked going to the markets and watching the haggling, or to the garrisons on the wall and watching the fishermen at work on the lake, or into one of the squares to watch people chatting around the central fountain and eating late, leisurely lunches in the shade of the city's many pergolas. Once his wings were strong enough, he'd sneak out to the largest of the palace's courtyards, where one side was open to the wind, and take flight, soaring over the city and lake and surrounding lands. And sometimes, when conditions were just right, he was able to sneak into the basilica when Maddok held court, seeing to affairs, listening to advisors and officials and the problems of everyday avians.

Lena treasured every detail, every image of a young Bel making up his own adventures. Even though he was a prince, an Adiiron, he'd been left to himself so much—Lena ached for him, but as he spoke, he didn't seem sad, more bittersweet. He'd made the best of his isolation, she realized, just as he had at Finhöln.

As Bel finished his final story, his gaze turned, unfocused, to the windows overlooking the great expanse of Aeriand below them.

"So, did you sneak girls in here, right under Eamon's nose?" she asked, just to see what he'd say, just to lighten his heart a little.

He blinked at her in confused amusement, his lips creeping up. It didn't reach his eyes—those still looked too dark, too deeply set in his face, but it was something.

"No," he said before a slight frown lowered his brow. "Though, there were a few girls who snuck themselves in."

Lena snorted a laugh.

"Oh, and no other squires tried sneaking into your room?" he teased.

"Of course not," she replied, "my mother is the most feared knight in Vagora. They wouldn't dare."

"I can imagine," he chuckled.

His gaze met hers, genuine amusement crinkling around his eyes, and Lena's breath caught.

Yes, he could. He could imagine what such a life was like. Nobody daring to come close.

He knew what it was to have a charmed childhood, to have every want met. And he knew, too, what it was to have a deep, aching loneliness, one that only grew when guilt came up on its heels, scolding that he had everything he could need, how could he long for more. But he did. Oh, he longed for more and felt guilty for it, but that couldn't stop him.

Lena felt a little tug in her chest, that golden thread that tied her heart to his. She'd felt it almost since knowing him, this lost avian prince. In those early days, he may have been her prisoner and she his warden, but there had always been something in his eyes that resonated within her. Holding a haunting kind of wisdom, his eyes had seen too much, underscored with lines, not of age but of loss. Her broken heart had called out to his, to the kinship it sensed within, just as it did now.

That bottomless pit of loneliness in her heart wasn't so deep when it was with his. She held no guilt for tying her heart to his, either, because how could that be wrong? In this shell of a city that bore the scars of genocide, beside its prince who bore the same scars, how could her lonely heart finding a mate, a kindred soul, ever be wrong?

18

The wind tugged at Bel's hair, making the locks billow and catch on the pointed tips of his ears. It was always windy here, so high up in Aeriand. The steady updraft made this the perfect drop-off, and for centuries the main courtyard of the Mount had been where all sovereigns and their courts took off from and returned home.

Bel's legs dangled over the edge, knees hooked on the ledge so that when a strong enough breeze caught in his partially open wings, he didn't go sailing backward.

The crisp morning wind felt good against his feathers, shifting through the barbs and rustling the down. He took comfort in the way it chapped and stung his skin. They were familiar sensations, dredged up from memories he'd spent many years hiding away. Like so many other memories of this place. *Maybe too many.*

The wind brought with it smells from the lake and floodplain beyond, water and sweet grasses and wildflowers. Smells from the city should've floated up too, foods cooking, smoke plumes from hearths, forges, and kilns, all tinged with the subtle sweetness of wisteria. Now, all that came up from the city below was dust.

Two full days they'd been in Aeriand and Bel hadn't grown used to the stillness. He thought perhaps after his long years in Finhöln, he'd be used to such quiet, but his memories of Aeriand were potent despite being buried deep, and it was hard to reconcile the differences between memory and reality.

A red sun rose over the land, sliced into sections by a low bank of swelling purple clouds. Bel didn't believe in the superstitions of the old scryers, who divined fortunes and futures with bits of bones and feathers, but nothing about the morning sky seemed auspicious. At the very least, he suspected thunderstorms that afternoon.

He, Lena, and Alix spent their days wandering the city, peering into homes, barracks, offices, potteries, workshops, and theaters to see if they could find...something. He didn't know what, didn't expect to actually *find* anything, yet it continued to disappoint, each time they didn't find...anything.

What little was left behind had long since moldered, rotted, or been consumed by the desperate packs of animals that now claimed the streets. More than just coyotes had tracked them as they explored, reflective cougar eyes following them from the shadows, making it necessary to retreat back to the Mount at night. It felt safer to sleep behind the gates and walls, and they'd taken chambers in the staff quarters; small, easily defended rooms deep within the Mount. The only things that bothered them there were the occasional lost bat, crow, or owl.

Aeriand had loomed large in his thoughts so long now, the deep, molten core of his determination to one day escape Finhöln. It'd been a desire so strong, so palpable, that not even the whipping post and interminable winters could extinguish it.

Now that he was here...his heart found little solace in the familiar. It wasn't truly familiar, not anymore, not after so much time and so much destruction. He looked around Aeriand and felt only despair and anger, a combination that bred a sucking hopelessness deep in his gut. What did it matter an Adiiron stood once again in the Mount? He wasn't the right Adiiron, and worse, he was years too late.

Quiet footsteps drew him from the storm of his thoughts, and Bel looked over his shoulder to find Lena carefully edging along the curved railing of the drop-off. She'd pulled on her quilted overcoat and had her hands stuffed in the pockets as she tried to hide her nervousness at the height.

She made it as far as the end of the railing, eyes darting over the side to the sheer drop below. Bel saw the concave shadow in her cheek that meant she was chewing the inside of it. He scooted closer to the railing, legs still dangling and wings still partially open to catch the breeze, but enough that, when she breathed a relieved sigh and plopped down to put her back against the railing, he could reach out and grasp her hand.

"The wind's...bracing up here," she said. She'd pulled her thick hair back into a tight, serviceable plait, but already small wisps tugged free to dance along her ears and cheeks.

"That's what makes it perfect."

She cast him a dubious smile as her eyes skittered to the sheer drop then away again.

"Don't like heights?" he asked.

"I hadn't thought about it, really. I've never been up so high like this."

She settled against the railing and brought the hand she held to her lap and the warmth of her coat. The pulse at her neck evened out, and though Bel knew she didn't like being so close to the edge, he appreciated her sitting with him. He needed the company.

"Where are we going today?" she asked, tracing his fingers.

Where indeed.

"It may storm this afternoon. Aeriand gets thunderstorms, not something we want to get caught in."

"So we're sticking close."

"There may be something to salvage in the lower levels of the Mount."

They both knew it wasn't likely, not with how thoroughly the rest of the Mount had been stripped bare. The bowels of the Mount held mostly storage, wines and grains and dried fruits and roots—a valuable target for an invading army with mouths to feed. Still, they hadn't gone there yet.

Lena lapsed into silence, still tracing his fingers, and he could feel the questions brewing inside her.

He had them himself. They could check the inner chambers of the Mount today, maybe the market district tomorrow. They could inspect the lake beyond the wall, climb into the hills at Aeriand's back. They could gather all the scraps left in the city and do...something.

"Bel," she said slowly, considering each word, "do you want to stay here, in Aeriand?"

He pulled in a long breath and looked back out over the riverplain. The sun had risen but still hid behind the bank of clouds, taking with it the meager morning warmth.

"I'm not sure," he admitted. "It doesn't...feel right." The words were inadequate, but he didn't know how else to say it. Aeriand was dead, and there was nothing he could do about it on his own.

"As in it's a bad idea or as in it's not what you want to do?"

"I'm not sure," he said again, wincing. "It feels hopeless here. The silence echoes."

She considered a moment before saying, "A city like this isn't meant to be empty. But, if we stayed, we'd make it better. Make it comfortable for us. We could do it."

Bel didn't like that the first answer that jumped up his throat was a refusal. Something about the emptiness made his skin crawl, made him want to hurry Lena and Alix away, but as they sat there, Lena playing idly with his fingers, he made himself swallow his reticence and truly consider.

"There's shelter," he admitted, which was more than most of their nights of travel could boast.

"Mm," she agreed. "I'd been thinking about a homestead somewhere, but here at least, we wouldn't have to start from nothing. There may not be many comforts left here, but those things can be made again or bought."

"The lake should have plenty of fish." And fresh water, too.

"We'd have the summer to make the most needed repairs and gather supplies for winter. And..." She looked up at him, searching his face before she said, "It won't always be like this. Aeriand. Someday it..." Her words ran out, and he saw the struggle in her eyes to voice any hopes or ideas about what the city's future could be.

It was a touching sentiment, but Bel was knee-deep in his pessimism this morning. Perhaps one day Aeriand could house more than just roving packs of quail, but not for a long time yet.

Still, he didn't let his doubts show, or at least, tried not to.

Lena cleared her throat and looked back down at their tangled hands. "It'd be a lot of work," she said, "but we could do it. Make a home here."

He didn't miss or think he imagined the way she forced *home* from her lips. She struggled with the idea just as much as he did.

It wasn't that they couldn't do it. They could. And it wasn't that Aeriand had nothing to offer them. It did.

It was just...

This didn't feel like the end, whatever that meant.

But perhaps this was just his pessimism and bruised hopes talking. He supposed, even days later, with every new sight proving what had been done to Aeriand and the avians, he hadn't yet worked through the pain of his homecoming. The echoes of their trauma and desperation still rang clear, and Bel, for all that he'd gone through himself these last years, hadn't had to reconcile with anyone's grief but his own for a very long time.

"It couldn't hurt to stay a while," he decided.

Perhaps, if they breathed a little life back into Aeriand, that gutting hopelessness deep inside him would fade.

Lena nodded, looking out over the city but pointedly not down at the drop below her. "We can stay in the rooms we have or choose something else up here. I think being high is best. Securing supplies will be important. But we may need to consider patching the wall as best we can."

"The wall...?"

She nodded again. "To make it defensible. I don't know why King Artemian withdrew, but that doesn't mean he's completely abandoned it. I'd assume, at least. Not after all it took..."

Bel couldn't hold her gaze. Logically, he knew the wall didn't come down by his hands. Bel couldn't have guessed the human king's mind, nor that the mistranslations would have any impact on his strategy. That didn't change the ache in his heart, though, that somehow that wall was his fault. For all that he'd believed himself completely cut off from his home and people, somehow, his words had reached them. And look at what they'd accomplished. Perhaps he'd bought them more time. Perhaps he'd galvanized the humans to attack the wall when they wouldn't have otherwise.

Bel's eyes slid closed and he hung his head.

Lena's hands squeezed his. "What is it?"

The words clogged his throat, and his mouth was too dry to swallow them back down. He didn't want to lie, or lie by omission, or hurt her with the truth. But...he didn't want to break his promises more.

And this grief...this was one burden she shared. She'd known the horrors firsthand, and perhaps it was worth something, knowing that nothing that happened in that siege was her or her comrades' fault.

"You remember what I did for Artemian, with the translations?"

A long beat passed, and he could almost hear her mind working to figure out what he intended with such a question. "Yes," she said finally, "maps and stories and such."

"I didn't really know why he ever wanted these things. Gods knows where he got some of it. It wasn't clear what the aim was at the beginning. But really, whatever it was, that didn't matter to me. He wanted my people's words, and after taking everything else, I didn't want to give them to him."

He looked up then, finding her eyes riveted to him. Her brows had drawn low into a pensive frown, the look of someone anticipating a blow and trying to determine where it would come from.

"You put in mistakes," she said slowly, not looking entirely surprised.

Bel nodded. She was clever and would've figured this out with a little more time at Finhöln. Most of the wardens who'd come to guard him had found his task odd, but in the face of the long, harsh winters, few cared enough to think on it more. Lena would've been the exception. She always was for him.

From the careful way she watched him now, Bel suspected she'd had her suspicions already.

"I couldn't help him. At first it was rebellion, a way to stay sane and feel like I was doing something. But then it...it was more about protecting the documents and the knowledge they held. It wasn't his to take."

He clung to her hands as he spoke and watched every wrinkle of her face and flick of her eyes, desperate to know if the truth was better than omission.

The sympathetic set of her brows didn't change, and Bel gathered his courage to finish.

"I put in errors purposefully on everything I translated. I thought someone would eventually catch on, but I was only ever sent more. So I kept doing it. I never thought he'd truly use what I gave him."

Lena turned her face toward the city, searching out the wall in the near distance. Her lips parted, but no words came for a long, horrible moment.

"We got bad intelligence..." she murmured.

"You got a lie."

"We thought we were attacking a weak point."

"No. It was one of the thickest points and the most heavily guarded."

She blinked rapidly in the way of someone keeping back tears. When her lip trembled and Bel could see all those memories playing behind her eyes, he couldn't stop from using their entwined hands to pull her into his arms and wings.

He cloaked her in feathers, shielding her from the worst of the wind, and buried his nose in the ridge of her braid.

Lena filled her fists with his jerkin, the leather crackling at the abuse, but she didn't push him away. He held her as the sun broke through the clouds, climbing higher in the sky to bathe Aeriand in morning light.

The growing warmth had burned off the low clouds by the time Lena moved again.

"You didn't know," she murmured.

"No," Bel sighed. "But I wouldn't have stopped even if I had."

She shook her head against his chest. "No. I know." The long breath she took had the wet stutter of unshed tears. "What was the point, then," she asked in a small voice, "of all of this?"

Bel couldn't answer, for he feared the reasons only made sense to one mind.

They sat in a somber quiet for a long while, holding each other in the brightening day, but with their faces to the wind, the air still had a cold bite to it.

"It cost too much," Lena finally said. "Whatever his plans are...it's costing too much."

All Bel could do was hold her as the ideals of her king came crumbling down around her. She'd remained loyal to a king who didn't deserve it, who punished her for doing what was right and noble, even into her wardenship. Bel suspected that even as they'd fled through the forest as fugitives, she still bore some sense of duty and loyalty to the figure of the human king.

But the truth was stark with everything they'd seen since leaving Finhöln. King Artemian was fortunate that this proof was so far away from the eyes of his people. If Lena's loyalty could be broken, anyone's could, for how could a king keep it when the cost of destroying one people was slowly killing his own.

All these lives destroyed, and what did Artemian have to show for it?

It made his guts twist uneasily, wondering about Artemian's aims. He'd met the human king only once but had received many of his missives. He didn't think the man was mad, and he couldn't say with any certainty that he was overly desperate, either. Bel didn't like the possibilities that left.

"The work and directions you brought me when you came to Fin-höln were focused on Hadria. Everything from poems to old maps. He's hoping to find a route through the old mines into the mountain."

Lena leaned back just enough to frown up at him. "We already tried the mines." Her throat bobbed on a swallow. "We lost good people in there."

He pulled her into his side and kissed her hair. "It isn't written down. Only an avian can find their way. Provided they remember the way at all."

"But if he's looking through avian documents to find answers..." Lena sat up to level him with serious eyes. "There's no other way to take Hadria. We can't climb up. The war machines can't throw high enough. Getting inside through the mines is the only option."

There was another option, to stop the campaign altogether, but taking it would truly make the last decade of war worthless. *Which is why Artemian can't take it.*

"Nothing they have can lead them through," Bel said.

Lena shook her head. "Maybe not, but he's got numbers." She clutched at his sleeve, her sudden panicked energy bleeding into him, and Bel's heart began to beat faster. "There's no other way, so he'll devote everything to finding a way through the tunnels. I was on the last rotation home almost two years ago, he's keeping everyone there. He even pulled soldiers out of Aeriand."

"He doesn't know the way, but throw enough soldiers at it, and one will eventually get lucky," Bel said through numb lips.

Lena nodded grimly.

Another silence gripped them, the horror of the king's plan and what it would cost breathtaking. Perhaps Bel had been wrong, perhaps Artemian truly was that desperate.

But *why*? Humans and avians had had plenty of wars in the past, usually over lands far away from the center of their kingdoms. But in the past decades, the humans had encroached, taking more, claiming what had never before been theirs. Still, avians only fought for what had been their territory since the first flocks. They'd never marched into the heart of the human kingdom. They'd never destroyed the human capital or slaughtered a human king.

A burning frustration joined the dark hopelessness inside him, roiling like a storm-tossed sea.

Lena picked up his hand again and brought it to her chest, over her heart.

"Bel, if this is true, then maybe..." She grimaced, and he knew what she thought before she finished, "maybe we need to go to Hadria."

He hated the idea, and he hated that his initial reaction was agreement. A frustrated grumble left his chest.

"Dartegn must know they're trying to go through the mines."

"But does he know about Aeriand being completely abandoned?"

Bel doubted it. But, "I don't owe my cousin anything." He didn't mean it, not truly, but the shamefully small shrine for his brother haunted him.

Lena's lips pressed thin in displeasure. "And what about everyone else in that mountain?"

He winced. He didn't owe avians anything either, but they were his kind. They asked for this war no more than Bel asked to spend ten years in captivity.

"It'd be dangerous," he said, "so, so dangerous." The mountain was an unforgiving place, and the mines beneath a warren of stale air, rockfalls, and pits so deep they had to go all the way to the underworld. He'd only been a fledgling the last time he visited with Maddok; his throat closed at the idea of having to lead Lena and Alix through those dark tunnels on his fragments of memory. To a nest full of avians who'd be apathetic at best to see him but wrathful at the sight of two humans, the first ever to reach inside Hadria.

Lena nodded slowly. "I know. But I think we could make it. And I think...I think *you* need to go."

When she met his gaze, he saw what she truly said.

"I'm not a prince, not anymore. I don't want a destiny or to play the hero."

Lena smiled sadly. "I know that, too. But that doesn't mean you don't still have things you must do. They're your people, Bel."

Gods, this woman might as well have driven a dagger through his heart, a heart that was hers in every way.

For so long all he'd had to do was survive. His life had no certainty, no real purpose other than to avoid harm and stay alive. These past weeks, he'd learned a new purpose—to keep Lena and Alix safe and find a place for them. He wanted to keep his promises to them, even unspoken as they were, with a fierceness that almost scared him. Lena had given him something to live for again, had shown him *how* to live again, and what she suggested now would put all of that—would put *her* in danger.

Going to Hadria, seeking out his kin, meant risking everything he loved for a cousin and a people who'd risked nothing for him.

Bel could hardly stomach it. Putting a mate, his *c'vana*, in danger went against every instinct, every moral.

Lena gazed out over the city again, giving him a moment to consider her words. He traced the sharp profile of her face with his eyes, heart aching in his chest at how dear, how familiar every contour, every freckle, every scar was.

She sat with back straight, proud nose and firm lips set against the wind.

This possible, probable danger wasn't a question for her. It didn't matter to her what was or wasn't owed. Lena helped people—gods, she was the one suggesting they go to the aid of avians, a people she'd only ever met across the battlefield.

Her goodness humbled him. It was why he'd never deserve her and why he'd never let her go, too. She was everything.

It was because he was watching her so closely that he saw when her expression hardened, eyes suddenly alert.

"What is that?" she said stiffly.

Bel searched the city below then out to the riverplain.

There, movement in the plain outside the city wall. He focused his

eyes, able to see farther than Lena, and sat stunned as he counted six riders headed for Aeriand.

What were the chances of any other group of six humans being so
far into avian country?

"It's Joran."

19

Lena always hated an ambush. Certainly when it was her unit being ambushed but also being the one lying in wait. She understood the sound strategy of it and didn't truly begrudge anyone, from commander to hunter to predator, using it.

It was the waiting she hated, the knowing that violence was soon to be done. That she would be the one to impart it on an enemy who, if the ambush was successful, would otherwise be unawares and unready. She didn't like meeting opponents that way, jumping out and pressing an advantage that had little to do with her prowess and much more with finding a good shadow and keeping your breathing quiet.

None of this would stop her from jumping on the knight walking toward her once the other woman got in just...the right...spot...

The knight stopped two paces back from where Lena needed her. She planted her fists on her hips, huffed, and looked around the abandoned granary she'd entered and Lena hid in the rafters of.

A bead of sweat trickled from the crown of Lena's head, down her forehead, across her brow, and pooled at her temple as she tried to keep her breathing even, willing the knight to find something interesting to inspect further inside.

Ambushing Joran and his knights hadn't been Lena's idea. She'd voted for slipping away as quickly and quietly as they could, leaving no trace they'd been there. Let Joran think coming here was a mistake, that he'd gambled the avian prince would want to return home and lost his own bet.

She hadn't wanted another fight with Joran—her hip still ached from the last—and hadn't wanted to risk their own gamble going sideways. They only had the upper hand for a preciously small time. Just thinking about Alix and Bel in their own hideaways, waiting for an opening, just as she did, had another trickle of sweat sluicing down her cheek.

The knight shifted her weight from foot to foot and grumbled something Lena didn't catch. She shifted forward...one step...peered further into the empty, cavernous space...and stopped, scowling into the shadows.

Lena bit down on her cheek and her frustration, holding still in her crouch between two beams. The weight of the weapons strapped to her —a sword and bow across her back, daggers at her waist, and a small quiver at her thigh—wasn't much, *"Packing light,"* as Alix put it, but it still pulled her down, as if eager for a fight.

She'd been out-voted. There were merits to her plan, but ultimately, Alix and Bel both agreed Joran and as many of his knights as possible needed to be dealt with here, where Bel knew every nook, cranny, blind spot, and dead-end alley. *"We'll never have a better chance,"* Alix had reasoned, *"at least here, it won't matter so much there's only three of us and six of them."*

Lena had held her tongue, fighting the urge to immediately deny that Alix would take any part in any possible ambush.

"We can't let them follow us to Hadria," Bel had added, his face a series of worried, downturned lines.

She hadn't liked it, but she couldn't argue with their logic. It would be dangerous enough getting to Hadria; they didn't need the continued threat of a knight errant who should've been hundreds of miles away doing his duty, protecting the prince, rather than chasing fugitives across the continent.

So they'd kept hidden, high up in the Mount, and watched as Joran and the knights systematically began searching the city. Joran could never be accused of sloppiness; they swept through the lower levels for two days as Lena, Bel, and Alix spied from above.

As the knights continued through Aeriand finding nothing, they began to fan out, spread wider to cover more ground. When they'd seen the knights splitting up that morning, Bel had looked at Lena with a grim determination.

"*Let's get this done,*" was all she'd said.

They'd each chosen a location to spring their traps. Lena picked a granary for its open space. Bel chose a block of mid-level homes, where the trellises were still sturdy and the wisteria leaves thick. And Alix had opted to get as close to their camp as possible, lying in wait for the first one back.

She'd made Alix swear to Matella, Her Maidens, and on her own hide that she'd stay out of a fight and stick to the heavy fishing nets Bel found her. Alix had rolled her eyes, sighed, protested she never got to have any fun, and then shook on it.

"*I won't be disappointed if some important things of theirs go...missing, though,*" Lena had offered.

Alix grinned up at her with wide, beatific eyes. "*It'd be a real shame if the horses got loose.*"

Lena liked stealing even less than ambushing, but she had to remind herself that these knights, given the chance, would steal something much more precious than rations or trinkets or weapons. This wasn't even just for Bel and his freedom anymore—sitting with him that morning at the drop-off, Lena had felt the heavy hand of purpose settle on her shoulders.

They could do something about this horrible war, and her part in it was to get Bel to Hadria safely without compromising the avian stronghold.

That's what she told her roiling stomach over and over again to try settling it.

The knight shifted her weight forward half a step, and then...yes!

Lena pounced, swooping down onto the unsuspecting knight like a raptor on silent wings before *thwack!* The knight toppled to the ground with an "Oof!" and Lena on top of her.

She only got a precious moment to lock her arm around the woman, before the knight and all her training snapped to attention. With a heave, the knight twisted and bucked, trying to unseat Lena.

She held on but only just. They were evenly matched, Lena a bit taller but the other woman wider with muscle. But Lena had two very important advantages—she'd already wrapped her arms around the woman's chest and she had much more to protect.

It was quick but brutal. Lena let the woman struggle and scrabble, wearing herself out as Lena bore most of her weight down. She grunted and grimaced at elbows to the guts, and she narrowly avoided a broken nose when the woman's head lurched back like a battering ram.

Lena held on, a snake constricting its prey, and both she and the knight felt when the other woman's strength began to wane. Her shoulder sagged, but she showed her training when, rather than fighting harder, she took a moment to try catching her breath and think.

But Lena had the same training—perhaps even better. Every young cadet dreamed of being Lady Margot Montcaer's squire. Well, everyone but Lena. The irony wasn't lost on her. And while Margot had trained many greenlings into strapping knights, none of them had been Maddalena, her daughter, her legacy. She poured everything into Lena, her knowledge, her ambitions, her determination to win.

It'd been enough to keep Lena alive when she stood with Prince Arion for years at the bleak base of the mountain stronghold, avian arrows raining down on them for hours.

Her mother had honed her. The war had sharpened her.

Her love for Bel made her brutal.

Sweeping the knight's legs out, she pulled the woman down and hammered a knee into her gut. All the air left her in a horrid gasp, and then Lena was behind her, drawing her arm back. Lena smashed the woman's right arm, her sword arm, on that knee.

The woman's guttural scream drew a whimper from Lena as she felt the knight's radial bone shatter in her hands.

The knight slumped to the stone floor, dazed with pain, and Lena, throat burning with bile, followed her down. She wrapped an arm around the knight's neck and squeezed, watching for the right purplish-pink flush. "*There's an art to suffocating someone,*" Margot liked to say, "*it takes longer than people think. Watch the colors. There are choking colors, fainting colors, and dying colors. Know which you want.*"

The fight slipped out of the knight as purple tones overtook her face. Lena counted in her head before finally releasing her.

The woman fell forward unceremoniously, unconscious.

Lena stumbled a step back, her hands and breath shaky. She tried to swallow on a dry throat but felt only the scratch of guilt clawing its way up.

Gritting her teeth, Lena took one long breath and then held it as she went to work unbuckling the broadsword strapped to the knight's hip and collecting all her knives. When Lena stood, the knight's sword weighed heavy in the hand that had broken her sword arm.

Guilt was a living, writhing thing just beneath her skin, and Lena fought to keep down all she'd had for breakfast and what little honor she had left.

Sparing one last glance to reassure herself that the knight's natural color was returning and her chest rose unrestricted, Lena turned and ran from the granary.

She set herself a pitiless pace, letting the burn of her legs and lungs lull her into that sharp place where all fighters wanted to be, senses heightened and emotions dulled. It lent her focus and a barrier between her and the guilt and grief at striking down a fellow knight.

Lena skirted the great buildings of what must have been a trade district, its granaries and storehouses and silos silent sentinels. They offered their long shadows as she sprinted down the streets in search of the other knight who'd been assigned this area.

———— •◆•• ————

She found him early in the afternoon walking down a side street peering into windows, a big man with closely cropped hair and a war hammer strapped to his back.

Lena sucked in a gulp of air and charged him, pressing the only advantages she'd have on him—surprise and speed.

His head was just turning to inspect the noise of her pounding feet when a sheathed sword smacked him across the cheek.

The stolen sword she'd thrown at him clattered to the cobblestones. The man stumbled back, a whuffing grunt rumbling in his throat, blood dribbling from his cracked-open cheek. He could do little but open his mouth in surprise before Lena was there.

Their bodies met in a heavy, reverberating *smack*, and Lena clung on as the force sent the knight tumbling backwards. One hand scrabbled across her back, looking for purchase, and Lena batted away the other as it tried to grab her hair.

The man hit the cobblestones with a sickening *thud*, his head bouncing twice off his war hammer. Teeth bared in a wild snarl, hands snatched at Lena in a dazed struggle, like a fox caught in a trap.

There would be no breaking the man's arm over her knee.

Lena drove one of her pilfered daggers through the meaty part of the man's right shoulder, between tendon and clavicle. He howled in pain, arching and bucking and throwing Lena off.

She lunged for him when he made to roll over and drove the heel of another dagger down onto the back of his right hand, crushing the delicate bones between metal and stone.

His howl this time was silent, his face a rictus of agony. Lena gripped him by the ears and smashed his head on the pavers. It took only one strong blow, and the knight went limp. She told herself it was a mercy.

Lena slumped to the side, chest heaving as breath sawed in and out of her. She gave herself only a moment and then staggered upright to collect the sword she'd thrown at the man and his own blades. It was no use getting at the war hammer, so she left it under him where he lay and the dagger in his shoulder so he wouldn't bleed out.

She set off through the city again but couldn't keep the same pace as before, weighed down with the stolen swords. As she jogged back through the market district, she didn't think of the two knights laid low and left for scavengers. She was only pumping arms and pounding feet

and grim determination.

By the time Lena made it to the rings of stately homes nestled below the Mount and its gate, she'd unloaded the stolen weapons in a dilapidated shop. Her hip throbbed, reminding her with every step how many times she'd fallen on it lately, and her legs ached in that way that if she stopped, she wouldn't be able to start again. So she kept going, her pulse thrumming and her breaths burning in—

She caught the unmistakable slap of shod hooves just in time to put on a burst of speed through the empty, exposed square and dove behind a limestone building as Joran rode in from the opposite side.

Lena slumped back against the wall, trying to hear over her panting. Run now and he'd surely hear her, if he hadn't already seen her. And she was too close to the Mount, couldn't risk being pursued back to their hideaway.

The clip of hooves stopped, and Lena held her breath even as her lungs wailed.

"I knew you'd bring him here," Joran called. "What I don't understand is why."

Lena let the held breath hiss from her teeth. *Damn it all.*

She could run now. He'd pursue, of course he would, no hunter chased their prey so long and got so close to abandon the hunt now, but she'd be a rabbit in a warren, lead him away from the Mount until dark, when she could slip back to their hideaway, collect Bel and Alix, and hurry out of Aeriand. It could work. She could probably outlast and outwit him for a few more hours.

Or...or she could finish what she'd started and do what needed to be done.

Let's get this done, she heard herself saying, not to Bel this time.

"Everyone deserves the chance to go home," she answered Joran over the rustle of unstrapping her bow and nocking an arrow.

"Even traitors?"

Flexing her fingers, Lena rolled her shoulders before stepping halfway out from the protection of the wall. She drew back the bowstring, aiming for the large target of Joran's chest. Archery had never been her strongest skill, but she was good, better when she knew she couldn't afford to miss.

Joran stiffened in the saddle, bow and arrow in his hands but unready.

Lena took a step closer, improving her aim.

"I knew I'd never go home again. I accept that. Some things are more important."

"More important than your duty?" he spat. "You took an *oath*, Maddalena."

"He's killing us, Joran. To destroy the avians, he'll sacrifice us all. And for what? It doesn't have to be this way."

"It isn't for us to decide. We follow orders, we serve our king and country. We protect our people." His face, always so stern and hard, cracked into a withering frown she'd rarely seen. "But you, you protect *him* and his kind. You're a disgrace."

She knew his words were meant to disarm her, to wound her as surely as any weapon, to create an opening. She knew there would be no reasoning with a knight like Joran, a man who'd dedicated himself to the code and to service for so long, he'd be nothing without them. She knew to a man like him, she was worse than the grime scraped off the bottom of a boot—oath-breaker, deserter, traitor.

She knew all this, yet the words, *disgrace*, burned her insides as surely as her arm burned holding back the nocked arrow.

Get this done.

"I hope one day you understand that duty doesn't outweigh compassion," she told him, "nor does following orders without question or conscience make you a good knight."

But she knew too that he'd never understand this, wasn't capable of it. Her words, while the truth, were just as much a distraction as his.

Joran's frown deepened and his mouth opened in outrage, to protest, to quote the knight's code at her again, and Lena let her arrow fly.

The bowstring snapped against her cheek, a sharp pinch of pain.

Joran jerked to the side, his years of experience saving him from worse, and the arrow slid home into his upper arm.

He grunted in pain but immediately reached for the arrow to pull it out as his horse danced uneasily beneath him.

Lena nocked another arrow and let it loose higher on his shoulder.

Joran bared his teeth in pain, one arm dangling while the other grabbed for the reins.

She nocked one last arrow. "This traitor spared you twice," she called to him. "Remember that." And, hating it and herself, she shot his horse in the flank.

The horse reared in pain, its outraged scream a horrible sound that would haunt Lena's sleep.

Joran tumbled from the saddle, landing heavily on his side. He groaned in pain but rolled out of the way of his horse, dancing in agony.

Lena held her breath, fingers hesitating on another arrow.

Joran lumbered to his feet and ripped out the arrows in his arm with a roar. A long breath shuddered through him, lips pulled back over gritted teeth.

He moved fast for a man his age, turning and sprinting for her.

She shot him in the other arm.

He just kept coming.

Screaming, Lena nocked her last arrow and sent it sailing into his chest.

Joran lurched and tumbled to the pavers with a *smack*. He didn't get up.

Lena ran.

She ran until her legs howled in pain. She ran until they went silent or she went numb, she wasn't sure.

Her path back to the Mount wended and doubled back, even if no one followed, *making sure* no one followed, maybe to punish herself a little. When she finally burst into the lower level of the royal quarters, it was dark and empty.

Lena only made it a few paces inside before she had to stop.

Her legs wanted to give out, but she locked her knees, the only thing she could do against the shaking and spasms. Her stomach rebelled next. Bile churned and bubbled, burning her insides.

Lena swallowed air even after her heart had stopped racing from the run, trying to cool and suppress all that wanted to spill out of her.

But it got out, one way or another.

———•◆••———

Bel was the next back. He found her there in the corridor, shaking, with tears dripping from her chin and knees quaking.

"Lena?"

He came around to stand before her. Through her tears and the gloom of the corridor, she could just see the red pattern of a deep scrape bisecting his cheek. Dirt caked one side of his head, and a few wisteria petals clung to his hair, but otherwise he looked unharmed.

She opened her mouth to tell him—something. Her relief? Her success? Her heartache?

Nothing came except a fresh gush of tears that scalded her cheeks.

Then his arms were there to take her weight. Lena collapsed into Bel and let him take her anguish.

"I know," he murmured, "I know."

He chanted it to her, nothing more, nothing less, nothing about how it needed to be done or how the knights would've done worse. She needed exactly what he gave, using his understanding to shore up her breaking heart.

When he turned to lead her to the room they'd claimed, Lena let him take her. She gave over her hurt, her grief, her stained honor to him and let him bear them for a while.

———•◆••———

By the gray light of dawn, they left Aeriand for the northern hills. The tall grasses blanketing the gentle slopes swayed in the breeze, as if waving them goodbye. Lena didn't speak and Bel didn't look back as the tall spires and towers of the Mount disappeared behind the rolling hills.

20

The time he'd spent inside the hood made Bel's hearing sharper than ever before. With his sight gone and sense of smell reduced to just his own breath and sweat, Bel heard every distant footfall, every leaf that fell on the roof, every mouse scrabbling in the walls.

He wished they'd all just shut up. Leave him alone.

His body ached from sitting in the same position for days, arms shackled before him in irons and wings pinned to his back with thick leather straps. That ache, and the sound of his own breath, overloud in this fucking hood, were the only things that reminded him he still lived.

He hated being reminded.

Days of no food and little water rendered the world fuzzy, even the sounds he thought he heard. His mind had unattached from his body a long time ago, and sometimes, Bel welcomed the hazy swirl.

But he couldn't stop himself from tonguing the cut in his lip. It'd healed over days ago, or should have if he didn't gnaw and worry it with his teeth. The bite of pain and blood kept him awake, kept him *angry*.

They'd kept him here, alone in some sort of room or tent. Alone with the memory of what he'd last seen—Maddok's face, contorted in agony, the blade thrust through his chest. Bel had watched a drop of blood fall from the sword tip spearing from his brother's chest as if in a dream, surreal, unreal. Maddok's hand had slipped from his shoulder, the strength leaving his grip, the light leaving his—

Stop, stop, he had to stop thinking about it.

He needed to figure out where he was. They'd get nothing from him. If that's why they'd taken him, they should've cut him down like everyone else, left him where he belonged.

He'd make them sorry for making him live. He'd gut every single one of those bastards who'd sprung up from the dark canyon like the wraiths the old tales talked of, set to steal and drag souls to the underworld, swarming from places he'd *checked*, he was *sure* he'd checked, as if they'd materialized from shadows *because he'd checked*—

A new sound, a group of footfalls, headed this way and fast.

Bel held his breath, a momentary relief from the humidity of the hood.

Footfalls and his own raging heartbeat drumming in his ears was all he heard until a tent flap or door slapped open. The footfalls came for him, too many to count or discern.

He tensed, the ache in his limbs ratcheting to a painful tightness.

"...back now and no reports of the survivors," one human was saying. A man, older, not a voice he'd heard before.

"Then we should move," another said, this one a woman's, "before they can mount a counterattack. The soldiers have had their fun. It's starting to go bad in the sun. Not even the pigs will want it soon."

"Very well," said a third voice, another man. "Make the arrangements to have what's left sent back with me."

"Artem..." said another woman as if she disapproved.

"And this one, my lord?" a fifth said, attached to a set of footfalls that came toward him.

Bel braced, ready when hands reached out to grab him. His body wailed from the violent rearrangement, knees popping and back cracking.

"He's no use to us, let's put him on the spit with the—"

"He could be worth something."

"My lord, perhaps there was a mistake and—"

"—we don't know what they'll do if—"

"He's just a boy, what could he—"

"—kill and be done with it."

"You're sure that's him?" said the voice with the air of command, the one who was so concerned over arrangements.

"We believe so, my lord. They're only rumors, he wasn't spotted until a few weeks prior."

"No one's talked to him?"

"Refuses to talk. But he doesn't need to, looks just like an Adiiron."

"Show me."

A fist grabbed the hood, yanking it off with some of Bel's hair. It made his eyes water, as if he were crying. Bel hated that.

Whatever room he was in was dim, but Bel had to shut his sensitive eyes to it anyway. Torchlight stabbed at his head even behind closed lids, a headache pounding against his temples. He shivered in the much cooler air, skin damp from the heat of his trapped breath.

The humans had gone hushed, eyes roving over him like beetle legs. He twitched and squirmed, trying to get his eyes to open, head sloshing under its own weight.

A sharp inhale to his left. "He certainly has the look of one. He'll do, then."

Bel managed to get his eyes open enough to see the watery shape of a man standing above him, long curls of brown hair falling over his shoulders and a gold breastplate catching the low light of the room.

That gaudy gold breastplate seared into his mind as the hood came back over his head to plunge him into darkness and stale air.

"Your Highness," said yet another man, his voice reminding Bel of a peeping chick. "Perhaps Highclere isn't wise. Perhaps it would—"

"You know you won't have support," said the woman. "And where would you keep him?"

"Many of your nobles prefer not to be reminded of the war."

"He may draw sympathy with how young he is."

"And what do we even need him for?"

Bel's throat clenched shut in panic, and he bit his lip to taste a trickle of blood.

"To make them feel the loss," the man with the breastplate said, "to make them feel the humiliation of knowing we killed their king and now we have their heir. They'll yield."

"And if they don't?"

"They will."

"But to take him to Highclere—"

"I have uses for him."

"Perhaps somewhere farther afield, Your Highness?" said the meek voice. "Out of sight. Secret. Leaving our people unworried."

"But *they* will know," another agreed.

"Fine," the armored man snapped. "Find me a suitable place, then. And get him ready to travel."

"Artem, there's no reason to—"

"He'll go there because I *fucking want him to*, Ilona. That's reason enough."

Clothes rustled and boots squeaked as the humans turned their heels. The flap or door slapped open again, the voices trailing with them.

Bel held perfectly still, sensing not all had left the room. He canted his head to hear better, to brace for a strike or grab, in case he needed to dodge or kick or—

"You know how he is about this," the woman sighed. "He won't stop."

"Better somewhere far away, from Aeriand and Highclere, if he's going to be kept alive."

"But *where?* Where can we keep the Adiiron heir where no one will find him?"

"In your tours of the north, did you ever visit the old demesne of Finhöln?"

21

Breath misting in the chilly highland morning, Bel switched from his left to right side, easing into the stretch. His back and wing bases moved and ached deliciously as Lena led them through the regimen. Behind him, the sun began to rise, saturating the thick blankets of lichen and heather that swathed the craggy landscape. The rolling highland hills turned into a riot of purples and greens in the early light, burning away the last of the night shadows in blinding color.

"Greetings," Bel said, pushing further into his stretch.

"*Ai'eda,*" chorused Lena and Alex.

"I mean no harm," he prompted.

"*A ruttan zival'an,*" Lena answered.

"*Zival'ana,*" Alix corrected.

Lena let out an irritated puff and twisted away.

As they made for Hadria, Bel couldn't help his growing anxiety at reuniting with his people, and he channeled those nerves into teaching Lena and Alix as much of his language, *alvani*, as he could. It wasn't perfect; his own memory of a language he'd only written, not spoken, in over ten years had grown cobwebs, and it became apparent quickly that Lena had little aptitude for languages. Alix picked it up enthusiastically, but Bel doubted Lena would be able to conjugate verbs before the highland hills turned to steep mountains.

But she persisted and so did Bel—he couldn't know what awaited them in Hadria, and this was the only advantage he could give them.

Well, that, and trying to ensure it was a friendly face they met first.

Their vocabulary lesson went on as the sun continued to rise, Bel sticking to easier words and verbs to bolster Lena's confidence—*help* and *stop* and *not enemy* were the first things he'd taught them. Then they practiced names, starting with his own; it was odd to hear it on another's lips when, for so long, the only fragment of Arubel Adiiron left had been in his own mind. He taught them how to roll the sounds like an avian would, not clumsily like they'd heard it in passing. It felt important, that they be able to say Adiiron right, if only to catch an avian by surprise.

They finished their stretches, Alix rolling up from between her legs in a hideous display of flexibility, to the sound of a great caw from the east.

Shielding his eyes, Bel looked to the sky, just catching a shadow against the sun.

"What is it?" Lena asked warily. Her eyes were lined and sunken, proof of his suspicions that she again wasn't sleeping. After so long in the dense northern forests, the treeless highlands made her anxious. Bel tried assuring her that anyone who could see them they could see right back—no surprises. Alix added that "*That lot isn't coming after us with all the broken bones between them.*" The comment only made Lena wince and go quiet for the afternoon.

Bel angled his right wing, feeling the dull pinch that he'd likely always have, but damn if it didn't feel incredible to be able to angle it at all. Light caught on the barbs, shimmering in the sun, and another caw echoed from high above.

The eagle began its descent.

"It's a volunteer," Bel explained.

Lena and Alix watched curiously as Bel stepped forward. He unrolled his sleeve, ready when wicked talons wrapped around his forearm.

The eagle was a large male, and Bel's outstretched arm bobbed under his weight as he twitched his mottled tail feathers and folded his gray wings. Eyes as dark and bottomless as the pits of Hadria blinked at him, and a crest of gray feathers stood up on the eagle's head.

"Thank you for coming, my friend," he said to it.

The eagle clacked his black beak, crest feathers rustling.

"Yes, I know it's too early for migration."

The eagle squeezed his taloned toes around Bel's forearm, one after the other.

"No, I'm not lost. Though the hunting is good here, many mice run through the grass."

The eagle ruffled his crest feathers in interest.

"I called because I need a message taken to the Hollow Mountain."

The eagle let out a shrill coo, angling his head to blink at Bel with those black eyes.

"It's important, my friend. It requires a fast, strong flier. Can you do it?"

A rumbling crackle reverberated in the eagle's chest, a bird sigh if Bel ever heard one.

He told the eagle to fly to Hadria, the Hollow Mountain, and seek out an old warrior named Eamon. Bel described Eamon's gray wings and crystalline eyes but warned that the message was for him alone, no one else.

"Tell him," said Bel, "to meet us at the Falls in the mountain in a fortnight."

The eagle shook out his tail feathers and whistled in assent.

"Thank you, my friend," Bel said and gave the eagle a few landmarks to look for where he'd spotted a colony of mice.

Pleased, the eagle cawed in farewell and opened his great wings. Bel threw the bird into the air, and with a mighty flap of his wings, the eagle ascended to the sky.

He watched the eagle fly in the direction of the mice warren for a moment before turning to find Lena and Alix staring at him oddly.

"What?"

"I'd heard stories of avians talking to birds," Alix said in awe. "I've never seen it before."

That's because it was a guarded secret amongst the feathered folk.

But Bel was curious. "What did it sound like?" he wondered. To avians, it was mostly like speaking with another avian; the words were the same, but somehow, it felt different to speak them.

The women frowned at him.

"Like chirping," Alix said in that tone that told him he'd asked something obvious.

"Hmm." That likely would look strange to an observer.

Folding her hands behind her back and wearing a mischievous expression, Alix strolled toward him.

"So, does this mean you're really just a big bird?" she joked.

Bel rolled his eyes. It was the eighth time they'd have this little bout, and judging by her smirk, Alix still enjoyed it just as much as the first.

"Those are just fanciful tales you humans tell to hide your jealousy." He fluffed his wings, feathers catching the light.

"If it has wings like a bird and flaps like a bird and chirps like a bird..." Alix rolled her wrist.

Bel sighed. Then he pounced for her, but the squire was slippery. He chased her around the crags, letting her slip from his grasp with whooping, maniacal laughs. He boxed her gently with his wings, making her snort, then let her swing up on his back and take him to the ground.

They play-fought the morning away, and Lena let them.

Bel teased and laughed with Alix, a welcome distraction from whatever awaited them at Hadria. The days of travel would eventually run out, and then there would be nothing to do but try their luck with the tunnels and his cousin's mercy.

The thought of making Lena and Alix so vulnerable made his guts clench, and he suspected it was one of the worries that stole Lena's sleep.

So he laughed with Alix, and when Lena ventured too close, he grabbed her, too. If only for a moment's distraction. Soon there would be none, and while he could, he wanted to make them smile.

22

Yvain's warm breath puffed against her chest as Lena stroked his forehead. His warm, musky smell was familiar and dear and dredged tears from behind the guard of her clenched jaw.

Pulling back, Lena wiped at her tears. Yvain nipped at her brow and hair with his velvet lips, as if trying to tell her it would be all right.

Two days ago, the grassy hills had given way to windswept crags that climbed to the skies. Jagged mountains rose from the earth like the spines of some long-dead behemoth, littered with dark rockfalls and sharp crevices that seemed to fall to the underworld itself.

It took a full day to reach the mountain that was Hadria, and though Lena had spent the better part of three years at its base, she didn't recognize it while they approached. From the northeast, the direction they came, the mountain linked with three other peaks to form a sort of rocky corona, crowned in light fog.

Bel had admitted his memory wasn't precise on the routes, but without realizing it until she was looking right at it, Lena was closer to Hadria's north side than ever before, despite many missions exploring secret passages inside. It took him little time to find a way inside, proving her suspicion that humans had no hope of infiltrating the stronghold without guidance.

The black, yawning mouth of the narrow cave was everything Lena had been dreading. All night, she'd kept the memories at bay of the missions she'd gone on with Arion and his guard, trying to find a way inside.

But in the gray light of morning, heartsick already to be leaving behind the horses, that gnawing dread and memories of dark, bottomless places wrapped tendrils of fear around her heart.

Lena petted one of the gray freckles along Yvain's muzzle.

"Take care of them," she whispered.

He rumbled in that equine way, another hot puff against her hand assuring her he would.

With one last pat, Lena pulled herself away.

Bel and Alix were similarly affected, eyes glassy and downcast as they hid their tack under extra blankets in a little hidey-hole between a cluster of boulders. It left the horses bare, like the wild cousins they'd spied on their travels through the highlands.

"*We'll come back for them,*" Bel had promised. "*We just have to get through first.*"

"*Still, we can't leave them saddled. Just in case.*"

Shouldering her overloaded pack, Lena looked back at their little herd. Between the two big males, they should be safe enough from predators. She swallowed hard, feeling as though she was forgetting something. She'd rarely been without a horse in her adulthood, and in their journeying here, Yvain and the horses had become as constant of companions as Bel and Alix. Sometimes Lena even preferred the horses because they were quieter. She'd rather leave her sword and weapons behind than Yvain, but where they went now was no place for a warhorse.

It's no place for a human, either.

Hence why she kept the weapons.

Giving her braid a tug, Lena stepped up to the narrow cave mouth. A dank breeze ruffled the hem of her overcoat.

A hand wrapped around hers and squeezed. She looked up at Bel to find his expression as somber as she felt. He didn't try to offer consoling smiles or platitudes, but he did lean down to kiss her brow. The simple touch bolstered her courage, and she squeezed his hand back.

On her other side, Alix blew out a breath. "Well, let's get going."

She handed Lena one of the torches she'd lit and Bel the other.

He took it wordlessly, and with a nod, he led the way inside the mountain.

———————— •• ◆ •• ————————

At first, the snaking tunnels leading into the bowels of the mountain were easy enough to navigate. Some places were wide enough that they didn't have to walk single-file, and on the first night, they made camp where the tunnel widened into a cavern. They laid their bedrolls amongst the stalagmites, the only sounds the soft echoes of the crackling fire.

Lena watched the shadows dance for hours, sleep refusing to come. Every flicker of the fire that was a little louder than the rest had her jumping in place, sure she heard more.

She fought the memories of other deep shadows, of scrambling through the mines with Arion and his guard. There'd been many missions to try and find the mines, but none had been as horrible as the last push, ordered by Artemian and finally carried out by Arion and his guard. He hadn't wanted to sacrifice the integrity of the army and so had sent them, a special force capable of slipping inside without the avians noticing.

She lay stiffly, remembering the harsh sounds of disembodied grunts and gasps as she and the other knights scrabbled through narrow chasms. She felt the odd, glowing lichen that grew in the dark slip across her palms, leaving a filmy wetness that made gripping rock difficult. The scrape of metal scratched at her ears, and she grew overwarm remembering the stifling stickiness of her sweat against her gambeson and mail.

All this she could manage if she lay still and quiet, listening to the soft breathing of Alix and Bel. But it was the darkest memories she feared most, the ones that were only flashes of light on steel plate, the feel of sweaty hands slipping through her own, the sound of Catrin's scream as she plunged beyond Lena's grasp, beyond saving, beyond the world of the living.

Catrin wasn't the first fellow knight they'd lost to the dark tunnels, but the woman had slipped through Lena's own fingers, had clutched at

Lena in her last moments. Lena had been the last thing she saw before endless darkness.

Lena's stomach flipped with nausea, and she forced herself up quietly to stoke the fire.

The routine of it settled her and her stomach a little, and with a few deep breaths, she regained her composure. If she stared at the shadows the fire cast a little too long, it was only because she was a human in avian territory. It didn't matter that she no longer wore Prince Arion's banner. She'd still be considered the enemy.

It was easier to think about what could go wrong in the future rather than what had gone wrong in her past, and Lena settled back down between Alix and Bel.

She'd barely pulled the blanket over her when feathers slithered up her body. She turned to find Bel watching her with heavy-lidded eyes.

Rolling closer, Bel slipped an arm around her, and Lena went happily into the curve of his body. His feathers rustled again, and then they were entirely cocooned under a wing.

The fire glowed dully through the warm canopy of feathers, and Lena took immediate comfort in the familiar smell of them, musky and a little nutty from the oil. There was just enough light to make out Bel's face, but these shadows didn't dance, just threw his striking features into soft relief.

"Pretend we're outside," he whispered, sliding his hand up her back to bury his fingers in her hair. Lena nearly moaned as he began gently working along her scalp, slowly massaging her head as he continued, "The stars are shining, and the moon is almost at its peak."

She settled into his words and illusion, tucking her face against his throat as he carded his fingers through her hair and told her how the fire would burn all night, keeping away any hungry beasts. She believed it when he told her how the sun would rise in the morning, all brilliant pinks and golds. He'd wake her to see it, he promised.

In the end, it was less his words and more the soft rumble of them against her lips that coaxed her, finally, to sleep.

The second day under the mountain reminded Lena very much of the dark weeks she'd spent crawling through other tunnels. The passages grew ever tighter, demanded odd angles and maneuvering to get through or around. Stalactites dangled like daggers above their heads, tiny water droplets clinging to their points. The water caught their torchlight in flickers, winking like will-o-wisps. A constant, damp chill clung to the air, making her hair cling to her neck.

The memories of the last time she'd done this were a hand on her throat, but the steady pace Bel kept assuaged the worst of her fears. His steps were sure as he led them through the labyrinthine tunnels; no fumbling in the dark dreading there was no solid rock to hold your next step.

That was, until their path widened and split into two passages, looming like darkened, unseeing eye sockets. The hand at her throat tightened, and the darkness seemed to bend and grow, yawning wide to devour them.

Bel stepped forward, looking between the two routes. He ruffled the feathers, as if to catch some unseen sense. She wondered what it would be to feel with wings, if the feathers were as sensitive as fingertips.

As the moments stretched and Bel remained quiet, she distracted herself by counting his feathers. But as the number grew higher, so did her quiet terror.

Bel's wings suddenly fluffed and gave a small flap before he folded them neatly against his back.

"It's that way."

"How d'you know?" Alix asked curiously.

"The air feels better that way."

Alix shrugged and followed Bel into the left passageway.

It took a moment for Lena to get her feet moving again. Mouth dry, she brought up the rear, telling herself that she didn't know what it was to feel with wings. That they must know something she didn't. But the hand at her throat gripped a little tighter, and all around, the shadows began to dance as if they too knew something she didn't.

When her knees became wobbly, she adjusted her stride, determined not to be the reason they stopped.

When her breaths went quick and shallow, she tried breathing through her mouth.

It worked for a time.

The day, or what felt like it must have been the day, stretched and narrowed all at once. There was a timelessness to the dark, not just the sleeping mass of ancient rock, but that anything or nothing could exist beyond the meager light of their torches. They were but a flicker of light in a dark, bottomless sea, a pinprick of time moving through endless vastness. There was no way of telling what lay behind or ahead of them, nor when or if the darkness would ever end.

Her pulse throbbed in her throat.

She barely heard it when Alix exclaimed in surprise at the dead end that emerged from the dark, but when she saw the solid rockface illuminated by their torches, that hand choked the breath out of her.

"Did we go the wrong way?" she faintly heard Alix ask over the ringing in her ears.

"No..." Bel said, running his hands along the rock.

The shadows nipped and flitted around him as he searched. At first she thought her mind played tricks when the fire of his torch swirled and bent, but then Bel saw it, too.

"Ah!" He stepped up on a boulder and angled his head into what had appeared to be merely a large crack in the rockface. But then his arm disappeared, followed by a shoulder and his torch.

"Thought so," he said, jumping back down. "Up we go."

Lena and Alix drew closer, raising their torches to reveal a hole in the rock leading up at an angle. There looked to be just enough room for one person to clamber up at a time, and the stone within had been worn almost smooth, as if many had passed this way before.

It didn't hearten her as Bel handed over his torch and shrugged off his pack. Tucking his wings tight to his back, Bel climbed into the hole, scrabbling blindly for purchase. She and Alix stood in nervous silence as he pulled himself up, his legs then feet then finally wing tips disappearing into the dark.

The ringing in her ears grew louder, nearly drowning out Bel's echoing call that he made it out, the hole was only about the length of him, and where the handholds would be. She watched her hands as if they were someone else's while she helped Alix pass up the packs and torches and then boosted the girl up.

Alix scrambled up easily, Bel there to hoist her out.

He reached down for her next, spanning almost half the distance. "Lena."

Swallowing on a dry throat, she passed up her torch first.

Her eyes watered as the dead-end cavern plunged into darkness. Through the tears, she stared at the flickering light above, silhouetting Bel's golden head.

"Your turn," he said gently.

She drew in a long breath that didn't reach her lungs. Her fingertips were cold, nearly numb as they slid into the handholds to pull herself up. She balanced her weight on her stomach, and pushed herself further along.

Her feet left the ground, dangling in the darkness. With her belly pressed against the rock, Lena couldn't draw a new breath.

Her heart thudded painfully in her chest and her vision swam. Bel's face above her blurred, shadows swirling around him until he was only a pair of haunting, inhuman blue eyes.

Her legs jerked against nothing—or was it something—more than just the wind—

Blood rushed in her ears, drowning out everything but the scream that tore from Catrin's throat—Lena could hear it, surrounding her, growing louder even as Catrin slipped away, into the darkness.

She kicked wildly, her fingers scraping to hold onto the rock—if she let go now, she'd fall—fall forever, into nothing, into darkness, never-ending—

Something brushed the crown of her head.

Lena reared back, yelping, tears soaking her cheeks.

"Lena!" he called. "Lena, it's me! Just reach out!"

She shook her head, not sure if she imagined the voice or the screaming or all of it. The rock bore down on her, squeezing her shoulders, and soon the mountain itself would come down on them, bury them under an eternity of rubble, never to be found again, lost like Catrin to the dark, crushed beneath all this rock and and and—

"Lena...!"

Something warm touched her head again, and Lena jerked up to see inhumanly blue eyes staring at her.

A hand lay palm-up just a few inches away, fingers splayed, reaching for her.

With a breathless sob, she clasped the hand, just wanting out. It grasped hers in a firm, warm grip, and then she was moving up, dragged along the smoothed rock until she was out of the hole, back into the firelight. She scrabbled out, legs wobbly, but hands were there before she fell.

She couldn't stop trembling, her hands shaking, and Bel bore her gently to the ground. Lena gasped and shuddered, unable to close her jaw as she took great gulping mouthfuls of air. Fat tears splashed onto the rock below her, but she couldn't cry, her lungs too needy for air.

A hand made soothing circles on her back, and Lena focused on the light pressure. When he spoke, she listened hard to his voice, using it to soften the sharp ring in her ears.

"It's all right, I've got you. Just breathe. Lena? Can you hear me? Breathe with me, one two three in...one two out...one...that's it...one two three in..."

She did what he said, forcing herself to breathe in and out in a steady rhythm. At first her lungs burned, needing more, but she kept his pace, and slowly, her heart began to calm and the spots faded from her vision.

He led her through the breathing, and after another moment she realized it was his breathing exercise, the one he did with his *ariant* forms.

It felt like a long time before she was truly ready to sit up, but when she did, his hands were there to support her without crowding. Her head swam, but as her blood settled back where it was supposed to be, she regained her balance and her senses calmed.

She blinked slowly at Bel and Alix hovering behind him. Their eyes were wide and uneasy, and the lines under Bel's told her she'd scared him.

Alix offered her waterskin, and Lena took it with hands that still trembled. The water was divine on her dry throat, but she didn't try more than a few sips in case her stomach rebelled.

Bel watched her closely with eyes darkened under a worried frown. When she capped the waterskin, he said softly, "Should we turn back?"

Yes! she wanted to scream but bit her cheek.

"No. I'll be fine." She didn't convince them or herself, but she said it anyway. They couldn't turn back now. And if she was honest…she didn't think she could get back in that hole just yet, even if it meant getting out from under the mountain.

Bel's mouth thinned unhappy, and when he stood and pulled Lena up after him, he held onto her hand and touched his forehead to hers. He ran his nose down one side of hers and up the other in a small *ashita*.

"We don't have to do this," he whispered.

"Yes, we do," she whispered back.

"Lena…"

"They're just memories," she told him as much as herself.

His throat bobbed as he swallowed, but finally Bel nodded. "It isn't much further to the Falls."

Rallying her courage, Lena set her shoulders. "Lead the way."

⸺⸺◆⸺⸺

In this new passage through the darkness, Lena finally saw evidence that Hadria had indeed once been a mine. The twisting, craggy tunnels carved by water and time soon smoothed to wider mineshafts carved with chisels and picks. Bel could stand to his full height and not need to tuck his wings.

The further in, the more intersections they passed, more and more mines linking up, all leading inwards. Old broken and abandoned tools littered the sides of the passage, and the air began to acquire a damp tang.

At first Lena thought it was her blood rushing in her ears again, and her heart lurched. She breathed in through her nose out through her mouth once, twice.

Bel's steps quickened, and Alix looked over her shoulder at Lena before trotting off after him. Lena kept her pace, matching it to her breathing.

Alix's exclamation came echoing back to her, and as Lena finally stepped out of the tunnel, she discovered the source of the noise.

A cavern wider and taller than any basilica stretched out before them, a cathedral of rock and minerals. At its center roared a great waterfall, a hundred feet high, spilling into a dark pool below. Water lapped at the edges of the pool, where it glowed an ethereal blue. Misty vapor filled the cavern, diffusing the eerie glow.

"The mountain has its own water," Lena said in wonder.

"An underground river," Bel confirmed, having to talk louder than the gushing water.

"We always wondered how..."

Bel nodded. "If my message got through, Eamon will meet us here."

They decided on a drier area to put down their supplies. As Alix and Bel explored the cavern and examined the glowing water, Lena made herself comfortable with a nest of blankets and kept watch. She didn't like setting up in so open a space, one that must have avians coming and going, but as the hours passed, no one disturbed them.

She tried to ignore the pounding of the water and how the mist sat on her skin in a damp sheen. Clammy from her panic in the hole, her skin was uncomfortable and sticky. Still, something about the darkness of the pool and ferocious roar of the Falls kept her stomach on the verge of queasiness, overriding her temptation to wash off, so she sat still and watched the shadows.

Alix jogged over to plop down beside her. She rifled through her pack before popping a hunk of jerky in her mouth. Lena declined when she offered one.

Bel knelt on her other side, his gaze careful as he looked her over.

"You all right?" he asked.

She managed a half-grin and nodded, about to answer *at least they were out of the tighter tunnels*, when something caught her eye over his shoulder.

For a moment, she thought her mind was playing tricks again, that between the mist and her memories, another panic was about to overwhelm her. She blinked, watching a small flame flicker from behind the waterfall.

"Bel..."

Seeing her wide eyes, Bel sprang up, wings spread to block her and Alix from whatever emerged from the shadows.

She watched his tense shoulders as they waited, silent, the mist churning and water roaring. Her mind gathered ideas of all the ancient creatures it could be, of the monsters that lived in deep holes and dark shadows and the pages of old books.

Alix's hand reached for hers.

Another moment passed, another, and then Lena thought she heard it—footsteps. Then...a sharp inhale.

Bel's wings shivered.

"Eamon."

23

The torch Eamon held clattered to the stone floor, sparks quickly snuffed in the mist. From the ground, the firelight cast stark shadows across Eamon's face.

It was an older face than Bel remembered, craggier. He'd heard it said that Eamon had been a handsome male in his youth, but as a boy, Bel always thought Eamon looked weathered. The lines beneath his gray eyes had always been there, though they'd deepened these past years. His dark hair was struck through with white, and his wings seemed more gray than the silvery hue he remembered.

But it *was* Eamon. And all Bel did was blink at him, his mouth unsure what to do.

Eamon swallowed thickly, his eyes moving over every inch of Bel and coming back for another pass, as if he couldn't quite believe what he saw.

"I didn't let myself hope. I didn't think it could be true, but I had to know..." The words hovered there between them, a divide, a distance. They were the first words Bel had heard in *alvani* spoken by an avian, uttered by the first avian he'd seen in years. There was a foreignness to them, or if not foreign than different, or perhaps just that they sounded off when they should've sounded right.

Eamon stepped over the discarded torch, closing the distance.

For the first time, Bel stared down into the eyes of his mentor, caretaker, and guardian—his *at'tan*. When he'd last seen Eamon, more than ten years ago, he'd yet to finish training or growing. Standing above the male who'd stood so tall in his life and memories had his chest aching.

Scarred hands reached for Bel, hesitating a moment, trembling in the space between them, before Eamon clasped Bel's face, his tears catching the firelight. "It is you. Arubel. *Ad'ana.*"

Ad'ana. Little hawk.

An angry knot pulled tight in Bel's throat. *Why didn't you come for me?*

The thought was unbidden and ugly, but it was there and wouldn't leave. He clenched his teeth, not sure what to do or say, not sure why, in this moment, when he should've flung his arms and wings around a male as good as family to him, his heart warred with joy and grief.

"I've missed you, *at'tan.*" He forced the words out.

Eamon shuddered, as if the words had reached out and touched him. "I've thought of you every day. You must know...if I could have, I..." He shook his head and pinched the bridge of his nose, stymieing the tears that gathered at his lashes.

What was there to say to that? That he forgave Eamon? That he understood? He didn't.

His tongue stuck to his palate, mouth dry as he clenched his teeth. Perhaps it was petulance, long ago buried when as a youth he'd realized no one would be coming to free him from Finhöln, rising now at the sight of the male who'd once been his everything as a fledgling. But Bel couldn't help the anger and tears that bubbled and boiled inside him; he couldn't help feeling like that youth all over again, lost, broken, abandoned.

He never wanted to be that boy again.

A hand touched his back, between his wing bases. Lena made small, soothing circles there, and finally, Bel swallowed the knot in his throat, down further into his chest where it clenched behind his heart.

Bel didn't mean for the dormant resentment to flare now, hadn't known it was even there anymore. He was glad to see Eamon, deeper down under the hurt, but it already wasn't a homecoming.

Not that he'd ever thought it would be, or that his kind would welcome him back like the Adiiron heir he truly was. He'd be foolish to hope that. Which was why he didn't.

When Bel still found nothing to say, Eamon grimaced. "What did they do to you, Arubel?"

"Kept me captive in a castle translating."

"Kept captive…" Eamon frowned over Bel's shoulder. "Your wing."

Bel only nodded. He didn't want pity.

He hadn't considered what it would mean to be in the presence of another avian like this—crippled but healing, intact but not the same. Between Lena resetting his right wing base and the stretches she put him through, it was on its way to healing fully. Whether or not that meant it could ever be what it was before being broken for years, he didn't know.

Yes, he'd flown, sort of, with Lena, and he was damn proud of it, too. And it might be impressive to a human, a creature of the land who could only dream of clouds and sun and sky—but to his kind, he was be broken.

"I came with information," he said, not wanting to talk about his wing or Eamon's regrets. "I need to see Dartegn." Not that he wanted to talk of his cousin, either, but they'd come all this way for a reason. He couldn't have put Lena through these days of darkness for nothing.

Eamon stared at him, as if he'd forgotten Bel came with a purpose.

"How are you here? How did you escape?"

"With help." He took a half-step to the side and pulled his wings in, revealing the two humans behind him.

Eamon reared back, hissing through his teeth, "*Valzan!*" *Enemy.* "You would bring them here?"

"I'm only here because of them."

The older avian's eyes narrowed, and he took another step back. Bel tensed when he palmed the hilt of the sword strapped to his hip.

Bel heard the soft creak of leather as Lena gripped her own hilt.

Holding up his hands, Bel explained, "They saved me. I wouldn't be here without their aid."

"They let you go and followed you back to Hadria. How do you know you haven't brought an army behind you?" Eamon demanded.

Bel flinched at the accusation. It wasn't that it was outlandish—if Lena had been anyone else, he might have suspected just such a plot. Eamon's immediate distrust, even in the face of the fledgling he'd raised, saddened Bel, as did the way the lines under his eyes deepened as he kept a defensive stance and looked between Lena and Alix.

The last ten years had been just as long for his old mentor. Bel had been away a long time, fighting his own kind of battle—but Eamon and the surviving avians had been living this war every day. Its toll was evident in the dark cast of Eamon's face, mouth a harsh, suspicious line.

"I know better than that. You taught me better than that, *at'tan*." He hoped the moniker might soften Eamon. He hadn't considered what they'd do if Eamon refused them; there was little chance of Bel making it inside Hadria, let alone to Dartegn, without avian help. "I trust them. And..."

Bel draped a wing across Lena's shoulders, Eamon watching on in choked horror.

"She is *c'vana*, Eamon. My *c'vana*."

Three pairs of eyes cut to him. Eamon and Alix knew its significance, and Lena had heard him say it before. The familiar word had the slightest frown creeping along Lena's face, and he could see the thoughts whirring behind her eyes, trying to figure out what he and Eamon said.

"She's a knight," Eamon hissed.

"Yes. And a good one. We wouldn't have made it here otherwise."

"It isn't possible. Not with a human."

"I don't want to argue with you. I only speak the truth. She is the best, most noble female I've ever met, and I chose her."

"You're an Adiiron!"

Bel bared his teeth. "Why should that matter?" *It hasn't before.*

Eamon wisely closed his mouth. What could he say to that? Nothing.

"*A ruttan zival'ana.*"

Bel looked at Lena in surprise. She gazed steadfastly at Eamon, her expression guarded and shoulders tense, but she'd made an effort to let go of her sword and remain in a neutral stance.

"*A ruttan zival'ana,*" she said again. *I mean no harm.*

Alix took a small step forward and repeated the words.

Eamon seemed struck by the sight of a human girl-child, his mouth and shoulders falling.

"We came, all of us," Bel said, banking his anger, "because we want this war to end. Enough have died."

"And you think you can end it by bringing humans here?" Eamon asked, though there was none of the previous heat.

"No. I don't know. We came with information. I don't know how useful it will be; that's for Dartegn to decide. All we wanted was to offer it to him in case it may help stop this."

That glassy, haunted look came to Eamon's eyes again. "I don't know that anything can stop it now."

"But does that make it not worth trying?"

Eamon sighed, looking away for a long time. Long enough that Bel began to worry he'd dragged Lena and Alix through the dark all for nothing.

"I'll take you to Dartegn," Eamon said finally, sounding as though he hadn't quite come around to the decision. "It would be best to go to him directly without being seen. And for the humans to stay behind."

"I'm not leaving them here," Bel growled, body rebelling at the very thought.

"Then send them back the way they came."

"What is he saying?" Lena murmured to him.

Bel canted his head to her, marking the growing worry creasing her brow.

"He'll take me but doesn't want to bring you and Alix."

Lena's lips pursed, and one cheek went concave as she chewed it. "I figured that's what would happen."

"I'm not leaving you here."

Lena's eyes pulled away from Eamon to look up at him, the green of them dark as emeralds.

"I don't want to be left," she agreed, "but...we could go back."

Bel sighed, frustrated to have the same argument with both her and Eamon. "You think you could find your way?"

Even in the dimness, he saw how her warm golden skin paled at the thought of heading back, alone. But he knew her answer before she said it because she was Lena.

"We'd manage. You need to go with him."

Bel pushed a lock of loose hair behind her ear with his fingertips. Her cheek was warm under his thumb and palm, and she gazed up at him with more determination than he knew she truly felt.

"I won't be parted from you," he said. "If Eamon won't take all of us, then we'll just tell him what we know and leave."

Lena gripped his wrist. "Your cousin needs to hear it from you."

Bel knew that. He also knew that Dartegn would rage at the sight of him and may never listen to what Bel had come to say. His presence would lend credence to what he said, but he didn't know if what they offered was worth opening old wounds nor if it could even help the avians end this war. He'd never sacrifice Lena as she sacrificed herself, especially not to the darkness under the mountain.

She was *c'vana*. Everything. She came first.

Bel looked up to find Eamon watching them carefully.

"You take all of us or none of us."

Eamon's mouth folded into an unhappy line. "Arubel..."

"She would let you leave her here, in the darkness. She knows how important this is and is willing to stay behind. But I'm not."

For a long moment, the only sound was the crash of the waterfall, reverberating in blue effervescence and long shadows.

Finally Eamon said, "I know," barely loud enough to hear over the roar.

Bel realized what he'd forgotten. It was Eamon who'd taught him both high and low Vagoran, so that he might understand what the humans shouted across a battlefield.

Another long moment passed before Eamon scooped up his torch from the ground and regarded them with resignation.

"No weapons on either of them. I'll take them now."

"All right."

"And I can't guarantee their safety. Or yours, if you defend them."

"I know," Bel said. "Just get us to Dartegn and we'll explain to him."

Eamon laughed once, humorlessly. "If he doesn't gut you first."

24

Bel had vague memories of the damp stairwell behind the waterfall. He'd been here once before, with Eamon, a bored fledgling with nothing to do while his brother inspected possible new mineral veins. He hadn't made it far, too unnerved by the deafening rush of water.

His ears ached, the tips nearly vibrating with the pounding rhythm of the Falls, amplified in the hollowed-out tube of the stairwell. They took the climb slowly, watching their footfalls, as the shallow steps led gradually up into the mountain.

The roar of the waterfall faded little by little, until the ringing of his own ears was the loudest noise. Still they climbed, Eamon leading the way and Bel bringing up the rear. By the time they made it to the mouth of the stairs, the ringing had faded, though an ache gathered in his thighs.

Eamon led them not into a rocky tunnel or mineshaft but an empty corridor, the stone worked to a high polish. The torches cast glistening shadows on the dark stone. Columns stretched in either direction, taller than the light could penetrate.

Bel remembered this place, too. It'd been a hub for the miners, all those years ago; a place to gather and plan and rest. To a younger Bel, it'd looked like a crypt.

Now, he was just glad for the open space. Bel extended his wings, shaking off the lingering dampness and stretching the tight muscles of his wing bases. When he closed them again, the feathers settled with a comfortable *snick*.

He caught Eamon watching him and couldn't help adjusting his stance, hiding his wings.

Wordlessly, Eamon led them to one of the stairways carved into the rock wall. Starting up the first step, he said in high Vagoran, "I suppose we'll find out if humans can climb a mountain in a day."

"We'll keep up," Alix replied, her face grim but determined.

Eamon considered her for a long moment before his gaze cut to Lena.

"We've come this far. We can't turn back now," said Lena.

"You may yet change your mind." He said it without heat or venom, casting a significant look at Bel.

When Bel said nothing in return, only nodded, Eamon began up the stairs, up into the stronghold of Hadria.

━━━◆◆◆━━━

They stopped three times before reaching the upper levels of the mountain. Only one was for rest, and they spent it easing their aching legs. Eamon looked on with mild disquiet as Lena led the three of them through a few stretches and again while he declined the hank of jerky Alix offered.

The first and third were to avoid the guards.

The first time was a near thing, Bel, Lena, and Alix scuttling into a dark threshold with moments to spare before two guards met Eamon on the stairway. Backs to the cold rock, they waited breathlessly as Eamon traded news with the warriors.

Over his thundering heart, he heard Lena beginning to breathe in that rhythmic way he'd done with her before. He slowed his own breathing to match.

Finally, the guards moved on with their rounds. Eamon whispered all was clear, and they began climbing again.

It wasn't until later, much later—though how late Bel couldn't say inside the mountain, where time was kept by torch and lantern oil—that another sphere of light descended the stairway.

"Who's there?" called the avian.

"Just Eamon."

"Your turn for the mines, eh?"

"Just came back from there."

"Anything?"

"As dark and drafty as it always is."

Without another threshold to duck into, and the avian close enough to hear their retreating footsteps, Bel took Lena's torch and ushered her and Alix behind him. He felt them twist and hunch against his back, making themselves as small as possible. Bel fluffed his wings, hoping the golds and whites would reflect the torchlight and conceal any legs or feet.

"Thought you said it was just you."

The guard held his torch higher as he approached, illuminating the handful of steps that separated him and Eamon.

Eamon looked at Bel over his shoulder before letting out a grumbling laugh. "Ah, I forgot. I've been on my own so long. I was just showing the new recruit the mines—what to look out for, where not to stick your nose."

The other avian drew another step closer, torchlight flickering off his battered bronze helmet. The worked metal of the decorative feathers at the sides had been beaten down or broken off. Bel realized the rest of his armor hadn't fared any better; his cuirass had a dent in the side that had to bother him if he breathed too hard, and his vambraces were too large, extra leather stuffed in the elbow.

"You're not in uniform, lad."

The warrior didn't look much older than Bel, but then again, yes he did. Even beneath the helmet, Bel saw the concave angles of his cheeks and bags weighing down his eyes. This male wore weariness like another piece of armor, hard and ill-fitting.

Still, his eyes were sharp as he assessed Bel. They were a shade of light blue, almost steely, and the hair and down at Bel's neck prickled to be looked upon by another avian. He'd nearly forgotten what it was like, the sharp cut of his own kind's gaze. He wondered what the other male saw—and hoped it wasn't too much.

"They didn't have anything for me yet," Bel replied.

"Haven't seen you around before."

Eamon nodded. "That's how green he is."

The guard cast Eamon an odd look, one that bore a significance Bel didn't understand. When he looked at Bel again, it wasn't with suspicion, but he seemed unconvinced.

"Just make sure he doesn't fall into a chasm. We need every sword arm available."

"Survived his first descent. I call that a success," said Eamon. "Don't let us keep you."

The guard nodded but didn't make to move, so Eamon took the choice from him. Drawing alongside Bel, they made room for the guard to pass on his way down.

Bel eased back, crowding Lena and Alix into the wall behind them. They stayed perfectly still as the guard passed, and Bel resisted reaching for Lena's hip.

Eamon exchanged a few more jibes with the guard until his torchlight faded and finally disappeared around a bend.

Still they waited, listening for any approaching footsteps, before Lena and Alix emerged from behind Bel.

"He's suspicious," Lena stated, not even needing to understand what was said.

"We need to find Dartegn before he finishes his rounds," said Eamon.

"Won't people be happy it's Bel?" asked Alix. "I understand not so much for us." She gestured between her and Lena. "But Bel's a prince. Why not tell them?"

"I haven't been a prince, or anything to them, for a long time," was the only answer Bel had. He didn't know how any avian would react to his name and sudden return. Likely with disbelief. "*Who?*" they'd probably say. He'd spent so little time outside the Mount or Maddok's retinue as a fledgling; he'd heard avians exclaim before that they'd completely forgotten about the spare prince. He'd barely warranted remembering then; he doubted he would now, after all that had happened.

But Dartegn would know. He would remember. And Bel counted down the moments with dread, feeling like the rock that fell from the mountain, every moment plummeting to an inevitable, disastrous crash that would shatter everything.

———————◆———————

They refueled their torches what must have been hours later, when Bel swore the corridors were beginning to seem familiar, or if not then like something he could remember, or at least like something he could have seen once, in his life before.

They climbed but didn't pass another guard. Nor anyone at all. Up they went, passing empty chambers and corridors, all silent, concealed in shadow. No sconces illuminated their way, no signs of inhabitance crossed their path.

"Why aren't there more patrols?" Bel quietly asked Eamon.

His old *at'tan* peered at him with a weary gaze. "It's all we have."

Not knowing what to say, not wanting to comprehend what that meant, Bel could only shake his head. He caught Lena gazing at him over her shoulder, her mouth a thin, grave line. She looked exactly as he felt— like the higher they went, the closer they came to a truth more horrible than Bel could ever have imagined.

———————◆———————

For all that the winding corridors and undulating stairways were cut and cobbled from the same dark gray stone, Bel knew when they approached the summit. Something to the air changed, a tinge of freshness that hadn't been there before. The air felt lighter, and the corridors looked it too, lit by the occasional sconce.

The first bubble of warm light surprised Bel, accustomed now to the dimness of their spiraling ascent. His pulse thrummed, realizing that, yes, they had to be getting close.

Before long, Eamon instructed Lena and Alix to put their cloaks on over their packs with their hoods up. It wouldn't fool anyone for long, but having at least the look of something on their backs offered the brief chance of not raising suspicion.

His legs cried with soreness, his wings trembled with anticipation, but Bel climbed to the top of Hadria, a dreadful excitement gripping his heart like a fist.

Finally, the empty corridors gave way to real signs of the city Hadria truly was. The lower levels of mines, cisterns, storerooms, stairwells, passages, and pits sat at the base like a bed of snakes knotted together for winter. Nearing the summit, the warren of corridors widened into grand passageways, their thresholds limned in peaked arches. The stones were smoothed, not just by time but craftsmen, with intricate carvings of tales and sagas at shoulder height.

They followed a wending passage up, Alix shadowed by Eamon's body and wings and Lena obscured behind Bel's. Though the hall was ornate and large enough to walk side by side, it was a back way up to the Round, the top of Hadria. The main procession way had room for ten columns of avian warriors to march in formation and another ten to fly above them. Bel remembered walking that route as a fledgling, flanked by his brother's personal guards. It'd seemed big enough to be a basilica itself, but compared to the real heart of Hadria, it was a mere hallway.

Bel's heartbeat quickened as Eamon's pace slowed.

They were here.

Lena's silent gasp ruffled the down at his neck.

Bel stepped cautiously past the last archway, out into the Round.

For days the rock bore down on them, but here, it gave way to a vast open space, large enough to house the Mount in Aeriand. Birds and avians alike soared through the air, catching the shafts of light let in through the canopy of rock above.

Hadria had begun life as a volcano, spewing fire and ash. It wasn't until long after it finally grew quiet and cold that the first miners had arrived to chisel away at the rich deposits left behind. For centuries the avians had mined, carved, and explored Hadria, shaping its stones into a great stronghold.

The Round was hewn from the massive caldera formed by the last great eruption and final collapse and death of the fire mountain. The flat center, the arena, had been smoothed and cleared, leaving an expansive open area to gather. At the eastern edge, two statues had been carved into the rock, standing ten avians tall, one holding a sword and the other a war hammer. The weapons crossed over the dark mouth of a chasm as deep as the mountain itself. The Pit, where the arena dropped down past the mines and bedrock into primordial shadow.

At the northern side, five shallow circles of stacked stone, each smaller than the last, formed steps to a platform for the avian sovereign. A great beam of light shone directly before the platform from the oculus high above. When his ancestors had begun building here, they smoothed away the rough edges of the caldera and brought the best stone from the mines far below, great blocks with diamond dust and amethyst shards to catch the light. A rounded dome now capped the caldera, the open oculus at its center letting in a pure column of light that illuminated the whole space.

Archways in the dome led to shaded arcades and porticos, outside spaces for landing and perching. Gardens and small orchards grew on the southern and western sides, and mirrors caught light to reflect back into the Round.

Into the original rock of the caldera itself, rooms, dwellings, and passages had been hewn. Hundreds of archways and thresholds had been carved into the western walls, spilling out onto dozens of stepped terraces that lined the Round in concentric semicircles like great steps that all led down to the open arena. The drop from one terrace to the next was twice the height of the tallest avian, but small stairs linked the levels.

A hive. That's what Hadria was.

Or, at least, should have been.

Stepping further onto the stone terrace, Bel focused on the far side of the Round, trying to count avians. There was a small squadron high above, likely about to leave through an opening in the dome. Several groups milled about on the arena, and a handful more came and went through various passages.

They were here, his kin. But the air didn't whoosh with the rush of hundreds of wings, the light didn't flash as hundreds of avians flew past, so few voices filled the great open space.

They were here, but the Round was eerily quiet.

His gaze cut to Eamon, and the older warrior only looked back with grim affirmation.

"Dartegn will be here somewhere," Eamon said. "There are no attacks planned today."

Eamon headed for one of the small stairs leading down to the next terrace.

Bel looked back to Lena, and she took the hand he offered.

She watched Eamon's retreating back with a small frown. "He knows where to find your cousin?"

"He said Dartegn's somewhere here."

Lena's lips thinned as she took another look at the vast Round. "Fantastic."

When they got to the stairs, Alix groaned. "Not more…"

Bel threw her an apologetic grimace over his shoulder.

She sighed and trudged down the steps.

Lena followed, reminding Alix to "Stick close."

They snaked down the terraces, catching the nearest stairs down to the next. They hadn't begun on the highest level, but it was slow going working their way down. The trek felt more like a labyrinth than the maze of mines they'd already traversed.

Perhaps it was because it was the end of the journey—the last steps always felt longer with the impending end. Perhaps it was that, unlike in the mines, where ahead was only the circumference of their torchlight, here Bel could see what they approached.

An old pain, one Bel hadn't felt since Finhöln, gripped him between the ribs. It was that gnarled knot of grief, the scar tissue that sat on his heart, pulling at him tighter with every terrace, every step closer to—

"There," Eamon said, nodding to the far side of the Round.

Bel looked where Eamon indicated and watched as, a terrace down, nearing the soaring archway of the main promenade, came Dartegn and his guard.

Even flanked by warriors clad in the same armor, Bel found Dar in a moment. His black wings and hair cut a striking contrast against the silver plates armoring his limbs and chest. Even from this distance, Bel marked the scowl shadowing Dartegn's face, his dark eyes cutting across the Round in a sweep.

He was bigger than Bel remembered, chest and shoulders wide with hardened muscle. He was a proper warrior, just as he'd always wanted to be, training long into the night when the other fledglings retreated happily to bed. All so he could serve alongside his cousin, his king.

But now a gold circlet ringed his head, marking him as different from the warriors at his back.

Maddok's crown.

Bel tried to swallow but nearly choked, his throat closed up with sorrow.

The hand he held squeezed his, and he felt Lena's chest press into his arm, leaning close so her words were only for him.

"One foot in front of the other. That's all you have to do."

He realized they'd come to a stop, Eamon and Alix looking back at him from a few paces ahead. Lena stood beside him, back straight, chin tilted up with resolve. Not tugging him along, not hurrying him.

He squeezed her hand back and did as she said, one foot, then the other, again, until they were walking.

But Bel didn't feel as though he walked. It didn't feel like flying, either. Once he'd started again, the steps rushed past him, as if he didn't move his own feet.

Freefalling. That's what it was, his stomach lodged up in his throat.

They followed the curve of the last terrace, Eamon keeping their pace steady, unhurried but determined—neither of which Bel felt.

They approached the wide opening from the promenade, and

Eamon picked up speed to intercept Dartegn, headed for the wide steps down onto the arena floor. He raised his arm to draw attention, to—

"My king! A word—I bring important news."

Dartegn stopped but turned only his head to find who'd spoken. Eamon drew closer and bowed.

Dar nodded in acknowledgement. "Captain."

Eamon hesitated, perhaps hoping Dartegn would come to him, or at least closer, a few steps away from his warriors. When the king made no move, Eamon drew closer.

"Get behind me," Bel murmured through numb lips.

Lena and Alix moved swiftly, disappearing behind his wings.

"My lord," Eamon was saying, "I bring..." He huffed and shook his head. What could he say?

I bring your cousin, back from the dead. The one you forsook. The one whose crown you now wear.

Eamon side-stepped, gesturing behind him. Ushering Bel out from the shadows.

Bel came slowly, to not startle the guards, to give Lena and Alix time to move with him, to give himself time to wrestle down the well of bitterness and joy that vied in his throat.

Dartegn's scowl fell away, his dark eyes glittering as he watched Bel step forward and push the hood from his head.

Bel didn't know which was greater, the desire to hit Dartegn—*how could you lose Aeriand, why didn't you come*—or to embrace him—*you're alive, kin, cousin.* The resentment in him was strong, the old scars on his back from the dozens of lashes prickling in a phantom sting, but the relief was stronger.

Because here he was, Bel's cousin and kin. A fixture of his life before, as tempestuous as a thundercloud, as brave as a wild stallion protecting his herd. He still had that one freckle just below his left eye; his nose was still a little crooked from when he'd broken it in a bad, drunken landing when he and Maddok were boys. The face that stared back at him was different, squarer, scarred, but those eyes—Bel could never forget the dark flurry of them, as black as night and deep as Hadria.

Dar staggered forward, disbelief slackening his jaw.

"Maddok..."

Bel's stomach lurched.

He wished it could've been Maddok that Eamon brought back from the dead, but the world wasn't that kind.

All he could do was shake his head.

Bel watched recognition register in Dartegn, that glimmer of hope in his eyes and in Bel's heart chased away by devastation.

"You..."

Dartegn straightened, and Bel could almost see him harden. The scowl returned but was worse than he ever remembered, not just a thundercloud but a tempest itself, churning and violent.

"Prince...Arubel?" asked one of the guards in disbelief.

Bel kept Dar's gaze as he replied, "Yes."

The warriors were too well trained to shuffle or murmur, but they traded looks and stole others at their king.

"You were supposed to be dead," said another.

"No." What else could he say?

Dartegn's dark gaze cut to Eamon, sharper than a blade. "What have you done?"

Before Eamon had raised Bel, he'd been *at'tan* Dartegn and Maddok. Dar's scowl didn't move Eamon.

"Your kin has returned," he said, his tone just above scolding.

"I didn't agree to any trade."

He'd known all along. He'd been offered and refused.

Bel bared his teeth in a brutal grin, advancing on Dar. "You get me for free, I'm afraid."

His cousin sneered. "What trick is—?"

"Human!"

A gauntleted hand snatched Dartegn back into the safety of armored bodies, and suddenly the Round echoed with ringing steel. The warriors drew their blades, flowing into formation with Dar at the center.

"No!"

Bel fell back to Lena and Alix, angry that he'd left them vulnerable. Lena had an arm crossed in front of Alix, drawing the girl behind her, and the other raised in submission.

A half-dozen warriors advanced, blades first.

Bel threw his right wing around Lena and Alix, drawing them into his side.

"You've brought humans here?" Dartegn hissed. "Traitor!"

Bel snarled back, pulling the females tighter to him.

Eamon put himself between the warriors and Bel, hands up and splayed. "Dartegn, my king, please, you must—"

"You've done enough, Eamon," Dartegn growled. "Take them."

25

Alix watched Lena pace the darkness of their room, making a disgruntled noise every time she walked too fast by the candle and sent the flame dancing and flickering. It was their only light in the windowless, rough-hewn room they'd been deposited in.

Lena supposed she should be grateful. It could've been a literal hole in the ground. Or a bottomless pit. At least this had a door, a candle, a bed, and a chair.

Alix had claimed that chair almost immediately, slumping off her weary feet with an appreciative groan. They'd both looked to the door after stumbling inside, listening with trepidation as a bolt on the other side slid home, locking them in. But then Alix had stretched out, making herself comfortable.

Lena had kept at the ready since she and Alix were left here with one candle and no Bel. Was the bed a siren's song that called to her every time she glanced at it? Assuredly yes. Was she fantasizing about sitting down and taking the luxurious pleasure of not being on her feet? Most definitely.

Her legs shook with exhaustion from their climb, and the strain of the mines and confrontation with King Dartegn, but Lena kept vigil. When her legs grew too tired to pace, she locked her knees just so and was able to stay upright. When she had a little energy, she paced.

"How're you still on your feet?" Alix wondered after a while.

Perhaps it was silly or foolish to Alix, but Lena knew once she was down, it'd be a struggle to get back up. And she wouldn't be caught down when an avian came through that door.

It was all the defense she'd have when it happened. They'd both been stripped down to shirts and trous, even had their boots and vambraces taken. The cold of the stone seeped through her wool socks, and a lingering damp had her wishing she'd grabbed her thicker coat before they took away her pack.

After...well, she couldn't say precisely how long, about an inch of candle, her legs finally couldn't pace anymore. Setting a wide stance, Lena balanced on the balls of her feet and focused on the door, ignoring the way her knees knocked.

"Where do you think Bel is?" Alix asked.

Lena looked over at her, a little surprised she hadn't dozed off. Alix could sleep anywhere, and the exhaustion was apparent in her sunken eyes and limp curls.

"I don't know," was all Lena could say. She wished she knew. She wished she was there with him, wherever it was.

"You don't...think they'd hurt him, do you?"

"I don't know." She didn't know enough about avian history to say whether politics often led to bloodshed. Vagoran history was full of aunts and uncles slaying or being slain by nieces or nephews, usurpers and true heirs both.

"They don't look much alike. Bel and the king."

"No."

Only one of them had the storied look of an Adiiron, and it wasn't the one wearing a crown. Her stomach churned remembering the dark wells of King Dartegn's eyes and the vast pain behind them. Their arrival had torn away the scab of a deep wound, and it wasn't that humans were in Hadria.

King Dartegn had seen a ghost.

The chair creaked as Alix leaned forward, elbows on her knees and head in her hands.

"Can you believe the size of this place?" Lena asked, realizing the girl needed to fill their dark hole with more than meager candlelight.

Alix snorted ruefully. "King Artemian would shit himself if he knew."

Lena choked on a laugh. "None of us fighting down there could've imagined it was *this*."

"What'd you imagine?" Alix peered at her with the hint of a smirk. "It was just one big bird's nest?"

Lena blushed.

Alix snickered.

"You thought Bel would have a beak," Lena retorted.

"Yeah, but—"

The bolt shrieked and the room flooded with light.

Lena moved blindly, putting herself between Alix and the open door. She took a defensive stance, feeling naked without her armor.

Her forearms were wrenched forward, and within a breath, the cold grip of iron shackles encircled her wrists. Lena shuddered from the feel of them, one she'd vowed to herself to never feel again.

She'd stood before King Artemian like this once, shackled and demeaned.

The metal wasn't uncomfortable, but the three inches of iron did encase her wrists in a firm grip. A short length of chain connected the shackles, enough to hold her arms down somewhat naturally, not enough to throw over someone's head and choke them with.

"You'll have to make it tighter," Alix chirped at the avian shackling her. "Slim wrists."

The guard grunted but didn't seem to tighten the metal much more.

Another guard entered to light more candles and one of the lanterns hung near the door. Then, as quickly as they'd entered, the guards left.

Blinking against the sudden brightness, Lena saw a shadow fall across the doorway. Great black wings consumed the light like the darkest part of the night sky.

Her limbs trembled with old memories, of days past when those wings had been harbingers of destruction and death. She swore she heard the heavy *thud* of avian arrows sinking through flesh and the screams of her comrades echoing behind her. Her arms twitched, wanting to raise a shield that wasn't there.

The avian king ducked his dark head to enter the little cell.

Backlit from light outside the cell, King Dartegn loomed over them, his features nearly hidden by shadow. The blood drained from Lena's face, leaving her cold as she looked upon the face that haunted the nightmares of every soldier and knight camped at the foot of Hadria. The Black Blade. The Shadow. The Scourge. That's what they called this black-winged wraith who darted through the air almost too quick to see.

He'd ruled for nearly as long as his predecessor, Bel's brother, a tumultuous ten years filled with nothing but battlefields and wargames. Those bottomless black eyes, with their hard, dangerous glint, were far older than the face they sat in.

Before her stood the greatest enemy of Vagora, the fox who'd outlasted every hunter, every trap laid for him. He may have lost the battle for Aeriand, but he may yet win the war.

He wasn't quite as tall as Bel, but his shoulders were wider, his chest and legs thick with slabs of muscle. King Artemian would go apoplectic knowing she was within striking distance of Dartegn Adiiron, one theoretical dagger jab away from turning the tide.

Her fists clenched, wanting to raise a sword that wasn't there. She couldn't help it, the years of screams and wails of the dying ringing in her ears.

Those dark eyes marked the minute movement, eating away at her under slashing brows.

Her pulse beat a thready, rapid tattoo in her neck, and she worked to loosen her tensed muscles. Dartegn Adiiron had been her enemy a long while, but it remained to be seen what he'd be to Bel. So she swallowed her memories and straightened from her stance to face the avian king.

He watched her for a long moment, waiting for her to squirm. She held his gaze, keeping in her terror by sheer will.

Finally, in a rumbling voice that could fill a mountain, he said in *al-vani*, "I'm told you understand our language."

"And I know you understand mine," she bluffed in her own.

King Dartegn tipped his head back slightly, looking down his nose.

"Who sent you here?" he asked in high Vagoran, his voice a tightly coiled thrum of anger.

"I came with Bel," she replied. "Where is he?"

The king's nostrils flared. "I am the one asking questions, human. Who sent you?"

"No one. We came with Bel. To help."

"Help? You want to help, human?" He took another step closer, a shadow looming over her. "Then tell me how to defeat the army below. Tell me how to crush them."

Lena swallowed on a dry throat. "I won't help you kill my kind. We came here to help if we could. To bring Bel home."

"Out of the goodness of your hearts? After keeping him for ten years?"

"So you knew he was alive."

He bared his teeth in a snarl. "And how did you meet my cousin? What brought your paths together?"

Lena worked to keep the frown from her face. Given the time she and Alix had been in locked away, it stood to reason Bel had already been asked these questions, too. She dreaded telling the avian king this truth, but she dreaded the consequences of their stories not matching more.

"I was sent to guard him," she said.

"So my cousin brings his captor and you both assume I will meet it with good will?"

"No. We never assumed that."

The king snorted and took a step forward. With his bulk and wings flared behind him, he took up most of the front half of the room and blocked much of the light from outside.

Lena held her ground, saying through her dry throat, "He came to speak with you about important things."

"Such as?"

"That's for him to say." Lena knew it had to come from Bel, that anything she might say wouldn't be believed. And more, he needed to do this, for his people and for himself. Whether or not they believed him.

"What he says is that you are *c'vana*."

Lena blinked at the sudden turn. "Yes."

"And you know what this means?"

"That he loves me."

"And you love him in return?"

"Yes. Very much."

King Dartegn sneered. "She says with no love in her voice."

Lena's jaw ticked. "Would it matter if I collapsed to the ground and wailed and beat my breast proclaiming my love? Would it sway you? Or would you feel even more confident that I'm lying?"

"It would show me how much skill you have. All that time spent captive, my poor cousin must have been weak enough to fall for your lies. Or is it just that human cunt is better than nothing—"

"Fuck off with that!" roared Alix, leaping to her feet.

King Dartegn's eyes snapped to her, but nothing else.

"She's my squire," Lena hurried to explain. "And you won't harm her."

That dark gaze flitted back to her, and Lena clenched her teeth. Her cheeks still burned with his ugly accusation, but she understood that in an interrogation, anything would be seized upon, most especially her upset.

"I am the lord of this mountain, human knight," King Dartegn said in a voice so dangerously low, it was more vibration than words. "I will say who lives and who is thrown into the Pit."

His eyes flicked to Alix again, and Lena couldn't help shifting her weight, getting that much more in between them. When he looked back to Lena, his cold, expressionless face terrified her. "What's to stop me from throwing that one off the mountainside? You say you'll give me nothing, so why should I let you live?"

"Because then you'd truly be the monster my people believe. I didn't say I'd give you nothing, just that I wouldn't help you kill my kind. But if you harm her, you'll get nothing from me but a blade in your gut."

"Careful with the threats you make, human," he said. "You'll remain here while my cousin's mess is sorted." With a snap of his finger, another guard stepped into the small room, leaving little space or air left.

Lena worked to keep the surprise from her face to see a female avian beneath the warrior's helmet. Crystal blue eyes stared dispassionately at her, and what would've been a plush, feminine mouth was set firmly, a scar bisecting the right side.

"We shall see how you enjoy being *guarded*, human knight," said King Dartegn, using the word she had before. "You won't eat, sleep, or breathe without Phaedra seeing it. And the moment you try, the instant you're a threat to my people, I will throw you both into the Pit." He loomed closer with every word, taking up her vision and all the air in the small chamber. "It's a long way down, knight. But I will happily wait to hear the sound of you breaking apart at the bottom."

And with a sweep of cloak and wings, King Dartegn quit the chamber, the female guard on his heels. The smack of the door reverberated against Lena's ears.

It wasn't the door or the bolt grating into place she heard in her head, though. No, it was Catrin's scream as she fell, slipping through Lena's fingers.

But it wasn't Catrin's face she saw in her mind.

Breathing through her nose to quell the bubbling nausea, all Lena could hear and see was Alix cast into darkness, falling down a chasm with no end.

Panic clutched at her chest. Goddess, what had they done?

26

Bel chewed the tasteless bread, grimacing when it was time to swallow the dry mash. He washed it down with the last of the water he'd been given before Dar and his councilors left him in this room alone.

There'd been something of an argument over what to feed him. Dartegn hadn't wanted to waste rations on him at all; several councilors had seemed agitated at the idea of letting an alleged Adiiron go hungry; and Bel had attempted to offer eating his own food, secured in the pack he'd had taken away from him hours ago.

That option had been summarily denied. He was being kept from Lena and Alix as well as his own supplies, as if anything that might have touched the humans could be influencing him. As though time apart could "*Maybe bring you to your senses,*" as Dar had put it.

A ration of hardtack had been found for him as a compromise. "*And be grateful for it,*" Dar said as if it were a threat before sweeping from the room.

As he waited in the quiet, dim chamber, Bel wished he'd saved another sip of water. His voice had rubbed raw hours ago, repeating his story again and again for Dartegn and the councilors. They asked him different questions that had the same answer, thinking to catch him in lies.

"*You had free run of the castle?*"

"*Why didn't you escape?*"

"*How did you not escape?*"

"What kept you there if you could run?"

"Didn't you want to escape? Didn't you try?"

They wanted to know how he'd spent his ten years of captivity. Bel still prickled at their apathetic, even disapproving faces at his answer of, *"Yes, I tried. It never ended well. So I kept out of the way and survived."* As if there was more he could've done. As if they expected more from the broken, beaten fledgling they'd left to rot there.

There should've been something else, he should've done something *more*; he saw the thought in all their eyes as they listened to his relatively short tale of his ten years. There was little else to say about what he did.

Those ten years were a blurry swathe, full of nothing worth remembering. He'd numbed himself, detached from the world and any life he'd known, because it was the only way to also numb the grief, pain, and utter loneliness of his captivity. If he'd tried to fill those days with anything but mindless survival, the boredom would've eaten him alive.

He'd survived. That was all.

Bel hadn't come alive again until a few years ago, and even then, it'd been a slow thaw. Spring always came slowly to Finhöln, and in picking up his *ariant* training again, he'd found that small spark to keep on going —purpose. When Aeriand fell, Bel couldn't abide doing nothing anymore.

And Lena...Lena was his summer, his sun, his star.

But they wouldn't understand. *Why didn't you escape once you found out, then? Why didn't you come to us sooner?* they'd ask.

There wasn't a way to answer without sounding like the scared fledgling he'd been.

Because there was so much more to say about what had been *done to* him. But none of them asked. None of the denizens of avian society, handpicked by the king himself, a few of whom Bel faintly recognized from Maddok's time on the throne, asked what the humans had done to Bel. He could tell them in great detail about every lash stripe and burn scar and pockmark that patterned his skin.

But they didn't ask. And Bel didn't tell them.

He knew what they'd think, even if they didn't say it.

The price paid for failing the king, for failing his own brother. For living when he should have died.

Cosmic justice. His due.

Bel scrubbed his hands over his face then tugged his fingers through his hair. The sharp ache as his knuckles met resistance from the tangles centered him for a moment.

Dartegn's interrogation had dragged and stretched for hours, though precisely how long he couldn't tell. He marked time by the growing ache in his chest at being separated from Lena. His questions over her and Alix went unanswered when he'd managed to fit them in between rapid demands.

He had to hope Dar wouldn't harm them or worse, not when they were such an anomaly and possible opportunity. They would keep Bel compliant. And Lena was a potential font of information.

Not that Bel ever saw her breaking, no matter the interrogation method.

Bel stood from the stool he'd been sat in upon arriving in this chamber, perturbed at the thought of what Dar would do if he truly wanted information from Lena. Dar had always had a temper, and there was something about him now.

There was a jaggedness to Dartegn that made Bel uneasy, like overworked metal that had gone brittle. He'd never relished the idea of throwing both himself and Lena on the mercy of Dar, and not knowing if their gamble would work, not knowing how or where she was, grated against him like sand.

Agitation dogged him, and he set to pacing the long chamber.

It was a meeting room of some kind. Not grand enough to be the actual council chambers where Maddok would—where Dartegn would hold council, plan attacks, and hear grievances. Still, it was a fine chamber, the stones smoothed to a high polish and the sconces finely tooled. A long table had been carved from a single block of obsidian, ringed by a dozen backless chairs of a dark, rich wood.

On the far wall, etched into the rockface, was the story of the slave uprising that marked Hadria's beginnings as an avian stronghold. Carved to varying depths, the effect cast light and shadow over the reliefs, making them look as if they marched in a great mass for the summit, where the slavelord and freedom waited. In the far corner the slavelord stood, his whip raised. He'd been depicted as avian, telling Bel that this was an old carving. Earlier stories were mixed on whether the avians had been slaves to humans, other avian flocks, or perhaps one of the extinct races. Orcs, possibly. But as the centuries wore on, further from the event and the truth, the story had made the slavelord human, sometimes even a king of a fallen human kingdom.

The *click* of the door drew Bel from the relief and its distraction. He put the long table between himself and the door and folded his wings behind him again.

Dartegn entered with as much force as he'd left with, making Bel wonder if he always swept into rooms, all fluttering wings and severe glower. The impact it had on Bel was less from the intensity of all that movement and more the sudden sight of a cousin he hadn't laid eyes on since his life before.

After years apart, the sight of Dar was a shock. A bittersweet moment of recognition. A face so familiar and yet so changed. A face he wanted to hit more often than not.

That hadn't changed.

A handful of guards and councilors entered behind him, but not as many as before. And this time, Eamon was allowed into the room, coming to stand quietly in the corner.

He met Bel's questioning gaze with only the thinning of his mouth.

What does that mean?

"Where were you born?" Dartegn asked.

Bel frowned, glancing at Eamon.

"He can't help you," Dartegn snapped. "Answer the question."

"In Aeriand," said Bel, turning his frown on his cousin. "Just like you."

"Yes, but where?"

"In the Mount, inside Queen Immora's chambers. From the queen's own womb, if you want to be that precise."

The few councilors grumbled, as if the mention of the dead queen's womb and Bel coming from it were somehow in bad taste.

"Who were your tutors? Starting from the earliest."

Bel rattled off the few names, finishing with, "And Eamon from then on."

"When was your first flight?"

"I was twelve. Not that you'd know or remember. You weren't there."

Dar bared his teeth in a snarling smile.

What was his favorite sweet as a fledgling? *Candied nuts.* What bedtime tale did he have his nursemaid tell him the most? *Yvain and the Green Dragon.* What did his father call him? *Arubel or boy.* How many freckles did Maddok have on his left cheek? *Six.*

"And what about this?" Dartegn pointed to the ghost of a scar on his cheek.

"I was playing with my first bow and the arrow got away from me," answered Bel. He took a step toward Dar, tiring of these questions. Why ask him to prove his identity now? Had his account of his captivity been so lackluster and underwhelming that they now doubted it could truly be Arubel Adiiron returned?

He touched the faint scar and bump on the upper ridge of his own nose, where the skin had split apart and bone beneath broken.

"And this I got when you pushed me on the stairs to the kitchens. It needed four stitches."

Dar tipped his head back, peering down his nose. Except Bel was a little taller now, a fact he took great pleasure in when he'd realized. He stood before Dartegn now, stance wide and expression bored. They could play this game for as long as Dar wanted, but it wouldn't change anything.

The chamber fell silent waiting for the king's next question. The councilors looked on with a sort of interested dread, a quiet chorus behind their king. The only movement came from Eamon, his eyes darting between Bel and Dartegn.

Bel could read his expression now, meaning all too clear. *Don't antagonize. Don't be stupid.*

"The human females..."

Bel worked to keep the emotion from his face, but his wings bristled and everyone saw it.

Dar smirked, and Bel wanted nothing more in that moment than to wipe it off his face with a fist.

It wasn't the first time Dar brought up Lena and Alix. They'd been one of the first topics, a source of fear and fascination both that demanded answers. That Lena was his *c'vana* had been met with a horrified silence. Then questions to determine if he was insane or deviant.

"Where are they?" Bel asked. Again.

Dar ignored it. Again. "The knight was much less forthcoming than someone in her position should be. Though, I suspected nothing less from a human like her. What I can't understand is the girl."

"Lena is her *at'tan*. Alix is loyal to her and my friend. She wanted to help us."

Dartegn paced away, his lips curling up in a malicious grin. Bel braced himself, but he still wasn't prepared for the ugliness that came out of Dar's mouth.

"The knight may make some sense, she could be comely enough for a human. It was a lonely ten years, no doubt. But do your tastes really run so young and scrawny?"

Bel lunged, catching Dartegn under his pauldron before he could dodge or his guards could intervene. Bel dragged Dar forward with a grunt, and he would've taken great pleasure at the look of surprise on Dar's face then if his rage wasn't so all-consuming.

Shouts rang out, and then Eamon was there, a hand across Bel's chest, pulling him back.

Bel only released Dar once Eamon pulled him far enough away.

"Say something like that again and I'll throw you from the dome myself," Bel growled.

Straightening his armor and waving away the guards, Dartegn sneered. "I'd very much like to see you try." His wings rustled behind him, arching and fluffing to make him appear bigger.

Bel's wings twitched in response, instinctively wanting to rise to challenge Dar's petty show of dominance. But he knew he couldn't hold his wings aloft like that for long and so didn't try.

"Don't speak of Alix like that. Either of them."

"I fail to see what other use you'd have for a human."

"And all the use humans have for us is fine quills. If that's all that can be between our kinds, then we really are doomed."

Dartegn snorted contemptuously. "I didn't realize you'd become a philosopher in your captivity."

"There was little else to do but sit and think."

Dar's black eyes cut to him so quickly, Bel felt their impact, right at the center of his chest.

"And what did you sit and think about, Arubel? Hm? Did you think about that night?" Dartegn advanced, wings raised again, a mass of black feathers and outrage. "Did you think about all the places you should've checked before you told Maddok it was safe to move? Did you sit in your sad little cell and think how it should've been *you*, not Mad?"

A hot tear sluiced across Bel's cheek, but he held his ground as Dar bore down on him.

Eamon braced, as if Bel might strike out at Dar again, but there was no need. Not when the answer was, "Of course I did."

The admission bled some of the fury from Dartegn, but bitterness rushed to take its place.

"And in all that thinking you did," said Dar with curled lip, "did you really think, after all that, after *everything*, you'd be welcome here?"

"I knew not to expect any welcome," Bel said through gritted teeth. "Least of all from you."

"Then why come?" It was the first question posed by a councilor since they returned, and the sound of a third voice broke the tangled web spinning between Bel and Dar.

Dartegn turned his back, scrubbing a hand over his face. "A good question," he grumbled.

"To relay information," Bel said.

Dar waved his arm. "By all means."

Bel sighed. *Where to even begin?*

"It can keep," said Eamon suddenly, stepping between Bel and Dar. "Right?"

"Yes," said Bel.

"We've made enough progress for one day. We can all agree that this is indeed Prince Arubel Adiiron?"

"Just look at him," one of the councilors muttered.

Dar's wings bristled.

Several more reluctant yeses answered Eamon's question, but everyone looked to Dar for the final answer.

He took a long moment, fists on his hips as he glowered again at Bel. Bel stared back impassively, knowing that would annoy Dar more.

Finally Dar huffed, "It's him."

"Good." Eamon bowed his head. "Then perhaps we should all find some rest. Let tempers cool."

A quiet rumble of agreement came from the councilors.

Bel nodded, more than a little relieved for a reprieve. A headache had begun to bloom behind his right eye, and another cup of water wouldn't go amiss. He'd lose his voice entirely with much more of this.

Really though, it was a play for time. If he divulged everything now, what use did Dartegn have for him—or Lena and Alix. Perhaps he'd let them simply leave again, and it wasn't a small part of Bel that wished dearly for just that, but that black glare made clear that hope was folly. Dar would fight him on everything.

Right then, he only wanted to fight on one more thing.

"I wish to see the humans. You've kept us apart long enough."

"Say he's a prince and he's immediately making demands," Dartegn scoffed.

"She's my *c'vana*, Dar."

Dartegn's mouth twisted with distaste, but something in his look shifted, a small crease below his eyes at the thought of a *c'vana*.

"Perhaps the king should come with the prince," suggested Eamon, "to see for himself how much influence the human knight may have."

Dartegn cast Eamon a thin-lipped look, knowing when he was being managed. Still, after a sigh, Dar said, "Fine. But the humans stay where they are—and you aren't staying with them." He strode forward, invading Bel's space to slap a hand on his shoulder. "You'll stay with me in the royal quarters. Cousin."

◆

Lena and Alix were being kept in one of a disused cluster of rooms down on one of the lowest terraces. Leading the way out into the Round, Dartegn launched into the air, preceding his guards and a few curious councilors in a gliding descent.

Bel gritted his teeth and extended his wings.

"Can you…?" Eamon's mouth clicked closed at the glare Bel lobbed at him.

It wasn't a pretty or easy descent. Bel could feel the weak muscles in his right wing straining, cramped from days in the mines and still sore with healing from ten years of brokenness. It was easy to pretend, while they'd done their morning stretches alone in the vast wilderness, that he'd one day fly like an avian should again.

Seeing other avians fly, he was reminded of just how far he'd yet to go.

Eamon kept at his side, landing when Bel landed, running to take off with him, gliding over another few terraces before touching down once more to do it all again.

It took twice as long as Dar's descent, and his cousin watched with a smug satisfaction as Bel landed gracelessly near the small party.

Bel huffed, shaking out his wings before folding them tightly to his back. Eamon came alongside him, silent support against the half-dozen sets of assessing gazes. Bel didn't know if he wanted it, but it was a buffer at least, something between him and all the eyes looking for more weakness, more disappointment.

In the human world, he'd tucked his wings away to avoid the vicious gazes of his former wardens. They marked his difference, his otherness.

It was no different here. Even in a city full of winged kin, he was still other.

These gazes weren't malicious or calculating, yet somehow the pity and aversion in them was worse. In Finhöln, he'd nurtured a stubborn pride for his wings, the mark of his difference and avianness. They could break his wings all they wanted, they were still his, still proof of who he was. Under the dour gazes of the councilors and guards, shame left a sourness on his tongue.

"They're here?" he said, striding for the arched entryway Dar had stopped before. He shook off the stares by keeping moving, not waiting for Dar's answer.

Unlike most of the rest of the lower levels, this corridor was brightly illuminated, every sconce lit, banishing all but the deepest shadows from the far corners. It was a long, straight hallway, a handful of closed doors standing sentry. At the end, under the light of two sconces and a lantern sat a female avian.

She wore the armor of Dar's guards, though her helm sat neatly at her feet, leaving her head of ruddy brown hair exposed. A thick plait lay over her shoulder like a rope, the warm light catching on the auburns and ambers. All of her natural colors were warm, her wings a spotted pattern of brown and cream, like the owls of the southern forests. Her face was tanned and flushed, a thick smattering of freckles patterning her nose and cheeks.

Her hands kept busy with something, and she didn't mark Bel as he approached, though he knew she counted his steps, waiting to see what he'd do.

Bel stopped a few paces away, and the female finally looked up to regard him. Her brows were a shade lighter than her hair and arched in mild surprise. Eyes the steely gray of newly forged steel ran over him in quick passes.

"It's uncanny," she muttered.

"Sorry?"

"How much you look like him."

"Phaedra."

The female nodded to Dar, who came up behind Bel. She stood easily from her stool, putting away what Bel realized were knitting needles and a small ball of yarn to stand at attention.

"Anything?"

"No, my king. Very quiet. They're either asleep or plotting."

Dar huffed. "Bring them out. My cousin wants to see them."

"Sir."

Phaedra went to the last door on the right, opening it to reveal a glimpse of a dim bedchamber. Dar hooked a wing over Bel's shoulder to stop him when he would've moved to follow her.

"You'll see them best in the light," said Dar. "Make this quick."

"Fine." Bel rolled his shoulder, knocking off Dar's wing.

"Visitors for you, humans," Phaedra called into the chamber, not unkindly.

Bel held his breath, and the moment it took Alix to appear in the doorway seemed to last a horrible eternity. She blinked at the brightness, grumbling as she sidestepped to let Lena take the lead.

Lena emerged warily, squinting against the sudden light but no doubt determined to assess as much as she could.

His breath came out in a relieved rush, and he stepped forward.

"Bel!"

Alix threw herself at him, and Bel wrapped her up in a wing. She buried her face in his side, and when she made no move to step back, Bel gently laid his hand on her head of flattened curls.

He reached for Lena with his other hand, and she came at a measured pace, eyes flicking over all the avians who'd come to gawk.

Dark circles underscored her eyes, and she stood before him in a wide, stiff stance. Exhaustion clearly pulled at her, but there was a flintiness to her gaze, as if the smallest thing would shatter her.

He wanted to wrap her in his other wing, draw her into his body where he could hold her and scent her and feel her with his own hands. His chest ached with wanting it, but her guarded posture told him how close she was to breaking apart.

Too much softness now might make her break, even if comfort was all she wanted.

Bel understood. Too much and everything would come out, all the fear and frustration and exhaustion, and it wouldn't stop.

She couldn't do that here, in front of so many curious eyes. She couldn't show weakness.

Bel needed to touch her, so he offered what comfort he could, cupping her face in his palm and drawing her to him. He touched his forehead to hers in a small *ashita* and breathed her in. He kissed her temple, running his thumb in soothing little circles at the other.

"It'll be all right," he murmured to her.

He felt her shudder under his lips.

"They didn't hurt you?" she whispered, though Dar was close enough to hear.

"No," he said, tucking a lock of her hair behind an ear. "Not unless you count the hardtack. And you...?"

When he reached down to grasp her hand, his fingers met smooth metal. His heart lurched in his chest, and he drew her hands up, knowing what he'd find.

Shackles cuffed both her wrists, a few links of chain connecting them.

Bel ran a hand down Alix's arm, realizing she hadn't put them around him. Another set of shackles, smaller but still not small enough for her. They slid down her arms when he held them up to see.

He rounded on Dar, but that was as far as he got.

Phaedra was there, her shoulder and wing blocking him. Eamon and several guards took half a step forward, hands on their hilts. Dar looked on, eyes cool and assessing.

What truly stopped Bel was the fists buried in the material of his shirt. Lena held him back, hands over his thundering heart.

Bel covered her hands with his.

She shook her head once.

Still, he couldn't help spitting, "Shackles?"

Dar's nose wrinkled like a roaring cat's. "Be grateful it's only that."

"We came in good faith to—"

"She's a *knight*, you fucking fool!" Dar's shout bounded down the corridor, echoing long after he'd clamped his jaw closed. "How many of us has she killed?" he hissed through gritted teeth. "You're lucky I don't throw her in the Pit and be done with it. If you were anyone else, I would."

And Bel knew, from the dangerous glint in Dar's eyes, that he didn't mean if they weren't cousins. It was his Adiiron name and coloring— only one of which Dar himself had.

It was on the tip of his tongue to tell Dar not to do him any favors, but he bit it back. A fledgling would say that, would goad an already irate Dar. But Bel wasn't a fledgling anymore, and Dar wasn't his older, brooding cousin anymore, either. He was king, and a king's threats were never idle ones.

Instead, Bel forced himself to say, "How long?"

Dar snorted. "For however long I fucking feel like, Arubel."

A muscle ticked in Dar's jaw, and Bel realized finally that they'd reached the end of his cousin's patience. Growing up, Dar's temper would've erupted by now, but instead, he simmered and bubbled, a kettle left too long on the heat.

"It's fine," Lena said quietly, tugging on his shirt again. "I wouldn't trust me, either."

Guilt gnawed him raw; he'd brought her into a den of enemies, where she was to be kept shackled in a dark room, entombed in rock. He didn't deserve this woman.

Her statement was met with a cold glare by Dar.

"Please." Bel infused the word with as much sincerity as he could and saw the flicker of surprise in Dar's expression. "We came here to help. I'll do as you say, go where you say, tell you everything I know. We'll prove ourselves to you. But please, don't keep them locked up in the dark. Let them prove that not every human is our enemy."

"Any more requests?" Dar asked.

"Just one." They all looked to Lena in surprise. She lifted her chin and met Dartegn's dark gaze. "Please, unchain Alix. She's just a girl—a fledgling. She's not a threat."

Bel drew Alix from his side but kept a protective hand on her shoulder. She looked uneasily around at the avians with large eyes, and he didn't think she feigned all of it.

"They're too big anyway," Alix said in a voice much smaller than Bel was used to from her. He squeezed her shoulder gently, offering what support he could. "I could probably get out of them after a while."

One of the guards coughed to cover his guffaw.

It was the last sound made in the corridor for a long moment, even the crackle of the burning sconces muffled as they waited for Dar's decision.

He looked Alix over, and the girl stared back. She didn't make herself look smaller or bat her eyes to seem innocent. Alix stood her ground, face neutral, and let the avian king take her measure.

Dar shook his head. "Fine."

Phaedra stepped forward, unlocking the shackles in a few efficient movements. Alix sighed in relief as she rubbed her wrists.

Bel turned to Dar to say, "Thank you."

Dar shook his head again. "Don't." The look he levelled on Bel and then Lena was near menacing, not a hot anger but a cold fury that scared Bel much worse. "We aren't the savages your kind accuses us of. But one mistake, one threat, and I won't hesitate to give you to the Pit. All of you. I'll see what my long-lost cousin has to say and decide if it's worth his keep. And the humans will stay out of the way."

It was generous, Bel knew that, but he still clenched his teeth at the terms. He never expected a warm welcome, but somehow, he hadn't imagined being separated from Lena. Bel had thought Dartegn more likely to throw him in a cell alongside her. Like this, he couldn't protect her or Alix; in fact, they were likely safer the further away he was. And that rankled.

But he could bear it. For them. For his kin. For Maddok.

Without waiting for either Bel or Lena to speak, Dar turned on his heel and began striding back down the corridor.

"We're done here."

The councilors and guards filed out behind him, and Phaedra retook her stool and knitting.

Lena forced a small grin when he looked down to her.

"We'll be all right," she told him softly.

Bel dropped his mouth to hers, claiming one quick kiss to take her taste with him.

"You say it and we'll leave," he murmured against her lips.

"You have to do this," she murmured back. Then there were no more words, just the hot press of her lips and tongue to his, one last warm touch he'd need in the—

"*Now*, Arubel!"

They shared a grimace, and Bel finally stepped back.

"Be safe," she said.

"I love you, *c'vana*."

27

S he didn't see Bel for days, or anything beyond the small chamber she and Alix shared, for that matter. The first day, they sat glumly by the light of their two candles, not wanting to move too quickly should they blow out. Alix slept and Lena pretended to, lost to the timelessness of the underground.

On the second day, they had the small comfort of receiving their things. Well, their packs at least. Everything sharp and useful had been removed, leaving mostly clothing, bedding, and what was left of the food. Still, Lena enjoyed the familiar taste of their food and textures of her own blankets. She enjoyed the change of clothes and shedding their dark journey through the mines. And most of all, she enjoyed the small bowl of water provided, thankful to scrub herself off before slipping into clean clothes.

Their guard, a female avian called Phaedra, left their door open to let in the light from the corridor. They were treated to an excellent view of Phaedra on her stool, just outside their door. She sat quietly, unbothered by their moving about the chamber, but one pointed ear was always angled in their direction, noting every noise.

Still, she exuded calm and didn't glower the few times they traded glances. The steady *click* of her knitting needles was oddly soothing, and to pass the time, Lena cleaned and oiled her boots in time.

But when that was done, there was nothing left to do but lie on the bed and close her eyes. Alix snored softly beside her through the night—

or what must have been the night, as another guard came to relieve Phaedra. She took the empty room across from them, and the new guard closed and bolted their door, plunging the chamber back into gloom.

Lena got up and blew out the candles, not wanting to waste them.

So she lay in the dark, wondering how many hundreds of thousands of stones separated her from Bel and how many more than that from the sky above.

She wondered too what she was to do now—and came to the unsettling thought that her part was done. She'd gotten Bel here, returned him to his people. Besides the little homestead she'd been building in her mind, there were no other plans, no other ideas for the future.

So, Lena lay there, the only thing she could do. Stay out of trouble. Stay out of the way. Stay in the dark.

<hr>

There was little other way to mark time than the shift changes. Lena and Alix figured it must be day when Phaedra opened their door, called out a friendly, "Up with you now, humans!" and resumed her knitting.

However long it was, it must have been enough time for Bel to explain what he knew. Giving the king what information they had was the only reason Lena could find for when, on what may have been the fourth day, or the fifth, they were allowed out from the chamber—to walk.

"We are?" Lena couldn't help asking.

Phaedra nodded easily, setting down the mitten she'd been working on all yesterday. "From the king's mouth."

Alix and Lena exchanged looks.

"And this walk isn't straight to the Pit?" Alix asked.

Phaedra chuckled. "If it was, you'd be hearing it from the king himself. He isn't one to give orders he wouldn't carry out himself."

She said this with a sort of pride, and Lena supposed she couldn't fault the king for that. It was the same quality she'd admired in Arion.

Still, the darkness of King Dartegn's gaze haunted her. She couldn't forget his savagery on the battlefield nor the grim seriousness with which he'd promised to throw her and Alix into the bowels of the mountain.

She recognized some of that intensity in Bel, but where it made him a cunning, reserved male, like a dagger through shadow, it'd forged King Dartegn into something sharp as an axe and more brutal than a war hammer.

If it weren't for being told they were kin and a hint of similarity in the angle of their jaws and shape of their mouths, she wouldn't have guessed they shared the Adiiron name. Day and night, shining bronze and inky night.

There was so little between them...Lena hadn't imagined it would be such a wide gap to have to bridge.

So she had to take heart that there was this small concession, whatever it meant.

Alix made a show of stretching and popping her knuckles as Phaedra followed them from the corridor out into the vast open space beneath the domed summit of Hadria.

"We call it the Round," Phaedra answered when Alix asked. She explained the flattened circle in the center was the arena, a gathering place and where the sovereign met their people. A handful of avians stood on the arena, clustered in small groups. Some seemed to be talking, others looked to be walking leisurely. A few pairs sparred on the far side, and as they watched, a squadron of avians alighted, circling to gain height before darting between the columned openings in the dome.

As they walked the stone terrace, Alix grew in confidence, jogging ahead to see something closer or peer into a new corridor. They came across no other walkers, and Lena realized they were on one of the lowest terraces, nearly parallel to the arena. Everyone on the arena or the higher terraces could see them, and once she realized, she couldn't shake the feeling of dozens of eyes watching.

Despite the shackles, she picked at her thumb with a nail.

She and Phaedra walked in silence, watching Alix dart from one thing to the next. Phaedra let her, so Lena did too, not sensing any immediate threat. Still, it warranted saying, "I've no right to ask, but if it comes to it, do what you must to me. I know it will be orders and I understand. But please, spare her."

She felt Phaedra's eyes land on her, but she kept walking, leaving her request hanging between them.

"We aren't in the habit of killing fledglings," was Phaedra's answer.

"She isn't a fledgling," Lena said. "She's a human girl. Nearly an adult, by our laws. But none of this is her fault, and she shouldn't suffer the consequences of our war."

Phaedra was silent for a long moment, and Lena couldn't help stealing a glance from the corner of her eye.

"You are odd, for a human."

"Mm. Perhaps, perhaps not. There are many good humans." She stopped and turned to Phaedra. "There are many bad ones, too."

"I've killed at least twenty humans," said Phaedra, her tone and expression still easy, but Lena didn't miss the hard glint to her eyes. "It didn't matter to me if they were good or bad."

Lena swallowed on a dry throat. "No, it wouldn't. Not across a battlefield. I've delivered the killing blow to at least fifteen avians. I helped bring down many more."

"Iron nets."

"Yes."

Phaedra considered her for a long while, those steely eyes piercing her as surely as an arrowhead.

"You know I'm to report everything back to King Dartegn."

"Yes. You can tell him any number you like; one will be too many for him, anyway."

"True enough. Why tell me, then?"

"I don't see a reason to lie. I'll admit, as a soldier down there, I hated every single one of you. I had to. I carried out my orders and killed before someone could kill me. It's war. But I could never hate Bel, even from the beginning. And if I didn't hate him, I realized that I couldn't hate his kind, either."

One side of Phaedra's mouth kicked up into a grin, startling Lena.

"You know, there are bets being placed on why Prince Arubel came back now. The leading bet is that you'll try to assassinate King Dartegn."

"From my cell?"

"It's hardly a cell. But yes, odds are good that you're an assassin who's manipulated the prince. Warped his mind with deviant human sex rituals."

"That again," groaned Lena.

"Mm. The next one is that Prince Arubel is here to assassinate the king and retake the throne, but that he'll surrender to the humans once he does."

"None of that is true," Lena insisted. "Bel would never, not after what's been done to him. He just wants to help his people."

"Good," said Phaedra, that little grin still on her lips. "Then I won't lose any of my coin."

<hr />

They were allowed two walks a day, and Lena kept her pace slow, giving Alix more time to zip about. It took Lena days to untense her shoulders on their walks, feeling dozens of eyes watch every step they took. Avians came to the terrace edges to observe them, their moods ranging from curious to malicious.

"Just push the human into the Pit, Phae!" another female warrior shouted one day from three terraces up.

Phaedra just shook her head. "That's the king's decision, Maron."

The other avian had sneered, spitting at Lena though it landed nowhere near her.

"Hey!" Alix yelped. "Why don't you come and say that to—"

"Alix," Lena admonished. "Don't."

"But—"

"Retaliation is what she wants. Don't give it to her."

Alix pouted, throwing a deadly look up the terraces, but held her tongue.

They'd begun walking again when a rock smashed at their feet, scattering shards against their boots. Alix yowled, a bigger piece hitting her knee.

Phaedra scowled up at the other female. "Maron—"

Lena advanced on the terrace wall, glaring at the female, who met it with her own. She tossed another rock idly between her hands.

"Don't you dare hurt my squire. If you have to throw rocks to satisfy your petty anger, throw them at me."

She wasn't sure how much the female understood Vagoran, but it must've been enough when her lip peeled back and the rock went sailing at Lena. It hit her in the gut, sending her back a step with a pained grunt.

"Lena!" Alix rushed to her side.

She shook her head, drawing Alix behind her. With a final stare up at the female warrior, Lena spat on the rock she'd thrown and turned her back.

It wasn't every time they went for a walk that that female and her friends harassed them, so Lena didn't deny them the chance to get out of that little room. Some walks were uneventful, a true chance to stretch their legs and acclimate to the mountain. Some walks it wasn't rocks thrown but insults, some in Vagoran and some in *alvani*. Lena didn't ask Phaedra for a translation.

When Phaedra intervened at another rock thrown, they instead turned to dried apple cores and rancid bones. The wet slap of rotten food still hurt but left less of a bruise.

She took it without comment, though Alix had choice things to yell. They didn't target Alix, and so Lena let it be. Even if her heart was sick with all of this.

"Not all are like Maron," Phaedra told her. "The war has been long and—"

"I know," she said, understanding all the ugly feelings that came with bitterness.

She just had to endure. That was her part to play now.

Lena saw nothing of Bel, and she could only assume that he was being kept away purposefully. The thought stirred her uneasiness, but she grit her teeth and pushed it down when she could. There was nothing for it now; they were at the mercy of King Dartegn. And really, perhaps it was best that Bel not be seen with her and Alix. Perhaps it'd strengthen his position, whatever that may be, to distance himself from them.

It made the most political sense.

Not that Bel was one for politics. Still, it made a sort of bleak sense to her, and Lena resigned herself to it.

Wherever he was, whatever he did, she hoped he was safe.

———◆———

Gnawing fears dogged her through the days and nights, robbing her of sleep. She could almost hear Bel imploring her to rest, but she just couldn't stop the litany of worries that marched through her mind like an army off to battle, row upon row, stretching to the horizon. She didn't like the look of their nighttime guard, just a hard visage under a helm. Lena spent every night with Alix wedged between her and the wall. It was the only protection she could offer.

After days of this, she didn't need to feign walking slowly. Her feet dragged, and the black circles under her eyes ached. She barely felt or reacted when struck with a new insult or half-eaten fruit.

Even Phaedra noted, "You aren't looking well, human."

"Underground doesn't seem to suit," was Lena's mild answer.

Phaedra hummed a wistful sound. "True enough. Most beings need a little sun."

Lena looked askance at their guard. It was easy to forget that, while an avian city, Hadria was firstly a stronghold of last resort. The hollow mountain was impressive but dreary compared to Aeriand, even in ruins. They could slip through the slats in the dome for some sun, but they couldn't truly leave, hemmed in by the human position below.

Hadria was a safe place but not where avians were meant to be.

After years of this, it shouldn't have been a surprise that their kind had grown so dour.

But not Phaedra.

Their guard wasn't at all what she'd thought an avian warrior would be, at least not when it came to her treatment of Lena and Alix. The night guard, He of the Scowl as Alix called him, wasn't a surprise. Phaedra's easy manner in comparison was flabbergasting.

At first, Lena wondered if King Dartegn meant for Phaedra to gain their confidence, to put them at ease in hopes of sussing out any more information. Lena knew the kind, people with flattering tongues and pleasing manners; they'd flocked around Arion, always vying for his attention or favor or to report back to his father. But Lena hadn't sensed anything like that from the female avian.

Her face was open and honest, a mildly amused grin often adorning it. She radiated a kind of warmth with her ruddy coloring; the warm browns of her hair and wings, the pretty flush of her cheeks, the charming freckles that dotted her nose and cheekbones. Even those sharp, steely eyes were crinkled at the corners more often than not, framed by long auburn lashes.

It was baffling, and Lena had exhausted herself debating whether it was all just a very convincing ploy.

"Why are you so kind to us?" she finally asked on their next walk. It was one worry she could resolve, or at least answer. And the tiredness left her with little tact.

Phaedra's wings gave a little flick, a gesture Lena was coming to realize meant surprise.

She'd come to learn how expressive avian wings were. Lena knew Bel's little tells, what his flaps and flutters meant. But compared to all the little gestures Phaedra made and the ones Lena observed on their walks, Bel's wings only whispered when everyone else's shouted. His wings were quiet, subdued, tucked away.

It saddened her to think. *What had his wings done before he was captured?*

Phaedra's auburn brows arched over genuinely surprised eyes. "I'm just doing my duty. Nothing kind about it."

Lena shook her head. "You could do all of it without talking with us. You leave the door open for us during the day."

"Makes it easier to keep an eye on you."

"You tell them to stop throwing things at us."

"Your language has a saying..." Phaedra thought a moment. "Not to kick a dog when it's down. I don't like downed dogs getting kicked."

"You let Alix run ahead. You don't get impatient or yell."

Phaedra shrugged. "You make the job easy, I suppose. You've done as the king said."

"I'm not a threat. I want to prove it."

Phaedra nodded. "All right."

Without knowing where to go after another of Phaedra's easy agreements, Lena left it there.

They walked in silence for a while. Lena lifted her head to watch the avians flitting to and from the dome, flashing in the slants of late afternoon sunlight. She ached to feel the sun on her skin, but their terrace was too low to catch even the smallest shaft of light.

"Of the avians you've killed...did one have red wings?" Phaedra asked, almost too quietly to hear. "Red like a fox, not scarlet."

"No." It was difficult to remember the faces, covered as they were in the helms avians preferred. This made it easier to imagine them not as people but merely enemies, faceless and evil. She was grateful not to remember the faces of those she'd killed, but she remembered all the colors.

Red wasn't one of them.

The more broken and brutal soldiers kept feathers from their kills, stringing them into colorful mantels or headdresses they'd wear to tell stories of those kills around the bonfire.

The memory curdled her stomach in disgust.

Phaedra nodded again, a little jerk of her head. "Then I don't have a quarrel with you, human. I don't hate your kind, despite everything. I'd just exhaust myself doing so." She said all this without heat or venom, just a bleak resignation that tugged painfully at Lena's chest.

If she'd had enough sleep, she might not have asked, "Who was it?"

They came to a stop, having reached the far side of the terrace, where the semicircle simply ended at a craggy rockface. Alix stood at the uncut rock, holding on with one hand to lean over the edge of the terrace and look down onto the arena below.

"My twin," Phaedra finally answered, eyes cast to the wide Round. "I want my people to survive, so I fight in this war and slay the human enemy. Those are my orders, and I take no pleasure in it. But the one who killed my sister, them I *hate*. And I will relish their death when I claim it." The hard face she turned on Lena then gave her a glimpse of the fierce warrior who terrorized every human soldier who saw her.

Lena nodded. What else could she do? She understood Phaedra's pain, and really, to her it seemed fair to hate the one who took away what Phaedra loved. But as Lena looked about the Round, sparsely populated with the dwindling avian race, she had to wonder how many felt just as Phaedra did. How many had lost their kin, their mate, their child? And even if they only sought revenge on the human who'd caused that loss, how could they not end up hating every human? For the avians' losses were so many and so deep.

There could never be recompense for such loss.

It made what she and Bel had that much more precious...or perhaps that much more futile. All Lena could do was promise herself that she'd cause no such loss ever again.

———— •◆•• ————

It was a week, or perhaps more—she'd lost most sense of time as sleepless nights and turns about the Round blurred into an endless cycle—before she finally caught a glimpse of Bel.

From so far away, she might've missed him were it not for the striking color of his wings. Even amongst his kind, the gilded bronze of the base and shimmering white at the tips marked his wings as exquisite, a pearl amongst marbles. They weren't the full gold his brother and Adii-ron ancestors were known for, but they still stood out against all the browns, grays, and blacks.

She watched his golden head as he went through his forms with a handful of others down on the arena floor. If it weren't for his hair and wings, she might've mistook him for another avian warrior. She couldn't see detail from her terrace, but the cut of his clothes was unmistakable. Avian-made garments had been found for him.

Gone was the overlarge shirt with slits cut in the back. A fitted jacket had replaced it, tight to his chest but more generous at the back to allow his wings movement. The large belt at his hips, the kind avians favored to support their backs and wings, was of a finely worked leather that gleamed in the morning light. Dark trous molded to his strong legs and boots to the knee looked new.

Even from afar, he cut a fine figure.

And as they continued walking, Alix running ahead to get a better look at the warriors Bel trained with, Lena saw she wasn't the only one who noticed.

More than one female warrior approached him through their prac-tice, standing close to him, letting their wings brush.

Heat flushed Lena's cheeks, and she chided herself.

This sudden stab of jealousy wasn't helpful.

Of course they'd admire him. He was a strong, handsome male. A prince.

It didn't matter. She knew it didn't. He'd find the attention curious at best. Lena remembered his stories of Aeriand, of girls his age being thrown in his way when he neared manhood. She'd seen it enough with Arion, too.

None of it made the sight easier to bear.

"Can we go down there?" Alix asked as she bounded back to them.

Phaedra cringed. "The king wouldn't like it."

"It's fine. Leave him be, Alix."

Alix pulled a face. "Don't you want to—"

"Yes. But he's doing what he needs to do. We need to keep our heads down."

Alix's face scrunched into a sour frown. "Fine," she sighed.

They resumed their walk, and Lena tried not to look where she knew Bel was.

Her heart cried out, wishing her voice could too, that it would somehow reach him across the distance.

The sight of him drew forth all she'd been working to push down. She longed for his touch, for him to tell her it was all worth it. That it would be over soon.

Lena told herself it was the tiredness that drew the stinging tears to her eyes. Perhaps it was. And perhaps it was the reason too for the growing despondency inside her, a sucking hole in her chest that was becoming harder to ignore than the blisters beneath her shackles.

It didn't matter. She repeated that to herself and drew herself up and the tears back inside.

Play her part. Do her duty.

She'd trained for that her whole life. She could bear this a while longer.

There was no other choice.

28

What took Bel the most getting used to again was the clothes. He didn't mourn his billowing tunics from Finhöln, and there was something utterly delicious about slipping his arms into and wings through the back of an avian shirt. It was odd to see himself in the mirror, the clothes accentuating the contours of him rather than hiding them away.

Alone, in the silence of the chamber Dar had him put in, he'd fluffed his wings and peered at himself from every angle. He hadn't had a mirror in Finhöln, and even if he did, rarely would he have wanted to look at himself. The scars he could see were ugly enough; he didn't need to know how the rest of him fared. Especially his back and shoulders.

His first night, he'd finally looked at the damage by candlelight, hoping to soften whatever he found. The stripes on his back were exactly what he expected and yet not as bad. Most had gone a silvery white, the angry reddish-purple of fresh wounds long since faded. The knot on his right wing base wasn't the ugly lump he'd feared it would be.

Overall, the sight of himself peering back hadn't been the surprise or disappointment he'd expected. It was almost curious to see himself so clearly. Oh he'd known what he looked like well enough, but to see every feature together, not just an eye or nose or mouth in the curve of a pot, was...curious.

What he didn't find was Maddok looking back at him.

That Dar had mistaken him for Maddok at first, that others gawked at him as he passed and whispered his brother's name, had made Bel think, even hope, that perhaps now that he was fully grown, he'd grown into the Adiiron name, too.

Perhaps he had—but he didn't see Maddok in his own face.

Curiosity sated, Bel donned the clothes Eamon provided, reacquainting himself with avian garments.

"*Where did you find these?*" Bel had asked Eamon, surprised they fit so well.

"*There are many to go around of late,*" was Eamon's answer.

The comment stuck with Bel, only deepening his worries and suspicions. His kind was dwindling; not just on the end of a human sword, but everything together, all the tragedies one after the other...there was only so much a people could bear.

Fastening the last of the buttons tucked neatly into the center seam of his fitted coat, Bel followed Eamon down to the arena. The fine boots Eamon had found him absorbed the shock of every step, the leather cushioning his foot and calf. He hadn't had such good boots since...before.

The easy fit of the boots and soft rasp of the jacket never quite faded from Bel's consciousness; so used to the flap and slide of the overlarge human tunics he'd been provided, the cut and fit of clothes made to suit him were almost unnerving in their quietness and ease. Everything Eamon found for him was of the best quality, sturdy yet soft, luxurious yet effective. With the welcome he'd gotten from Dar, he'd expected to be left in his dirty, patched human clothes or even a used sack.

It was certainly an improvement, and Bel had no complaints, but it did make him curious.

It'd been almost a fortnight since they made it to Hadria, and every day, Eamon kept him busy meeting this commander and that councilor. All the while Bel had to remember not to caress his own arm, just to feel the supple texture of the leather or softness of the velvet. There was little hope of him remembering all the names and faces Eamon brought before him, and Bel had yet to figure out the reasoning behind which avians he was introduced to.

Curiouser still, each morning, Eamon brought him down to the arena. At first it was to reacclimate him to the Round and find everywhere he needed to go. He'd spent the better part of his first morning just watching the comings and goings of other avians, marveling at the everyday beauty of them.

It was fascinating to watch all the ways wings moved. With humans, Bel had come to learn it was the eyes and brows he needed to pay most attention to. For avians, expression often came from their wings. They were the unruliest of the limbs, wont to flutter and ruffle with each changing emotion. The cacophony of little movements overwhelmed him, and Bel unconsciously tucked his wings tighter to his back.

On the second morning, Eamon told him, "*We can go out there, you know. Talk with others. Your cousin hasn't restricted your movements.*"

Talk with others? The idea horrified him. What would he even say?

The constant stream of avians Eamon had him meeting was more contact and conversation than Bel had had in ten full years at Finhöln. And those meetings felt loaded, not just pleasantries and sating curiosity. It wore on his nerves. Between that and his growing impatience at being separated from Lena and Alix, he retreated to his assigned chamber feeling rubbed raw. He was in awe of Hadria and being amongst his people again, but being expected to throw himself back in exhausted his nerves and patience.

His frown must have been clear enough for Eamon. He didn't suggest it again.

Instead, he introduced Bel to one of the avian squadrons, bringing Bel to them during their time to train, spar, and do their forms. Eamon did it so neatly, Bel hadn't realized at first. A spark of frustration, vaguely familiar, heated his chest.

It was like being a fledgling again, Eamon managing his time.

He would've fostered that frustration longer if he hadn't come to enjoy his mornings with the squadron so quickly.

They were all a few years older than him, a patchwork of warriors from across avian country. Della with her gray wings, flushed cheeks, and loud laugh. Burly Diarmund, tall and wide as a bear with a deep growl and black-brown wings to match. Amaranthe and Maron, sisters, one with wings white and speckled like a snow owl and the other a rich brown with auburn bands up the barbs; they had tempers to match, though, and were fearsome to watch spar when they got each other going. And last there was Rurie, a willowy male with pale hair that contrasted sharply with his blue-black wings.

They welcomed him easily, curious more than anything after hearing the rumors of his return. The first day of *ariant* forms was sloppy at best, as Bel fielded questions about where he'd been and how he'd come to be here.

"*They said you brought captives with you. Human knights.*" Maron had sounded impressed, and Bel didn't miss the appreciative way her eyes passed over the width of his shoulders.

"*Just one knight and her squire. And they aren't captives.*"

Maron and Ama had exchanged looks. "*So, they aren't being held on the lower terrace?*"

"*Yes, but she's my—*"

"*And switch!*" Eamon called.

Bel regarded Eamon, trying to gauge his *at'tan*. But the older male led them through their forms and nothing else was said about the humans.

His mornings now started with training, and Bel had begun to look forward to it. He wished it could have been Lena and Alix he trained with; that was one of the things he'd liked most about their journey through the forest, stretching and practicing together.

The thought of Lena never failed to set his heart to aching.

So he set himself to training and staying near the arena in the hopes of catching his cousin. Dartegn hadn't spoken with him after those first days and hearing the information he had.

"*Is that it?*" Dartegn had said after Bel finished explaining what he and Lena believed of the human king's plan. *"You came all this way just to tell me the human king wants to kill us all?"*

Bel hadn't taken the bait, and he didn't believe Dar's disinterest, either. The councilors had been agitated at the news of the shuffling human forces and stunned to hear Aeriand now sat empty and abandoned.

The information had been considered, and while he received no true acknowledgement from Dar, patrols were stepped up in the outer mines to ensure the humans hadn't found their way into one of the derelict shafts.

That was the last Bel had seen of Dar, and the only councilors he met with were those Eamon introduced him to. Those older avians were less interested to hear about Bel's captivity and his thoughts on the human king's mindset, instead asking over his feelings towards humans, what he remembered of his brother's education, how he felt about Aeriand being abandoned three years ago.

Bel's answers were careful, though each confounding question deepened his frustration. The answers didn't matter, not to him. They wouldn't get him to Dar or protect Lena and Alix.

So Bel trained, keeping himself out in the open hoping for...something.

It was much more enjoyable too than meeting in dark, out-of-the-way rooms to have whispered conversations about nothing.

If Bel didn't know better, he'd think Eamon had designs for a coup.

But Bel put that from his mind. Eamon had trained Dar and Maddok, just as he had Bel. It wasn't impossible, but it felt improbable—and not as important as dodging the wooden sword swinging at his head.

Bel ducked and leapt to the side, using his right wing as balance to catch himself and roll to his feet. Diarmund was there, catching Bel in the vambrace as he blocked and rolled away again.

Diarmund pursued, never quite letting him get to standing, keeping him rolling and dodging in a wide circle.

The others cheered and jeered nearby, and Bel felt Eamon's assessing gaze. Could almost feel him mouthing pointers.

Parrying another strike, Bel hooked a wing behind Diarmund's leg and knocked him off balance. It gave him the needed moment to regain his footing and take a stance.

He was ready when Diarmund leapt through the air, wings beating to carry him the distance, legs wheeling. It was a classic avian attack, effective and devastating.

But rather than dancing backward, out of the way, as expected, Bel pitched forward, knocking Diarmund's sword away and putting his shoulder into the male's gut.

Diarmund grunted and wheezed, thrown back the way he'd come. He landed on the arena floor with a hearty *smack*, wings splayed.

The male laughed and coughed as Bel offered a hand up.

"That's new," remarked Ama as the rest of the squadron joined them.

"Boniest shoulder I ever felt," Diarmund wheezed.

"You did well, training on your own," said Maron with a smile that was more than friendly.

Bel nodded, taking the compliment. He was more than a little proud that keeping up with his *ariant* forms and taking the time to do the training properly had served him well. There was no real substitute for sparring, pitting one's skills against another, but he'd held his own so far, and the squadron didn't seem to be going easier on him.

"That's not from *ariant* training," Rurie noted.

"No," Bel agreed. "It's a trick Lena taught me."

The squadron fell silent, casting looks between themselves.

Bel held his ground, knowing that if he and Lena were ever to be accepted, it had to start somewhere.

"The human knight?" Ama said carefully.

"Yes. She—"

"I think that's enough for today," said Eamon, striding quickly to where they stood in a loose circle. He clapped Bel's shoulder, turning him toward the north steps of the arena. "The prince has duties to see to."

"Are we finally seeing Dar?"

Eamon's eyes flicked over the squadron before he nodded behind him, indicating for Bel to walk with him.

When Bel didn't move, Eamon's mouth thinned.

"The king is on patrol."

"Then I'll wait for him here," said Bel.

Eamon shook his head and held out an arm, indicating again for Bel to follow him off the arena.

"There are more important things for you to do. First we'll—"

"BEL!"

His feathers stood up in surprise as his name ricocheted across the Round. He twisted his head, looking for who called him, the voice sounding like—

"Prince Arubel, we should be going." Eamon motioned again for the north stairs.

"Bel! Bel, over here!"

He followed the shout to finally find Alix, two terraces up, waving her arms like a madwoman. Even from afar he saw the big, mischievous grin on her face.

A few paces behind her was the female avian, Phaedra, as well as Lena.

His heart picked up pace, and his feet began moving without thought.

A hand grabbed his arm, pulling him back.

"Bel, don't." Eamon drew alongside him, his frown grave. "As you can see, they're fine. Let them be. The sooner everyone forgets about them, the better."

Bel pulled his arm out of Eamon's grip. "I won't forget, Eamon."

"No, of course not. But you must keep your distance. The best thing you can do is sway others to your side. Let the people come to know you. Let them admire your resilience and determination to return and serve."

"Haven't I been? Isn't that what you've been parading me around for?"

"These things take time, Arubel. You've been gone a long time, much has changed. There was never much love for humans, and there's certainly no good will left after everything they've done. You strengthen your position keeping your distance from them."

"My position," Bel repeated. "My position to do what, exactly?"

Eamon's eyes went tight, little lines fanning from the corners. "Your place as prince. As an Adiiron."

The softness of his coat rubbed against his arm, and Bel looked down at the fine weave and embroidery. The garments were far better than the human castoffs he'd worn for ten years, and they were finer too than anything the squadron wore. All their clothes were well kept, cut for avians, but nowhere near the fineness of what Eamon had found for him.

Gods, he really was letting Eamon lead him by the nose again. Deciding his schedule. Laying out his clothes.

Clothes for a prince.

"I didn't come here to play politics or at being prince," Bel growled. "We have a king. What do we need a prince for?"

Eamon stepped closer, voice cast low so only Bel could hear. "*You* are Maddok's heir. The true Adiiron heir. But a claim like that will take time to strengthen."

A cold rage gripped Bel's heart, and he couldn't suppress the memory of Maddok's cry, the awful death knell he made as he shielded Bel with his own body.

"I already took my brother's life," Bel hissed. "What makes you think I want his throne?"

He looked over Eamon's shoulder at the squadron, all watching silently, their curiosity apparent and intense.

"Lena, the human knight," he said loudly to them, over Eamon's cringe, "she's my *c'vana*."

Ama's wings fluffed and Maron and Rurie's bristled. Eyes widened and mouths fell open.

"There," said Bel to Eamon, "I've made my position clear."

He turned on his heel, making for the west steps up to the first terrace. Alix still waved at him from the second, her smile growing when she saw him headed their way.

"Bel—Bel, listen." Eamon gripped his shoulder, pulling him to a stop again. "It's the only way. Help your people and you help them, too."

Bel shook him off and kept going. He didn't want to believe Eamon meant anything traitorous; his *at'tan* had always been protective of Bel and wanted to see him recognized in a court that often forgot he existed. But Bel wasn't a fledgling anymore. Nor a spare.

He took the steps two at a time, hurrying along the terrace to where Alix stood on the edge of the next one. When he got close, he took a running leap, pumping his wings to propel him high enough to catch the lip and pull himself up.

Alix smirked at him from a few paces away as he got to his feet.

"Showoff."

"Brat."

She bounced into his embrace, and he wrapped her up in arms and wings. Bel was relieved when she stepped back after a moment, not because he didn't want her touch but because it was such a difference from the last time he'd seen her, quiet and meek tucked into his side.

"You're well?" he asked, holding her face in his hands.

"All right. Forgetting what the sun looks like, though."

Lena joined them, though she hung back a step, and Phaedra watched on from a few paces away.

"Prince Arubel," said Phaedra with a respectful nod.

Not knowing what to do with that, Bel nodded back.

Alix whistled, holding up his wrist to inspect the fine embroidery on the cuff. "All right, now I can believe all this prince business. You clean up nice."

The tips of his ears pinkened. He tried not to be too annoyed at how effectively Eamon had dressed him for the part.

"Just found clothes that fit," he said, letting Alix sate her curiosity.

After a few moments, his attention was all for Lena.

He closed the distance between them, wings lifting without thought to curl around and draw her to him. He took her face between his palms, thumbs tracing the curve of her cheeks. His forehead touched hers, and Bel breathed her in as he ran his nose up hers in a small *ashita*.

"I've missed you, *c'vana*," he whispered.

A small shudder passed through her, and she swayed toward him—making him realize she hadn't stepped forward but stood stiffly in the circle of his wings.

"Bel, they'll see."

His brows slammed down in a dangerous frown. "Let them see."

But Lena shook her head and stepped back. "You shouldn't be seen with us."

"I won't let anything happen to you," he promised her.

"It's not me I'm worried about."

She retreated another step, pulling taut on the chain she had around his heart.

Alix came up beside her, arms crossed over her narrow chest and ferocious frown on her face. "They're throwing things at her," she told him, tapping a finger on her breastbone.

Icy fury drenched him. His gaze searched Lena where Alix had indicated on her own chest and saw it, a fresh bruise blooming just below Lena's right clavicle, half-hidden under her shirt.

"Who did this?" he hissed, hearing the cold rage in his own voice.

Lena winced but remained silent.

Alix huffed. "That one." She pointed at the arena. "Maron."

Fists clenched, Bel turned back toward the arena.

"Bel, don't," Lena said, reaching to intercept him. "She's allowed her anger."

"She's allowed *nothing*. Not from you."

He clutched her hands to his chest. His palms clasped around warm metal, and Bel grit his teeth against his searing outrage at her shackles. He lifted her hands to see, not letting her tug them from his grip.

They'd been secured over her shirtsleeves, but he could still see where the skin had rubbed raw and red at her wrists. Small blisters dotted the delicate skin of her inner wrist.

"Do they come off at night at least?" He lobbied this question at Phaedra.

To her credit, she merely blinked at his scowl. Perhaps he wasn't so intimidating, not to a warrior, especially one who served beside his cousin.

"Yes, Prince Arubel. While they're inside."

Inspecting Lena's wrists again, he said, "I'll have salve sent down."

"I'll be fine," Lena insisted. "I've endured much worse. Bel, you shouldn't make a fuss over me. You're not in a position to make demands."

"Why am I the only one who doesn't give a damn about my *position?*" He spat the word and immediately regretted it when Lena's eyes went tight.

"I'm sorry," he murmured, a little soothed when she didn't rebuff him as he drew her into his arms again. He felt her soften, just a little, and buried his nose in her hair.

All he wanted was to protect this precious woman who'd already given him everything—her love, her loyalty, her life. Even amongst his kind, she was still the only one who didn't ask anything of him in return. She'd gotten them here, chosen him over her life and duty.

Bel could damn well do the same. He'd pledged himself to her; he was her man first.

A bit of salve and warning Maron off was the least he could do.

As he held her, soaking in her touch and scent and textures, he hardened his resolve. He'd lost it these past days, overwhelmed from being back amongst his kind. Perhaps he could be forgiven for the lapse, but he wouldn't forgive himself. And he wouldn't let Eamon dictate where he went and who he talked to and what he wore anymore.

He wasn't a fledgling.

He wasn't Arubel Adiiron—but if that name got him where he

needed to go, fine.

He'd do what needed to be done. He'd take the initiative, help where he could, find his cousin, make him listen, figure out a place for both him and Lena here.

He'd get those damn shackles off. And if one more thing was thrown at her, even a feather, he'd bring this mountain down.

Because a *c'vana*—because *Lena*—deserved nothing less.

29

Bel decided to make a first move at a council meeting. They were irregular, arbitrary, and it took several days to figure out the signs to look for. When he felt sure there would be one called that day, he slipped inside the council chamber well before anyone was due to arrive. And waited.

Without fail, each councilor who filed into the chamber stopped to gawk at him, standing out of the way against the back wall. They blinked at him and he blinked back, but otherwise, they let him be.

The councilors trickled in through the morning, none questioning why Bel was there. He felt their curious gazes flick over him now and again, and conversation never rose above an awkward, stilted buzz of pleasantries. With his status as an Adiiron confirmed but no Dartegn in the room, Bel's presence couldn't quite be questioned.

He'd been betting on this. His family was one of the longest, strongest dynasties in avian history, the most illustrious in a line that went back to the joining of the first flocks. Prosperous in peace and effective in battle, the Adiirons had earned the loyalty of all avians over the centuries.

Bel had come to find, over the days in Hadria, that this had grown to a sort of reverence. Perhaps it'd always had a kind of fervor and he'd just been too young and sheltered to notice, but he thought it was more than that. The Adiiron name was said with such respect, as if they spoke of Halva herself.

He didn't care much about his name. It'd brought him nothing but misery for a long time, but if it could be helpful now, he'd use it.

Bel kept his casual yet watchful position as more councilors came. Eamon eventually found his way inside, and he nodded to Bel, looking pleased. Bel nodded back but kept his face neutral.

He wasn't doing this for Eamon.

It was nearly another half-hour before Dartegn finally arrived, sweeping inside in a flurry of black feathers and thunderous frowns. He brought with him his normal retinue of guards as well as several other councilors.

They all wore armor splattered with grime and blood. As if they were just back from battle.

They are, Bel realized.

Dartegn's dark hair was slicked back against his skull with sweat, and a fresh cut sliced across his cheek. It no longer bled, but the pink of it was stark, the edges gleaming with whatever salve had been applied to speed healing.

Dar brought a wave of energy with him, the councilors' wings fluttering as they gained their feet. Some called out to the king, asking how they'd fared, what news there was.

Dartegn answered none of them, instead accepting the cup one of his guards passed him. He drained it in a single long draught, his black eyes scanning the chamber. When they fell on Bel, he stilled, the cup halfway from his mouth.

"What are you doing here?" he grumbled.

Pushing off from the wall, Bel stepped forward with a shrug. "You didn't say I couldn't. I'd like to be of use, if I can."

He expected immediate refusal from Dar, but his cousin was quiet, scowl deepening. Bel didn't miss the lines carved beneath his eyes, pulling his whole face down with weariness.

Dar didn't like it, but he was too tired to fight it.

Then Eamon said, "Prince Arubel may have some insight, given the new developments."

Everyone's interest piqued, curious eyes landing on Dartegn.

Dar snorted, nostrils flaring, knowing he'd been neatly outmaneuvered.

"If my cousin wishes to finally understand everything the humans have done and plan to do, then by all means."

Bel bit his tongue against reminding Dar it was him who'd informed everyone here what the humans planned to do. He wasn't here to quarrel.

Guards and councilors moved about into familiar positions, finding allies and turning to hear what the king had to say. Bel watched several councilors drift toward Eamon, and he thought he recognized them as ones Eamon had introduced him to.

Dar stepped forward to the table, setting aside his cup. With a flick of his hand, two guards pulled out a thick roll of vellum. Carefully they unraveled the leather, revealing a map that stretched nearly from one end of the table to the other. The guards weighed down the corners with polished stones.

Bel couldn't help edging closer to the table, amazed at the detail. The entire Gogona mountain range had been painstakingly copied in brown ink, every ridge, every crevasse. Not quite in the center stood Hadria and the three surrounding peaks, shielding her dome from the west. Dozens of scores and strikethroughs surrounded the peaks and nearby ranges. As Bel admired the map, the guards laid smaller stones over the marks, red granite and gold-veined marble in neat semicircles around the base of Hadria. And along the peaks, they placed a handful of black obsidian chips.

"We confirmed what we'd thought," said Dartegn without preamble. He moved two red stones south.

"You saw the digging?" asked a councilor. Bel thought his name was Faros; he'd been quite taken with Bel's wings in his meeting with Bel and Eamon. It'd left Bel's skin crawling.

"No. They didn't let us get that far. Put up quite the defense at the west ridge," he moved another stone, "more than they should have. They want to deter us."

"But, my king, if you didn't *see* the new tunnels..."

Dar's eyes flicked up to the councilor, killing the words in the older male's throat.

"They've no other reason to be there," said another councilor, a younger female who'd come in with Dar. "They're defending the diggers."

Dar tapped a finger along the western peak of Hadria. "The question is whether they're stupid enough to dig their way through the mountain or aim to find an existing mineshaft."

A rustle of parchment, and then another map was laid out, this one a chaotic network of lines branching out under the mountain.

"We don't believe there are any viable passages that far to the southwest," said the councilor who'd laid out the map. Bannion? Bannon? Bannor, yes, Bannor. Eamon had mentioned this male kept the archives of Hadria. "No worthwhile veins had been found for years, so they looked elsewhere."

"The maps the human king has have mines going that far southwest. He must have taken them from Aeriand."

Bel's statement was met with utter silence. He couldn't tell if it was from his talking at all or the mention of Aeriand. He watched a tick under the skin of Dar's jaw and held his tongue, waiting for someone to speak.

"Saw them in your work for him, did you?" Dartegn hissed.

"Yes. Altered them, too." The councilors murmured and fluttered at that. "Those maps showed mines going southwest. I can't say if they were accurate or not; the records here would likely be more precise. But that's what the human king is working off of. I extended the maps to run further southwest."

His speech was met with a moment of silence before councilors began talking over one another. They consulted maps, moved stones about, and argued over whether the archives of Hadria or Aeriand would be more accurate. Through it all, Dar held Bel's gaze.

His stare was neither cold nor angry. Instead, Dar considered him, and Bel gazed back, hoping, just for a moment, he'd done something right.

"If that's the case, they could be digging for months and not hit any true mineshaft," said one councilor.

"*If*," Bannor emphasized. "The human king could have gotten those maps from anywhere."

"We should send a party out there," said another. "Determine just how far out the southwest passages go."

"We could see then how far out the humans are," agreed another.

"And do what with that information?"

The council went quiet again at Dartegn's question.

He looked about at the avians gathered, a hard frown set on his sharp face.

"If the mineshafts are there, then we wait for the humans to get in. Draw their forces inside. And then we collapse it. All of it." Dar's declaration grew in vehemence with each word, as if he could pull boulders down on the humans with his command alone.

Bel tucked his wings tight to his back, observing the others. Many councilors avoided the king's gaze while others stared back grimly, resolute. Bel's gaze snagged on Eamon. His *at'tan* shot him a significant look, though Bel didn't entirely understand that significance.

"It could work," one of the councilors said carefully. "That far out, there would likely be less risk to Hadria herself."

"We don't know that," grumbled the archivist. "The mineshafts go everywhere under this mountain. We don't know how the collapse of one may affect the others."

Another of the councilors who'd entered with Dar pushed forward, a rangy male with a shaven head and black wings. Memories of that unsmiling mouth flooded Bel. It was Ophir, former Head of the Guards to Maddok.

Bel had always thought he looked more like a wraith than an avian, all sinew and bone. His black wings gleamed with a purplish-blue undertone, emphasizing the dark browns in Dar's.

Ophir's face barely moved; indeed, it'd barely changed from Bel's memories as a fledgling. The distaste was still plain in Ophir's hard stare as the older male came alongside Dar to say, "Why wait for the humans to tunnel into the mountain; we risk them finding a way we don't know about. We save time and effort executing the king's original plan. It'd literally crush the humans and rid us of them forever."

"And possibly take us with it," said Eamon.

Bel tried to keep the confusion from his face, a sickening feeling swirling in his gut. "How would you do this?" he asked slowly.

"A rockslide, down onto the human position. One final blow, to end this war."

The air rushed from Bel's lungs, and he felt the color drain from his face.

"It's suicide," argued the archivist, voicing Bel's first thought. "The mountain is hollow. Such a cataclysm could bring the whole mountain down on us, too."

"Hadria has stood for generations. She's seen rockslides and collapsed mineshafts before," said Ophir.

"Natural movement of the rocks," replied Bannor. "Nothing like what's being proposed."

"Which begs the question," said another councilor, "how would this even be done?"

"We're working on a way," Dartegn said.

This was met with another tense silence, councilors exchanging looks.

Bel could feel Eamon trying to catch his eye, but he wouldn't look that way. Instead, he kept his face neutral, knowing Dar and Ophir watched for any response from him.

Dartegn finally took stock of the avians gathered. It was clear even to Bel that the council hadn't yet developed a taste for Dar's plan. As king, as an Adiiron, Dar's word was final, without question, but the avian sovereign had always taken the advice of a council. Acting against that advice never boded well.

Neither did councilors meeting in deserted corridors with Eamon and the returned Adiiron heir.

Bel's unease knotted in his guts and squeezed.

With a sharp sigh that flared his nostrils, Dar stepped back from the table. "That's enough for today. We know now what the humans are about." He turned his head to address Ophir. "Gather a party to check the southwest passages. Take maps and account for every possible passage that leads into the mountain."

"It will be done, my king." Ophir bowed and left, wasting no time to see it done.

With Ophir's departure, the council meeting dissolved into quiet conversations between groups. Some left to see to other duties while others spoke furtively in whispers, and a few guards began gathering the stones and carefully rolling the vellum map back up.

Eamon weaved between bodies, headed for Bel.

Bel let him come but didn't move to meet him.

Drawing close, Eamon put a hand on Bel's shoulder, pitching his voice low so only Bel could hear him say, "Now you understand. You see the danger in this?"

"I think everyone does," Bel replied.

"Such a plan could destroy us all."

"Then alternatives better be found."

"Bel..." he said with that sigh Bel knew so well from childhood. The sound of Eamon's patience wearing thinner.

"What do you expect me to do about it, Eamon?" He met Eamon's gaze, holding it, waiting for him to say the words. He wanted to know how far Eamon was willing to push, but the older male was clever enough not to voice any such suggestion here, in a room full of councilors and guards and the king himself.

When Eamon said nothing, Bel shook his head and pulled away.

He slipped between councilors, and no one stopped him, though he felt their curious, assessing eyes following him.

Bel searched for the dark head of his cousin, hoping he'd been waylaid by a councilor, but didn't see Dartegn. Gritting his teeth in frustration, Bel left the council chamber, striding out into the corridor.

A happy gurgle caught his ear.

Bel stopped and turned to see Dartegn standing a ways down the corridor that led back into the royal quarters of the Round. The guards had left him, and instead he stood with a slight avian female. Her wings arched elegantly from her delicate shoulders, bared in the low back of a traditional avian dress. They were of the purest white, glowing almost blue at the edges in the torchlight. A diadem of silver feathers was woven through hair so pale blonde it was nearly white. Her limbs were slim and graceful, her small hands delicate as one cupped Dartegn's face, turning it to the light to inspect the cut.

"You promised," the female chided softly.

"It's nothing," Dar assured her, taking her hand to press to his chest.

Another gurgle, and Bel finally saw what made the noise. The female shifted, revealing a small baby nestled in the blue velvet folds of her dress. A shock of black hair marked the child as Dartegn's, and Bel couldn't pull his gaze away.

A baby. A fledgling. His own kin.

Hadria was full of warriors and those needed to support them. He'd seen so few families, even fewer fledglings. None younger than perhaps nine or ten years. The sight of a new, precious life shattered Bel to his core for reasons he didn't quite understand.

"She worries about you, too," the female said, face soft with affection for her child.

Dar leaned down to nuzzle his daughter's head. The baby squeaked happily and grasped at Dar's feathers.

Bel could only stand in stunned silence as he watched the coldness melt from Dartegn. Lines fanned from the corners of his eyes, spreading a warmth across his face.

He'd heard of Dartegn's mate and child, that the king had a queen and heir. He realized he'd seen the pale female before, too, but hadn't been introduced. Cira. He had vague memories of her as a fledgling in

Aeriand, a quiet female whose family served at court. She was older than him and always seemed unapproachable, as if any attention paid to her would send her to tears. With her pale coloring, she'd reminded Bel of the human stories of ghosts; he'd see her haunting the library sometimes or escaping court functions down a private corridor.

She cut a sharp contrast standing before Dartegn, all pales to his darkness. As Bel watched them together, Dartegn bent to receive her whispers, he had the feeling it was Cira, in all her quietness, who commanded.

"Come rest," Cira was saying. "You've done enough today. Bathe and come to bed."

"Are you offering to bathe me, my queen?" Dar said in a warm rumble that wasn't for Bel's ears.

Cira flushed a pretty pink, the color saturated against her pale skin.

Bel took half a step back, unsure he wanted to interrupt. He had his own *c'vana* to fight for, but seeing this softened Dartegn, not a king but a mate and father, made him hesitate.

Bel knew what it was to have so few moments of softness and joy, how precious they were because of their rarity. Those he'd had he always wished lasted just a little longer, to be that much more perfect. He may not have understood or even really liked Dar, but he couldn't begrudge him that.

His boot made no noise on the stone floor, but Dar's ear twitched, and suddenly those black eyes trained on Bel, hard mask sliding back into place. Dar snarled at him, an animalistic sound that had Bel's feathers standing on end. He faced not a king but a mate and father whose family was threatened.

A black wing snapped around the little family, hiding away all but the top of Cira's pale head.

Bel held up his hands, knowing how foolish it was to make a male avian angry when protecting his mate and child.

"Forgive me," Bel said.

Dartegn huffed, the feral look leaving his eyes, but his scowl remained.

"I would speak with you, cousin, when you have—"

"Not now, Arubel," Dar growled. He used his wing to turn Cira and ushered her quickly down the corridor.

Through Dar's black feathers, Bel glimpsed Cira looking back at him.

"Is that...?" he heard her whisper before they turned the corner and were gone.

Left alone in the corridor, the serene little face of Dartegn's daughter seared his mind. That little life was the next Adiiron heir. It made Eamon's unspoken insinuations that much more troubling.

He was distracted enough that it took a second hissing whisper slithering down the corridor to get his attention.

At the other end of the corridor, at the entrance leading out to the Round, Bel spotted Phaedra, her face tight with displeasure.

He hurried to them when a curly head peered around the corner.

"Alix," he murmured in surprise. He met them at the entrance, following when Phaedra motioned them into a recessed alcove. It offered little cover, but Alix was small.

"What are you doing here?" he asked, not sure if he was more angry or impressed.

"I needed to see you," Alix replied.

"Are you even allowed up here?"

"*No*," Phaedra said. "But this one's slipperier than an otter and just as ruthless. She told me she'd get to you with or without my help." She glared down at Alix with a look of utter betrayal.

Alix shrugged. "And I would've."

"What's the matter?" Bel asked. Alix was smart enough not to risk such a move without cause. "Where's Lena?"

"It's about her," Alix said. "Bel, she's not all right."

30

Lena hadn't wanted to get up, no matter what Alix said about not getting up the day before, either. A headache thrummed beneath her left brow for a third day, and she cried off going for a walk, waving Alix on. Phaedra hadn't liked it—not able to keep an eye on both of them at the same time, Lena supposed.

Alix had left reluctantly, and Phaedra locked the door behind them.

Lena lay there in almost darkness, the light of one candle all she could bear. She hoped if she lay there long enough, in the quiet, alone, her body would succumb finally to sleep.

She'd snatched a few hours here and there through the nights, but the smallest sound had her eyes flying open and heart racing. More than once she'd stumbled from the bed, half-awake, thinking King Dartegn had finally come to throw them in the Pit. Alix had had to coax her back to bed, assure her no one was there, they were safe, that if the king was going to cast them into the Pit, he would've done it by now.

None of it was restful, just enough to keep going. She closed her eyes and then Phaedra was opening the door with her, *"Up with you now, humans!"*

If she could just sleep...

The ghost of a noise pricked her ears, and Lena tensed. It was hard to tell at first the difference between someone walking past the corridor and someone entering the corridor; both bounded down the tunnel in a resounding echo that grated at her ears.

She listened in the dark, eyes wide, but heard nothing else.

Shifting on the bed, Lena dug her toes further into the blankets and tried to find the place on the pillow where her head throbbed the least.

She lay perfectly still, timing her breathing in counterpoint to the pulsing beat of her headache. The pain dulled her thoughts, but that didn't stop them from rushing like a river that'd breached its banks. She drowned in her worries, each a stone weighing her down.

Another noise.

Lena strained her ears over her pounding heart and headache.

Someone was coming.

But then...

No, it was nothing.

But what if it wasn't?

She held her breath and pressed a hand over her chest.

No, nothing.

Goddess, look at her. Scared of the smallest noise. Bedridden with her fears. Hot tears gathered at her lashes, partly from the pain of her head, partly in shame.

How had Bel done it? How had he gone so long in captivity, never safe, never at ease? Waiting for the next blow, never able to trust what was said or done?

Lena had barely lasted a fortnight or however long they'd been here. She didn't even know that anymore.

She'd known what she walked into coming with Bel. She'd made this bed when she decided to push onward with him, even when Eamon told them to go back. She lay in that bed now, her cheek chewed raw and her nails bitten to the quick.

She didn't regret it, but she wasn't sure how long she could bear it.

This interminable waiting...laying here, useless...

She was only a weight around Bel's neck, a target, a weakness. King Dartegn held all the power and there was nothing to be done about it.

She hated that most. How could she even help or be useful in a place like this, where everyone looked at her with hatred. And for good reason.

How could Bel ever retake his place among his people when he was always associated with their greatest enemy?

I'm a liability, Lena admitted to herself and the shadows.

The tears came faster now, soaking into the pillow. Her face grew
hot and her nose clogged, adding pressure to her head.

If she could just sleep...

Another noise. She wanted to scream in frustration, her eyes stinging with tears and tiredness. She carefully wiped at the tears, and it was
only when she'd mopped up most of them that she realized—it *had* been
noise this time.

Several pairs of feet.

She tried to calm her racing heart. *Just Alix and Phaedra.*

Lena was ready when the door cracked open, shielding her eyes from
the light.

"Lena?" Alix whispered.

"Hmm?"

But the girl retreated back outside.

Then Lena heard more voices, Phaedra talking in low tones with
someone. A male rumble replied, setting her pulse pounding again, but
when she made herself listen harder, she discovered it was Bel's voice.

The door opened again, and through her lashes Lena watched Bel's
silhouette slip into the chamber. He closed the door but left a sliver of
light.

In a moment he was there, kneeling beside her bed. His warm hand
cupped the side of her head, and she moaned softly as his thumb traced
soothing circles at her temple. A rustle of feathers, and then his wing was
draped over her like a second blanket, bringing with it the familiar scent
of him, musk and oil and Bel.

"Sweetheart, *c'vana*," he whispered to her, as if she was breaking his
heart.

The sound of his voice, the comfort of his hands and wing and presence, the imagined safety of their dark little bubble tipped her over the

edge. She fell into her tears, unable to stop, the salty heat burning tracks down her cheeks and nose.

Bel cooed and made soothing noises as she sobbed. He nuzzled her temple, and Lena buried her face in the hollow of his throat, breathing him in. Her fingers found the hair and down at his nape, and she clutched at him, needing him to stay, never wanting to let go.

He knelt over her, taking her in his arms, wrapping her up. One of his hands found her head again, and he held it in his warm palm, taking the weight from her neck. Lena hung on, desperate to hold him and be held, terrified he'd let go.

"I d-don't—know h-how—y-you did it," she sobbed and gasped.

"Did what, sweetheart?"

"*Survive*." She shook her head, gritting her teeth through another pulse of pain at her temple. "Always under threat. Away from your ki-kind."

Bel sighed, his breath warm against her cheek. "I did what I had to. I bore it. And it hurt, it hurt so damn much. So many nights, I lay in the dark and cried and raged at what happened."

"You were brave."

"No. Sometimes I was stupid. Sometimes it was defiance."

"Bel, I..." She didn't know what, just that she was so grateful and relieved to have him here.

"I know, *c'vana*. I'm sorry. I've asked so much of you."

"I'd do it again."

Bel cursed, and then his mouth found hers. His kiss wasn't passionate but full of love and comfort. His lips caressed hers, then her cheek, her jaw, her ear, her temple, before his forehead fell to hers.

"I don't deserve you. You're the brave one, Lena. You always have been. I swear, I'll make things right."

Lena wiped at her eyes, feeling raw and hollowed out. Her head throbbed even worse and her nose ran, but her heart was a little lighter for the shed tears.

"You shouldn't anger your cousin."

"It's worth the risk. *You're* worth it, *c'vana*. And if they still won't listen, we'll leave."

"Bel..."

"I've told them what I came to say. If this is all that comes of it, fine. This isn't a life, Lena. I want one for us, and if it isn't here, so be it."

He pushed himself up, and Lena immediately missed his warmth. He didn't move far and kept his wing over her and a hand for her to hold. With the other he picked up a waterskin and placed it near her head.

As Lena unscrewed the stopper, Bel inspected her unshackled wrists.

"Where's the salve I sent?"

"Here. But you don't have to."

"Yes, I do. Now, drink."

"Is that an order?" Her joke was as tired as she was, but it sparked a little mischief in his eyes, and he grinned down at her, giving her just what she wanted.

"I am a prince in these parts. People are supposed to do as I say."

Lena was too tired to laugh, but a comforting warmth bloomed in her chest, filling the gaping maw of worry that'd opened up inside her.

Bel rubbed the salve into her wrists, leaving behind a pleasant coolness on her skin and healing blisters.

"No new bruises?" he said neutrally, but she knew what he was really asking.

"No. They've stopped."

"Good."

When she finished with the water, she settled back down as Bel made himself comfortable on the floor beside her. He hooked an arm over her waist and blanketed her with his wing. Lena curled into him, her head already a little better from the water. Bel traced her brows and forehead in soothing circles with his thumb and gently kneaded her head and neck. If she'd been less tired, she might've been embarrassed at how quickly she melted for him as he petted her.

"Go to sleep, *c'vana*," he murmured.

"Don't leave," she whispered, lids already heavy.

"I'll be right here. I promise."

<hr>

Finally, Lena slept.

At some point, she was aware of Alix gingerly climbing over her to the far side of the bed. But then Bel kissed her lids and brows and whispered to her, coaxing her back to sleep.

When she next woke, pleasantly drowsy and her headache dulled, she found his head resting close to hers, face easy in sleep. He was still sat on the floor leaning against the bed, arm and wing draped over her and now Alix, too.

The candle had burned down to a nub, but there was enough light to see the contours of his face. She gently brushed a golden curl off his forehead. He nuzzled into her hand without waking, and Lena rested her head beside his, sharing breath.

She fell asleep again with her lips pressed to his cheek.

<hr>

Phaedra's, "Up with you now!" was a whisper the next morning. Rather than the door thrown open wide, it remained almost-closed, just ajar enough for Phaedra to peek inside.

Behind her, Alix grumbled, not quite roused, and rooted further under the blankets.

Lena heard Bel inhale sharply. "Does she do that every morning?" he whispered, voice deep and thick with sleep. His head lolled to the side, closer to her, his eyes still closed.

"Yes. Usually much louder."

Bel rumbled deep in his throat, a sultry, sleepy sound that made her toes curl. "Mm. The perks of being with a prince, no doubt."

She hummed her agreement, and they lapsed back into a peaceful quiet.

The candle had long since melted away, but the crack of light from the door was enough for Lena to trace Bel's profile with her eyes and then her fingertips. His breathing eased, but she'd slept beside him enough to know he didn't fall back to sleep. He seemed as content to receive her touch as she was to give it, and Lena took her time, not wanting the morning to find them and take Bel away.

Her hand wandered down his neck to the curve of one wing. Silky feathers slid beneath her fingers as she traced the bone, avoiding the overly sensitive wing base. Every so often, she felt a little knot or ridge, all the places where his wing had been broken at one time or another.

He'd spread the wing over her and Alix, a position he wouldn't have been capable of months ago. She was so proud of him for coming as far as he had, working to strengthen the wing as it healed, but with that pride was a shadow of shame. She'd never forget what rebreaking his right wing base felt like, the bone cracking under her own hands.

It needed to be done; there was no other way to heal it.

That didn't mean she hadn't fled the cell as soon as she'd done it and vomited her guts up in the corridor. It didn't mean she hadn't had nightmares about it for days afterward, hearing the *crack* in her dreams.

She'd left her mark on him, just like all the other wardens of Finhöln.

"You're thinking very loudly," Bel rumbled.

"I can finally hear my own thoughts again."

His warm palm cupped the side of her head. "Your head's better?"

"Much."

"Good. Do you think you can bear outside light?"

"Just be gentle with me."

He huffed a laugh, kissed her, and stood. Even under layers of blankets, she felt the loss of his wing, the weight and warmth of it leaving a cool absence behind.

Behind her, Alix grumbled.

Bel stretched, spine popping and wings flexing.

"All right," he said, taking her hand and drawing her from the bed, "put your boots on."

"Why?"

"I'm taking you somewhere."

"Bel, I doubt that's allowed."

"So?"

She opened her mouth but nothing came out, unused to this cavalier Bel.

Crossing the chamber, Bel eased the door open and stepped outside to speak with Phaedra, leaving Lena to dress.

When she joined him at the door, she found an unamused Phaedra sitting on her stool, knitting abandoned to frown up at Bel.

"The king won't like it."

"The king doesn't like anything," Bel countered. "Certainly nothing I do or say. Please, she needs this. I'll take responsibility."

Phaedra's lips pursed, and her gaze turned to Lena.

She blinked in surprise as the female avian looked her over.

"She's been looking unwell lately," Phaedra allowed.

"I'll stay," Alix called from the chamber. Bel opened the door wider so they could all see the mop of curls poking from the blankets. "Let Lena go with him. I'll stay here the whole time. Insurance. She'd never leave without me." And after declaring all this, Alix rolled over, her back turned to the light.

"That's very true," Bel said.

Phaedra sighed. "Very well. But these stay on," she said, holding up the shackles. "It won't be my head that rolls for this."

"Thank you, Phaedra," Lena said, though she didn't quite know what she was thanking her for. She held her arms out nonetheless, used to the feel and sound of the shackles clicking closed around her wrists.

Bel glared at the iron but didn't argue. He thanked Phaedra too, adding, "We'll just be an hour or two."

"See that you are. I'm not covering for you, Adiiron or not."

• • ◆ • •

When Bel had said *outside*, Lena thought he'd meant the Round, perhaps even the arena. Instead, Bel led her through a network of narrow passages all leading up. Her legs burned from the steep steps, but curiosity kept her going.

She knew they were close when Bel grinned at her over his shoulder.

In another moment, they turned a corner and were bathed in sunlight.

The steps led to a small landing with an arched threshold carved into the dome. Leading *outside*. She followed Bel in wonder, eyes watering at the sudden brightness of true light.

"Oh, Bel..."

He smiled at the awe in her voice. A shadow passed over her, making the strong sunlight easier to bear. He balanced his wing on her head and a hand on her hip, drawing her into his side.

Wind whipped at their hair and his feathers, and the spring sun shone down on them as they stepped out onto a wide, flat terrace. Unseen from the base of the mountain, stone terraces had been carved or cobbled between several peaks and ridges of Hadria, creating space for gardens. A riot of green spilled out over dozens of stepped terraces, leaves and branches blowing in the breeze and irrigated channels reflecting the sun in sparkling ripples. Birds and clouds floated by, passing between peaks and levels of the hanging gardens.

They were so high up here, well within the clouds, with nothing to protect them from the wind. The conditions were mild now but the cold still nipped at her exposed skin—it was incredible.

Taking her hands, Bel led her into an orchard, high above the ground.

They passed through rows of apple and persimmon trees, delicate white blossoms perfuming the air and dancing in little swirls at their feet. The air smelled sweet and green and fresh, invigorating her senses. She took great gulps of it, filling her lungs to expel the dank air of the mountain.

They walked along little stone pathways that wended through the trees, their pace never more than an amble. She could almost feel her skin soaking up the sun, saving away a little of its radiance for when she had to go back to the dark.

It felt as though they stood at the top of the world, just them, alone like two creation gods surveying their divine work.

Until Bel drew up short, wings fluttering.

Lena looked around him to see what had suddenly caught his attention.

Back in a copse of apple trees, several warriors stood with a group of fledglings. At their center sat a delicate avian female nursing an infant. The child's dark hair stood out against its mother's pale skin and hair.

Lena could only blink in wonder before Bel was tucking her into his side and covering her with a wing, the crook balanced on her head.

He bowed his head to the female sitting amongst the fledglings. "My lady," he said, not waiting for a response before leading them down another path, deeper into the trees.

She opened her mouth to ask, but the further they got from the little group, the easier Bel became. He regained his bright smile, even winking as he drew his wing back. So Lena left her thoughts on the mysterious female behind, content to let Bel lead her.

Her soul felt lighter as they came to the end of the terrace. They hung back in the last row of trees, sheltered a little from the wind. There weren't any fruits to pluck yet, but the sweet smell of their blossoms filled her up.

Together they looked out over the jagged spine of the Gogona Mountains. Dark gray and treacherous, all the sharp crags and sheer cliffs were missing was a swirling mass of gray and purple clouds above to make it truly ominous. Instead, the day was mostly clear, the sky almost painfully blue.

Below, more terraces full of growing things sprawled out in organized rows. Beds of squash and tomato, cabbage and turnips. Yet, for all the bounty, many sat unsown, blank brown breaks in the rock that yielded nothing but dirt. For whatever reason, the avians weren't using all the beds.

Lena shivered, partly from the cold but also in sheer happiness.

She'd never thought something as simple as the sun could change her mood so quickly and drastically. In that moment, she longed to be a lazy cat, able to stretch out in a warm sunbeam and nap all afternoon.

Bel moved behind her, folding his arms over her chest and waist then draping his wings over them both. Immediately the cold bite of the wind disappeared, and Lena melted into the soft warmth.

"It's beautiful here," she said, voice barely above a whisper. There didn't seem to be a need for more. "This must be how they've borne it, all these years."

"Hadria is full of little wonders. But it was never meant to be a capital. A few lived here in times of peace, and it's been used as a stronghold many times. It hasn't been occupied for so long by so many before, though." He took a deep breath before he said, "It's not a place for us. Not to stay, anyway."

"After seeing Aeriand, I understand." Hadria was whatever the avians needed it to be in the moment—but the limits of that were apparent. They weren't thriving here; even Lena could see it.

It was more than the tragedy of losing Aeriand and the human threat at the foot of the mountain. The avians could only bear this campaign for so long, and the mountain could only bear them a little while yet.

"Yes. But I meant us. You and me."

Brows arched, Lena canted her head to peer at him. He hooked his chin over her shoulder, gaze cast to the craggy horizon.

"You don't want to stay here?"

Bel was slow in answering, and she watched him gather his thoughts.

"There are many things I like about being here," he said finally. "It's a relief to be among my kind again. To not be the only one."

Lena could understand that—she thought she'd been lonely before, as a cadet but the headmaster's daughter at Lindenfaire, as a squire but her own mother's squire, as a guard and lover to Prince Arion but avoided by the others for fear that she'd repeat something to him. All of that loneliness was real and tangible inside her, lonely but not alone, but it was still viscerally so different from being only one of two humans inside the whole mountain. Having Alix with her was a relief in so many ways; just having the same number of limbs and speaking the same language were small comforts when they were surrounded by difference.

Again, she didn't know how Bel had borne it as long as he did. Her admiration for his strength and resilience grew tenfold, and her heart swelled with pride. This male was broody, cagey, but so, so clever and strong. He survived what many wouldn't have. He'd been apart from his kind so long, in many ways he needed to relearn what it meant to be avian.

"But there are many things I don't," he continued, holding her hands and tracing where her skin disappeared under the shackle.

"They trust you because they trust their king. Hopefully, given enough time, they'll come to trust me too, because they trust you."

"You sound like Eamon," he grumbled.

It was on the tip of her tongue to ask, but something told her he didn't want to talk about Eamon just then.

"I really am all right," she said after a little while. "Maybe not as all right as I could be," she amended, "but this helps. I'll get used to it, and they'll get used to me. We don't have to leave."

If we even could. Another something told her King Dartegn wasn't likely to let them leave the way they'd come and slip back into the wilderness.

"We've done what we came here to do," Bel said. "I want to help my people if I can, but I don't know how or if they'd let me."

"You'll figure something out."

"Maybe. There's just not...I didn't truly belong, even before. I don't have a purpose here other than another body to send to battle."

Lena's heart lurched. It was sometimes easy to forget that a war waged on the other side of the mountain, with battles and skirmishes often daily occurrences. Bel was strong and able; he couldn't fly like the others, but he could fight.

She clutched at his forearm.

"I don't think Dartegn will let us leave," Bel said, voicing her own thoughts, "but he doesn't trust me with anything. I'm a problem to leave for later. I've lived that life before and it's not one I want again."

"What do you mean?" she said.

"In Aeriand, I was looked after, and a few people genuinely cared for me. But many blamed me for my mother's death, my father included. When he followed her a few years later, I was blamed for that, too. And then Maddok..." His throat bobbed, and Lena turned to press her face to the side of his, kissing his cheek.

"It's not your fault," she told him. "You were just a boy."

"I tell myself that same thing about my mother and father. But Maddok *was* my fault. It's a burden I'll always bear, and it's why Dartegn hates me. It's why he'll never trust me. To my kind, I'm to blame for the death of my family, one after the other. And really, they aren't wrong to think that."

"Bel..."

"I was so excited to serve with my brother. To finally be useful," he said, the words coming faster now, like the river that'd finally breached the dam. "I was finally going to *live*. But just when my life began, it ended. I got my brother killed. I ruined Dar's life. And I got thrown in an even smaller prison. But ask any avian what they think and they'll tell you I deserved it. Maybe I did."

Lena rebelled against the thought, the injustice of what had been done to Bel still a thorn irritating her sense of honor.

His words gave her pause, though. For truly, hadn't it been her greatest fear since coming here to Hadria, that "I don't want to be another prison for you."

"What?" His sound of surprise puffed against her skin.

"It may be easier to readjust to your kind without the burden of a human."

"You aren't a burden," he growled, vehement.

Lena shook her head. "Here, I am. I'm a liability."

"Not to me. You freed me, Lena. With you, I'm not a spare or a nuisance. I'm a man. That's all I want to be. I'd give you the same, the life you want. It's no less than you deserve."

Bittersweet tears pricked her eyes. "But with me, there's no life, not really. Outside Hadria, it would always be isolated, even nomadic." That little homestead she'd been building in her mind had begun to lose its appeal; yes it was safe enough, a place where she and Bel could just *be*, but most of its qualities were those she'd been desperate for as they trudged through the forest and unknown—safety, defensibility, secrecy. Beyond that..."I don't think you want that, Bel. And honestly, I'm not sure I do, either."

A safe place of peace and quiet appealed greatly to her, but at the cost of being kept apart from everything and everyone? It was a steep price.

"I want a life. A *real* life," Bel said. "I don't know what that looks like yet, but it has you in it. I loved my brother and I want to help my kind, but *you* are my people, Lena. *You* are my home." He hugged her tighter, pressing their cheeks together. "I don't want to hide away or always be on the run. That's not living, not truly. I want a life where I can stand beside you and no one will gawk or sneer. And I think if we want such a life...we're going to have to make it."

"Changing minds is difficult."

"But that doesn't mean it isn't worth trying. I want to make a world for us, Lena. I think it starts with our people no longer at war."

Something firm lodged in Lena's chest, a sense of resolve that eased her worries and sharpened her mind.

"This war has to end," Lena agreed.

"Whatever we do, however we can help, I think we have to try making a new world and a place for us in it. And if we can make such a world, my place will always be beside you."

"I just don't want you to feel..." she grimaced, forcing out the word, "beholden."

"Oh, I'm beholden to you, sweetheart. And besotted and beguiled and bewitched and—"

"Shh," she hushed him, "or they really will think I've used deviant human sex rituals on you."

His snort of laughter puffed against her fingers. "That one's my favorite."

"Mm-hmm." Lena hadn't worked out yet if she should be flattered the avians thought her capable of such a thing or insulted that they thought she needed supposed sex magic to influence Bel.

Still chuckling, Bel kissed from her neck to her shoulder then ran his nose and lips back up in an *ashita*.

"I want a life with you, *c'vana*. Hopefully one full of deviant human sex rituals—oof!" He wheezed when her elbow connected with his gut.

"Seductress," he laughed.

"For a prince, you aren't very gallant," she teased.

"That's because I'm not a prince, not really." He leaned in close, lips just grazing her ear to whisper, "Just say you'll stay with me, Lena. That's all I want. If it means helping end this war, securing peace, changing minds, fine. We'll do it. Together."

31

Lena's hands were still a little raw and smelled of potatoes from that morning's chores when Phaedra came to collect her and Alix for their afternoon walk. Lately, in an effort to endear, or if not endear then prove herself, or if not that then at least show she meant no harm, Lena and Alix sat outside the corridor to their chamber, in full view of the Round, performing important but menial tasks; darning socks, twining thread, peeling potatoes.

Bel often joined them, and it proved to be enjoyable enough. It alleviated the worst of her anxiousness, seeing him every day, assuring herself he hadn't been murdered in his sleep.

The tedious rhythm of the tasks had their own soothing quality, and it made the time pass faster, hurrying them along towards...something. Lena wasn't quite sure yet.

An incessant current of anticipation ran through Hadria, a buzz of nervous energy that never quite dissipated. Always looking to the next day, the next battle. Soon, it superseded worries over the two humans inside the mountain. There were many more to worry about down the mountain.

"Where are we going?" asked Alix, an excited note to her voice.

Lena looked up from her hands, realizing she'd been mindlessly following Alix and Phaedra. They'd walked their terrace so many times now, Lena could do it blind.

Phaedra diverted from their known path, instead heading for the narrow steps leading up to the next terrace.

"Prince Arubel has gotten permission for you to visit one other place. I thought you might like to see it." The avian guard looked back at them, a secret sparkling in her eyes. "I think it will cheer your sad faces."

Alix made a rude sound with her tongue but followed behind Phaedra merrily. Lena did too, just more subdued.

She was better for the night spent with Bel and their excursion outside a few days ago. He and the sun had done her a world of good—but it didn't solve their problems.

Lena resolved to take it a day at a time; she repeated this to herself at night and was able to catch a few more hours of rest.

She was *trying*.

It unnerved her somewhat that their avian guard had come to read their moods and thoughts so well. She and Alix had spent so much time with Phaedra that if it weren't for the shackles Lena wore, she might even think Phaedra liked them a little. At least Alix. It was easy to like Alix.

Phaedra led the way, catching several sets of stairs up at least three terraces. Lena lost count as her legs began to burn.

Her interest piqued alongside her unease as they entered a passage, dimly lit by the occasional torch. Their footsteps echoed in the tunnel, and cool air raised the hair at the back of Lena's neck.

"Is this the way to the kitchens?" Alix asked, all innocence.

Phaedra snorted. "Not a chance. You're not allowed anywhere near there, her," she nodded at Lena, "because...well, you know, but *you*," she pointed accusingly at Alix, "because of the damage you could do."

Alix chuckled smugly. "That's true."

Lena didn't take the insinuation that she'd possibly try to poison the food to heart. At least, she *tried*.

They turned a bend in the passage and were struck by sunlight and the pungent, musky smell of livestock.

Phaedra led them out into a wide cavern. A long time ago, it was likely a cave of some sort, but over the centuries, the avians had polished down the rock, smoothed the floors and carved alcoves, stalls, and paddocks for all manner of animals. Wood and ceramic had been added to create an enormous stable. On the far side, a set of shallow steps led up to a cavemouth, teethed with thick columns. Shocks of green lit by sunlight filtered in from outside, giving the space a glowing warmth that was as immediately comforting as the sounds and smells of the animals.

"You can care for all of these animals here?" Lena asked in wonder, counting hundreds of goats, donkeys, deer, chickens, ducks, pigs, and even a handful of dogs.

"Oh, yes. More, actually. This is just what we have left from…" Phaedra cleared her throat and ushered them on.

Lena didn't press, just squirreled away the unfinished comment in her pool of things that didn't quite make sense in Hadria.

The human forces had no idea how many avians they fought; in a hail of arrows and feathers, it was difficult to ever gauge. Many soldiers had grumbled there had to be a mountain full of avians in there, always another to take the place of a fallen.

Lena had seen nothing close to such numbers.

The hollow mountain truly felt hollow, like a cast made for something much larger than what filled it now.

A nicker drew her attention, the familiar sound of horses making her eyes sting. She hadn't seen horses at first, didn't know avians to use or ride them.

Lena's heart began to beat fast and hard, barely hearing Phaedra as she moved them along through the stable, saying, "We found them wandering the mountains and brought them here a while ago. They have settled nicely."

By the time they reached an alcove set up for horses, Lena's eyes dripped with heavy tears. Behind a rope, standing in a bed of hay and munching on packed grass, was their little herd; Yvain, Miri, Ruan, and the packhorses.

A sob burst from Lena, and she would've been mortified to make such a sound in front of Phaedra and the handful of other avians moving about the stables, but she was moving too fast, over the rope and to Yvain.

The great gray warhorse trotted forward to meet her, ears forward in greeting. He chuffed at her, breath warm on her face. She buried her face in his neck, tears unstoppable now, as his velveteen nose and lips nipped at her hair and shoulders.

She heard Alix's excited noises behind her as she cooed to Miri, but she couldn't tear her eyes away from Yvain. He lowered his head, looking at her with one liquid brown eye. His long lashes tickled her forehead, and Lena smoothed her hands down his neck and flank, needing to assure herself that he was well.

Yvain waited patiently as she patted him down, and the other horses gathered near, wanting attention, too. She petted noses and forelocks, cooed into soft ears and patted hearty flanks. They all looked wonderful, not like they'd crossed half the continent and then got lost in the mountains; their coats shone, their manes flowed untangled, their hooves were unshod but clean.

When she was done petting the other horses, Yvain pushed forward again, wanting more attention she was happy to give. Lena scratched his neck and chin, whispering to him, "I've missed you, my friend."

Yvain huffed happily.

"And you train them for battle?" Phaedra was asking Alix.

"For lots of things," said Alix. "Moving heavy things, farming, riding. But the big ones, like Lena's, he's a warhorse. His name's Yvain."

"Yvain...like Sir Yvain and the Green Dragon?"

The new voice had all of them turning, and Phaedra quickly dropped into a bow.

A few paces away from the rope hemming in the horses stood a petite avian female, one elegant white wing folded neatly behind her and the other draped over her right shoulder and side. A crown of silver feathers had been woven through her white-blonde hair, and with a start, Lena remembered where she'd seen the female before.

That day, outside, in the orchard. They'd disturbed her, and Bel had bowed to her, too.

My lady, he'd called her.

Lena swallowed on a dry throat.

"Queen Cira, I didn't hear you. My apologies," Phaedra rushed to say. "I didn't realize you'd be here. I'll take the humans back—"

"It's all right, Phae," the avian queen said gently, eyes crinkling at the corners as she smiled. "You know I like to sneak up on you. And I've been wanting to meet the humans." She turned that gentle face to Lena, wide avian eyes flicking over her in an assessing but not intrusive way. "Hello, human," she said in Vagoran.

"Your Majesty," Lena said, bowing her head, the movement so familiar from her years of court etiquette training.

"*You can slay someone as effectively with manners as you can with a blade*," her mother was known to say.

The avian queen smiled as if she was charmed. "They told me you were polite. Even when some yelled terrible things at you."

"And when they threw things," Alix muttered.

Queen Cira looked at Alix in surprise, delicate brows arching. "I've never seen a human child before."

"I'm not a child," Alix said, though thankfully without the usual gruffness when people called her that.

The queen frowned. "But you are small."

In truth, Alix wasn't that much smaller than the queen herself. Lena had never seen such a petite, delicate avian, hadn't known they came in anything but honed, muscled warrior. Those were the only kinds of avians she'd encountered on the battlefield, and it was the only kind she'd observed in Hadria.

This delicate creature, with her near-white hair and soft face, was the opposite of the morose, brooding King Dartegn. She imagined they must look striking together, their contrasts impossible to miss.

"She's young but not quite a child anymore," Lena explained to the queen. "Old enough to train."

Queen Cira nodded, seeming impressed. "It's best for those of us who are small to learn to fight. No one sees us coming." And she gave Alix a wink, making the girl smile.

A clamor echoed through the stables, the sound of pattering feet and childish laughs. The animals stirred, coming to the front of their stalls to see.

Lena watched in amazement as two more avians, tall and obviously warriors, shepherded a gaggle of avian fledglings inside. They bounced and bounded down the steps, giggling happily to see the animals, who bleated and brayed at them in welcome. Lena counted seven of them, the youngest a toddler, carried by one of the warriors, and the eldest around Alix's age.

"I bring the fledglings to visit the animals often," Queen Cira explained. "They've been curious about the horses. Perhaps you can answer their questions?"

Lena's mouth opened and closed without making a noise. She finally managed a nod because what could she do, deny the avian queen?

She looked askance at Phaedra, only to find the female warrior looking just as bemused as Lena was.

Alix caught her eye, and the girl just shrugged with a lopsided grin. Stepping up to the rope, Alix met the group of avian children and their wide, curious eyes with her most charming smile.

"Who wants to see the horses?" Alix asked them in *alvani*.

• ◆ •

Sometime later, when all the fledglings had run out of questions about the horses and had their turn sitting on Yvain's back, Queen Cira beckoned Lena over from her seat on a bench hewn from the cavern wall. Lena approached slowly, aware of the queen's two guards and Phaedra watching.

The queen patted the space beside her, and Lena sat on the edge, ready to jump up if a guard warned her away.

For a long moment, neither spoke, instead watching the younger children giggle and shout as they chased the goats in their paddock. Or was it the goats chasing them? Lena couldn't quite tell. Further down, Alix and a few of the older fledglings had made an obstacle course out of bales and barrels, trying to impress one another with how far and high they could jump.

Filled with the loud noises of happy children and animals, the scene before her was almost surreal in its peacefulness. She hadn't seen anything like it in...

"I'll tell you a truth," the queen finally said.

Lena turned her head to look at Queen Cira, leaving her hands relaxed on her lap, nonthreatening.

The queen leaned forward like she had a secret to share. "I don't usually bring the fledglings here on this day, but I'd heard you were headed this way and decided to finally see these mysterious humans for myself."

Not sure what to say to that, Lena kept silent, letting the queen look her over. At first, she'd been tempted to think the sweet demeanor was an act, even a trap, but it took less than an afternoon for Lena to decide that, no, it was just who the queen was. However, Lena didn't miss the sharp edge of cleverness in her eyes.

"I'm surprised and disappointed in equal measure."

Lena smiled hesitantly, replying in stilted *alvani*, "I'm pleased and insulted in equal measure."

The queen laughed. "Very good, human."

"I hope...I hope that you don't find us..." She didn't quite know the *alvani* word for what she meant. *Odious. Abhorrent. Disgusting.* "Alix and I both mean no one harm. We just came to help Bel."

"I understand. If I'd thought you were a danger, I wouldn't have let the fledglings anywhere near you. I came ahead to see just that." One fine brow ticked up. "If you were a threat, what better opportunity to show your hand than finding the little avian queen, alone."

Now horrified and impressed in equal measure, Lena insisted, "I would never—"

"Yes," the queen smiled, "I wanted to see that for myself. If it eases your worries, I knew Phaedra would stop you before anything happened. And though I'm small and don't wear warrior's garb, I wouldn't have let you touch me."

"I believe you," Lena said and meant it.

"Excellent. You may be the only one." The queen's face turned rueful, a joke at her own expense Lena didn't quite understand.

Lena had guarded a crown prince for years, one who was a seasoned warrior and could hold his own on the battlefield. She still wouldn't have trusted any stranger, let alone a perceived enemy, to approach him.

"I never heard you say," the queen said, "your horse, he's named after the Sir Yvain in the tale?"

"Yes, he is."

"Is it a popular story where you are from? It's a favorite among avians."

"It's an old story," Lena said, "but maybe not so popular anymore. You see more stories with..." Lena cleared her throat. "Stories that just have humans."

"Ah. Yes, I suppose that makes sense." Queen Cira smiled sadly. "Perhaps that's why it's still such a popular tale amongst my people. It helps us remember a time we weren't alone."

Stricken, Lena opened her mouth to...apologize? The weight and guilt of all that'd been done to not just the avians but every creature that once lived on the Vagoran continent—dragons and harpies, griffins and manticores, serpents and sirens—pressed down on her chest.

She wasn't responsible for most of it, but that some of the blame *could* be laid at her feet...it made her guts twist in regret.

Nothing she said could make it better. All she could do was swear to herself she'd never kill again if she could help it.

"It's always been my favorite tale," Lena admitted quietly. "Yvain was my first horse purchased with my own wages. I chose him. And when I first saw him, he just looked like an Yvain."

Some of the sadness left the queen's eyes. "He seems to have chosen you, too. He is much happier now that you're here. Before, he would stay in the back and not let the children pet him. With you, he is content.

Enough to let the fledglings climb all over him."

Lena couldn't help her grin, the show of loyalty from her warhorse easing some of the ache in her chest.

A little whine drew the queen's attention.

Lena had spied the baby throughout the afternoon, the queen's wings sometimes shifting just right to allow a glimpse of her child's dark head through her feathers. It was still a shock to see the infant, held protectively to her mother's shoulder, kept hidden and warm under her wing.

The baby fussed, tiny fist curling against Queen Cira's shoulder. The queen cooed and kissed her, rocking back and forth until the baby settled.

"She's beautiful," Lena murmured.

The queen's smile was radiant, full of maternal pride and pleasure. "We named her Aurelia, but I call her Elia."

More tears pricked Lena's eyes, her chest aching in an unfamiliar way as she looked at the baby avian, her dark hair wispy and her wings just two little tufts of down.

Elia. Lena knew that *alvani* word. *Hope.*

That's what this little princess was. Hope.

It took her a long time to tear her gaze away from the baby, and she looked up to find Queen Cira watching her. Not worried or wary but curious.

"Thank you," Lena said, understanding what a gift the queen had bestowed.

32

Bel was suspicious when, rather than taking him to the arena for morning training, Eamon led him into the warren of unused corridors in the lower levels of the Round. The passages grew dimmer as the sconces grew scarcer, the air cool and damp. Bel couldn't help asking, "Another secret meeting? This is getting very cloak and dagger."

Eamon threw a scolding look over his shoulder. "Just do this for me. It's important. I wouldn't ask if it wasn't."

Except Eamon hadn't asked, had he?

"It's important for me to be seen with Lena and Alix," Bel reminded him. He was having to miss their walk to accompany Eamon into the bowels of the mountain.

He'd taken to joining Lena and Alix on one of their daily walks, gliding down to their lower terrace in the afternoon. Phaedra had grumbled a bit but ultimately allowed it since the shackles stayed on and he hadn't tried to take Lena anywhere again. They strolled together, talked, and kissed, and Bel made sure every avian in the Round saw them. Especially Maron.

"A day away won't hurt," Eamon grumbled.

"You know as well as I do that even a day's difference could start gossip." And gossip like that meant a setback. He wanted to appear as a unit, a pair, as often as possible, the sight of them together eventually just an everyday sight. Nothing to gawk at or scorn.

Eamon wanted Lena and Alix to be hidden away, forgotten. Dar no doubt allowed the walks in the first place to remind everyone of the humans their long-lost and likely deranged prince had brought. Bel refused to let them be hidden away or separated from him again.

All these concessions were trying Dartegn's nerves; Bel could tell from the vein in Dar's forehead that popped every time he argued for more freedoms for Lena and Alix. He tried to ask for little things, a bit more time, a few more comforts. At every turn, Bel and Lena had done as they were asked, strengthening his claim that they'd come in good faith.

Still, he wasn't naïve—the main reason for time with Lena was likely Dartegn being called to battle more and more. The human army had renewed is attacks after several months of infrequent skirmishes, attempting to keep the avians occupied in the west while they dug into the southern ridge. Every day, Dartegn and his warriors flew out to inspect their progress and make a show of it, allowing the humans to think that they dug in secret.

Left without a cousin to scowl at him nor much supervision at all, Bel took advantage, making himself useful where he could and claiming more time with Lena. He helped repair armor and boots and furniture; he cooked and chopped firewood and stitched threadbare blankets. He brought Lena and Alix out into the Round to help him darn socks and twine thread and skin vegetables.

It was all under the watchful eyes of his kin, but more than that, Bel enjoyed the work. Keeping his hands busy quieted his mind and therefore his worries.

But because the work he did was menial and tedious, there was little reason to refuse when Eamon came asking him to come with him.

"It'll be fine," Eamon insisted, not slowing his pace.

Bel sighed and continued to follow, equal parts curious and suspicious. He'd no doubt for the purpose of Eamon leading him back this way, but he wanted to find out more about all this scheming, to finally understand its scope.

And…for all his resentment at being left to rot in Finhöln, Eamon was still Bel's *at'tan*—and he had a point that Dar's plan to start a rock-slide sounded terrible.

Eamon finally turned a corner and led the way through a steep archway. The air held the faint smell of stale grain, and inside the chamber, moldering sacks and piles of wheat littered the floor. A few torches had been lit and placed in the sconces, but deep shadows pooled in every niche and corner, little red eyes reflecting the firelight.

Almost a dozen avians awaited them—every important person Eamon had had Bel meet, as well as a few new faces.

He stopped a few steps inside as Eamon went to greet and gather the others.

Bel kept that position, the open archway at his back, as the councilors and warriors hushed, looking between him and Eamon.

"It really is a strong likeness," said one of the councilors, an older female whom Bel thought was called Linnea. "This just might work."

His wings drew up tight to his back.

"He's an Adiiron," said Eamon with pride. He looked over his shoulder and beckoned Bel closer.

Bel didn't move.

"More importantly, he's got the look of one," said the male named Faros.

Eamon waved him forward again, and again Bel refused.

"Bel…" he sighed.

"I thought my identity had been established," said Bel, willing to play ignorant for the moment.

"It's not in question at all," said Linnea. "In fact, it's just what we've needed."

Ah. Here it was. Finally said aloud.

"Needed for what?"

Eamon's grin dimmed, knowing Bel well enough to know when he was being obstinate.

"To take your rightful place," Eamon said.

"That's treason," Bel said easily.

"Prince Arubel, let me ask you this," said Faros, "do you know how many of us there are left?"

Bel kept the surprise from his face. "No. I admit, far fewer than I'd thought or hoped."

"We're dying inside this mountain," said Faros.

Eamon nodded. "Some time ago, a colony was sent to the eastern sea. The old and the fledglings. Some of the females and younger males. They deserved a chance. But even then, even with half our people outside the mountain, we number only fifty thousand."

The number was staggering, hitting him like a physical blow. During his brother's reign, Aeriand had numbered in the hundreds of thousands and had been close to a million in reigns past. Other cities and colonies had thousands.

To be whittled down to splinters...

"The loss of Aeriand was devastating," said Eamon, "a hard blow that many didn't survive. More have succumbed to Hadria. The air here —it isn't good. Fledglings grow without seeing the sun and stars. Not even the gardens have been safe, depending on where the human lines are."

"An end to the war seems in our best interest, then," said Bel.

"It isn't that simple."

"The human king won't broker a truce," said Bannor the archivist, stepping forward. "He isn't interested in treaties, just our destruction."

"With the information you brought to us, we understand now how far the human king is willing to push to destroy us. He'll sacrifice his own army to do it," Linnea said, eyes hard.

"It's the move of a desperate man," said Eamon. "But our king is no less desperate. You've heard his plan."

"A rockslide."

"More than that," Bannor corrected. "Collapse the western mountainside. Bury the whole human army and make Hadria impossible to approach."

"So you see, we have two kings, willing to destroy themselves to destroy the other." Eamon closed the distance between them, standing before Bel and leveling him with a gaze weary of death. "He may not mean to do it, but Dartegn will bring this whole mountain down on us."

"You don't know that," Bel protested.

"I don't. But Dartegn doesn't know that it will work. It's a gamble our people could pay for with their lives."

"We may save the human king the trouble of eradicating us," spat Faros.

"Then find a better plan," Bel insisted. "Give Dar another option."

Bel couldn't imagine Dartegn truly wanted to risk Hadria and all the avians inside, especially when two of them were his mate and fledgling. But Bel did know what it was to have no other options, how thankless it was to choose a path just because it was the only one there at his feet.

"You think we haven't tried?" Eamon grumbled. "Dartegn has always been impetuous. He can't see through his anger and bitterness."

Bel had many memories of Dar's hot temper growing up, but he didn't see an impetuous male now. Kingship had hardened Dartegn's heat, forging him into something stronger and sharper. There was still a fire burning inside, but Bel wondered if it was less that Dar couldn't see beyond his anger and more that Eamon couldn't see past the boy he'd trained.

"Then what do you propose?" Bel asked, wanting to hear the words.

Eamon drew himself up, looking about to the others before answering, "You're the true Adiiron heir, Bel. You were always Maddok's heir. You even look like him." A bittersweet grin kicked up one side of Eamon's mouth. "So like him."

"You have Adiiron blood and the coloring," said Bannor.

"And that will win us the war, will it?" Bel couldn't help the sneer in his voice.

"It may save us, yes," Eamon insisted.

"I fail to see how—"

"A true Adiiron would inspire, give the people hope."

"Dartegn has as much Adiiron blood as I do."

"Dartegn never had much of the look of his mother. He's his father through and through," argued Faros.

"But he's the one who's led you for ten years. You've all fought beside him. When Mad—" Bel's voice caught "—when Maddok fell, it was Dar who led. You'd repay him like this? Stabbing him in the back?" He had little love left for his cousin and no affection, but the ardent disloyalty by those sworn to support Dartegn had Bel's feathers bristling.

"Where has his leadership gotten us?" asked Faros. "Stuck in this mountain. Our capital destroyed."

"And it was all his fault, was it? He made every decision on his own, never listening to counsel?" Bel retorted.

Faros's lips thinned.

"Bel, think for a moment," Eamon cajoled. "You know Dar. He never wanted to be king. It was always meant to be *you*, if something happened to Maddok."

"You think I would've done better? I barely had my adult feathers, Eamon!"

"What I think is that you could do better now."

"How? You just said the human king will stop at nothing. What could I do that Dar hasn't?"

"You have insight into the human king's mind. You know about humans, what they want. You could be a great Adiiron king, if you just—"

"*I'm not Maddok!*"

Bel's shout echoed in the chamber, scaring away the little red eyes lurking in the shadows. The other avians looked on in stunned silence.

When none dared speak, Bel rasped, "If you wanted me as king, then you should've *come for me*."

Eamon made a choked sound. "*Ad'ana*, I..."

"If you thought I'd be a better leader than Dartegn, you knew where to find me. But you didn't."

Pain saturated Eamon's face, and Bel relished it.

"Prince Arubel, you know any rescue, so far into human territory, was impossible," Bannor tried to reason.

"It wasn't. I know it, you all know it, and Dartegn knows it, too. But I suppose that doesn't matter now." He said the words but didn't believe them, not when the hurt was still raw.

"We all have things to atone for," said Bannor. "We can't change the past. But we can try to make a better future."

"You think because I have the look of an Adiiron that I can lead like one? I can't fly, maybe never will again. How could I ever lead our warriors?"

"We don't need a warrior, we need a peacemaker," said Linnea.

"Artemian won't talk terms. If that's your gamble, you've already lost, and our people will pay for it."

"It's a *chance*, Arubel," insisted Eamon.

"What makes you think any avian outside this room would choose me, the lost spare no one wanted, over the king who's led you bravely for years? A king with an *heir*."

More than one councilor shifted anxiously at the mention of Dartegn's little daughter.

"The princess is the first fledgling born in almost a year," said Linnea. "The mountain...it isn't healthy for us."

"All the more reason to protect her," Bel said.

"The child is a blessing but also fragile. Weak," said Faros. "Should the king fall in battle, it'd be years before the princess is ready to be queen, if she even survived long enough."

Bel's blood went cold at Faros's words. All of it could be true, but the insinuation...He thought of that glimpse he'd caught of her and shook his head.

"And what of Dartegn? How will you make him abdicate?"

The councilors looked amongst themselves.

"We hope he sees reason," said Eamon.

Bel laughed humorlessly. "First you say he's tempestuous and now you hope he'll see reason? Which is it?"

"A controlled show of force will be enough," said Faros.

"An assassination," Bel corrected.

"Not if we can avoid it."

Bel turned his glare onto Eamon, not wanting to believe his *at'tan* would go along with any plan to assassinate a former pupil. Eamon wouldn't quite meet Bel's eyes, looking instead at his forehead.

"And the fledgling? Cira?" he insisted.

"They shouldn't be a threat to you," Eamon said, barely above a whisper.

"*Threat* to me?" Bel roared. "Our people won't accept this. *I* won't accept it!"

"They'll see, Arubel," Eamon insisted. "Your years away made you strong. I can see it. They will, too. And we'll guide you. Right now, what the people need most is hope."

Bel knew what a dangerous thing hope could be. He also hadn't seen an absence of it within Hadria. Weariness, yes. Frustration, yes. But hopelessness?

"Guide me," Bel repeated, casting his gaze about the chamber to meet the eyes of every councilor. Some met his stare defiantly, but more let their eyes fall to the floor. "I see. You don't want a king. You want an Adiiron puppet to say the things you whisper in my ear. The princess is too young and Queen Cira doesn't have a claim. None of you could do it. The people would see it for the coup it is."

Eamon sighed. "The sovereign has always had a council—"

"Not one that's been self-appointed," Bel hissed.

"Bel—gods-damnit!" Eamon nearly shouted. "We can make you sovereign. Let me make you king!"

Bel stared at his *at'tan*. Frustration pulled away the façade of patience and reasonableness Eamon affected to reveal a male red in the face with his desperate guilt.

Perhaps Bel would've felt sorry for him once, even felt that kingship, *recognition*, was his due for all the years spent captive and broken. But he didn't. He'd only ever wanted his brother's approval—never his throne.

"No," Bel said, willing to say it as many times as needed until Eamon heard.

The older warrior bared his teeth, betrayal plain in his feral snarl.

"If you won't think of your people, maybe you'll at least think of your *humans*," Faros spat the word.

Everything in Bel stilled. "What?"

"Our people will never truly accept humans here, not after everything they've done," said Faros. "Certainly not one of their knights."

"But if you were king..." added Bannor.

Bel snorted in incredulity, but it was Eamon who spoke next, his voice as unyielding as the mountain they stood in. "If Arubel were king, he could keep them safe." He looked over his shoulder at Bel to say, "But avians would never accept a human queen."

Bel's smile was all teeth. "All the more reason not to be king, then. She's my *c'vana*. I won't have another."

"And the people won't have her."

"Well, then."

"Sovereigns are allowed some...eccentricities," said Linnea. "Your queen need not be your *c'vana*."

"An avian queen, one from the old families, would strengthen your position," Eamon said in that pedagogic tone he took sometimes, when Bel needed more time to understand.

"This is treason," Bel told them. "You have a king. You have an heir. And neither is nor ever will be me."

Bel gave them his back, turning for the doorway and the corridor outside, wanting away. From their plans, their lunacy, their desperation. Gods, if the humans knew they held onto themselves by a thread...how close they were to consuming one another, self-immolating to annihilation...

"Prince Arubel," Faros called.

Bel stopped just outside the threshold, turning only his head.

"Think on what we've told you, but say nothing. You may not see it, but the king will lead us to ruin. We will stop him before that happens.

You'd be wise to help us, and your *c'vana* safer for it."

"The humans are vulnerable," said Linnea. "A weakness to you. We cannot afford weaknesses."

Bel turned so they could all see his eyes and the rage burning there when he said, "I won't speak of this because of what little respect I still have for my *at'tan*. But if you ever threaten Lena again or try to harm her, I'll pluck the wings from your backs and throw you in the Pit myself."

"Bel..." Eamon tried, but he was already marching out into the corridor, leaving them and their delusions behind.

Bel went straight to Lena, first to calm his fury with the sight and smell and feel of her, then to tell her what had happened, and then to tell Phaedra to remain vigilant. She no longer guarded the avians from Lena and Alix; now, he needed her to guard Lena and Alix from avians themselves.

33

In the days since Bel explained the conspiracy being laid in his name without his consent, Lena noticed an odd shift in the dynamics of those avians she saw day to day. Phaedra was as careful as ever, but rather than watching her and Alix for misconduct, her vigilance was instead devoted to watching all the avians that came near them. If it weren't for the shackles she still wore, it'd almost seem like Phaedra watched over them.

Their days had grown a little brighter, too; instead of a second walk through the Round, Lena and Alix spent most afternoons in the sunnier sanctuary of the stable, tending to the horses and other animals.

The avians who worked in the stables remained wary; they didn't protest the spare hands, but they didn't warm to her and Alix.

Not the way the fledglings had.

Most afternoons, Queen Cira, her two guards, and the gaggle of fledglings she looked after joined them. Lena learned from the queen that since she was one of the few who didn't go to battle and didn't have any critical tasks to perform like the cooks and guards and grooms, she oversaw those fledglings who needed looking after. Some had parents out working or fighting each day. Others had no one at all.

"I used to do more," Queen Cira told her one day as they watched over the playing children. She spoke in *alvani* but slowly, so that Lena could understand better. "Dar insisted I lessen my duties, rest more when I was with Elia. It was all right then, this child had me bigger than your horse. Elia is here now and I'm recovered, yet Dar insists still that I do less. That I do *nothing*."

The queen huffed an annoyed sound, and Lena remained quiet, allowing Queen Cira to fill the space. For all that she was soft and shy, the queen enjoyed chatter. She struck Lena as lonesome, the only avian with nothing to do despite the crown she wore.

"Anyway," the queen said, shaking her head, "this at least I could do."

"It's no small thing," Lena replied in Vagoran. "The children needed someone, and you provided."

"Your human queen wouldn't do the same?"

Lena thought of Queen Ilona, an imperious figure in her memory, sitting regal and still in her throne. Her mother Lady Margot had served with Ilona, back when both were merely middling knights looking to prove themselves. They'd been good friends, Margot liked to recount, before Ilona was chosen by Artemian and dutybound to marry him.

"I can't imagine her, no."

"Hm."

Then the children had gotten into an argument and the queen swept away in a rush of white feathers to soothe tempers.

It was something similar each day, a routine that took the sharp edges off the strangeness of spending her afternoons with the avian queen and a half-dozen fledglings. If Lena didn't let herself stop to think about it, she could forget the outlandishness of the avian queen treating her like a friend, happy to chatter away the afternoons as the children played.

There was even a day that Lena, Alix, and Phaedra accompanied the queen and fledglings outside. The cavemouth at the far side of the stables led onto a large terrace, blanketed in tall grasses and shaded by hardy trees. It was a space for the animals to graze every now and again, except for the goats, who were often taken to the other terraces to pick out the weeds in the growing beds.

The afternoon was painted in dappled sunshine filtering through the leaves, and sweetness hung in the air, crisp and green-smelling. Lena sat on a bed of loam and soaked in the spring sunlight, listening to Alix lead the fledglings through her favorite games.

It reminded Lena of the little gang Alix led back in Highclere, and she had to grin. Alix formed a little band with the older avian fledglings. They followed her through games and had her speaking fluent *alvani* in no time. With others near her age, Alix didn't have to worry over Lena so much, and Lena enjoyed watching Alix thrive in a group of kids, as well as her excited chatter while they returned to their room, recounting all she'd learned of avians that day.

———— ••◆•• ————

It took Lena several days to settle enough to speak more freely with the queen. Those first afternoons, she couldn't quite overcome the watchful eyes of the guards. They tracked her every movement, ready to stop what they no doubt all assumed was inevitable.

When she didn't attack or threaten the queen, and Lena grew used to the scrutiny, she allowed herself to actually converse with Cira.

That surreal feeling often struck her in the middle of a conversation with Queen Cira. The small female had a shy but easy nature, and talking came easily to her, especially when she could sate her curiosity by asking Lena questions. Her smiles were gentle and easy, her expression and voice soft. Lena could almost forget Cira was a queen, mated to a king waging war on her kind. But then an errant sunbeam would glint off the silver feathers of Cira's diadem or one of the fledglings would run up to her calling, "Queen Cira! Queen Cira! Look!"

And though she was open and friendly, the queen never ordered Lena's shackles be removed. She also never let anyone else carry the princess, and around Lena and even Alix, covered the baby with her wing.

It was a delicate dance, gauging the other, deciding what was true good will and what was perhaps guile instead.

Lena had once liked to think the best of others, that most weren't conniving or manipulative. Life had taught her differently, and those lessons still left a bitter taste in her mouth. Yet, they were what led her eventually to Bel.

As the days passed, Lena slowly began to believe that all the queen wanted was an ear. She likely could have anyone's she wanted, but there was something about speaking with a person on the outside. Queen Cira was lonely, and Lena knew what a smothering burden that was. So she listened to the queen chatter, letting it and the familiar stable work lull her.

E xplain something to me, if you'd be so good," the queen said one afternoon. She waved a hand in Alix's general direction, where she and the older fledglings were practicing mounting on Miri. "I still don't understand this squiring you do. It is training, but not of your own children? Must the training always be done outside the family?"

"Where a squire trains and with whom depends on many things," Lena said. "I'm not a good example. I squired for my own mother. But generally knights take on a squire who they see promise in." For such a rigid system that liked to claim foundations on the knight's code, it really was ambiguous when it came to squires. Still, it was something Lena knew much about and she gladly explained the process to the queen.

Cira listened with wide, interested eyes, her lips slightly parted. "And they're chosen that young? Taken away from their families? I'm not sure I could part with Elia that young and for that long."

Lena could only nod because she'd never been parted from her parents during training. Or, rather, they'd traded off when she became a squire, going from her father at Lindenfaire to serving as a squire with her mother. It'd been the starkest difference between her and the other cadets and squires.

"Not all children become squires," Lena felt the need to say. "Many stay with their families. It's just the way of becoming a knight. Training begins early."

"Hmm." Queen Cira looked over to the fledglings with consideration. "But they are at least happy, these squires? Even away from their families?"

"I think generally yes." It depended on the squire and the knight they served, certainly.

She thought she understood this preoccupation with sending children off so young. Avians only produced a few children between mates. One or two, rarely three. Every fledgling was precious, and they lived with their family for as long as possible. The parents were responsible for training and educating, it wasn't passed off to tutors or knights.

Well, most of the time, anyway.

She admired this aspect of avian culture, this emphasis on keeping the family together, but she couldn't help the twinge of bitterness she felt on Bel's behalf.

"So not all human children grow up thinking life is about combat."

"No, not at all."

Queen Cira smiled sadly. "I want that for avian children. To not have to live the way of the warrior. Those called to other lives should get to do so. How will we ever have poets, artists, builders, and philosophers if all fledglings must be warriors first?" She shook her head. "Training them up, teaching them to fight, just to send them to slaughter...I *hate* it."

Lena had no words other than, "I hate it, too." Because she did. And because there was nothing else to say.

Carefully, slowly, she put her hands over one of Cira's and gave a comforting squeeze. She pulled them back just as slowly, making no move that would agitate a guard.

Cira gave her a watery smile. "I never thought it'd be easy to speak with a human."

"Really, it isn't. I only understand about half the *alvani* words you say," Lena said, drawing the laugh she'd hoped for.

<hr>

It was fitting that the first time Lena saw King Dartegn again, it was storming outside. The animals huddled further into their stalls and paddocks, avoiding the rain splatter coming in from the cavemouth. Everyone's mood had dampened with the rain, and Cira told her that the human forces were trying to reclaim a higher position on the mountainside. Lena knew the place; they'd taken and retaken it several times throughout the long campaign.

Cira rarely spoke of the king, and when she did, it was as a husband and mate rather than a king and warrior. Her affection for the king was evident, as was her worry over him when he and his army were out battling the humans, but there was something else, too. As the days passed, Lena didn't miss the way Cira grew more forlorn, her smiles coming slower.

At first Lena thought it was that the king was off fighting, but this was more than Cira's usual worry.

"*There are some who are...unhappy with my mate,*" the queen had told Lena, her tone quiet and careful. "*I worry soon he'll not only have to fight the humans but watch his back against his own.*"

Guilt had cramped Lena's stomach, and when she next saw Bel, she'd whispered to him, "*You need to tell your cousin about the plot.*"

Bel had drawn her closer with a wing, nuzzling close in what looked like an *ashita* but really he whispered in her ear, "*They can't move without me. I don't want their blood on my hands.*"

Lena wasn't so sure; she saw the way Eamon watched Bel, and she knew how the people around royalty managed and moved them. Kings and queens held power, but so did anyone who could influence them. She worried that Eamon and his conspirators would give up trying to influence Bel and instead give him no choice. If they assassinated Dartegn and left the throne empty, could Bel truly walk away?

And what of Cira and little Elia?

When the avian king stormed into the stables that rainy afternoon, Lena was sure he'd found out. The look he levelled her was thunderous, his face a savage snarl as he took in their little group of humans, guards, and fledglings, an odd little mish-mashed retinue.

A shudder skated up Lena's spine, and she held perfectly still under the violent stare of a predator.

Cira didn't see the danger, or perhaps she didn't care, for when she realized King Dartegn stood there, a half-dozen guards at his back, she hurried to him without hesitation.

"Dar—what are you—are you all right?" She went to cup his face, still damp from the rain. He drew her hand away but kept it held in his.

"What are you doing?" he said, low and dangerous.

Cira frowned. "I told you, I bring the fledglings to the stables in the afternoons. They like to—"

"You didn't say the humans would be here. What were you thinking?" he hissed.

Cira's spine went rigid. "Don't insult my intelligence or Phaedra's skill. We wouldn't endanger the fledglings."

King Dartegn's black gaze flicked to Lena. "She's dangerous."

"She's shackled."

"I've asked you before, I've *begged* you, don't put yourself in danger. I can't fight this war and worry over you, too."

"And I've told you before, I won't stay in that room and stare at the wall waiting for you to come back," Cira said, her sharpness and sudden flush of color evidence of an argument that'd been had many times before.

A tendon popped into relief on Dartegn's cheek as he ground his teeth. "Enough," he growled and wrapped a wing around Cira, ushering her to the passage back to the Round. She disappeared behind his large black wing, but Lena heard her muffled protests as they went.

Long moments passed, the royal couple taking all the air with them.

Phaedra approached, a disconcerted frown pinching her brow. "Best we get back, humans."

They went quickly and silently, even Alix going without complaint.

———————— •◆•• ————————

The queen didn't return for two days, and when she did, Lena recognized the pallid appearance of someone who hadn't slept well in days. She didn't know what to make of this diminished Cira and kept her distance at first. The guards watched her more carefully than they had in days, but after setting up the children to play with the new goat kids born a week before, Cira came to her. She took up a brush and stood alongside Lena to groom the horses.

"I suppose you've heard Dar's plan." It wasn't a question.

"Yes." She'd barely slept the night after Bel told her. Visceral were her memories of arrows and rocks raining down on the human ranks, the whistling of missiles and the heavy, wet *thwack* of them connecting with flesh. Those sounds haunted her even outside her dreams; she couldn't imagine the terror of watching the whole mountainside tumble down on you, knowing there was nothing to do but wait and hope it would be quick, that your head would be crushed first.

Cira was quiet for long moments, her brushing more vigorous than necessary. Ruan was too good-natured to care, but Lena watched the queen carefully.

"It's not right," Cira muttered into Ruan's mane. "If we do such a thing, we're no better than..." Her eyes flicked up to meet Lena's before skittering away.

"The king's plan has some sense," Lena said through shards of guilt piercing her throat. "It could end this war. But it..." *At what cost? And how would the humans ever see past it?* If King Dartegn buried the human army under his mountain, Vagora would remember. King Artemian wouldn't be alone anymore in wanting the total destruction of the avians.

"It's cruel," Cira finished, her brows puckered with upset.

"War is cruel, my queen," Lena said gently. "It's not fair or just or noble. One side must always lose."

The queen was quiet for a long while, losing herself in the rhythm of brushing. It put baby Elia to sleep, and the queen eventually took to plaiting little braids in Ruan's mane to keep her fingers busy.

"It's the waiting that's the worst," she finally said. "I couldn't take the boredom of sitting in our chambers, left with nothing to do but *wait*."

"It's the same down the mountain. The hours, days, even weeks between something happening were almost worse than the actual fighting." Even a minor wound often seemed less painful than the endless waiting and the way it strung the mind along, fraying nerves and stealing sleep.

"It seems rather silly, both sides dreading the coming fight but still going off to do it."

Yes, perhaps it was, but Cira's words seemed more for herself, so Lena kept quiet.

Much later, after the stable descended into a peaceful quiet while the animals and fledglings ate their evening meal, Cira sat beside Lena, offering her half of the apple she cut up. Lena took it, relishing the sweet tang on her tongue. It was one of the first apples of the season, the orchards turning into a colorful swathe of red and green.

"You must think Dar and I are a strange match," said Cira.

Lena looked up with a smile. "Not any stranger than Bel and I."

Cira laughed. "You're right. Very strange, the two of you." Her smile grew thoughtful as she said, "I'd forgotten, honestly. That you and he were so different. When I see you together, you just…"

Lena blushed, filling her mouth with apple, but it wasn't entirely the tang that had her cheeks aching. Pleasure warmed her heart thinking of at least one avian looking at her and Bel and not seeing something to scorn.

"We're well suited," was what Lena finally said.

Cira cut her a wry look. "Oh, is that all you have to say? Fine, keep your secrets. I know more than one female is filled with envy for you. He has quite the crowd when he trains nowadays."

Lena couldn't help pursing her lips. She knew about Bel's growing popularity, could see it herself as she and Alix walked about the Round while he trained. If she had an ounce of spare room within her mind for more worries, she might've been a bit jealous, but really, there was nothing to be jealous of.

"Not that he sees any of them, mind you," Cira went on. "His eyes are only for you."

Lena fought her grin. "We've been through so much together. There's a bond that forms, nothing else like it."

Cira nodded, but her eyes and smile fell. Picking at the apple core with a nail, she asked, "But do you think that bond can weaken? What if it was never truly strong at all?"

She took a long breath to consider. "I think the king chose the right queen."

"I can't fight beside him," Cira whispered.

"Another warrior won't end the war."

A wet, shaky breath shuddered out of the queen and she fell silent. They said nothing more about it that day, nor in the days after. But Lena could see it, the way Cira frayed at the edges. Her eyes sunk and darkened. Her words and moods were subdued. And finally, she stopped wearing her crown.

———•◆•———

A rope left to fray and rot will always break under tension. When King Dartegn came in like a tempest the next day, face as dark as a thundercloud and wings whipping like trees in a gale, Lena could almost hear the *snap*.

"Queen Cira," she murmured, widening her stance.

Cira looked up from where she let Elia pet one of the goat kids. She straightened to stand, face hardening into something Lena had never seen before.

The king strode for them, punctuating each step with a clipped, vicious syllable, "I come back to find you gone and exactly where I *forbade you* to be. I told you to stay away from the humans."

Lena couldn't help angling herself toward the queen, so much smaller than the male who came for her. Yet for all that she barely came to the king's collar, Cira stood her ground. She met Dartegn's glower with an unimpressed mien.

"And I told you that I wouldn't be dictated to like one of your warriors. I'm not a child, you cannot *forbid me*."

"Cira—"

"No, Dar. I won't be ordered about. I won't be hidden away." When he went to reach for her arm, she stepped back. "And I won't be dragged around like a doll." Her eyes went glassy with tears and her cheeks reddened, but she kept her chin up, meeting her mate's dark glare. "You won't humiliate me like that again."

"*You're* humiliated?" he snarled, wings raising in a show of dominance. "How do you think it looks, my queen hiding herself away with the humans and the livestock?"

"At least they're good company," Cira shot back.

Dartegn's nostrils flared. "I've done everything you've asked of me, Cira. Everything. And yet you refuse to do the one thing I ask."

It was Cira who advanced, crowding Dartegn, making him cant his head down to look at her. "Yes. Because what you ask is for me and our daughter to wither in the dark, waiting for you to come home with nothing but shadows for company. I won't live like that, Dar. I won't punish our daughter with your fear."

The look that passed over the king's face Lena had seen many times before, on the faces of those struck suddenly by an arrow or lance, that last moment of pained shock before their life fell away into the mud.

The stable went silent, even the animals holding their breath.

A fast-approaching stride was the first noise to break it. Bel pushed his way past Dartegn's guards, wings twitching in agitation.

"Lena," he called, closing the distance with his long strides.

The sound broke whatever spell had woven itself around the king. Devastation carved deep lines under his eyes. With a bitter shake of his head, Dartegn turned and walked away.

His shoulder smacked into Bel's with a heavy *thud* as he went.

Bel didn't miss a step, though he threw his cousin a withering glare as they passed.

He hurried to Lena's side, wrapping a wing around her. "Are you all right?"

"I'm fine," Lena said, but she let Bel pull her closer. As he leaned in to kiss her temple, in his ear she whispered, "You have to tell him."

34

Bel followed Diarmund, the passage ahead hidden by the warrior's expansive shoulders. They climbed steadily, making way for other warriors headed back down to the Round.

He'd approached Diarmund to lead him up to where Dartegn would most likely be, an area called the Perch that offered a panoptic view of the Gogona Mountains, particularly to the south and west, exactly where the humans now clustered. The quiet warrior had agreed in his usual reserved manner, nodding and immediately heading off to the nearest stairwell. Bel had had to jog to catch up with him.

In a way, he was glad he couldn't see the way ahead and estimate how much longer the journey would take. With every step, his dread grew heavier in his gut. He didn't want to say the words to Dar, didn't want to expose Eamon, didn't want to defend against retribution on him or Lena.

He'd told Lena and Alix to go to the stables early to get them out of the trap of a corridor that offered no escape.

The cut of cold, fresh air burned his nostrils, and Bel clenched his fists.

He squinted against the bright light of a clear morning, following Diarmund out onto a network of narrow catwalks and pathways, all crisscrossing below the dome. Each led to different outposts and sentry stations, but all returned to the wider, rooved Perch. The stone of the gable had been fashioned to blend with the rock, hiding the Perch and its vantage point. It reminded Bel of those eels he'd seen as a fledgling, on a tour with Maddok to the east, a predator hidden in the rocks, waiting to strike.

Wind swirled and eddied around them, tossing his hair and cutting through his layers of clothes. Spring had gained a firm foothold here, the snows retreating to the higher peaks, but the cold was still biting.

The world spread out to Bel's left, curving toward the horizon. Mountains cut a swathe across the landscape, peaks spearing the sky like jagged teeth. The steep valleys and high ridges of the Gogona Mountains were all a brownish gray, broken only by the white snowcaps and occasional mountain lake, so blue and deep they had to burrow all the way under Hadria.

It was all breathtaking in a dizzying kind of way.

Shots of color darted across the sky between outposts, avian wings glinting like steel in the sunlight. Far below, taking up much of the valley laid out before Hadria, was the human camp.

Bel peered down at it, unnerved by the swarming mass. They were so small, yet many bodies clearly moved about down there. No fighting today, but Bel could see all manner of war detritus littering and pockmarking the western mountainside. The remains of catapults, ramparts, siege towers, ballista, battering rams, and scaffolding rotted in the sun, the wood splintered and desiccated. Warped iron pieces reached from the ground like nightmarish flowers, the red of their rust stark in the sunlight.

It was one thing to know and read about; it was another to see the human effort.

Why? was all he could think.

Hadria was what it was precisely for this reason, its near-impenetrability. And perhaps Dartegn could have sat back these years and let the humans seethe far below, but all the debris, some of it nearly halfway up the slope, spoke to the sheer determination, or insanity, of the human king to break this mountain open.

Hadria could be summited. It could be taken. It would cost the human king almost everything if not all, but it could be done.

So the humans were repelled at every turn.

Diarmund led Bel out onto the Perch, the air cooling in the shade of the craggy gable. Dartegn stood near the parapet, talking with two of his warriors, but Bel felt his dark gaze tracking him. So too did the handful of guards placed around the Perch, their bodies tensing as Bel stopped to stand at the back.

"Can you find your way back?" Diarmund asked him.

"Yes. Thank you, Diarmund."

The big male bowed his head and left without another word.

He'd chosen to ask Diarmund for this reason; the big male did it without comment or judgment. Della would've chatted the whole way, trying to suss out his reasons for needing to see the king. Ama would've asked pointed questions about Lena while Maron would try to seduce him. She hadn't been subtle in her appreciation of him nor her disdain for Lena. Bel telling her to leave Lena alone had worked, but she'd redoubled her efforts to tempt him away from his *c'vana*. And Rurie...the male tolerated him, but any mention of Lena set him to scowling. So it'd been Diarmund he asked.

Bel kept his stance loose, patient but ready. Dar and his warriors looked at him askance, continuing with their conversation. They pointed and debated, discussing lines and numbers. Dartegn asked several questions over again, drawing out the wait just to annoy Bel, but he remained in place.

Warriors came and went. The sun inched across the sky.

Finally, the warriors bowed to Dartegn and left. Dar remained at the parapet, looking out over the mountains.

No one moved, and Bel refused to look to the guards for permission.

He let Dartegn have his pettiness for a moment longer before he approached, his pace measured and deliberate.

"I don't remember sending for you, cousin," Dartegn said when Bel drew alongside him.

"You didn't forbid me from it. And it's where to find you, so it's where I came."

Dar sighed. "What do you want, Bel?"

"To speak to you."

"What does your human want now?"

"It's not about Lena. Though if you're feeling magnanimous today, then *I* will ask for her shackles to be taken off." He might as well try before telling Dar a faction of his own people plotted to assassinate him.

"I'm not feeling magnanimous today."

"Then I'd better get it over with." The comment drew Dar's gaze, his head turning infinitesimally toward Bel. Folding his hands and wings at his back, Bel told Dar everything. The councilors and warriors he'd met. Their discontent and insinuations; their threats and plots. Their desire to put Bel on the throne. He didn't emphasize Eamon's role but didn't spare his *at'tan*, either.

The words fell between them, and Dartegn listened in silence. He remained unmoving, unspeaking for a long while after Bel finished.

Bel waited, dry tongue stuck to the roof of his mouth, for Dar to shove him off the Perch into the graveyard of war machines below.

What finally came was a humorless, tired laugh.

"Gods, I knew they were desperate. I suppose Eamon had you meeting in secret passageways the first chance he got."

Bel's wings fluttered in surprise. "You knew?"

"Of course, I did," he replied without satisfaction or heat. "They think because they scheme when I'm off fighting our enemy that their secrets are well kept. They think because they whisper that I won't hear."

"Then why not confront them?"

Dar shrugged. "Because warriors will talk. Frustrations must have a release. That's all their plans could ever be. Until you came." He turned his head to regard Bel with a sharp but impassive face. "You served them exactly what they craved, coming here. And now they believe they can seize power. Make you king. Make you *their* king."

The calm, toneless way Dartegn said all this unnerved Bel more than if Dar had grabbed him by the throat to dangle him over the side of the mountain.

"I refused them. Over and over, I've told them it's treason."

"Only if they don't succeed."

"I don't want the throne. I've never wanted to be king. And I know neither did you."

Dar's eyes flashed with a quiet rage. "And yet."

"And yet." Bel shook his head. "If I could change it, if I could take his place, I would."

"If only." The stab had no heat to it, but Bel's heart clenched in pain even so.

"You have my support," Bel said thickly, throat tight. "I'll pledge my loyalty and fealty if you want."

"In exchange for what?"

The shrewd question took Bel by surprise. "For nothing. A show of good faith."

"Not for your human's freedom?"

"We already established you aren't feeling magnanimous today."

Dar huffed, the closest Bel had heard to a laugh from him. "I'm not. And I don't need your pledge, Arubel. I don't need anything from you. All you've brought to Hadria are false hopes and humans."

"You have it nevertheless."

They lapsed into silence again. Little hints of noise wafted up on the breeze from the human hive below. The wind caught in Bel's hair and feathers, but he remained alongside Dar, unwilling to concede just yet.

He was ready when Dar finally asked, "And what do you suppose I should do with you now? You're a threat to me and my heir, and I don't suffer threats to my child."

"I'm not a threat to you and especially not to your daughter."

Dar bared his teeth in a savage smile. "Then why come here at all? What do you *want*, Arubel?"

Bel clenched his jaw against all the childish wants that clambered up his throat, swallowing them back down where they belonged, deep inside, behind his heart.

"To help," Bel said. And since he had Dar's attention, he might as well add, "But if you want to bargain, I'd ask for you not to bring the mountain down and risk Hadria. I'd ask for my *c'vana* to be freed and protected. And I'd ask that Eamon and the others' lives be spared. Their motives are their own, but most just want an end to this war."

"And I don't?" Dartegn turned to regard Bel with a penetrating gaze. "It's good you won't be king. You don't have the stomach for it."

A wordless ire flared inside him, his patience fraying at all of Dar's dismissals and underestimations. He never wanted to test his mettle with kingship, but he didn't believe favoring mercy to be a weakness.

The downy feathers at Dar's neck bristled, sensing Bel's shift. One of his black brows flicked up, a dare, one that called viscerally to the boy Bel had been, the one who was Maddok's brother but not his friend, the one who was so intensely jealous of a cousin who got to be Maddok's age and his friend.

"King Dartegn!"

Dar jerked away from Bel, stepping aside to meet the warrior rushing to the Perch.

Bel turned in time to see Ophir hurdling the last distance, pumping his wings to land just a few steps from Dartegn.

"My lord, humans—in the mountain." The older warrior threw a baleful look at Bel.

Dar's wings shivered. "Where is the queen?"

"In the stables, with the..." Another glare from Ophir.

Worry knifed through Bel's chest.

"You said the southwest mines were impassable," Dar demanded, already moving, unfurling his wings.

"Not there. In the old passages," Ophir said.

In a moment, Dar had Bel by the throat, backing him up against the parapet. His fingers dug into skin and tendon, and Bel grabbed his wrist before Dar could crush his windpipe.

"You led them straight here, you fucking fool!"

35

Lena picked at a cuticle with her thumbnail until it bled, a knot of worry lodged in her throat.

"You didn't know?" she asked gently.

Queen Cira shook her head, the shock still plain on her face. "I knew Dar's plan displeased many councilors. And that morale has been low amongst the warriors, but this…" She stood, cradling her forehead in her hand, wings fluttering in distress.

Lena stayed seated though she wanted to offer comfort, sensing the gaze of the queen's guards drifting her way.

"I'm sorry," she said, "I didn't mean to upset you."

Cira shook her head. Color pinkened her cheeks as her pale brows drew low in a heartbroken frown. "Why didn't he tell me?"

Lena was relieved when the queen answered her own question.

"He never wants me to worry," Cira said. "He thinks I cannot handle the danger, that I'm made of glass."

"You're precious to him," Lena offered, though she didn't relish advocating for Dartegn. Still, in her time in Hadria, Lena had come to see the king not as a monster or a tyrant or a phantom dredged from the nightmares of human soldiers, but as a man, a man at his wit's end, desperate to protect his mate and child.

Desperation made people do stupid things.

"Before the baby, he trusted me. He told me everything. At least, I thought so. But now…" Cira shook her head.

"The king just wants to keep you safe, my queen," Lena soothed, guilt pricking at her as tears gathered in Cira's eyes. "And so do I. That's why I'm telling you this. Not to upset or anger you. I just want you and the baby to be safe."

The queen nodded, reining back her tears as baby Elia began to fuss, sensing her mother's distress. Cira swayed back and forth, humming to the baby, but her expression remained troubled.

"I believe you," she told Lena. "It just pains me that I have to hear it from you and not my own—"

Something loud echoed into the stables, making the animals shift and whicker. Lena stood up on instinct, attention trained on the smaller entrance to the stables from the Round. A rumbling noise vibrated through the passage, making the air quiver with agitation.

A slight movement of air beside her and then Alix whispered, "What's going on?"

"I don't know."

"Something's happened," murmured Cira, her mouth a grim line. To one of the guards she said, "Take the fledglings back; quickly now," and handed over Elia with an agonized grimace. To Lena and Alix she said, "Follow me."

Her guards protested, but Cira strode down the passageway, her other guard, Phaedra, Lena, and Alix hurrying to keep up.

The buzzing tension only grew as they passed into the Round. For the first time, it actually looked crowded, avians emerging from every archway and corridor, even flying in from openings in the dome. Murmurs of confusion tumbled like whitewater over falls, crashing below in a roar.

Bodies shifted and wings rustled; feathers caught errant shafts of light, color ricocheting in Lena's periphery, drawing her eyes every direction.

"Stay close," she told Alix.

"Down there," Alix said, pointing to the arena.

They all peered down, watching as a convulsing mass of bodies struggled onto the arena floor. Further away than they normally were on their low terrace, Lena couldn't clearly see or make sense of what she saw.

"Come," Cira whispered, making for the nearest stairs.

They moved as a unit down the terraces, drawing less attention than if the avians among them flew. Yet they didn't go unnoticed. Whispers darted through the air like animal chirps through the forest, warning of predators. *Humans* and *the queen* and *don't trust her.*

Two terraces down, Lena finally saw what happened on the arena. It stole the breath from her chest.

A squadron of avians wrestled with three humans, dragging them forcibly onto the arena. They'd struggled on the steps leading up to the arena, and now fought as the avians drew them closer to the burning, concentrated light of the oculus.

"Lena, is that...?"

"Joran."

The name fell from her numb lips, disbelief shocking her still.

Joran struggled between two avian warriors, hands bound before him. Two other knights came behind, fighting just as viciously to break free. Even from afar, Lena saw their gaunt faces and the grime that coated their skin. They'd been stripped of their gear, armor, and weapons, leaving only graying, threadbare shirts and trous.

Dismay sank its teeth into her heart.

"No..." Lena moaned. She thought she'd...she thought he'd...

Joran had followed them here. They'd led him to Hadria.

"*Fuck,*" she cursed.

Alix's curls bounced nervously as she shook her head. "How did they—?"

"You know these humans?" Cira demanded, eyes sharp as she looked between Lena and Alix.

"They pursued us from Vagora. We thought we lost them at Aeriand. I never thought..."

A hint of suspicion entered Cira's eyes, and Lena hated it.

The queen opened her mouth to ask something else, but a gasp went through the Round.

From the uppermost terrace came a shadow of black wings. It circled the highest reaches of the Round before cutting across the oculus, making the pillar of light flash. King Dartegn wheeled above the arena, warriors and councilors gathering on the floor below.

He came to land near the stepped dais on the arena, his long legs eating up ground as he strode for the struggling humans.

A glitter of gold caught Lena's eye, and she watched as Bel and a few more guards followed Dartegn down, gliding from the top terrace.

For one long, surreal moment, Lena watched as Joran and his knights stopped struggling, realizing suddenly who came for them. No guards or warriors at his back, Dartegn swept across the arena alone, his wings consuming the light of the oculus as they rose and flapped in outrage.

The human knights had gone still, but movement exploded on the far side of the arena.

Cira's hand clutched her arm. "They wouldn't—!"

Dread was a cold knife at Lena's throat. So far away, all they could do was watch as a half-dozen or more avians rushed the king.

"Dar," Cira moaned.

The avians gathered on the terraces gasped and shuddered, confusion thickening the air. Bodies rushed the king, flashes of steel and feathers converging in a clattering mass that sent shouts and the ring of metal echoing up the Round.

Movement caught Lena's eye—weaving between the dazed bodies across the terrace and the one above came at least four avians, eyes trained on her little group.

Eliminate the queen. Eliminate the human lover. Everything could be wrapped up so prettily.

Lena's stomach swooped, but she allowed herself only that one moment of terror.

"Move!" Lena yelled, throwing her body into Phaedra's.

Phaedra blinked as if coming awake, her sharp eyes taking a moment to look about and then she was moving, hurrying them to the stairs.

So many bodies stood in the way, unmoving even with their queen shoving past—then Lena saw them, two more fast approaching, overtaking the stairs they aimed for.

She filled her fist with Alix's shirt and pushed her into Phaedra. The girl stumbled with an *oof*, and Phaedra caught her, bewildered.

"Fly!" Lena demanded, crowding Cira toward the terrace edge. "Get out of here!"

Her guard caught Cira's arm and pulled her into the air. Their wings beat in Lena's face as she pushed at Phaedra, grappling with a squirming Alix.

"Lena, wait—!" Alix cried, but her voice was lost in a rush of feathers as Phaedra was forced to jump, wings unfurling to catch them.

And then it was just her on the terrace, a crowd of shocked avians looking on.

"She attacked the queen!" someone cried.

"Get the human cunt!"

An avian pushed forward, and Lena ran at them, putting all her weight into it as she drove her shoulder into their gut. She heard the avian grunt with a *whoomph*, all the air knocked out of them. They staggered, and Lena darted around, skipping past hands that grabbed at her.

She bounded down the steps, crashing into the bodies at the bottom. Wings spasmed below her and she scrabbled up, off the avians, and ran.

Hands and wings jumped out to catch her, a growing thrum vibrating through the Round.

"The human is attacking!"

Bodies jolted forward, blocking her way.

Lena skidded to a stop, turning to find even more behind her.

She sucked in a breath. Let it out.

Lena ran for the terrace edge. The avians nearby yelped and shouted, tried to slow her, stop her, but then she leapt, legs wheeling through the air, and the terrace below came up fast to meet her.

She landed hard, managed to roll through the worst of it, but came up gasping. Her left knee wailed, nearly giving out, but she forced herself up.

A set of stairs was just ahead, but so many stood in her way.

She tested the shackles, wishing she at least had her hands for combat. The chain held.

Cursing, Lena ran.

A body crashed into hers, catching her before she could jump. Tawny wings beat around her shoulders and hands caught her under the arms.

"Hold still!" Phaedra yelled. "*Fuck!*"

With a roar, she hefted Lena from the terrace, gliding down to the next. They took three running leaps together, Phaedra adjusting her grip, and jumped again, heading for the lowest terrace.

There, Alix, Cira, and her guard stood back-to-back, spears brandished against four circling attackers.

"Fuck," Phaedra grated again—and then dropped Lena, right onto a conspirator.

Lena yelped, shifting her weight to make the avian take her fall. They crashed to the ground together in a heap, weapons clattering.

Dark spots danced in her vision, but Lena rolled onto all fours and tried to get her feet under her.

A hand gripped her under the arm and hauled her up.

"How are you with a spear?" said Phaedra, not waiting for an answer.

The smooth shaft of a spear was thrust into her hands, and Lena gripped it with relief. She used the blunt end to hook Alix behind her, into the small pocket between her, Phaedra, and Cira's guard, and closed the gap.

"Get to the arena!" Phaedra called.

Lena stole a glance at the arena floor, thinking it'd be crowded with conspirators, gathered over King Dartegn's corpse.

But the Shadow hadn't fallen.

Now surrounded by guards, Dartegn fought off the conspirators who'd ambushed him, their threat stymied by evened odds. A ways away, another group had wrestled the human knights to the ground, keeping them from slipping away in the chaos.

She thought she saw Bel's golden head, but then an arcing sword took up her vision.

Lena caught it with the shaft of her spear, swirling it around and sending it flying out of the avian's hands.

They moved as a unit, slow and steady, keeping Alix and Cira near the middle. The sounds of battle echoed loud on the arena floor, nearly deafening her to anything else but her pounding heart. She could feel the battle behind them, pressing against her back as they neared.

Seeing their opportunity slipping away, the conspirators rushed at them in one final desperate gambit. Alix's spear was knocked aside and another rushed Phaedra. Too close to use the sharp end of her spear and limited by her shackles, Lena lowered her shoulder and rammed the male coming at her and Alix.

Their circle broke apart, leaving their flank exposed.

"Lena!" cried Alix somewhere behind her.

The male stumbled back, his face gone red from lack of air, but he slashed as he fell back, slicing Lena across the arm.

She grunted from the sting, feeling blood bloom across her sleeve.

Wings brushed her back, and she turned to find Cira knocking away the sword of a female avian, aimed for Lena. Cira deflected the next heavy strike but left herself open to the dagger the other female pulled from her belt.

Lena shoved Cira down, catching the dagger in the chain of her shackles.

"Human bitch!" the female roared. She pulled back her sword, readying to strike, when a spearhead caught her under the pauldron. Her sword clattered away as she dropped with a pained yowl.

Phaedra twisted her spear further in. "Stay down, Maron."

The other female hissed in outrage.

Lena just got her feet under her when the air around her crackled, sparks of static jumping from black feathers that consumed her periphery.

Her breath snagged in her throat. Somewhere distant, someone called her name.

A hand clutched her by the hair. Another wrapped around the chain of her shackles.

Feathers whipped past her in a soft sting and then her feet left the ground. King Dartegn wrenched her in an arc and slammed her down to the ground with a shattering smack. Something in her left arm popped.

Lena's mouth fell open in a gasp of pain, but she couldn't take air, couldn't stop him when he snarled at her, teeth bared and nose pulled back, and dragged her up and up and up—

A horrible, gutting howl slammed against her ears.

The hand on her chain disappeared, and Lena slumped to the ground.

Black and bronze feathers clashed as Bel caught Dartegn by the shoulder plate and shoved him away. Dartegn lashed out blindly, an animal attacked, and Bel put his shoulder into the king's chest.

Dartegn's hand swiped, pulling Bel down with him, and the two went tumbling to the ground in a tangle of limbs. Blades clattered to the stone floor as they grappled, the king's eyes wild and unseeing. Dartegn boxed Bel with his wings as his hands scrabbled for purchase, teeth gnashing.

Bel hooked a leg around the king, and though he was slightly smaller than Dartegn, he put his full weight into the push and sent them rolling. Bel fought his way atop his cousin, pinning his shoulder and pressing the crooks of his wings down on Dartegn's flailing black feathers.

He drew back his fist and smashed it into Dartegn's face, once, twice, again. He struck until he drew blood from the king's crooked nose.

"Finish it, Arubel!" she thought she heard Eamon cry.

Chest heaving, arm wound back to strike, Bel stopped.

Both males stared at the other, mouths open as they panted.

Soft feathers brushed over Lena's face, and for a moment she couldn't understand. Bel was over there. How...?

"Stop it!"

Dartegn jerked at the sound of his mate's voice. His lip curled in outrage to see Cira crouched over Lena, helping her sit up.

"Get away from her!" he growled, struggling again under Bel.

"No," said Cira, letting Lena lean on her as she got her bearings.

Shoulders and wings trembling, Bel stood to put himself between Lena and the king. Blood trickled from his mouth, and a cut oozed on the side of his neck, but he stood his ground.

Dartegn bounded to his feet. "Look at what they've done!" The king's shout echoed across the Round, silencing everything. "Humans in the Round, an attempt on my life, on *yours!*"

"She was defending me! She fought off *avians* to save me. It was *our kind* who did this."

The king shook his head once, vehement, and advanced on Lena and Cira.

Bel got in his way.

That black gaze swept up Bel, and the king cocked his head just to the right.

"Get out of my way, Arubel."

"No," Bel said.

Dartegn's lips peeled back in a snarl. "You may have fought beside me, but *you* caused this. Disaster always follows you."

Bel's wings shuddered, and if Lena could've gotten enough air in her bruised lungs, she would've argued, told him not to listen to or believe that venom.

The king took a deep breath, and the tension receded by a hair. He cast his eyes about, to those conspirators still alive, restrained and laid out on the ground. To the group that had brought Joran and his knights. To the thousands of avians watching on in horror.

Finally, he looked to his queen.

"Cira," he said.

But she shook her head.

Everything in Dartegn's face drained away except devastation. It gleamed in his eyes, hollowing his face. Her denial pained him infinitely more than this conspiracy ever could. It was hard to watch a heart being pierced without a blade.

In a ragged voice, the king said, "Take them all. We have to sort this mess."

"Wait," said Cira, but a guard was there to pull Lena away.

"Lena!" Bel cried, but warriors blocked his way.

In a moment, she was marched across the arena, losing sight of him. Her head swam and it was all she could do to get her feet to keep pace with the firm but not unkind grip on her arm.

Alex's head of curls bobbed beside her, and the girl took Lena's arm over her slim shoulders, as if she could bear Lena's weight.

"Come on then, human," Phaedra said on her other side. "Let's get that cleaned up."

36

In the aftermath of the assassination attempt, Bel was confined to the council chamber, not imprisoned but not allowed to leave. He was able to wipe the worst of the blood from his face and neck, though the slice below his ear stung under the salve a healer had taken two moments to slap on. Sitting in one of the seats to the rear, Bel balanced his elbows on his knees and clasped his hands in front of him so he wouldn't scratch the growing irritation.

That night and into the following day, Bel watched and waited for an opening Dar. Every moment he sat there, unmoving and useless, anything could be happening to Lena and Alix. He tugged at his hair when his fingers needed something to do, understanding better now Lena's need to fidget when she grew too anxious.

His worry and the rush from battle coursed through him, a potent mix that made him want to fight and punch and not wait to be given permission. He tried more than once to approach Dartegn in between meetings.

The guards intercepted him at every turn.

"He'll deal with you soon enough," one told him.

Bel bared his teeth but said nothing, fearing one wrong word would get Lena cast into the Pit. It didn't quell the agonized rage boiling inside him. He'd heard about what happened for mated avian pairs, how once a *c'vana* was chosen, they became the central focus of their mate. If he hadn't known already how deeply rooted his bond with Lena had become, this cruel separation from her and how it made him skirt insanity would've proved it.

So Bel bided his time, taking food and water when it was offered but refusing rest. Instead, he watched Dartegn as he dealt with the fallout, waiting.

Dar questioned the conspirators who'd attacked Cira first.

The howling rage in Bel only grew tenser every time a conspirator was led in, sat in a high-backed chair to negate their wings, and shackled to the arms. He felt no pity for them, but the dread of each conspirator was palpable as Dartegn circled them silently, a looming shadow that blocked out all else.

In the ensuing silence, under the unblinking stare of Dartegn Adii-ron, one by one, they cracked.

It started with babbling.

"We only meant to get the queen somewhere safe," some of them said.

"We didn't mean her harm, we just wanted to ensure she wouldn't interfere," most claimed.

Dar's disbelief was plain in the harsh, thin line of his downturned mouth.

Still he said nothing.

Then accusation.

"We were only trying to get to the human bitch," spat Maron. Bel hadn't been surprised to see her among the conspirators. "The queen got in the way. She's under the same spell as Prince Arubel, believing that witch's lies!"

"It was the human we were after, to protect her for Prince Arubel," said the next.

Bel's snort of derision got him a cutting glare from Dartegn.

"We were after the human knight. Her threat is intolerable and Prince Arubel won't see reason. Unfortunately, the queen's soft heart compelled her to defend the human."

When each conspirator had finally argued themselves out of breath, without saying anything, Dar would finally approach, taking up their vision. He didn't lean in. He didn't frown. Just stared, eyes trained and unblinking, holding his breath, a predator readying to strike.

Each and every conspirator leaned back in the seat, crushing their wings behind them.

"And what," Dartegn would finally say, "were your plans for my daughter? If the queen had had Princess Aurelia with her, what was your plan?"

The color drained from their faces. Mouths fell open. Terror gleamed in their eyes. Some shook their heads, whether in denial or grim acceptance, Bel didn't know.

He didn't care, either. The truth in their non-answers disgusted him.

It was all the answer Dartegn needed.

They were unshackled and marched from the room, bound for a dark cell deep in the bowels of Hadria to await execution. Some hung their heads in shame. A few, like Maron and Faros, threw venomous looks at Bel. And some like Linnea kept their heads held high, accepting their fate.

Eamon was left for last.

Bel braced himself for the sight but still found the red-soaked tunic and sweaty, pallid color of his old *at'tan* disturbing. Eamon had to be helped into the room, the strength and life clearly seeping out of him with every drip of blood onto the council room floor. Under his grimace of pain, he seemed neither frightened nor contrite, merely resigned.

He'd seen Eamon take the wound, had thought at first it was merely a glancing blow, until blood spurted from his side when the blade drew back.

So much blood...

Disquiet drew Dar's lips into a thin line at the sight of the old warrior, and he shook his head when the guards went to shackle Eamon to the chair. They left him sitting slumped, chest heaving to take thin, reedy breaths.

"Why, Eamon?" was all Dartegn said.

"Because you won't see reason," Eamon rasped with effort. "You've grown as desperate as the human king. You'll destroy us to destroy them."

"You don't know that."

"You don't know what bringing the mountain down will do, either."

"I begged the council for better ideas. I came to you, Eamon, my old *at'tan*, asking for what to do. And you gave me nothing."

"You refused to listen." Eamon's head lolled as he shook it. He slumped on the chairback, eyes tired but clear as he regarded Dartegn. "You'll never do what needs to be done. We must negotiate with the human king."

A sardonic smile broke across Dartegn's lips. "Of all your delusions, that's the biggest. The human king doesn't want to negotiate. He wants annihilation."

"Perhaps. But this war is growing costly for him. He may be ready to come to the table, but you'd never meet him there."

Dartegn stood to his full height and folded his hands behind his back. It was a considering stance, nonthreatening, but Bel didn't miss how Eamon tensed, waiting for impact.

"And you think Arubel would?"

"His female is human."

Bel bit back the growl rumbling in his throat. *Female*, Eamon said, as if Lena was just a temporary bedfellow to rut for a season.

"He was also kept captive by humans. Maimed by them. Why shouldn't Arubel hate them just as much as we do?"

"He knows how humans think." The answer was feeble, and they all knew it.

"Perhaps. Or was it that you thought you knew how Bel thought. How to control him."

"I've always wanted to help Bel take his place among our people," said Eamon. "His coming here now, it was a sign from Halva—that we haven't been completely abandoned by the old gods."

"His coming here is the will of a human knight, not our gods. You're a fool, Eamon. If you wanted to help Bel, you should have. I never forbid you from searching. But now, in your guilt, you'd sacrifice me, my mate, and my *child* to atone for something that can never be set right."

Eamon may have prepared for the impact of Dartegn's words but Bel hadn't. They hit him in the chest, a devastating blow full of jagged-edged truths. That beast in him that howled for its mate rumbled and roared, hurt and betrayed. But under it all, a sharp, insidious guilt pricked at his soul.

Disaster always follows you.

Dartegn motioned for Eamon to be taken away, and two guards came to haul him to his feet.

"Now let the healer see to you, you old fool," Dartegn grumbled.

"No point. We both know the skies call me home." Eamon turned to find Bel in the empty council seats, eyes heavy as he searched. His brows drew low in a troubled frown as he and Bel stared at each other.

Bel felt as though he should say something, before he couldn't, but nothing came to him.

Perhaps he'd regret it, but Bel sat in silence.

There was nothing left to say.

A wet breath shuddered through Eamon. His gaze fell and before the guards bore him away, to Dartegn he murmured, "I'm sorry it came to this."

<hr>

The conspirators sentenced to die gave their lives to serve those they claimed to want to protect. Forced to the front of the next attack, they fought the humans and sacrificed to save other warriors. "They died with honor," Dartegn told his commanders the next day, "so let it be done."

Eamon died of his wounds an hour after speaking with Dar.

With the mountain now secured, Dartegn issued commands and tried to calm the avians who'd seen the assassination plot all unfold. He made appearances. He met with commanders and captains and councilors and cooks.

Through it all, Bel lay in wait.

Brooding over being kept from his mate. Worrying that he'd regret saying nothing to Eamon. Feeling guilt over still finding nothing he wanted to say to his old *at'tan*.

Sometime on the third evening, Cira arrived with a tray of food. Dar's expression went blank as he watched her approach from where he sat at the far side of the table. He went completely still, as if the slightest movement might scare her away.

Cira placed a small tureen and cup in front of him. "Don't do their work by starving yourself," she said.

Dar nodded, his features carefully schooled as if he waited for censure or outrage. He got neither. Lifting a small hand, Cira drew his hair away from his eyes and traced the point of his ear.

"You need to rest."

"Yes, my queen."

Cira nodded and turned for the door.

"My queen," Bel entreated before she could leave, "how is Lena? Have you seen her?"

Cira shook her head, her features flat with fatigue. "I don't know."

Bel bit back his frustration, nodding at Cira as she left.

He looked back at Dartegn, impatience eating away at him. Head in his hand, Dar spooned soup from the tureen to his mouth in economical movements, eyes distant. He was a male in desperate need of rest. The weight of the past days hovered over Dar, a malignant heaviness that hung about his shoulders.

Perhaps Bel should've taken pity on him. The past few days had been grueling. Watching Dar deal with the fallout of the conspiracy only made Bel that much more grateful he'd never be king.

But the howling in his chest wasn't compassionate or reasonable or forgiving. He'd sat in this room for two days now, the memory of Dartegn tossing Lena about by her shackles seared into his mind.

Bel let Dartegn eat for a few more moments, a grand concession.

He rose from his spot, cracking his back and stretching his wings. The guards watched him come warily, but Bel didn't stop until he stood at Dartegn's side, impossible to ignore.

"And what about me, cousin? Can I go pick out my new cell now or are we done playing this game?"

"What game is that, Arubel?" Dar asked his soup.

"What do you want from me? I've done everything you asked. *Lena* has done everything you asked! We aren't a threat to you. Hell, I fought beside you and Lena defended your mate! What else do you want?"

Dartegn carefully placed his spoon beside the bowl, his movements calculated and infuriatingly slow.

"I want you not to be here," Dartegn said. "I want you to have never come back."

He went straight for the jugular of Bel's hurt, and it worked. But Bel would be damned if he let Dar see it.

"I've done what I came to do," Bel rasped. "I told you what I know. So let us go. We'll leave here and you'll never see me again."

"I can't do that. You know too much now."

Bel leaned forward to splay his hands on the table. "Dar, I can help you. I'm not your enemy. Let me be your ally."

Dar's eyes flicked up to Bel finally, running over his features as if he searched for something. Dread pooled in Bel's stomach, and he knew before Dar spoke what he'd say.

"You look just like him," Dar murmured, "and I *hate you* for it."

Bel's lip peeled back in a sneer, his patience hanging by a thread. "I know. And I hate you for attacking my *c'vana*. By all rights, I could seek retribution for that."

Dar shook his head, gaze dropping away, and Bel didn't dare think he'd caught a flicker of remorse in him.

"Go away, Bel," he said to his soup.

"No."

Dartegn sighed. "I just had my own people try to kill me. They attacked *my mate*. And you think I care about what you want?"

"They attacked mine too, you ass," Bel hissed. "You've punished everyone who threatened and attacked your mate. How do you think it's been, sitting here for days, unable to do the same for mine? Just because she's human doesn't make our bond any less real than yours and Cira's. Instead of comforting her and protecting her like I should be, I'm here, watching you *fucking eat*."

Anger sparked in Dartegn's eyes, and Bel welcomed it. He was past the point of caring what Dar did to him as long as he *did something*.

"I stood beside you against Eamon. I could've run you through while you attacked Lena, *my c'vana*. I would've been within my rights to. But I didn't. Lena didn't even fight back when *you attacked her*."

Dartegn was quiet for an unnerving moment, his thoughts unreadable, his expression inscrutable—but his eyes, they whorled with pain and rage, a potent mix that in Dar, always led to malice.

He thought he was ready for Dar's lash when it came, but he wasn't.

"Do you know what *her kind* did to Maddok?"

Bel bared his teeth, wings rustling in agitation. "I was *there*, Dar. Don't play, not about that."

"You *don't* know," Dar said, voice cold, even, terrifying. "They took you both that night. You alive, him for sport."

Bel tried to keep his expression from betraying his growing trepidation, but he could feel the color leaching from his face.

"They celebrated for days, made drinking games out of cutting him up. They skinned him, cooked him, fed him to the—"

"Stop," Bel murmured.

"They fed him to their animals, paraded his head on a spike. By the time we could mount a counterattack, that was all we recovered to bury."

Maddok's sarcophagus in Aeriand...little, plain, rushed, holding only the pieces left to bury...

Dar stood, the leather of his coat creaking.

He might've told Dar to stop, that he didn't want to hear whatever it was, but Dar had no mercy. "And his wings? Pulled off at the socket, bundled up, and sent to their king. Gilded and mounted on the fucking wall. And now they sit in the human king's palace, behind his throne. Strung up like a hunting trophy."

Saliva flooded Bel's mouth, and it was only by pounding his sternum that he stopped himself from retching.

"Your human told you none of this, but she knows."

Bel clenched his fists, fingers cold and numb against clammy, trembling palms. Bile burned his throat, but it was nothing to the anguish burning inside him.

Of course Lena knew. Of course she'd seen them.

Why hadn't she told him?

In Aeriand, she had to have known...

"Her kind did that to him. Human knights. Defiled Maddok, *destroyed* him." Angry tears gleamed in Dartegn's eyes as he glared at Bel and said, "And you brought them here."

"Lena's not like that," Bel insisted. He knew this to be true, but it didn't make the truth of Maddok's fate easier to swallow. He still wanted to punch his fist through something, wanted to rage and curse and beat everything and everyone who'd done that to his brother.

"I don't care if she's goodness fucking incarnate," Dartegn said. "She's a human, trained all her life to slaughter us. She can't be trusted."

"She didn't kill him," Bel told Dar as much as himself, "she's not responsible."

"Every single one of those bastards is responsible," Dartegn growled, eyes gleaming with old pain. "Every single one deserves to be slaughtered for what they did to him. An eye for an eye."

"Then by rights I should gut you for what you did to Lena."

Dartegn reared back, his neck flushed red with rage.

"If I ever have the chance," Bel swore through gritted teeth, "I'll kill the human king. I imagined all the ways I'd do it, locked up in that castle. Because he was *my* brother, too." A hot tear seared down his cheek, but Bel couldn't stop, crowding close to Dar. "Do you think I don't wish, every day, that he hadn't saved me? That I'd died and he lived? He was everything and I was nothing and *I should've died!*"

Bel grit his teeth against the wave of sorrow, dredged up to drown him.

"I should've died," he said again, "but I didn't. He saved me and I can't change that. I can't change…" He had to stop, suck in a breath, or else he'd sink beneath the tide of grief.

Dartegn looked on, his brows drawn low, almost as though he was troubled. Resting his fists on the table, Dar leaned forward, head hanging.

The ghost of Maddok stood between them, all their memories and jealousies and grief. They were bound by it, more than the Adiiron name, a bond neither wanted but couldn't change. Bel had spent most of his life resenting or hating his cousin; they'd almost nothing in common and little interest in each other. Maddok had always been the bind between them, and even now, it was true.

That didn't change his desire to pummel Dar's face for what he'd done to Lena.

Bel reached into his pocket to pull out the one thing he'd brought with him from Aeriand other than news. Shiny from the inside of his pocket and warm from his body, the rondel from Maddok's first set of armor gleamed in the torchlight. He ran his thumb over the embossed wings and stars before setting it on the table and sliding it to Dar.

Dar's nostrils flared when he recognized what it was.

"Then give us both what we want. Let me protect my mate and put an end to any more ideas of taking the throne from you."

Dar twisted his head to peer at Bel.

"I'll mate Lena, declare myself for her. Give her my name and protection. Then no one will support my claim with a human wife."

Gaze falling back to the rondel, Dar picked it up before straightening.

Ophir stepped closer, disapproval writ in the deep lines of his forehead. "My king, I'm not sure—"

Dar's hand cut through the air, a quick and brutal dismissal, as he stood.

After another moment of considering, Dartegn said, "You'll stand with your human in the Round, before your people, and take her as your mate. You'll both swear fealty to me and loyalty to my daughter."

"Yes."

Choosing to mate Lena would never take him a second thought or cause him a regret. Even as he howled to know why she hadn't told him about his brother's wings, it changed nothing. She was the one who'd rescued him, given him his life and freedom and courage back. The woman he'd choose above all others, human or avian. She was *c'vana*.

Dartegn nodded stiffly. "Take her to your chamber and keep her there. Both of you stay out of the way and come when you're called. There's still some of your mess to clean up." He couldn't give a concession without just a hint of spite.

With a sardonic twist of his mouth, Bel bowed his head. "My king," he said, and left Dartegn to his cold soup.

<hr>

"Leave us for a while."

Phaedra arched a brow at Bel, unimpressed. She had a bruise blooming on her left jaw and three scratches crisscrossing her right cheek but otherwise didn't look too worse for wear. She'd just sat down on her usual stool, yarn and knitting needles already halfway out of her pocket.

She'd accompanied them up to the higher terrace where Bel's chamber was, reassigned to guard Lena and Alix now rather than supervise. Phaedra had nodded easily at the news, collecting her stool while Lena and Alix shouldered their packs, following him in bemused silence after he'd come to fetch them.

He'd wasted no time getting them out from that trap of a corridor, dark and barely defensible. Yet all the frustration and anger of his exchange with Dar still bubbled inside, that howling thing in him not soothed just by being close to his mate.

Some of this must have shown on his face, as Phaedra finally shrugged, picked up her stool, and set up down the corridor a ways.

That would have to do.

He turned to Alix next, and the girl threw up her hands.

"I've always wanted to learn to knit," she said and beat a hasty retreat out of the chamber.

He shut the door after her, closing himself inside with an anxious Lena.

He'd been slightly mollified to find that she hadn't been concussed or broken any bones from Dar's attack, thank the gods, but bruises patterned her skin like leopard spots. Every single one just added fuel to his rage. And more, she looked bone tired. He could guess she'd barely slept, and as he stalked toward her, he knew she sensed something was wrong.

The need to comfort and care for her was strong, but so was his need to understand.

"Bel, what..."

"Why didn't you tell me about my brother's wings?"

Lena blinked at him before her eyes went wide. "You mean the...Oh, goddess, Bel...I..." She winced, turning away from him.

"In Aeriand—why didn't you tell me?"

Lena put a few paces between them.

"I didn't want to believe it was true. No one's sure how Artemian did it. Some think they're just a cast or impression. I didn't want to..."

Believe that her king, the man she'd sworn fealty, loyalty, and service to, could do such a horrific thing. She'd told herself that and many more lies; every knight, every person who served that man lied to themselves so they could rest at night.

"Artemian hangs dismembered limbs above his throne and then claims *we're* the savages?"

"I know, I know," Lena said, guilt cleaved across her face.

"How would humans feel if Maddok or Dartegn strung hands up like garlands?"

"I know..."

"How could—"

"I know." Lena shook her head, clenching her eyes tight against her tears. One slipped out, a small track of wetness sliding down her cheek.

The sight finally broke the spell of his anger, the red fading from his vision to let him see clearer. When he asked "Why, Lena?" it was without heat or reproach. He just wanted to understand.

"I just didn't want to hurt you more."

He hated how she wouldn't meet his eyes, hated how her arms twitched to cross over her chest, defensive. Gods, and he hated himself now, too, taking his anger out on her. She'd borne so much for him; exile, danger, ridicule. For all that she'd trained her whole life to fight, Lena wasn't the sword but the shield. She defended those she loved, and Bel knew how damn lucky he was to be one of them.

Still, she didn't need to swaddle him in wool. He wanted her care, her love, her devotion, and to give all those back to her tenfold.

"I should've told you," she murmured.

"Yes," he said, making her wince again.

He hated that, too.

Enough.

He couldn't stand to see her wounded, inside or out. Gods, he'd nearly made her cry. Intolerable.

Still, a restlessness prickled under his skin, aftershocks of the impotent rage for what happened to Maddok. It crackled inside him, a built-up heat that needed release. He could at least put it to use making it up to his mate. And helping her understand something once and for all.

"I'm not fragile," he said, closing the distance between them, moving into her space.

He took her hands and put them on his chest so she could feel the steady beat of his heart. When she finally looked up at him, he leaned down to fill his hands with her backside and pick her up, careful of where she hurt. Lena made something between a gasp and a giggle, a look of mock-horror crossing her face.

Bel guided her legs around him and hitched her up to his waist before leaning her back against the stone wall, pinning her. They were of equal height like this, eye to eye.

He'd distracted her, and he watched a surprised, bewildered grin twitch across her lips.

Enough guilt. Enough sadness. His *c'vana* was as safe as he could make her. Soon he'd mate with her and declare to everyone that he was hers. He forfeited a throne but got the world in return.

"I'm not fragile," he said again. "I'm not broken." He spread his wings to full length just to show her. "Because of you."

Her face crumpled, cracking his heart in two.

"Humans hurt you. Humans took everything away from you. And I'm—"

"The ones who killed my brother and broke my wing, yes. But you? Never. Never you." He dragged a hand up, took her weight in just one, just to show her. He touched her everywhere he could on the way up with gentle fingertips until he could move aside the collar of her shirt. He kissed the bare skin of her chest, just above her breasts, tasted the sharp inhale she took, felt the quick exhale through his hair.

"I broke your wing," she sobbed in a voice he never wanted to hear from her.

He groaned and kissed up her chest, her neck, to her ear, where he said with lips pressed to the shell so he knew she'd hear every word and feel the vibrations of them too, "You healed my wing. You healed *me* and you freed me and you brought me back. You're *good*, the best of your kind."

He caught her lips with his when she would've argued. He wanted her heat, her tongue, never her doubt, and he pressed her further back against the wall, letting her feel the heat of him between her legs.

She ran a hand up his neck and gripped the hair and down, sending a shiver through him that he felt in the tips of his fingers, ears, and toes.

"You understand what I agreed to?" he asked between hot presses of his mouth to her skin. He'd explained the deal on the journey up, but his words had been clipped and hurried.

"Yes." She gasped when his *ashita* turned into a long lick across her collarbone. Her hands pulled at his collar, and he was happy to yank off the shirt to offer his skin for her touch. She hummed happily, running a hand down his chest.

"Any objections?"

"Bel, you can't tie yourself to a human. An avian prince can't..."

Why was this woman always so determined to fall on her own sword? It infuriated him, but he loved her for it, too.

"I'm not a prince, not anymore. I don't want to be king."

"Then—"

"But I do want to keep you safe."

She shook her head and tipped it back against the wall. "That's not reason enough. I can take care of myself, of Alix, too. We can leave. Somehow."

"If you want to leave, then we'll leave."

Her head and gaze snapped back up to frown at him.

"You don't understand." He gathered her hands and held them again over his heart. "I'm already bound to you. Mating is just a formality. You have my heart, Lena, and I would be your mate. If you want me."

"But I'm human."

"You're Lena. That's what matters."

He took her mouth again, and where their kisses before had been heated and urgent, this was tender, coaxing, and he let her lead, let her touch him with delicate fingers. Her kiss was a question, and all he could be was open and let her find the truth of it. He'd long since been bound to her, and that greedy part of him, the part that always longed for good, soft things and grabbed at them when they chanced by, wanted her for himself. He wanted that moment of declaring he was for her and she would be his, as if saying the words would cleave them to each other, forever, inextricable.

He felt when she pushed away from the wall, giving him more of her weight, and he breathed a sigh into her mouth.

Fumbling with buttons, he opened her shirt enough to expose a breast and draw patterns with his tongue. Lena moaned, fisting at the down and hair at his neck.

She was so warm here, her smell strong and intoxicating as he drew it into his lungs. He played with her, sucking her other breast beneath the shirt while running his fingers over the first. He loved the pillowy softness of her here; everywhere else she was so strong and firm, but here, she filled his mouth and hand with soft, warm flesh that made him come undone.

He didn't quite know how, didn't see it himself because he was too busy laving attention on her perfect breasts, but he managed to peel her out of her breeches without putting her down. Perhaps just to show her. He balanced her against the wall so he could work on his own.

She moaned when he freed himself and teased her with the tip. Gods, she was hottest here, so slick for him. His teeth ached with how much he wanted to push inside, but first, "Will you be my mate?"

Lena made a choked sound, and her legs squeezed his hips, drawing him closer. He felt her shiver and nearly lost control when she rolled her hips, rubbing herself up and down, up and down.

It was hard, almost as hard as he was, but he palmed the firm globes of her backside and held her still.

She huffed at him and he smiled.

"Mate?" she said, that teasing tone he adored making his heart soar and blood burn.

"Mate," he agreed. "Your human tongue has several words for it. Husband and wife. Partners. Breeding pair." He teased her with the underside of his cock, feeling her core pulse.

"Bel!" She moaned again and he knew he couldn't tease her much longer, could barely keep his own control. But he wanted to hear the words.

Lena kissed him with such force their teeth clacked together. "Yes," she whispered against his lips, "yes, I'll be your mate." And then she tugged at his hair, not to draw him down to or away from her but to make her point. "Now finish what you start."

A laugh, a whoop, he didn't know, a noise of pure happiness and triumph rushed out of him, and then he was inside her, inside his mate, thrusting so hard and fast he couldn't stop. His heart thundered, fast and loud, as if it might grow and break free of him. Like it knew it didn't belong inside him anymore, but with her.

He pushed away from the wall, holding her up in the center of the room, and Lena gasped when he let her fall down the last few inches, impaled, taking all of him. Her heels dug into the small of his back and he could see the contours of her strong arms, wound around his neck to hold herself up. But he took her weight, moved her up and down, up and down, moving her hips to meet his.

His wings snapped around them, cocooning them and their heat. He felt the brush of her hot skin against every single feather and wisp of down.

She tightened around him, legs squeezing, and Bel watched her come undone. She was magnificent, head tossed back, haloed in his feathers, her neck long and arched. She ground herself down one final time, and then Bel came apart at the seams.

He thrust and pushed and pulsed, watching her bounce on him, and he only wanted more, forever, everything. And he had it—in that moment, Bel had everything. He had his mate, held in the strength of his arms and wings. She was everything, everything to him, and as she went limp in her pleasure, head resting on his heaving chest, just over the heart that beat for her, Bel felt something he never truly had before.

All the pieces of himself, his heart and soul and grief and love, settled.

37

Lena watched in a daze as Cira finished the last delicate button at her wrist. The silky fabric was soft against her skin, a delicate embrace compared to the shackles that'd left red stripes and blister scabs. The sleeves hid the marks as well as the bandage high on her arm.

Cira stepped away, allowing Lena to see herself in the mirror.

It was her own face staring back, but that was the only thing she recognized about her image. Cira and another female had brushed Lena's hair until it shone, weaving little braids together with small downy feathers from Bel's own wings. It fell in a cascade of heavy, dark curls, the ends tickling her exposed back.

Cira had gone to great lengths to locate a dress that would work, commandeering wardrobes both used and abandoned to find the dusky blue gown that now molded to Lena's frame. The neckline scooped low to complement how the stays lifted her breasts, creating warm shadows and contours. Long embroidered sleeves attached to thin straps, the silver thread glittering in the light. And the back...

It was an avian gown, cut for someone with wings. The back neckline fell past her shoulder blades, leaving her skin exposed. Her hair and the feathers in it brushed softly at her skin, an oddly delicious sensation, as did the silvery gossamer cape that cascaded from below her arms down to the ground in a sparkling waterfall of translucent fabric.

The bodice clung to her form, nipped in at her waist, then fell in soft lines past her hips, the dusky blue folds gathered at her feet like the shimmering surface of a mountain lake.

Looking at herself, Lena had the distant thought that the female staring back was a water nymph, rising from the water, skin glistening and limbs limned in starlight.

Her wrists were still itchy with healing skin and her left side still smarted from being thrown around by Dartegn; her left knee still ached and a dull pain throbbed in her arm. Two days sequestered in Bel's chamber hadn't changed much. She felt all of it and more, yet when she looked at herself...she didn't see it.

Cira smiled sweetly. "Look at you! Just beautiful." She fussed over the already perfect folds, making sure everything lay just right, even though any moment now they'd be called away to the arena and Lena would have to undo all the artful draping.

A low whistle from the door drew Lena's attention. She met Alix's wide eyes in the mirror and couldn't help blushing.

She'd so rarely seen herself in a gown. Never one this fine. Never on her own wedding day.

Goddess, it still didn't sound real.

Weren't brides supposed to be happy on their wedding days?

Lena wasn't *un*happy. She wasn't quite sure what she was, honestly, past the ball of nerves that even now knotted and writhed in her chest.

Alix stepped further into the room, making approving sounds as she walked a circuit around Lena. Her hair and face were freshly scrubbed, her cheeks rosy and curls bouncy.

"You look good," said Alix.

"I look different."

"Good different. Fancy." She waggled her eyebrows. "Meanwhile, *I* look dashing."

Her squire had been kitted out in a fine leather jerkin, a blue velvet doublet tucked neatly underneath. Her trous were of a fine dark wool, and her leather boots looked new, shiny in the warm light of the chamber. A leather bandolier crossed her chest, strapping a sheathed sword to her back.

"They let you have my sword back?" Lena asked.

Alix snorted. "Of course not. It's a nice wooden one. I asked for the best they had." She did a little spin, showing off the fine scabbard. Her smile was beaming when she said, "It's what squires are supposed to do during big ceremonies. So I had to look the part."

Leaning down, Lena caught Alix in tight hug. Alix threw her arms around Lena's neck, holding on with all the strength in her scrawny arms.

Lena would never fully shed the guilt of putting Alix in so much danger—in Balderak's demesne, at Finhöln, in the forest, Aeriand, the mines, and now here. This scrap of a girl had taken it all with a cocky little grin, and goddess did Lena love her for it.

When Alix pulled back, her eyes glittered with happy tears. She wiped at them quickly, pulling on one of the small braids in Lena's hair.

"I like these," Alix said. "Think I could have feathers, too?"

"There are a few spares," Lena agreed.

Alix went to stand dutifully in front of Cira, who seemed equal parts charmed and baffled by their exchange. Cira set to weaving a few of the feathers left over into Alix's curls, humming absentmindedly.

It gave Lena the chance to take one last look at herself.

Perhaps it wasn't quite a stranger staring back. Maybe it was just another her, a newer self who was fundamentally the same yet *more*.

Yes, Lena thought, smoothing a hand down her middle, the fabric under her palms rippling silkily, *not different or changed or bad. Just more.*

From outside, Phaedra knocked three times. "Best get moving, humans. It's almost time."

Lena hid the burst of nerves in her belly by fiddling with the folds of her dress.

Cira laid a gentle hand on her unhurt arm. "Phaedra will take you down. I'll be standing with Dar if you need a friendly face. You remember what I told you about the ceremony?"

"Yes, I think so."

Cira took her hand and squeezed. "It will be all right. Just remember, for all the politics, this is still a love match. That's what I reminded myself when I walked out to all those eyes watching me. It didn't matter because Dar was waiting for me, there at the end." The smile she gave was wistful and just a little bit sad.

There was some sort of truce between the king and queen, but nothing had been truly mended as far as Lena could tell.

With one last good luck, the queen left them to fly down to the arena and join her mate. After Alix admired the feathers in her hair in the mirror for a moment, she and Lena joined Phaedra out in the corridor.

The female warrior gave her a once over. "You look nice. But do you think you can do the stairs with all those skirts?"

Alix snorted and Lena let herself laugh, too. "I think I'll manage," she said. "But just in case, walk in front of me so I have something soft to fall on. We wouldn't want to wrinkle the dress."

• • ◆ • •

The nerves that assailed her were like those she had staring across what would become the battlefield, the enemy lines amassing on the horizon. She stood with shoulders squared at the steps to the arena, staring down the hundreds of avians who waited on either side of a cleared aisle. Thousands more ringed her on the terraces, all holding their breath.

At the far side, standing at the raised dais, she could just see three figures—Dartegn, the tallest and in all black; Cira at his side, small and almost glowing in the light from the oculus; and Bel.

She focused on him as she put one foot in front of the other, ascending the steps and gliding between the avians with Alix and Phaedra behind her. Her heartbeat was thready, waiting for someone to jump from the crowd. No doubt King Dartegn thought it one last good opportunity to suss out any lingering dissenters.

Her tongue stuck to the roof of her mouth, and her fingers twitched, wanting to fidget.

The further she walked, the more clearly she could see him, waiting for her.

Bel stood on the first step of the concentric dais, eyes fastened on her. Brushed back from his face, his hair was all leonine golden waves that framed his sharp, striking face. His blue eyes burned clear and intense as they watched her approach, the stark pride, lust, and love in them making her blush. His lips parted slightly as she came closer, and Lena's pulse quickened—not from fear or unease but the sharp *need* to touch him.

Bel cut a fine figure, looking like he belonged there at the head of the crowd alongside the king. He was every inch the Adiiron whispered about with awe. Mane of golden hair, his white-and-bronze wings oiled to a glossy shine. A fitted coat stretched across his wide chest, the rich sapphire blue making his eyes almost ethereal. Silver thread decorated the high collar and cuffs, royal emblems and feather motifs embroidered down the center and his arms. Trous of the softest gray wool covered his thick thighs, and his leather boots had been polished to gleaming.

The king and queen stood behind him, higher on the dais, but Lena barely noticed. Perhaps they looked finer, perhaps they wore crowns. She didn't see. She couldn't see anything but him.

Cira's words came back to her as she neared Bel, almost able to touch him. *A love match*. That's what this was. Beyond all odds. The war, the politics, the glowering avian king behind him—it didn't matter.

The only thing that did was taking the hand Bel offered her.

She shivered when their fingers met, and she watched his pupils expand, his expression growing almost hungry. She became aware of her breasts pushing at the neckline of her almost-too-tight bodice and didn't miss when his eyes dipped there.

Somehow, as one of two humans in a sea of avians, coerced there to marry before them all, Lena went almost dizzy with lust.

Bel pulled her closer, a little grin on his devilishly handsome face just for her. "You're so damn beautiful," he leaned in to whisper.

"So are you," she said, blushing, placing a hand on his warm chest to feel the softness of his jacket and the beat of his heart.

Bel covered it with his own and drew her up to the second step of the dais.

They faced each other, hand in hand. As she looked at Bel, this whole surreal day became a little more tangible. Her mind still moved as if through syrup, but her thoughts and mood were nothing but sweet.

Not even the king's severe face could sour it for her.

Dartegn looked between them, his dark eyes inscrutable. She didn't know what she expected him to do or say, be pleased with himself and his plan perhaps, but after another moment, the king merely took a long breath and began.

"You have come here to witness the joining of Prince Arubel Adiiron to this human woman. He has claimed she is *c'vana* to him and will prove what he says is true. He will mate this human, take her to wife, and forsake all others, avian and human both."

A few murmurs flitted through the crowd, as if some hadn't believed the king's reason for summoning them or that Bel would truly go through with this.

"As head of his family and his king, I will join Prince Arubel with his human chosen. What say you, Arubel?"

"I accept and am willing."

"And you, human?"

"I accept and am willing," Lena repeated.

"Prince Arubel, do you swear to keep this human, defend her, choose her above all others, and love her through the end days? Do you promise her the strength of your back, the whole of your heart, and the protection of your wing?" The oath wasn't quite the one Cira had explained to her, but it was faithful enough to the traditional avian mating promise while still serving Dartegn's plan.

Running his thumbs over her knuckles in a gentle caress, telling her without words it was all right, Bel lifted his right wing and wrapped it around her. A twinge of pain made him twitch, and she felt him lower the crook of the wing onto her left shoulder.

A few more murmurs went through the crowd.

Cira had been specific about this part, that the intended were meant to hold their right wings aloft around each other, a sign of strength and devotion.

Healed though it was, Bel's wing would never truly be right, and some positions pained him, like holding it aloft, unmoving.

Bel swallowed, letting the annoyance ease from his face. He used his wing to pull her a little closer, nearly chest to chest, their held hands between them.

"I, Prince Arubel Adiiron, swear to keep Maddalena, defend her, choose her above all others, and love her through the end days. I promise her the strength of my back, the whole of my heart, and the protection of my wing. I promise her everything I am and will be."

Lena bit her cheek to keep the tears from falling. She wished intensely to be out from under all these eyes, for this to be a small, intimate ceremony where they could both speak their hearts. Yet another part of her, the side that coveted praise and winning and proving herself, relished that he said the words in front of so many, claiming her, giving himself to *her*.

"And do you, human, swear to keep Arubel, defend him, choose him above all others, and love him through the end days? Do you promise him the strength of your back, the whole of your heart, and the protection of your..."

Louder murmurs now, a few laughs muffled behind hands.

A muscle ticked in Bel's jaw.

Lena glared up at Dartegn from under her lashes. She wouldn't be humiliated like this on her wedding day. She wouldn't let her mate be shamed, by her or by a king.

Letting go of Bel's hand, Lena turned to gesture at her squire. "Alix."

Alix's frown turned into a smirk. Unlooping the strap from her shoulder, she tossed Lena the scabbard and sword.

She caught it to a chorus of gasps and murmurs. But they didn't matter. All that did was the male looking at her now like the love he had for her almost pained him. His hand slid around her waist to rest on her back, the pads of his fingers tracing little patterns on her skin.

Lena wrapped her right arm around him, grasping the sword in her fist.

"I, Maddalena Montcaer, swear to keep Arubel, defend him, choose him above all others, and love him through the end days. I promise him the strength of my back, the whole of my heart, and the protection of my sword arm. I will fight for him and die for him, but first, I'll live for him."

Bel didn't smile. He didn't grin or laugh or murmur tenderly. His eyes, though, they never left hers, and she felt the pads of his fingers dig into her back and his heart thundering beneath her fist. He shuddered, struck by her promise, and his gaze roved over her, like only the barest thread kept him from consuming her whole.

Her declaration was met with stunned silence until a whoop went up from Alix, clapping wildly. A few more joined in, and when the queen herself clapped, more hesitantly began to applaud.

"By the sight of Halva, the first flocks, and your sovereign, I declare this mating final," declared the king over the din.

Lena barely heard and barely cared. Bel splayed his hand on her back, claiming the small distance between them, and she rose on her toes to meet him.

His mouth slid over hers in a warm, deep kiss she felt everywhere, her head, her toes, her past, her future. She poured herself into that kiss and the promises she'd made to him. It didn't matter how or why they were said.

It only mattered that she meant them—now, tomorrow, and always. And she did.

———— •◆•• ————

It took far too long to finally be alone with her new mate. Dartegn had made more speeches about loyalty, fealty, and family bonds. Both she and Bel had sworn up and down, though Lena couldn't help the terseness of her voice. She'd done it for Bel and no one else. When the king finally seemed satisfied, celebrations were held, with feasting and dancing and singing.

Well, avian dancing and singing. Avians didn't sing with words like humans; instead, they hummed tunes, adding slaps of their hands and wings to create rhythm. And the dancing...most of it took place in the air, partners darting together and away and together again, a dazzling aerial display that had Lena's heart in her throat every time one of them dove or spun away with wings tucked to their backs, only to flare them wide and swoop up to their partner. She'd nearly gone dizzy watching them.

She and Bel finally slipped away as the food and wine flowed, the reveling avians eventually forgetting why they'd come to celebrate in the first place. All that mattered in times like these was taking moments of happiness and pleasure.

They chose to claim theirs in private.

Phaedra followed them at a polite distance, having promised to see to Alix for the night.

Inside Bel's chambers, Lena stole a look at herself in the mirror again. Some of her curls had fallen or frizzed, and some feathers tangled with the braids. The dress creased with wrinkles where she'd folded her legs to sit.

Her cheeks glowed a rosy pink, and her lips were just a bit swollen from the kisses Bel had managed to steal. Between his quiet affection and the wine, she couldn't feel her pains and aches anymore; or, rather, didn't care to. Not when the woman staring back at her looked and felt so effervescently happy.

She watched Bel come up behind her in the mirror, his arms slipping under hers to pull her back into the warm solidity of his body. His head fell to the curve of her shoulder, and he ran his nose up and down, up and down, *ashita* and kisses. A hand came to rest on her belly, holding her against him, while the other played with the neckline of her dress.

She hadn't missed how often his eyes strayed to her breasts through the evening. She'd enjoyed taking every opportunity to lean over him, reaching for this or that, teasing him. It almost made her consider wearing dresses more often. Almost.

In the mirror, his fingers danced between skin and bodice, teasing her now. Her breathing grew deeper, breasts rising to meet his touch, but he never gave her more than a glancing caress.

"You're magnificent," he whispered into her neck.

She reached back to cup his head, burying her fingers in his hair. It drew her breasts just a little higher, just a little further out, taunting, tempting. Finally he filled his hand with one, thumbing her nipple through the fabric. He groaned low and deep as her nails scraped along his scalp, the vibration at her back making her bite her lip in delight.

Entranced, she watched him strum and stroke her, play with and pleasure her, under heavy-lidded eyes. Every caress and flick and squeeze went straight to her core, where she burned and ached for him.

"Bel," she moaned.

Breath hot on her skin, he rumbled, "I won't be distracted. I've fantasized about peeling you out of this all night, one skirt at a time."

Lena hummed in pleasure and let him turn her by the hips. Her hands immediately went to his chest, feeling all the coiled heat and strength there, just under a few layers of fabric. She'd had her own fantasies through the celebration, dreaming of popping open each little cloth button that closed his coat.

She set about doing just that but had only undone two when Bel took her face in his hands.

Meeting his gaze, she nearly melted under the tenderness she found there.

"I never wanted a crown," he said quietly, "but gods would I love to see one on your head. You'd make such a queen." He leaned in to capture her lips, parted in surprise. "Princess Maddalena," he murmured, and she felt his smile on her lips.

Lena blushed, not sure what to do with being called princess or how much pleasure it gave her.

She didn't want to be one. At least, not to anyone but him.

They didn't bother with words after that, at least, not full sentences. In the quiet of their chamber and glow of candlelight, they didn't need more as they slowly undressed each other. For all the heat and lust thrumming under her skin, Lena dared not rush anything, not a single moment.

Her bodice went first, peeled off her shoulders to bare her breasts to his appreciative gaze. He lavished them with his attention and tongue, stopping only when she undid the last of his buttons. She pushed the coat off his shoulders and hooked the soft shirt underneath with a finger, drawing it up over his head.

With each discarded garment, they touched and kissed and nuzzled every exposed inch of skin. Lena hummed with desire, her need for release almost unbearable by the time Bel freed her of her skirts. He lay her back on the bed, soft furs and velvets caressing her skin. She loved the softness, loved that Bel always wanted such things for his nest. He deserved everything soft and good.

She opened her arms to him, taking his weight, taking him inside. He never rushed and she never urged him, even as she smoldered inside, ready to combust. His pace was a slow, sensual build, flesh meeting in a warm slide again and again, breathtaking but never quite enough.

They made it last, not knowing what tomorrow would bring. Lena didn't belong in Hadria yesterday and wouldn't tomorrow, either—but today, she belonged exactly where she was, with Bel, holding her mate, taking him and adoring him and whispering in his ear when she finally came apart, "I love you, *c'vana*."

38

A summons to the council chamber to attend a meeting already underway caught Bel by surprise. He and Lena had exchanged glances, a dart of worry popping the bubble they'd created around themselves the past two nights. Lena's movements were still restricted and Bel was still scrutinized everywhere he went, so they'd gone nowhere, indulging in time alone.

Now, they hurried behind Phaedra to the council chamber, shirts just tucked, coats just buttoned. Outside the doors to the chamber, Lena straightened her sleeves and Bel fluffed his wings. Phaedra looked over her shoulder for confirmation, and with a nod from Bel, opened the door to usher them inside.

They walked in together, Lena's hand tucked in the crook of his arm. Bel felt the tension in her fingers, but she walked inside the room full of avians with the warrior's grace he'd come to expect of her. Poised, brave, she met the stares with her own.

Walking into the council chamber with her beside him made him think of all those important avians he'd watched enter the Mount as a fledgling, their names announced as they swept inside. They'd seemed to float, even with their wings draping behind them, buoyed by their own regality.

He felt that way now, buoyed by her. Undaunted, they bowed to the council and then to Dartegn, standing at the head of the long stone table. Beside him, sitting in the sovereign's seat, was Cira, her feather crown weaved through her hair.

The council looked on with a range of expressions, from disapproval to curiosity to animosity. Their numbers were markedly smaller with all the conspirators culled.

Tension crackled like a thunderstorm gathering over the mountains, though no one looked too red in the face, as though they'd been shouting their point. Dartegn wore his usual scowl, nothing out of the ordinary, but he ruined it looking down at his mate every few moments. The sight of her softened his gaze, though she didn't see it herself.

Once Bel and Lena reached the table, Dartegn straightened. "You both swore before everyone that you meant no harm and came only to help us. We've decided to test those oaths now."

"He means your opinion on matters would be useful," said Cira.

Several councilors grumbled and Dar shot his mate a disgruntled look, all of which she met with a mere arch of her delicate brows.

"We've been discussing this for hours now. Let's not tarry over the point," Cira said, rearranging the folds of her dress.

Bel worked to conceal his amused grin as he said, "We want to help. What can we do for the council?"

Their attention, heavy with expectancy, shifted to Lena at his side. Her fingers tightened on his arm.

"We have questions for the human," a councilor said.

"That human is my mate. You'll address her with civility, especially if you want something from her."

The councilor sneered and remained silent.

Another huffed, rolling her eyes. "The council would appreciate your insight, human. First of which, who are the humans found in the mines?"

Lena squared her shoulders and adjusted her stance to address the councilor, a posture Bel had seen her take before when speaking with superiors. He didn't think she even realized she did it.

"I only saw them for a moment, but I believe one is Captain Joran Farland. He's captain of the guard to Crown Prince Arion."

"And what is a man like that doing skulking about the old mines?"

"He pursued Bel and me from Finhöln," she said, explaining their flight through the forest and later ambush in Aeriand. "We thought we'd dealt with them there."

"You didn't kill them all when you had the chance," noted Ophir. "And now they're here."

"I didn't think he..."

"They didn't get further than any other human has," Bel thought it worth reminding them.

"No human without help," Ophir corrected.

Bel ignored him. "They were lost for days and never would've found Hadria on their own. They would've starved if they weren't found."

"They've yet to show any gratitude for that," grumbled Dartegn. "Perhaps they should have been left down there. It'd make this much simpler." He fixed Lena with a calculating gaze. "If they're no allies of yours, then you won't care if they're cast into the Pit."

Lena swayed, her jaw ticking with how hard she clenched it. "I do care," she said thickly.

"They're mouths we can't afford to feed. They cannot be released and they cannot be kept," said Dartegn. "Unless...there's something you can offer worth their lives."

Bel glowered at Dartegn for playing with her.

"I told you before I wouldn't help you slaughter my kind," Lena said.

"Then you condemn them to the Pit."

"No, cousin, *you* do," Bel interjected. He wouldn't let blame be laid at Lena's feet for any of this.

Dartegn's cool façade slipped when he turned to Bel. Frustration bled into his features, carving stark lines across his face.

"I'll do what I have to. Nobility doesn't keep people alive and fed. I use what I have because we're at a disadvantage." To Lena he said, "If you have anything to say, anything that could help us, say it now. You claimed you wanted to help. I'm trying to keep my people alive,

Maddalena. If you know something that could help me do that, then I'll consider letting these humans live. It's a better offer than any avian ever got."

Lena's fingers twitched on his arm when Dartegn said her name for the first time. Her frown eased into something more pensive.

Bel put his hand over hers. "Tell them what you can, *c'vana*. Please." It would take sacrifice to end the war, and he hated asking Lena to sacrifice any more than she already had for him—but the avians had little left to give.

Her throat bobbed with a hard swallow, and he saw the anguish inside her, everything she'd been told, everything she'd been trained to be crying out against it. But Bel also saw her resolve, that forged steel inside her that made Lena unbreakable. She nodded.

"I don't know how worthwhile it is, but I'll tell you what I remember. I want this war to end with as many spared as possible."

Dartegn extended his hand.

Lena and Bel approached the large map of the Gogona Mountains laid out with all its marks and stones. A new archivist helped Lena detail where she thought the humans had tried before to traverse the mines and caves. Most of the expeditions had been on the northern side, and Bel saw a few flickers of sympathy in the eyes of the councilors listening to her short, efficient explanations. The northern tunnels were mostly caves, ancient and treacherous. Few mines extended that way, not worth the dangerous chasms and crevasses. No one actually knew how far or deep they went.

The humans had no way of approaching the mountains from the east, exactly where the old mines were and where Bel had led them in. So with the north and west failed, all that was left was the south, where the humans now dug and searched.

"The human king is convinced that the way in is under the mountain," Bel said, recounting the documents he'd translated for King Artemian.

"He's not wrong," allowed one of the councilors. "It just can't be done from there."

"He doesn't know that," said Lena. "Or won't believe it. King Artemian will throw all the resources of Vagora into conquering this mountain. Even at the expense of his army. He nearly did so to take Aeriand. It will destroy him eventually, but..."

"Not before it destroys us," Bel finished grimly.

Dartegn's wings twitched in frustration. "Then we should bring the mountain down to him."

"We'd bring it down on ourselves, too," Bel said without heat. "Between the caves to the north, the old mines, and the new tunnels the humans are digging, how do we know we won't bring the whole mountain down?"

Dar's nostrils flared, feathers bristling, but then a small hand reached up to touch his arm. He looked down at Cira and her beseeching face. For a long moment, the king and queen conversed without words, Dartegn curving his wing around the chair and Cira seated in it.

Finally, Dartegn sighed. "Then what else is there? Wait for the humans to break through? What else do we have left?"

The king's demand hung in the air, unanswered. The faces of the councilors pinched in dismay and shame. Bringing the mountain down could destroy the last thing avians had, Hadria herself—but what else was there?

"Aeriand," Bel heard himself say. "We still have Aeriand."

"We lost it," Dar said, "and the humans left it in ruins."

"But not destroyed." Bel stepped forward, wings fluttering. "They stole the trappings and decoration, but Aeriand is *there*. It can be rebuilt, refortified. The city could live again."

Dartegn looked on with a considering frown, and Bel was encouraged when he didn't outright refuse.

Murmurs and looks of interest thrummed through the council.

"If Aeriand was taken back, Hadria could be evacuated. A rockslide wouldn't risk our people," suggested one councilor.

"A small force could stay behind," said another, "while others evacuate. The humans would never know until it was too late."

"They could occupy the humans here while the wall is rebuilt."

"The cisterns can be fixed."

"As can the aqueducts and roads."

"And who will do all this?" asked Dartegn, quelling the building excitement. "Who will lead a colony back to Aeriand?"

"I will."

A hush fell over the chamber, everyone staring at Queen Cira. She gazed at Lena for a moment before looking up to her mate.

"I will go to Aeriand. We can collect the colony on the eastern sea and return home."

When Dartegn said nothing, the council shifted restlessly.

Eyes only for his mate, Dartegn knelt beside the chair, putting their heads level. Cira reached out to gently brush the hair from his forehead.

"I can do this, Dar," she whispered.

Bel's ears heated, and his gaze fell away, turning instead to his own mate. Lena rested her cheek on his shoulder, looking up at him. Bel kissed her brow. Everyone else in the chamber looked anywhere but at the royal couple, affording that small privacy, but Bel didn't think they noticed anyone else as they gazed at each other.

"I don't want to be without you," Dartegn admitted quietly.

"I know. I don't wish to part from you. And Elia will miss you. But I think...I think it will be good, for us and for our people. I can be useful and you can focus on the battle without worrying over me."

"I'll always worry over you, *c'vana*," Dar rasped. "You and Elia are my heart."

Soft, intimate sounds tugged at Bel's chest, and he caught Lena wiping her eyes. The king and queen shared a few more whispers, but when Dartegn stood, his face had hardened once again.

"Aeriand could be reclaimed," he said, "but I won't send my family back there only to be attacked again. The human army must be defeated here. We can't allow them to destroy Aeriand a second time."

"Once we've evacuated all who can be, we bring down the

mountain," suggested Ophir, seeing where Dartegn's thoughts headed. "Bury them so they can't follow."

"You do that and you'll face a fresh army at Aeriand."

Heads swung to stare at Lena.

"If you destroy the whole army," she continued, "Vagora will never forgive you."

"I don't need the humans' forgiveness," said Dar.

"But they'll remember," Bel said, understanding what Lena was saying. "This war has become painful to humans even deep inside Vagora. Many have fled north to avoid taxes and conscriptions. The people we talked to on our travels here, they didn't support the war, nor did they seem to consider avians some great enemy. King Artemian is the only one who truly wants this war. His nobles collect heavy taxes for the war effort, so they don't oppose him."

"But if you destroy the human army, kill everyone..." Lena's throat worked as if the thought made her need to be sick, "every single one of those soldiers down there has a family. Someone to remember them. Someone who will answer the call for revenge. Artemian will raise another army and he'll have the full support of Vagora this time."

"Then what can be done?" demanded Dartegn.

"If King Artemian was gone, the war effort would lose its momentum."

"The human king is perfectly content to wage his war from afar," said a councilor, his tone accusing, as if it was Lena's fault Artemian couldn't brave his own choices.

"If there was ever an opportunity to kill him, I would've taken it," said Dartegn darkly.

From his periphery, Bel saw Lena glance up at him. He turned to catch her chewing the inside of her cheek, regarding him with a look he didn't understand.

She turned back to Dartegn to say, "You risk making Artemian a martyr that way. But if he was deposed..."

Bel went stiff, memories of a charming smile and golden head making an ugly jealousy rumble inside him.

"His son, Crown Prince Arion, is a good man. He's fought here at the front; he knows the toll it's taking. He doesn't believe in the war, but he serves to ensure it isn't led poorly."

"How do you know all this?" asked the grumbling councilor, his eyes narrowed in suspicion.

"I served under him for years," said Lena.

Bel worked to keep his face impassive, knowing that if his jealousy showed, if they knew how truly well Lena knew the human prince, they'd never listen to her.

He couldn't stop the swirl of resentment and jealousy brewing inside him, though. It was irrational and unneeded, but that didn't mean all those ugly feelings weren't lodging between his ribs, tightening his chest.

"He's well-loved by the people," Lena continued, "and more popular than his father. I'm not sure of his support amongst the nobility, but he's unmarried, so anyone with a daughter of eligible age will likely support him."

"What are you suggesting?" asked Cira.

Licking her lips, Lena explained, "If we could infiltrate the palace at Highclere, speak with Prince Arion, we may be able to convince him to depose his father."

The room exploded with noise, from guffaws to scoffs to questions.

Dar silenced it all with a mighty flap of his wings.

When the chamber was silent again, he asked Lena, "What makes you think he'll agree?"

"Prince Arion doesn't support this push Artemian is making to get inside the mountain. Even if it succeeds, the cost of life will be catastrophic. Arion doesn't want that."

"You speak as though you know him," Dartegn observed.

"We were friends," said Lena, and Bel didn't think anyone would notice the slight hitch in her voice as she said it. "War creates bonds that are hard to break or recreate."

"How would you even get to him?" asked another councilor. "He must be heavily guarded."

"He will be. But I know the capital and the palace. And you have the captain of his guard in your dungeon. He's...vulnerable."

Dartegn seemed unconvinced. "And you think if you go and ask him nicely, he'll overthrow his father and end the war?"

"No. It won't be that simple."

"Then how?"

"We force his hand. Leave him no choice," she said thickly, the words no doubt paining her to say.

⸻ ◆ ⸻

Many hours later, after they were finally dismissed and sent back to their chamber, a tired Phaedra came to fetch Bel and Lena once more. It was the small hours of the night, well past time to blow out candles and seek the comfort of bed.

Neither of them had been able to sleep, and they'd spent the intervening hours in relative silence. Part of Bel hoped this plan could finally be the solution they'd been waiting for—but another part, the one that coveted his mate and wanted to drive his fist into the face of the prince who'd come before him, didn't want to go anywhere near Vagora again.

Phaedra led them not to the council chamber but to the royal quarters. They passed two guards and a set of heavy double doors to find Dartegn and Cira still awake, seated with backs to a crackling fire at a small table in the jade-tiled sitting room. Parchments were spread out between them, and baby Elia slept soundly in her mother's arms.

Long shadows danced over their faces, the weight of every day of this war playing across Dartegn's tired eyes. He regarded them for a moment before beckoning them closer.

When Bel and Lena were settled at the table across from the king and queen, Dartegn took Cira's hand and said quietly, "We'll try this. You leave in three days for Vagora, to infiltrate the palace and give the human prince our terms." He moved a parchment in front of him, reading, "We will support his bid for the throne and recognize his claim. In return, this war must end. And Maddok's wings must be returned."

Under the table, Lena's hand found his.

"If he refuses," said Cira, "we'll bring this mountain down on the human army. We'll also ally with his enemies to the south."

"If he loves his people as you say, he'll accept our terms. He will if he loves his father, too." Dartegn's face hardened as he told them, "Ophir and Phaedra will accompany you. I need warriors there I can implicitly trust. If you fail, if your prince refuses, they have my orders to kill Artemian. Either way, he'll no longer be king."

Lena shifted in her seat, but Bel squeezed her hand.

This had to be done. Whether she liked it or not.

Bel had no qualms about assassinating the king who'd ruined his life. He remembered only the man's voice and his shadow; both had sustained his hate for many cold winters in Finhöln. But this wasn't about hate or even vengeance. As he looked between Dartegn and Cira, holding their child, Bel understood this mission was about hope—for peace, for their people.

To Lena, Dartegn said, "If you do this, I will spare the human captives, but I expect them to give any information they have. I'll also delay the rockslides as long as I can. We'll hit the human forces hard, make them believe we're at full strength, to give Cira time to get to Aeriand and you to get to the human capital."

"Thank you," Lena murmured.

"Phaedra is a fast flier and will return with news. If you fail, I'll bring this mountain down whether your prince is a king or not."

"I understand."

The crackle of the fire was loud as silence descended. Dartegn turned to Bel next, the severe features of a king falling away to reveal the tired, hopeful, scarred male beneath. He looked younger somehow, a hint of that intense, tempestuous youth Bel remembered.

"Make this right, Arubel," he said.

Emotion clogged Bel's throat, and the long breath he took

shuddered through him.

"I won't fail again," Bel said, as much to Dar as to himself.

Decided and agreed, Dartegn slid the parchment across the table. It was a treatise, outlining everything he'd just told them but with more threatening overtures. It was half-bluff and entirely dangerous, this document.

It was the best chance the avians had had in years.

39

Lena straightened her jerkin for the fifth time. It was a fine thing, all buttery leather with tooled designs and decorative stitching. She just couldn't quite get used to the airiness of the back, the paneling left open from nape to lower shoulder blade. Made for someone with wings, the slight chill or the sudden swish of her hair against the shirt beneath distracted her. The avian garments took getting used to, but there was no denying their quality—and they made her feel a little less like she had no business standing beside Bel, the golden Adiiron prince with his family crest emblazoned in gold thread across his coat front.

Still, part of her desperately wanted to come wearing her own gear for this.

Maybe, if she wore her own jerkin, made by and for humans, Joran wouldn't see everything about her as a complete betrayal.

Ridiculous, of course. Nothing could redeem her in his eyes.

Lena swallowed hard, wishing her nerves would sink back into her stomach rather than clutching at her throat.

It doesn't matter what he thinks, she reminded herself, *only that he takes the offer.*

She waited with Bel, the king, Cira, and the council on the arena near the dais. With a pair of avian guards each, the three human knights were marched across the vast platform. They squinted and cringed in the sudden, intense light of the oculus.

Pulse thrumming in her throat, Lena tucked an errant lock of hair behind her ear.

A damp updraft from the Pit swirled around them, and they stood near enough to hear the faint wails of the wind, far below. The stony faces of the guardian statues, with their weapons crossed and eyes veiled, watched them in macabre silence.

She hadn't liked the decision to bring the knights here, but Dartegn wanted his terms and the consequences clear. He brooked no argument, from Lena or from the knights that needed to bend.

Lena finally got her first look at Joran and the other two knights, a man and woman, as they were brought before Dartegn and made to kneel.

The woman had had a plait of auburn hair once—now it was just a knotted reddish rope that hung limply from her shoulder. Scruffy beards had sprouted on both men, and dark stubble capped Joran's head. Used to her former commander always being mercilessly clean-shaven, the sight of Joran's growing hair and slightly receding hairline stirred the unease in Lena's belly.

All three knights were gaunt, their eye sockets and cheeks concave. They'd been fed meager rations but not bathed; even from a few paces away, Lena could smell the stench of them, their clothes stained from weeks of wear.

Lena didn't know the man and woman, and neither looked up from the floor. Exhaustion was written in their sagging shoulders and dull eyes. Neither seemed to know or care what they'd been brought here for.

Joran had pushed them past all duties, boundaries, and limits. The knights before her now were broken people, kept too long in the dark.

Lena hated Joran for it.

Her former commander kept his head up, eyes darting between all the gathered avians. His gaze skittered over her at first before swinging back and widening in disbelief. His mouth opened, but nothing passed his cracked lips.

Dartegn approached them, drawing a shudder from the knights.

"You were found six days ago in the northeastern tunnels," said Dartegn in stiff high Vagoran. "Know that you would not have made it to Hadria on your own. For all that you may hate us, we saved your lives bringing you here. Remember that."

He looked over his shoulder at Lena, expectant.

She drew herself up tall and stepped forward. Bel followed a step behind, supportive and warm.

Lena set her stance and folded her arms behind her back, a posture all knights would know. The other two knights barely noticed, only picking their eyes up from the floor to glance at her. Joran, though, scrutinized her from head to foot with eyes a little too wide, a little too manic.

"I am Maddalena Montcaer of Lindenfaire, daughter of Sir Warrek and Lady Margot Montcaer, mate to Arubel Adiiron. I speak to you now on behalf of King Dartegn Adiiron." The names tasted surreal falling from her lips, but she said them, claimed them. She knew how knights thought, knew stating her titles and intent would get her at least their attention.

The woman looked askance at Lena through her lashes for a moment, shifting on her knees, but the other man remained motionless.

Joran spat on the ground between them.

"*Mate?* You *married* that—"

A swift cuff to the head from a guard silenced him, but Lena held up her hand.

"Don't, please."

Joran only sneered at her.

"King Dartegn has decided to spare your lives. You'll be kept as prisoners here in the mountain until the war is over."

"So forever," mumbled the woman.

"No," Lena said. "Not forever. The war will end."

Her statement drew Joran and the woman's attention, their suspiciousness and disbelief plain. But she wasn't to reveal their plans, just say what Dartegn had told her to.

She had to convince them. If she could, if she could save them, it would be one small victory. If nothing else in their plans went right, at least Lena would have this.

"King Dartegn has agreed to keep you until your release. In exchange, you'll provide what useful information you can."

Joran snarled. "You fucking traitor!"

Feathers brushed her back, Bel's wings beating in an aggressive display.

"I'm not the only one who abandoned my post," Lena said to Joran. "You had no right to follow us, we both know your orders were to fortify Finhöln and await further instruction from Prince Arion. But you left that duty to chase us across the continent. For what? You've left your prince unguarded. You've gotten your knights wounded and worse. *For what*, captain?"

Lena's voice echoed in the Round, her outrage at everything Joran had done reverberating across every terrace. Avians began entering from many of the thresholds, drawn by her demands.

Demands that went unanswered.

"Catching fugitives from the law is every knight's duty," Joran hissed. "You betrayed your king and your country—you'll answer for that, Maddalena. Maybe not today and not by me, but one day soon, you'll pay for betraying your own *kind*."

"Perhaps. But I'll end this war first."

Joran's smile was ugly, something she'd never seen him wear before. The weeks of pursuit and darkness had done something to him, broken something fundamental. It wasn't the captain she'd admired glaring back at her now but the shriveled remains of obsession.

"Fucking princes doesn't win wars, you stupid girl. No cunt is that—"

"Enough!" Bel boomed.

Lena drew herself up, hardening against the insults. They stuck to her but didn't penetrate.

"You call us savages with the same mouth you insult the only person here keeping you alive," Dartegn hissed.

"I don't want your forgiveness or even your understanding," Lena said, more to the other two knights. She thought from the way the woman kept her head canted that she might be truly listening. "I just want you to live. So please, tell King Dartegn what you can. Help us end this war. Too many have died."

Her plea was met with resounding silence.

Lena held her breath, willing the man and woman to take the hand she offered.

Joran staggered to his feet, and the guard let him with a nod from Dartegn.

His shoulders drew back and his stance widened. For a moment, he was the captain she'd known, venerable and distinguished, the lines of him firm and straight. He regarded Dartegn and then her with a quiet censure, his frown unyielding.

She knew what he'd say before he said it.

"I took an oath to serve king and country. That *means something*. It doesn't matter if that duty is difficult or distasteful. My loyalty is to my king and my kind." His head tipped back just the slightest bit so he could look down his nose at her, just as he had when correcting her form or telling her to clean out the latrines. "You've betrayed your oath, your king, and your people. You're no knight."

Lena stood there and took his words, for there was truth to them. She'd betrayed the knight's code and the oaths she'd made to her king. But, "I refuse to serve a king who kills without reason and sacrifices his own people to hide his incompetence. You're right, Joran, fucking princes won't win this war—but neither will a knight."

Joran shook his head slowly. "Your honor, your word, they're worthless, and so is your offer. You're nothing, Maddalena. I'll never take the word of a traitor like you."

Lena winced, unprepared when Joran ducked and threw his shoulder into the guard to his right. He spun away from the stunned warrior, pushing off to get a running start. He ran straight for the Pit, nearing the edge, as if he would, as if he meant—

Her legs moved before she could think, trying to catch up, to stop him. A cry formed on her tongue, but then wings came around her, muffling her shout in feathers.

Bel caught her, stopping her as quick as she'd begun running. He pulled her into his heaving chest, wrapped her up in limbs, whispered fervently in her ear, "Don't look, Lena, don't look."

But she did, she had to. No one caught Joran before he made the edge of the Pit. Without hesitating, he threw himself into the void, legs wheeling. For a moment, he floated there, airborne, aloft in the updraft as if flying without wings beneath the eyes of the stone guardians.

And then the Pit swallowed him whole.

He didn't scream, just disappeared into the darkness with the hissing *whoosh* of parted air.

Lena's mouth opened, maybe to scream for him, she didn't know.

Bel pulled her away, lifted her off her feet to turn them around and block her view.

The avians standing there, even Dartegn himself, looked on in stunned silence. No one met her eyes.

Tears overflowed her lashes, the sharp edge of failure stabbing at her heart.

"Lena..." Bel murmured, a hum in her ear.

"Are you really going to end the fighting?"

Lena looked blearily at the other two knights. The woman peered up at her, eyes wide in an ashen, perturbed face.

"We're going to try," Lena replied.

Cracked lips twisting in consideration, the woman knocked the man's shoulder with hers. "Then we'll take your offer. We don't know much, but if it'll help end this..." Her eyes flicked to the Pit.

"Do as you're ordered, answer truthfully, and you won't be harmed, human," Dartegn said.

The woman nodded slowly.

And then there was little left to say. Lena let Bel usher her away, wanting to get far away from that open maw.

Her hands shook but were too stiff to clench into fists.

Two at least, she repeated to herself. She'd gotten two spared at least. Her first negotiation, neither a total success nor failure. Yet it felt like failure, the sight of Joran hanging in the air over that black abyss consuming her.

A wing settled along her shoulders, surrounding her in warmth and softness. Bel's embrace wasn't soft, though. He pulled her into his arms and held on tight, his solidity a comfort she could hardly bear.

His heart thundered in his chest, beating against her own, and his breath was hot as he nuzzled her hair. "You're everything, *c'vana,*" he rasped against her temple. "*Everything.*"

40

Three days later, Bel stood before the high gateway that connected the Round to the main promenade. A small party had gathered there to see them off, an odd assortment of beings if he paused to think about it.

The horses had been readied and fetched from the stables. Warriors tied off the last of the supplies to the packhorses, overseen by Ophir, while Lena, Alix, and Phaedra said their goodbyes to Cira and baby Elia. Several councilors and commanders formed a semicircle around them, waiting to be useful.

The smell of the horses, the feel of travelling clothes, and the rhythm of packing for a journey were like stepping into a worn pair of boots, stiff but familiar. The routine of it was almost surreal, nearly erasing his sense of the past weeks in Hadria.

Through the little gathered crowd, Bel spotted the person he'd been looking for.

Dartegn stood apart from the group, his eyes on Cira as she fussed over Lena, Alix, and Phaedra. Two of his guards flanked him, but otherwise, he seemed content to stand alone.

Having seen everything kingship demanded of Dartegn, Bel couldn't blame him.

Still, there was something left to be said. He didn't know when he'd see his cousin again, and Bel still bore the scars of leaving things unsaid to his kin.

Dar's gaze swung to him as he approached. He wore that bland expression Bel had come to associate with him when he played king. Never giving too much away, Dartegn kept a tight leash on his temper and moods, so tight that his duty encrusted him in a calcified shell of obligation. To the detriment of all that he was or could have been underneath.

It saddened Bel to see.

Kingship had hardened the fierce, impetuous, brash, sensitive boy Dartegn was, cooling his fire into something rigid. Bel thought he finally understood, gazing into that bland look, that many of the scars Dar bore were the same size and shape as his own.

Bel bowed his head but didn't wait to be acknowledged. "May I speak with you, cousin?"

Dartegn nodded. "Best make it quick," he said, turning to lead Bel along the lower terrace of the Round.

They walked in silence for a short time, distancing themselves from the others. It wasn't a comfortable silence nor a tense one. It just was.

Bel realized this was the first time he'd stood alongside Dar without animosity or frustration crackling between them. Like this, in the quiet, Dar wasn't his king or cousin or antagonist—he was just a male, one whose duties weighed heavily on his shoulders.

It saddened Bel, too.

"We'll have to turn around at this rate," Dartegn muttered.

Bel realized they'd nearly made it to the midpoint of the terrace without having said a word.

He couldn't help grinning at Dar's surliness. That hadn't changed.

"I promise you, Dar, I'll do this."

Dartegn looked at him askance from under that inscrutable shell. "You're finally the hero you always wanted to be."

Bel frowned. "I never wanted that."

In a contemplative tone, Dartegn said, "You mean you didn't dream of this? Returning to swoop in and play the hero? The savior of your people?"

"I've only ever wanted to belong, Dar."

Silence descended over them again, their footsteps loud now to Bel's ears.

When Dar spoke again, his voice rasped as if he pulled the words from deep in his chest. "It doesn't matter now how it happens or who does it. I don't care anymore who saves our people, so long as they're saved. I won't make them suffer for my pride."

He stopped, compelling Bel to stop. His brows drew together as though something troubled him.

Dar's jaw worked, tendons ticking, before he said, "I'm sorry you had to suffer."

The oldest of all Bel's scars throbbed inside him. It was one that never fully healed, left raw around the edges. He tasted the rejection he'd felt all his life on the back of his tongue, a sour bitterness.

Dar didn't apologize for not coming for Bel, nor for abandoning him, because he knew Dar wasn't sorry for that.

It'd taken a long time in his cold room at Finhöln to come to accept the truth—he wasn't important enough to his cousin, his kin, *anyone*. He'd held that resentment as tightly and deep as his hatred for King Artemian, in the very marrow of himself where it ate away at him.

He didn't think he'd ever truly be free of it, for some scars never truly healed. Seeing Dartegn and what he'd had to do to keep their people going removed the claws and fangs from that bitterness. Acknowledging it, accepting that no one had been in a position to help him leached the poison from all that resentment.

"We've all suffered from this war. From losing Maddok. I don't want to anymore."

He looked out across the Round, at the empty terraces and arena, then to their party, almost ready to leave Hadria.

"I want the chance to live, Dar. That's why I'm going. Not for glory or to play hero." For the first time in his life, his fate was in his own hands. "I belong now. With her. I want a world where I can stand beside her without fear of shame or threat."

Dartegn was quiet long enough that it finally drew Bel's gaze. He didn't know how to describe what he found on Dar's face, wasn't sure if he believed Dar could hold any affection for him.

"Maddok would be proud of you."

Bel's wings fluttered, almost coming around him to shield him from words that cut him to the quick. They lanced the hurts inside him, letting some of the acrid bile drain away.

"Tell me I've paid my penance, Dar," he murmured.

Dar's face crumpled, and he turned away, eyes shut tight.

"I don't know that I can ever forgive," Dar rasped, "but I'm tired of hating you. Maddok made his choice. He saved you. And I...I can't punish you any longer for his decision."

"I wish he hadn't, Dar, I wish he—"

Dartegn shook his head. "But he did." He closed the distance between them, clasping a heavy hand on Bel's shoulder. The male staring at him now was raw, eyes glassy and fierce. "I have to accept that, and it's the burden you have to bear. The crown was left to me but he gave you his life."

Bel swallowed thickly, understanding that both were heavy weights to bear.

"You've kept our people alive, Dar," Bel told him. "I know you never wanted it, but you're the king they've needed. Maddok would be proud of you, too."

A tear spilled across Dar's cheek, falling onto Bel's arm. "Let's make him proud, the both of us."

Bel squeezed Dar's shoulder. "Halva watch over you and your family, cousin."

"Take care, Arubel, and may the wind be at your back and the sun warm on your face."

41

Lena woke from her light sleep when Bel rejoined her after his watch. His movements were quick and efficient, barely jostling her, but she'd been waiting for him. As he pulled more blankets over himself and then her, Lena cracked an eye, surveying their camp through her lashes.

Bel had stoked the fire before ending his watch, the coals simmering and red. Alix lay tucked between the fire and Miri, just a few stray curls escaping her cocoon of blankets. Phaedra was next, laid on her stomach with her blankets bunched beneath her and her wings laid out over her like a cloak.

Across the fire, Ophir sat with a lantern for more light as he cleaned his sword and daggers. He'd slept little on their journey, even as it stretched into its second week. They'd passed into Vagora a few days ago, and now his blades shone like mirrors.

He sat with his back to the cart they'd purchased in another border village they'd happened upon before entering Vagora. Lena ended up buying a dozen barrels to go in the cart and filling them with wheat, barley, and dried fish.

"*We need something to sell,*" Lena had explained to Ophir when he protested that the cart would be weighed down and therefore slower.

Whatever warnings or gossip there might be travelling through the pubs and inns of Vagora about three fugitives from up north, Lena guaranteed they'd talk of two or three, a man and woman, possibly an older girl. What they wouldn't notice was a family travelling to the capital to sell their crop.

Ophir had snorted in distaste when they'd decided that he would play Lena, Phaedra, and Alix's father, if ever confronted on who they were.

So far they hadn't had to rely on the story and Ophir's acting abilities, thank Matella, having come across few others. Which was precisely why Lena had chosen the route they now took, a circuit of roads that curved south before heading west, to the capital of Highclere. Most travellers, as well as the army, used the more direct King's Road. The southern roads made for a longer journey with more ruts and fewer towns, but that suited them. Well, all but the ruts.

She and Alix learned many new colorful avian curses whenever the cart got stuck in a particularly bad rut.

Behind her, Bel settled down, blankets arranged to his liking. She heard the rustle of feathers and then felt the slight weight of his wing, crook resting on her arm.

Lena rolled to face him, letting her tired eyes fall shut as she nuzzled in close to find his mouth. His lips were cold from the night air, a chill still clinging to the spring nights. She warmed them with her own, soft, sleepy presses of welcome and affection.

He wrapped her up in an arm and wing, pulling her deeper into the curve of his body. Her fingers found the buttons of his shirt, opening a few so she could delve inside to feel the heat of his skin. His chest radiated warmth, captured by the insulation of his feathers, and he didn't begrudge it when she stuck her socked feet between his shins.

She hummed quietly, content with the easy intimacy. Cuddling under the blankets and stars and the occasional stolen kiss or *ashita* were all they had the past weeks. She refused to do anything within earshot of Ophir, and she doubted he'd appreciate stopping long enough for her and Bel to slip away into the woods so her mate could pin her against a tree and—

Goddess, she had to stop. Or else she wouldn't, whether Ophir was in earshot or not. And he was.

Perhaps it was being mated to Bel now, the formal ties of it, that had her hungering for him even more than before. She was raised as a knight by knights, with all the pomp and circumstance that came with it; she found comfort in formality and ceremony. It may not have happened how she or Bel would've chosen, but Lena would change nothing.

Or perhaps it was that every day dawned to meet them just a little quicker than the last, rushing them toward the unknown. She'd never found comfort or thrill in the unknown, and if she let them, her worries and fears would eat her alive.

She kept them down with the building sense of purpose that had taken root in her since leaving Hadria. Perhaps there truly was something bad in the air, as Cira had thought, because the further they travelled from the mountain, the more assured Lena became. The sun and fresh air were surely part of it, yes, but Lena also had budding confidence in their plan the closer they got to Highclere.

It may well be false hope and confidence, but she had to believe they could do this, could make Arion king. If she didn't, she couldn't stomach putting Alix and Bel in so much danger. If she didn't, those fears would cripple her.

So she drew confidence and comfort where she could and never missed a chance to steal a little time with her mate.

His wing drew higher, the bone coming to rest over their heads. She lost sight of his features, only the faintest glow from the fire penetrating his feathers, but she didn't need more. Using her fingers, she traced his throat and the hollow there between his clavicles.

"Did I wake you?" he whispered. His wing caught the warmth of their breath and words, and Lena loved how it always seemed like the world was just the two of them hidden under his wing.

"No," she mumbled, kissing his chin.

Bel maneuvered so her head was pillowed on his arm and he could bury his fingers in her hair. "How long until we reach the capital?" he said, taking the edge off the question by kneading her scalp.

Melting under his touch, she could barely form words as

contentment pulled her toward sleep again.

"About a week."

Bel made a soft hum of agreement. When he spoke next, it was thankfully after a series of long, slow kisses that had her toes curling between his legs.

"We can do this, *c'vana*. Make our better world," he murmured against her lips.

"We have to."

He smoothed a hand over her hair, catching her between his palms when she would've leaned in for another kiss.

"Whatever happens—"

"Bel..."

"Whatever happens, I at least got to be your mate for a little while. Everything will have been worth it, just for that."

Lena kissed him hard, occupying his mouth with her tongue so he couldn't say any more heartbreaking things. Her confidence was a fragile thing, and she shored it up with his kisses and touches and affection.

Her conviction, though, was much stronger. She'd seen enough battle to know plans went to shit the moment the fighting started, but she knew, without doubt, that they'd face it. Together.

42

Bel couldn't look at Highclere too long without being momentarily blinded. The great towers and citadels of the human capital rose from the sea cliffs like polished coral, gleaming white, gold, and rosy. Glossy tiles painted with intricate designs decorated the homes and buildings, glittering as brightly as the sea behind it.

Built atop cliffs that overlooked a protected bay, the palace and largest buildings of the city stood like white chess pieces, overseeing the board. The city followed the curved slope northwest, nearly rimming the entire bay. At its midpoint, the landscape and city with it naturally dipped, and here the humans built a great harbor, a forest of masts and sails.

That's where Alix said she'd be going, that depression in the cliffs. Cheapside, she'd called it. Where much of the work and industry of the city took place but also the only place where the people who did the work could afford to live.

A sea breeze had hit them as they made camp outside the city, in a shady copse of trees on a bluff to the north, making Alix turn her head west. She'd taken a long draw of air, humming to herself, *"Smells like home."*

Alix's connections to the place were the only reason Lena agreed to her squire's plan. Bel hadn't liked it either, but he agreed that Alix would look inconspicuous on her own. Lena had argued for another ten minutes that at least one more of them should go.

"The only other human is you, and you're wanted, remember? They've

probably got prints of your face all over. And I'm not taking one of them." She'd jabbed a thumb at the three avians, looking on with bemusement. *"We'd never get away with all the layers it'll take to disguise them during the day."*

Lena finally relented when faced with so much logic. So, Alix had left in her old clothes, carrying nothing but a light pack, a pocket full of coin, and all her hidden weapons. Lena stood sentry on the bluff ever since.

He approached his mate quietly, not wanting to startle her. She stood in the shade of the trees, face turned toward the setting sun. It'd be at least another hour before the sun even touched the watery horizon.

Highclere shone in the evening light, the stone and tiles and copper reflecting so much light, the citadels glowed like torches, calling the ships in from sea. Bel averted his sensitive eyes, instead looking at the wall that snaked around the vast boundaries of the city. There were multiple walls, another erected whenever the city had to expand. The outermost layer was a formidable thing, built of blonde granite and linking pairs of barbican gates. Yet, the gates never closed, not even at night.

"Never had to," Alix had said with a shrug when Phaedra asked over it. *"Honestly, people would probably get nervous if they did."*

A defensive wall they never had to use. Imagine.

Slipping an arm around Lena's shoulder, he pulled her into his side.

"She'll be fine," Bel reassured her. "You know she's smarter than all of us."

Lena grumbled in agreement, but her posture remained rigid, her arms crossed over her chest as if she needed to keep her worries restrained.

Bel kissed her temple and left her to her vigil, understanding reassurances and embraces weren't what she wanted right now. Tightly wound, Lena wouldn't come away until they'd seen the signal Alix promised. So Bel made himself useful helping the others prepare. When Alix called them, as he knew she would, they'd be ready to move.

———— •◆•• ————

Dusk settled on the water in streaks of lilac and rose, the sun winking out over the horizon in a flash of green. Windows all over the city flickered with light, illuminating it from within with a soft orange glow.

The signal came about an hour after full dark.

Alix had pointed out a tall, square tower made of brown and gray stone. *"See that? Used to be a belltower. Wait for three flashes, then I'll meet you at the east gate."*

Bel, Phaedra, and Ophir sat around two lanterns, not wanting to risk a fire. Not that they needed it; the air was warm here, the breeze from the sea pleasant but not cooling.

They didn't speak, instead keeping themselves busy with mindless tasks.

So Bel heard it, Lena's sharp inhale.

The *clack* of Phaedra's knitting needles went silent.

In just a handful of moments, they were moving, Lena and Bel riding while Ophir drove the cart with Phaedra and all their barrels, for the east gate.

———◆———

They met Alix just inside. Well, more like she found them. The horses and cart clattered on the cobblestones, a din loud enough that they hadn't seen Alix materialize from the shadows beside them until she'd bounced on the balls of her feet, cocky grin on her face.

"Welcome to Cheapside," she said with a wink.

Lena leaned down and grabbed her shoulder, giving it a squeeze. "You're all right?"

"Just fine," she said, her low Vagoran accent thicker than Bel had heard before. Alix tapped her head. "All in here. C'mon, got a spot for us for the night."

Leaping onto Miri, Alix drew alongside Lena at the front, giving her subtle directions through the lantern-lit streets.

Even at night, all the sights, sounds, and smells nearly overwhelmed Bel. Pubs and restaurants overfilled with patrons, their interiors warmly lit. They passed near a market, closed for the night, the stalls somnolent with their drawn-down tarpaulins. Some humans walked in groups, laughing or talking or arguing; others scurried down side-streets and alleyways, looking even more suspicious than their group; others lounged in window-seats or benches, enjoying the temperate evening.

It was overall a much merrier, jovial scene than he'd imagined.

Bel realized when they passed into Cheapside.

The lampposts became scarcer, their light a kind of murky haze behind grimy glass. Ophir and Phaedra muttered curses as the cart bumped along, cobbles missing from the streets. Shadows pooled in alleyways, too deep for even avian eyes. And the humans here...they looked up at the group of horses and cart askance, there and gone again, but Bel felt every swipe of their eyes, assessing, calculating.

The down at his nape stood up.

A shadow moved to his right.

"Alix..."

"Yeah, I see it. C'mon."

First they trotted, putting on a little speed, but still the shadow followed. And then there were two. Three. Six.

The streets narrowed, hemming them close. Bel drew Ruan behind Lena and Alix to make room and could feel the packhorses growing skittish at his back.

Shadowy silhouettes with hungry eyes gathered at every alleyway and crossroad. More followed behind, loping to keep up but not attacking.

"Almost there," Alix muttered.

Without warning, she tapped Miri's flanks. The horse flew forward, and then they all did, running down the dark street. The cart lurched and thundered behind him, but all Bel could do was hope the wheels held.

Cheapside flew by in a shapeless blur, the smell of salt and dead fish growing stronger. Bel could hear the waves when Alix turned right, heading straight into the black, yawning mouth of a warehouse.

Heart thudding in his ears, Bel passed into the darkness.

The cart came clattering close behind, and then Alix yelped, "Now!"

A sharp squeal and then something heavy dropped over the warehouse entrance, closing them in, enveloped in darkness.

Bel's feathers prickled.

Somewhere, a flint struck.

One by one, lanterns and candles were lit, little splashes of light in the boundless dark.

His breath caught in his throat.

The candlelight illuminated faces, childish faces. Large eyes stared up at them set in gaunt, hungry faces. At least a dozen human children hesitantly walked forward. Some looked as old or maybe older than Alix while others were barely walking age, toddling behind an older child.

They gathered together, their combined light giving shape to some of the building. Little houses of crates, barrels, and old carts had been piled into a ramshackle village. A central ring was marked with stones and broken bricks, the ashes of a bonfire still smoldering and an ancient looking cauldron still steaming over it.

Sadness stung Bel's heart to see this.

"Who are they?" he murmured.

"Kids like me," Alix answered softly. "Runaways. Street kids. Orphans of the war. Kids with bad fathers and drunk mothers." She met Bel's sad gaze, and he saw the old hurts there inside her. Hidden behind bravado and big curls, the truth of Alix's beginnings lay plain now for them to see, as did the hard knot of scars it left behind.

Her gaze cut away to the children and she plastered on a smile. Standing in the stirrups, she planted her hands on her hips and announced, "Flawless timing, as always!"

The tension in their thin shoulders eased, and some of the children laughed.

"Everyone, this here's Lena—you probably remember her—and this is Bel, and that's Phae..." Alix went down the line, introducing each of them, even the horses. The children blinked at the newcomers, not quite sure what to make of them.

Finally, one of the older youths stepped forward, a suspicious frown on his young face. "We did what you asked. So what'd you bring?"

"Good stuff," Alix said. "Let's get dinner going. Then I got some things we gotta find."

◆

Bel was equal parts charmed and dismayed at how efficiently the children unloaded the cart of goods, the foodstuffs disappearing into the shadows. A fish stew was quickly brewing over a hearty fire, older children cutting food while the littler ones tore apart the meat with tiny hands. Soon, bellies were full, and as some of the younger children gathered around Phaedra to pet her wings and ask more questions, Alix sent a few her own age out on their errands.

He met Lena's troubled gaze over the fire. It felt wrong to sit here and let children do this for them. Alix insisted they knew what they were doing, they'd be back in no time, don't worry, but Bel remembered those lurking alleyway shadows.

He didn't like this impotence, but there was nothing to do but trust Alix and her friends. He and the other avians had been lucky to make it this far into Highclere, and even hidden as they were, being surrounded by humans had his nerves itching.

Still, as they waited, Bel let the braver children come and touch his wings. They marveled at how the bronze barbs gleamed gold in the firelight and cooed appreciatively at the soft down.

It didn't take long for the children to start playing, running beneath and around and through Phaedra's wings. The female warrior laughed and clapped, encouraging them with what Vagoran words she knew. As the night wore on, a little boy even fell asleep in her lap.

Ophir stayed back from the fire, answering questions but none of the children seemed as interested in him with his wings kept tight to his back. Still, Bel didn't miss when Ophir handed one of the older girls a dagger to keep.

Through the night, Alix commanded her little army as competently as any commander, issuing orders, checking on supplies, asking after friends she didn't see. Some of the older youth seemed reluctant at first, and Bel assumed they'd been the ones in charge in Alix's absence. The ones her age and younger all listened with rapt attention, their loyalty evident in how they looked to and leaned toward her. His heart ached with pride for her, and he understood fully now what Lena had seen when she chose Alix.

———•—◆—•—•———

The fire burned low and the littlest ones had all fallen asleep when the youths Alix sent returned with their spoils—palace and royal guard uniforms, capes, helmets. Alix and Lena inspected each item, holding coats up to his chest to measure and quickly hemming a pair of trousers to fit Alix. The helmet was snug, pinching his pointed ears to his head, but they were hidden.

Enough was found for all of them, and after toying with the heavy cape over his wings for half an hour to see how best to hide all the avians' wings, there was nothing to do but bed down.

Children drifted into their crate houses, and Phaedra stoked the main fire.

Lena took his hand and led him deeper into the warehouse and shadows, away from prying eyes and innocent ears. They found a secluded corner, full of old crates and wagon wheels, good enough for hard kisses and desperate hands.

"Everything's ready," he told her between hot presses of his mouth to her throat. His nerves kept the words coming. "We won't—"

She nipped his tongue and drew it into her mouth, telling him what she needed right then. His mate needed a rough, desperate distraction from the impending day, and so that's what he gave her. No promises, no assurances, just him and the thundering heart that beat for her.

She helped him forget for an hour that tomorrow would either be the beginning...or the end.

43

Lena emerged from the back garden of the empty townhome Alix had scouted, a bundle of nerves prickling in her stomach. She contained them with a narrowed focus and didn't let herself think more than a few moments ahead. Nothing outside her line of vision mattered anymore.

It was how she found her feet marching into battle, the rhythm of it making everything else fall away.

Bel drew alongside her, striking in his royal guard uniform. Helmet pulled low over his eyes, he was the picture of an overdressed new recruit looking to make a good impression. Arion never stood on much formality when it came to uniforms, which was why Lena wore no helmet nor cape.

When Arion came for Lena at Finhöln, most of his knights had been new to Lena, her former comrades either reassigned after the horrors of the war or cut down by it. Between the losses and those Joran kept with him, those guards Arion had now would be new to him and therefore not know Lena's face. Still, Alix had helped darken her hair and brows with kohl, even added a thin line around her eyes and a few new freckles on her cheeks.

Alix and the other avians came next, kitted in the blue and gold of royal guards. Wings had been folded away under cloaks and bulky gambesons, down tucked into high collars, and pointed ears hidden by helmets. Lena still wasn't sure if they'd pass, but then, she knew there were avians beneath those tunics. She just had to trust Alix's advice.

"It's like any con. Walk in confident. Look like you know where you're going."

Lena did know, had walked the route to Arion's suite many times.

The avian's didn't, already wary and nervous for all that they stood ready, which was why Alix would go with them.

Alix tipped up her page's cap, meeting Lena's gaze with a grim determination.

They nodded to each other and set off in different directions for different entrances. On principle, knights of the royal guard didn't fraternize with palace guards much.

Lena watched them until they disappeared around the corner, assuring herself that Alix was safer with them. She had to hope their mission would end up merely a tense tour of the palace grounds, no one the wiser that avians hunted the king. She had to hope she and Bel got to Arion and made him king before Ophir got to Artemian and made him a martyr.

———— ·◆·· ————

She and Bel made the training yard without incident, passing onto the palace grounds through the eastern entrance. All around, knights and soldiers trained, chatted, and sparred. The familiar buzz of activity had her wanting to pick at a thumbnail, but she kept walking, stride confident and unhurried.

Bel was a silent force beside her, his nerves and determination palpable. He matched her pace, careful not to look about like this was all a new, overwhelming sensory onslaught for him.

Lena nodded to those whose gazes she met but didn't slow, joining the loose line of guards on their way deeper into the palace to start their shift. They moved with the current, and Lena sidestepped when she could to get Bel towards the edge of the group. One stumble into him would be enough to feel the bulk of his wings.

The smooth stone of the corridor gleamed in the morning light, the blonde granite illuminated by the rows of leaded windows lining the southern walls. Lena's pulse thrummed faster as the corridor narrowed, but one foot in front of the other, only a few steps to go until—a set of six steps led up to an arched, octagonal landing, a hub of hallways and corridors. They lost most of the crowd, each knight heading off to their duties.

It was just them and a handful of other knights who ascended the back staircase. They lost two on the second level and another on the third. By the time they made it to the fourth, where all the royal apartments were, it was just her, Bel, and another pair of knights.

Dread began to pool in Lena's stomach when the other pair followed them from the hidden warren of passages for servants, staff, and soldiers out into the lavish corridor used by the royal family and palace guests.

Glittering chandeliers reflected back in the polished parquet floors, lit with tall white candles and shining crystal teardrops. Gilt scrolling curled across the silk wallpaper like ivy, ushering passerby further down the corridor, past fireplaces of marble and tile with mantels of mahogany and cherrywood. Delicate treasures decorated every mantel, putting her mother's little hoard to shame. Flower arrangements set in porcelain vases bigger than Alix perfumed the air from their recessed alcoves of windows.

Lena met the eyes of one of the other knights. The man looked back at her curiously, the beginnings of a frown lowering his brows.

"Are you lost, lady?" asked the knight.

"No. We were assigned the next shift at Prince Arion's suite."

The knights exchanged looks.

"That's our shift. Has been for months."

"Ah. There must've been a mistake, then. We'll do a check of this floor and then go see where the error occurred."

"Very good."

The knight made to start again, but his partner, a younger man barely old enough to have earned his spurs, looked Bel up and down.

"Haven't seen you before."

"Just received his reassignment," Lena said. "May as well acquaint him with the royal quarters."

The knights nodded, still frowning, but she didn't sense any suspicion. She led Bel in the opposite direction, toward Queen Ilona's apartments.

Bel's frustration prodded at her as they made a circuit of the floor, using the main corridor to pass by the other suites. She refused to hurry, nodding at the guards they passed. No one stood outside Artemian's door, meaning the king was somewhere else in the palace.

They passed a handful of others, ladies in waiting, guards, and courtiers. Lena slowed for no one but nodded courteously to everyone. Her pulse quickened with each new person who saw her and Bel.

It only took one.

Finally, she recognized the corner they were about to turn as leading to Arion's rooms.

Alone in the hallway, she slowed down just enough to whisper to Bel, "Those knights from before will be around this corner. If they're alone, we have to move fast, all at once."

"And if they're not?"

Lena chewed her cheek. "Then we find Alix and try another day. It'll look too suspicious to come back again."

Bel nodded, though his scowl told her how much he disliked that idea.

She resumed her pace as they rounded the corner. Sunlight streamed in from a window directly down the hall from her, gleaming on the breastplates of the guards. She felt their eyes train on her, though she couldn't see them through the brightness.

They stopped before the pair, turning away from the glare.

"Nothing to report," Lena said. "We'll head down to the captain's office and see about our shift. Unless you had anything that needed done?"

The knights glanced at each other. Guards were always trying to shed chores and errands off on one another.

"Well, if you're headed that way anyway, there's a—"

Lena struck the older guard with her vambrace, metal cracking against bone. The younger knight's eyes went wide before Bel was on him, engulfing him in limbs and feathers, his grunts muffled.

She shoved the stunned knight against the wall, hitting him again. Blood splattered from his nose, and he rocked to the side. Lena blocked his wobbling strike, pinning his arm behind him and wrestling him to the ground. She got her knee on his back and pushed his face into the carpet, waiting for the right color.

Just out of her sight, the sounds of struggling suddenly went quiet. She glanced over to see Bel holding up a limp guard by an arm around his neck.

It took another handful of long, torturous moments before the knight she'd pinned went utterly still. She gave it another moment before turning him over and checking his color.

A little too dark but not dangerously so.

Checking the corridor, they entered Arion's apartments and dragged the limp, unconscious knights inside. The foyer was silent, shadows deep in the tall, arched ceiling.

Lena led the way around a small table laid out with flowers in the center, pulling the knight into Arion's sitting room. Also empty, she cut strips of drape to tie the knights at the wrists, knees, and ankles. Last they tied gags around their mouths and left them on their backs.

"You're sure he's here?" Bel whispered when they made the foyer again.

"They don't guard unoccupied suites."

Ignoring her fluttering pulse, Lena went to the far door.

She slipped inside Arion's bedchamber, catching the door before it whined. Arion never got the hinge fixed, saying it was a good warning.

Bel slid in behind her and kept the door ajar as she crept further in.

The room was dark and cool, the heavy drapes on the east side still drawn. Gossamer curtains fell in soft waves over the north windows, morning light filtering in through the blue fabric to cast the chamber in somber tones. She rounded the spacious four-post bed; the velvet duvet and cotton sheets were thrown back on one side, and when Lena touched the slight depression in the bedding, it was cool.

She'd been in Arion's bedchamber before, knew there was only one other place for him to be.

Lena hung back at the corner of the bed, watching as Arion emerged from the bathing room. His golden hair was wet and slicked back from his bath, the buttons of his shirt still undone as he strode barefoot into his bedroom.

He stopped to work on the buttons.

Lena stepped forward, steps muted by the plush carpet.

For all his smiles and good nature, Arion was a warrior—his eyes snapped up from his shirt immediately, shoulders gone tense.

She met his shocked gaze, holding her ground when, after a moment that stretched with every terrified thud of her heart, he closed the distance.

Lena widened her stance to meet him.

Arion threw his arms around her, pulling her to him in a tight, desperate embrace. He buried his face in her hair and curled himself around her.

"Lena," he choked.

"Arion, I..."

He pulled back only far enough to hold her face in his hands, his eyes frantically searching—for what, she didn't know.

"What's happened? Lena, where have you been?"

Lena gently took hold of his wrists. "East. To Aeriand and Hadria."

Arion stared at her, uncomprehending, eyes gone a little wild. "You went to avian country." His throat bobbed on a swallow. "You took him back?"

"Yes. What was done to him..."

"And now you've returned." His thumbs caressed her cheeks and his gaze fell to her lips. "To me."

Lena squeezed his wrists and pulled his hands away. "No, Arion. I've come back with a message." From her pocket she produced her copy of the treaty, one of four that had all been signed by Dartegn. She held it up, in his line of sight. "This is a treaty from King Dartegn Adiiron, written and signed in his own hand. He agrees to end this war if you'll meet his terms."

Arion looked at the folded paper she held before him without taking it. Even in the dimness of the room, Lena saw the color drain from his face.

"What've you done?" he murmured.

"What I thought was right." She pressed the parchment into his hand. "This war must end, Arion. You've seen Hadria, you know what it will cost to win. Is victory worth all that blood?"

"You know my father—"

"Your father started this war. You can end it."

Arion stepped back, the treaty falling to the floor.

"Careful," he said, "before you speak treason."

"I'm far beyond treason now. My loyalties aren't with a king who'd send his people to slaughter in the name of genocide. He says he wants to make Vagora and humans safe from the avian threat—what threat? The only threat to us is the lengths to which your father will go."

She picked up the treaty from the ground. "It's not just soldiers— I've been past the northern border, Arion. I've seen the villages full of refugees. *Our* people. Forced to choose between paying for the war or feeding their families."

Lena broke the seal, unfolding the parchment so he could see the words carefully written there in precise high Vagoran.

"You know how your father's war ends. The northern army decimated. The kingdom bankrupt. Will he be satisfied then? Or will he start another to distract from his disaster?"

Arion's mouth went hard, his once warm gaze shuttered. "You want me to overthrow my father. Seize the throne."

"Yes. You're a good man, Arion."

"Good men don't kill their fathers."

"I didn't say kill him. Enough blood has been shed. I'm asking you to stop more from being killed." She pressed the paper onto Arion's chest, where she could feel his heart beating through his skin. "The avian king will recognize your claim and make peace with you. No one else needs to die. Please."

Finally, Arion took the paper. Moving to his writing desk, he held the treaty out to the light of the window, eyes quickly running over King Dartegn's terms.

"He sounds just how I'd thought," Arion muttered after a long moment.

"He's...many things."

Arion's gaze cut to her, eyes glittering like gold coins in the light from the window. "You've spoken with him."

"Yes. Him and his queen. He's a king who wants to save his people. That's more than can be said of our king."

"He's brave, I'll give him that," said Arion. "But what you both seem to forget is that king you slander is my *father*. My loyalty, my duty is to him."

"And what of your duty to your knights and soldiers? The ones who've fought this war while your father sits here safe, playing pretend in his armor?"

"You really want to stand there and preach to me about duty?" Arion growled. "You abandoned your post." *You abandoned me* is what he meant.

"All I've ever done is my duty," Lena hissed, cheeks reddening with indignation. "When you sent me home out of your own fear, I went. When I was punished for *doing my duty*, I went. I've served your father loyally my whole life and only ever been punished for it."

"Lena..."

"My honor demands I do what I think is right, Arion. Not follow orders blindly because someone wearing a crown ordered it."

"And the avian king doesn't wear a crown?" He waved the treaty at her.

"I don't answer to him. I'm not doing it for him, either. This is for

Vagora. The kingdom is more than just the king in a throne. I brought this from Hadria because I thought you'd understand."

"Understand that I need to betray my own father? I may be prince and he may be king, but he's still my father, Lena."

"I know what I'm asking of you," she said, "but we aren't our parents, Arion. We don't have to walk their paths or fight their wars."

Arion remained silent, regarding her with that expression he reserved for when he didn't want to be read. His eyes flicked over the treaty once more before he folded it back up and turned to look out the window, giving Lena his profile.

"And what if I wanted my own terms?"

"That'd be reasonable."

Arion smiled without warmth, the closest thing she'd ever seen to a sneer on his face. It almost made her sick to see.

"I couldn't take and hold the throne alone." Lena very much doubted that, but she listened as Arion said, "If I do this, I'd want you as queen."

"What?" she murmured.

"Everyone is making demands—that's mine. You'd sit beside me as my wife and queen."

"You don't mean that."

"Don't tell me what I feel." He stalked forward, eating up the small distance between them. "I've loved you for years, Lena. I came for you at Finhöln. I've spent months arguing for your pardon. Goddess, I'm considering deposing my own father if it means I get *you*."

"Arion, I can't."

He took her face between his hands again, his pupils blown wide and golden irises overbright. "I've never cared about station. I'd have married you without this—but if this is what it takes—"

Arion's gaze snapped away, over her shoulder. Lena felt the air move behind her, then the warm, solid chest of her mate at her back.

"Prince Arion," Bel clipped, tilting his head in the barest nod.

"Prince Arubel," he said, manners so engrained he addressed Bel without thinking.

Bel took off the helmet, bearing his savage face, a possessive, wrathful fire burning like blue flame in his eyes.

"We'll hear your terms—after you get your hands off her."

"She's all I want," Arion said, not letting go. "The only thing that'll make it worth the betrayal—and having the throne before I have to."

"Then consider your people instead of yourself," Bel growled, "because you won't have my mate."

Arion reared back, gaze darting between Lena and Bel. "*Him...*" he groaned, the sound as tortured as though she'd slashed through his gut. "How could you—"

"Because I wanted to," Lena said, cutting off any thought that she'd been forced or unwilling. Yes, their mating ceremony had been a political orchestration, but none of its substance, the words and promises they exchanged, had been anything but true.

"We didn't come here to fight over Lena," Bel said, "although I'm more than willing to. We came to make you king."

It took Arion a long moment to drag his gaze, heartbroken and betrayed, from Lena to Bel. "And if I refuse?" he said.

"More lives will be lost. Lena has told me and my cousin that you are a leader who values his people. I'd hoped you'd prove her right."

"Nothing after Aeriand has gone to plan," Lena said, "and even there, the casualties were so high. It'll be nothing to the lives lost to summit Hadria."

"And even then, you'll never take it," Bel said. "If you don't claim the throne, if Lena and I are killed, my cousin will bring the mountain down."

The pulse in Arion's neck jumped. "What?"

"The mines you so desperately searched for, they're real. The whole mountain is hollow with them. My cousin has always known you searched for them, and I told him exactly where to look for your diggers. Your father's plans were easy enough to figure out from what he sent me to translate."

Arion cursed. "Those stupid translations…"

"I know exactly what your father plans, and now my cousin does, too. King Dartegn will bury your whole army in a rockslide as big as the mountain herself." Lena sensed the spiteful pleasure Bel took in having this power over Arion, his human counterpart. He'd waited ten long years for this, and though he was due a much more brutal vengeance, she couldn't help the prickle of unease as he bore down on Arion, taking what revenge he could.

"You're bluffing," Arion said.

"Perhaps. But you've played politics enough to know that the best bluffs are rooted in truth. So, are you willing to risk guessing which is truth and which isn't?"

Arion glared but didn't speak.

"If we lose the northern army," Lena said, more gently than Bel, "Vagora will be left vulnerable in the south. The barbarian hordes may be able to push north of the Dyne."

"They will when the avians ally with them. So take the throne," Bel said. "I can have an avian in the air tonight, flying back to Hadria. You can save your army and your people."

"At the price of my father."

"Everyone has sacrificed for his war," Bel growled. "Why can't he be sacrificed for peace? He's killed hundreds of thousands of my people and gotten thousands of his own killed doing it—without ever leaving this city. He's a *coward*. Unfit to rule. And you know it."

Arion's face remained stony and still, but Lena didn't miss the way his eyes flashed at Bel's accusation. Of course, Arion knew his father was weak. He mitigated and buttressed and smoothed over what he could.

But the damage had grown too great.

"If not for yourself or your people, then do it for this father you love so dearly," Bel hissed. "It isn't just me and Lena who walked right into your palace. Even now, avian warriors are following your father."

Arion's eyes went wide, and Bel smiled viciously to see it. The scars of Bel's pain were stark on his face, making his words and expression ugly. She could almost feel the writhing mass of it coiling beneath his skin, his rage building as he stood inside the sanctum of those who'd caused all his grief.

"They have orders to kill him. They could be even now—but you could stop it. Take the throne. End the war. Or we'll end it for you."

"You *fucking avian bastard*," Arion growled. "We should've killed you."

"Yes, you should've." Bel bared his teeth in a savage smile. "Isn't pleasant, is it? Being threatened in your own home."

Confronted with everything that had hurt him the last ten years, Lena could see Bel's control slipping.

"Enough," she murmured, placing her hand on his chest. His heart hammered beneath her fingers, and he nearly vibrated with how hard his wings fluttered, trapped beneath layers of cloth.

"Your father doesn't deserve your loyalty," she told Arion. "He'll always be your father, I understand, but he's not just your father and you're not just his son. You have a duty, Arion."

He looked at her without light in his eyes, face haggard from the weight of bearing a crown he didn't yet wear. The turmoil swirled inside him, made his shoulders sag with the burden.

Softly, he said, "For Lena's sake, I'll give you five minutes before I call the guards."

• • ◆ • •

*G*et out! Get Bel out!

Light flashed in Lena's periphery as windows whizzed past on her left. She ran down the corridor with Bel at her back, her nerves a high, wailing whistle in her head. No, wait—from somewhere deeper in the palace, the faint blare of a horn.

"We should've killed him."

Lena shot Bel a quelling look over her shoulder. She knew he didn't mean it, that was his anger talking, but she didn't need his rage right now.

She led them down the sumptuous gilt corridors, nearly empty for all their finery, passing ladies who waited for a mere glimpse of Arion and other courtiers waiting for a chance to catch Artemian. The painted eyes of Arion's ancestors watched them from ornate frames as they took the main staircase two steps at a time.

The horn blasted again, closer this time.

Damn him, he said five minutes. They'd made sure of it, tying Arion to a bedpost. He couldn't have gotten help that quickly, even if the guards had awoken too, which meant—

"This isn't for us!"

Something else was wrong.

Alix.

From a connecting hall came running another guard, barely noticing them in his haste to catch the next turn. To the basilica.

Lena skid on the polished stone, pivoting to follow.

They heard the fighting before they saw it, the sound of steel echoing inside the grand basilica. The other guard charged inside, nearly knocking over a willowy page hurrying from the room.

"Alix!"

Alix's head swung her way, and seeing Lena and Bel sprinting for her, she waved them over frantically, her big eyes impossibly wide.

"What's happened?" Lena demanded before she'd even made it to the tall arched doorway.

"Finally found the king," Alix panted, quickly explaining how Ophir hadn't waited, just went straight for Artemian. He'd almost delivered a killing blow, but a guard pulled Artemian back just in time. "What do we do?" she asked, sounding more scared than Lena had ever heard her.

"We finish this," Bel said. He pulled his sword from its scabbard and a dagger from his belt, striding into the basilica.

Lena rushed to follow him.

Vast and impossibly tall, the basilica glowed in the light from the eastern windows overlooking the bay. Fluted columns rose higher than trees, stone fingers splayed to hold up a roof full of arches and colorful frescoes. Oil lamps larger than cauldrons hung from the ceiling by delicate chains, and scarlet rugs all led to a central aisle.

The fighting spilled across the basilica, combatants darting between columns. The avians were easy to find, their wings out and catching the light. Feathers flashed as sharp as blades, the two of them drawn into a defensive formation Lena had seen before.

At least a half-dozen palace guards jostled around them, looking for an opening.

Movement to her right caught Lena's eye, and she looked to see Artemian, flanked by four other guards, backing up toward the dais. Up four shallow steps sat the thrones. Behind them, framed by two-story windows blazing with light, hung—

A terrible sound ripped across the basilica. A wail of pain, like an animal caught in a trap, agony so acute it defied any other expression.

Her heart broke hearing Bel make that sound.

He'd seen his brother's wings, preserved in gold and hung like a hunted deer head.

For a moment, everything and everyone stopped, shocked still from the sound of Bel's grief. No one breathed, his scream taking up all the air, demanding all the empty space of the basilica.

Then he was moving.

Blades in either hand, Bel charged the king and his guards.

Lena cursed, looking between Ophir and Phaedra, defiant but pinned down, and Bel as he crashed into the wall the guards made of their bodies to meet him.

She sucked in a breath, fingers tingling as she felt the momentum shift.

She looked down at her squire, those jade eyes wide but fierce. Alix had pulled out her shortsword, holding it loose and ready, knees slightly bent, balanced on the balls of her feet.

Lena was so damn proud.

"Come on," she said, grabbing Alix's arm.

She hurried them to the south side, where a long window wall looked out over the gardens. Wrenching at the old clasp, she threw open a window.

Alix looked on in bewilderment. "What—?"

Lena grabbed her by the tunic and heaved her out the window.

Alix landed with an *oof* in the hedges several feet down. She went rolling onto the grass, cursing the whole way, and sprang up the moment she came to a stop.

"Get somewhere safe!" Lena called.

Face red, Alix ran at the hedge. "Don't you *fucking dare*—!"

Lena shut the window and locked it.

Her blade rang as she pulled it free of its sheath. Lena took one deep breath—*take the air wherever you go*—and then she ran, full on, headlong, straight into the heart of battle.

44

Bel howled.

Ten years of grief and shame, ten years of torture, abuse, and mourning—twenty-seven of loving his brother—ripped from his very soul, out his mouth, hitting the humans like a physical blow.

His sword was next, crashing on the armor they raised, their own plated limbs sacrificed to a king who'd take them and gild them and string them up like garland. He didn't hear the screams nor wet slap of flesh hitting the stone floor. He didn't feel the warm splash of blood across his face nor the gauntleted fists that struck him.

All he heard and felt and saw was his rage.

All he smelled was blood.

All he tasted was his own anguish.

Hands ripped at him, clawed at his back and chest. His wings burst free, smacking away two guards. The others rushed him, blades arching above their heads. Sparks spurt across their hands, Bel's sword catching the others in a defiant show.

He smashed his helmet into the face of one guard and slashed his dagger at the other.

More pressed him from behind, but there was someone there, guarding his back.

Lena. Mate.

He caught a glimpse of her from the corner of his eye, her face rigid and focused, braid swishing behind her. *Magnificent.*

Bel pushed forward, through more bodies. He met a guard with either arm, dagger and sword flashing, his wings beating at them, boxing their heads and catching their eyes.

The glare of gold was what Bel saw.

Behind another guard stood the human king, adorned in that stupid gold armor like he was a sun god himself. Sword held in front of him, ready for attack, Artemian edged toward a side door tucked behind the dais.

Coward.

A sword caught him in the shoulder, sending him stumbling.

Bel spun, the sound of ripping fabric loud in his ear. His shoulder stung where the blade sliced, caught between his gambeson and breastplate strap. The thin armor sagged on his chest, cut away from his shoulder.

He spun again, a swirling gale of feathers, keeping the guards away, and wrenched the broken breastplate off. He stopped suddenly, momentum carried in the breastplate as he threw it at a guard, catching him in the chest. The man *whoomphed* and crumpled.

And then there was no one else.

No one else to come save him.

Bel watched the king realize this, eyes darting around the basilica. To Lena, who battled his last two royal guards standing. To the dozen palace guards kept occupied by Ophir and Phaedra, unable to break their formation or to breakaway themselves, caught with a wing to keep them in the central aisle.

Artemian bared his teeth in a grimace and turned to flee.

Bel bounded up the dais steps, arms pumping, wings flaring. He took two running leaps across the raised platform, kicking off the thrones, and was airborne. His wings propelled him up in a high arc—then he tucked as he dove, plummeting for his target like a bird of prey.

The king spun at the last moment, catching Bel's sword, but Bel's dagger drove home.

Artemian yelped, pierced just below the pauldron, and they crashed to the stones, armor and swords clattering.

For all that he'd stood behind his guards and tried to flee, Artemian knew how to fight. Or at least, he sensed the predator above him, hungry for blood and retribution, and fought hard, knowing it was that or die.

Artemian smashed a fist into Bel's face, sending them sprawling. Bel lost his sword and grunted when his wing folded badly under them. He could feel the newly healed bone bending, could imagine all those little threads snapping until the whole thing gave.

His stomach and shoulders heaved, tossing Artemian back. The king landed hard, and then Bel was there, knocking him down again when he tried to get up. They brawled and scrabbled across the ground, reaching for weapons, hitting their opponent with fists and elbows and knees. Bel fought for the high ground, and Artemian lurched, face contorted in a wretched snarl as Bel wedged the dagger further under his armor. Artemian's long hair knotted at his neck and stuck to his face with spittle.

Bel wrenched the king's arm up and pinned it with his knee. Artemian filled his fist with Bel's feathers, yanking at his wing. He felt the tear of feathers giving but didn't care.

Bel grabbed the dagger from the king's shoulder and ripped it out. Artemian hissed, head flailing, bucking and grasping at Bel's wing.

Clenching the hilt in his fist, sticky with blood, Bel held it above the human's throat.

"Bel, no! Wait!"

An animal growl rumbled from his chest, a predator denied. Artemian squirmed and writhed beneath him as Bel looked up at the only person brave enough to deny him his revenge.

Lena stood a dozen paces away, her face and breastplate splattered with blood. A cut ran across her left cheek, and her braid had come loose at her right temple. She held her sword with one hand and reached out for him with the other.

He growled again, nostrils flaring.

"I know," she said, "I know. But if you kill him now, like this, you'll make a martyr of him."

"Don't listen to her!" screamed Ophir. "Kill the bastard!"

Lena took a step closer, her hand out, pleading, fingers splayed as if she could reach the dagger from all the way over there.

"I know you want revenge. I want you to have it, too. But it'll cost you your life, Bel, and everything we've done. Please."

So noble. She was good, all goodness, *goodness incarnate.*

He *knew* she'd ask this of him.

And he *hated* it.

He hated that he couldn't have both. He hated that she made him choose. He hated that she had to be so good and that she demanded it of him, too.

He wasn't good. Didn't want to be.

He roared, screaming until his lungs couldn't bear it, until his mouth couldn't stretch wider. He emptied his lungs and his soul, everything inside him, howling until he thought he could bring the basilica down on them—until the humans' sun goddess herself could hear him.

Echoing silence met his cry. His chest heaved, hollowed out and empty.

He loomed over Artemian, sweat and tears plinking on the man's gold cuirass.

"Do it," Artemian murmured even as he shook under Bel, "or don't you have the spine, boy?"

Bel bared his teeth. "Surviving can be worse than death," he hissed.

Quicker than Artemian or Lena could stop, Bel pinned the king's chest with his other knee and drove the dagger into it.

Through the thin gold armor.

Through the skin.

Through the first layer of muscle.

But not all the way. Not as far as he wanted to go.

"Stop," Bel shouted. "*Stop!*"

The sounds of fighting ebbed, the guards going still when they realized they'd already failed.

"Get Arion," he demanded. "NOW!"

———— ••◆•• ————

The minutes slipped by in an agonizing march, no one daring to move quickly. Lena had drawn closer but not too close, seeing the darkness in his eyes. Ophir and Phaedra worked their way to the dais, taking higher ground. Guards grabbed their wounded and pulled them further into the basilica, forming a defensive line.

They didn't get too close, but they watched.

He could see it in their eyes, that they waited for him to tire, to give up. They only needed one moment, one opening. There were more of them, so many more, ready to die for the worthless man under Bel's knee.

What they didn't understand was the depths of Bel's rage—he'd waited ten years for this; what were a few more moments? They'd crystallized his pain, gilded it, made sure it would never rust or tarnish. Gold lasted forever.

Arion burst into the basilica, an explosion of noise. A handful of knights came in behind him, wearing royal guard colors, but they didn't move to join the others.

The prince rushed forward, but Bel shook his head, making him draw up short, close to where Lena looked on warily.

"Throw it away," Bel said, eyes flicking over the sheathed sword Arion held.

Mouth a taut, angry line, Arion tossed the sword down.

"I warned you that if you didn't end this war, we would." Bel dug the dagger a little deeper, making Artemian gasp and Arion wince. "If you love your father, then take his throne and save him. The crown or his life, it's your choice."

"Fucking avian," Artemian wheezed.

Bel put more of his weight on his knee, pressing on Artemian's chest, making him breathe deeper and every single breath agony.

"I'm granting you mercy where you never gave it," Bel said through clenched teeth. "The brother of a slaughtered king. The prince of a murdered people. I should gut you from throat to cock—it's what you deserve."

He looked to Arion, awaiting an answer. He didn't miss how the cold cruelty in his voice made Lena flinch. If he let himself feel anything but his searing rage, he might've been frightened by it, too.

But Bel wasn't good and he wasn't frightened.

"If I do this, you'll spare him?" Arion said carefully.

"Yes," Bel promised, the word tearing his throat like shattered glass. "You have my word."

"It won't work," Artemian rasped. "He'll never hold the nobles in line." His lip pulled back in a sneer. "And you can't trust the word of an avian."

Bel returned the sneer with his own. Under his gilt casing, Artemian was no more than a human man. Without his crown or his guards, he was nothing, a weakling who harmed others to distract from his own mistakes. Somehow, it was more upsetting that such a man could do so much harm. All he'd been given was the opportunity, the power. And look at all he'd made of it.

Artemian was nothing, and if Bel lived past today, he'd make sure that's exactly what history remembered of him. Nothing.

"Yes or no," Bel called to Arion.

With a sharp breath, Arion said, "Yes."

Artemian threw a baleful look at Bel. "My son won't—"

"Shut up," Bel growled, twisting the dagger.

Arion moved for the dais, though his eyes remained on Bel. "I'll have him restrained. Just let him up so someone can see to him."

"No."

"He'll bleed to death."

"Then you'd better hurry."

"*End this, Arubel!*" Ophir cried.

"Bel..." Lena took a step toward him.

A hand grasped his own, nails digging in, while another wrenched at his wing. His wing base howled in pain, tendons nearly snapping.

Artemian knocked Bel's hand away to free the dagger from his shoulder. Still wet with his blood, he plunged it into Bel's side.

Bel howled, listing to the right. Artemian grabbed the dagger, twisting it before pulling it out with a spurt of blood.

Bel rolled away, missing the next strike. He got his feet under him and his wings behind him, only to see the glint of the blade coming for his face. He wouldn't be fast enough this time.

Lena collided with Artemian, taking the slice across the chest. They stumbled together across the dais steps, grappling for the dagger.

Bel staggered upright, hand clutched to his side, palm filling with blood.

The western doors to the basilica crashed open with a resounding *boom*, making the windows rattle and dust cascade off the oil lamps. The din of dozens of knights swarming inside drowned out all but Bel's thundering heart.

He watched through swimming vision as his mate fought for him, fending off Artemian's attacks, trying to disarm him while he tried to kill her.

Bel pressed his hand firmer to his side, feeling the blood ooze between his fingers and the wet, exposed flesh pulse. It was all he could do to keep his innards inside as he lowered his shoulder and charged Artemian.

45

Lena threw her weight forward, not letting Artemian topple her to the dais steps. Her grip on his wrist slid as blood dripped from the dagger down his arm.

Bel's blood.

Outrage fueled her, made her hands strike hard and vicious. She swept her leg between his and clubbed the back of his knee with her heel. Artemian grunted, staggering into Lena. His arm dropped, the flat of the dagger pressing against her face, sticky and cold.

He grabbed the strap of her breastplate, pulling her down and himself up.

She felt the air move around her, the rustle of rasping feathers so familiar now. Bel tackled Artemian, sending them staggering on the dais steps.

Artemian held on, dagger wedged in the strap buckle of her breastplate. She felt the force of his arm pushing down and the tip of the blade eek through the metal, just scratching her skin. He let go of her other shoulder to grind his elbow into Bel's side.

Bel grunted in pain, blood gushing from his wound. He didn't fend off the strikes, fighting instead to get his arms under Artemian's.

"Lena!"

Heart dropping into her stomach, she looked over her shoulder, frantically hoping she'd imagined Alix calling her.

But no, there was her scrappy little squire, rushing through a growing fray. Her dark curls bounced as she ran across the basilica, dozens of knights behind her, converging on the confused mass of guards.

Just behind strode Margot Montcaer.

Those eyes of steel moved over her and then Bel and Artemian. Her mother came in with the force of a tidal wave, sweeping everything and everyone aside. It was Alix who ran, but Margot made it to the dais at almost the same moment.

A bite of pain at her shoulder reminded Lena that a dagger still hovered at her throat.

She clawed her way up Artemian's arm, to the fist clenched round the hilt. Digging her thumb into his wrist, Lena pressed down between the tendons and twisted.

Artemian's wrist snapped.

He yowled in pain, hand going limp, and Lena knocked the dagger out of his slackening grip and away from her neck. She heard it clatter somewhere as she lurched away.

Bel took the opening, wrapping his arms around Artemian and locking his hands behind the king's head. Strung up like a scarecrow, the king's face immediately began to redden. With enough pressure, Bel could render him unconscious. Or snap his neck.

Artemian struggled for a moment, but Bel held, even as his gambeson and trou leg soaked with blood.

"Enough," Lena said, spitting out blood. She rounded on Arion, stood stock still on the dais. "Do it."

"Do what, Maddalena?" came the cool voice of Margot.

Lena grit her teeth. "Take the throne," she told her mother, giving her a defiant glare. "Artemian is unfit to rule."

Margot said nothing, just arched her brows and looked over Bel and Artemian again.

Arion looked between them, his brows knit with turmoil. He'd moved close to where she and Artemian had grappled on the steps, unsure who to help. Now, he looked on at Bel holding his father, his face gone red but his eyes glinting with angry desperation.

"Arion—you can't—" Artemian croaked.

Bel applied more pressure, his leathers crackling. Artemian gurgled, tongue spearing from his gaping mouth.

Arion's gaze met Lena's. She nodded.

He moved to the center of the dais, the thrones at his back and dozens of knights and guards before him. Gazing out over them all, Arion's shoulders squared, and Lena watched the mantle of kingship slip over them.

"This isn't what I wanted, nor how I wanted to assume the throne. But this war with the avians has gone on too long. I fought with many of you on the battlefield; I know you understand the cost of this war. The avian king has offered terms for peace. I intend to take them. My lord father—" his voice caught, jaw working to get the words out, "the king will never accept these terms. He'll never accept peace. So in the name of Vagora and all our people, I declare Artemian unfit. Who will support my claim?"

The basilica echoed with silence, every face turned to Arion in incredulity. Vagora hadn't seen a deposed monarch in over a hundred years.

Alix stepped to Lena's side, her grim face trying to hide the obvious worry. They watched the basilica full of knights and guards anxiously, and with every moment no one stepped forward to recognize Arion's claim and declare their loyalty, Lena's heart sank deeper into her chest.

It was silent so long, she began to hear the soft patter of Bel's blood dripping on the floor.

She tried to catch his gaze, to tell him to stop, to stem the bleeding, to not fucking die for this, but Bel wasn't the male staring back at her, gone to his rage. She'd seen it before, soldiers burying themselves under mental walls to preserve some of their soul as their anger and violence unleashed. Though his eyes shone bright, nothing of the male she loved was there, just a vicious determination as he held onto Artemian.

"I will support your claim."

Lena stared at her mother as she knelt before the dais. Margot kept her chin up and eyes forward, her voice resounding through the basilica as she declared, "I, Lady Margot Montcaer, swear fealty to you. I will be your shield and your sword. I pledge my loyalty and my service to you, King Arion."

Arion stared at Margot with such astonishment, he didn't notice the other knights stepping forward at first.

Those knights who'd come with him to the basilica and all those who served in his royal guard knelt before him and swore their fealty, loyalty, and service to King Arion.

Many knights of Artemian's own guard came forward next, and the palace guard, too. One by one, all but a handful of knights knelt before the new king.

He received their pledges with eyes that'd gone glassy, moved by the loyalty of all these knights.

When those loyal to Artemian had been corralled to the north wall, Arion took a long, deep breath. His gaze flitted over Lena as he turned to take the throne.

"All hail King Arion!" Margot cried.

"King Arion! King Arion!" the knights cried back, filling the basilica with their support.

Arion nodded to them, and Lena's heart ached as surely as she knew his did. It wasn't what or how he wanted, but Arion would be king. And a good one. It began with these knights, and she knew the kingdom would follow. He was beloved by so many because they saw exactly what Lena did, a king who'd care about the lives of his people.

Right now, though, there was only one life Lena cared about.

As Arion issued orders to secure the palace before word spread and to find and contain his mother Ilona, Lena carefully approached Bel.

"It's over," she told him. "Bel, you can let go now."

His nostrils flared, brows lowered in a severe frown. His eyes flicked to Arion, who stood from the throne and walked toward them.

"We did it," she whispered. "You did it. You avenged Maddok. You saved your people."

Artemian jerked in Bel's hold, teeth bared. "This won't stand—no one will—"

"Bring healers and surgeons," Arion ordered. "They've both bled too much." He carefully descended the steps, hands splayed in front of him. "I'll take my father to be held in his rooms. He'll be under guard. Just, please, let us see to him."

"I'll take him there and secure him myself," Margot said.

"Once he leaves here, what's to stop him from taking power back?" Bel said, voice rasping with overuse.

"We keep him secured until I declare my father's poor health and call on the nobles to swear loyalty. Then he'll be sent into exile."

Bel rumbled in displeasure.

Lena saw the way his body shook and how pale he'd gone. He'd lost so much blood, his left side completely drenched in red.

"Please," she begged him.

Those intense blue eyes trained on her, the pupils dilating inhumanly. He stared at her with that monstrous face, nose and lips curled back in a leonine snarl.

For a moment, she thought he'd refuse.

For a moment, she thought she'd lost him.

Then he looked to Arion and demanded, "I want my brother's wings taken down and returned to Aeriand."

"Done."

Bel grunted, then his arms fell away from Artemian. The man slumped, face gone nearly purple, but Margot and another knight rushed forward to secure him. They held the deposed king up, and for one tense moment, everyone looked on to see if those promises of loyalty were truly any good.

Margot pressed a handkerchief to Artemian's chest, stymieing the bleeding, but ignored him as he hissed promises and demands and insults at her.

Lena hurried to Bel, who staggered, unsteady on his feet. She put her shoulder under his arm and took his weight. Alix quickly handed over a clean handkerchief, and Lena pressed it into Bel's side.

He leaned into her, head lolling forward.

"Stay with me, damnit," she growled, terrified and furious with him.

"Yes, *c'vana*," he murmured just before going limp in her arms.

46

In the ensuing days, Arion first secured the palace and the pledges of everyone who lived and worked there. Pockets of discontent amongst the old council, Artemian's guards and personal secretaries, and even a few of the kitchen staff were rooted out, smoothed over, bribed, or sent away, but for the most part, the palace staff and hundreds of knights and guards took Arion's ascension less as a coup and more of an inevitability. He was always going to be their king—many had happily awaited the day and were pleased not to have to wait any longer.

His next vote of support was from his own mother.

Some had whispered behind furtive hands that the queen might rally support to her husband, all of which made Margot chuckle. When Lena arched a brow at her, Margot just grinned. "The only thing Ilona likes about Artemian is the son he gave her. She'll support Arion."

And so it was. Queen Ilona recognized her son's claim, pledged loyalty to him, and accepted her new station as the Queen Mother.

Lena didn't know the queen well, but her small smile had seemed almost relieved as she watched Ilona kiss Arion's cheek, take off her crown, and place it in her empty throne. It seemed like unnecessary ceremony between a mother and son, but the performance wasn't lost on the few dozen holdout nobles and knights gathered before the dais. All swore their loyalty and recognized Arion's claim by nightfall.

In just a few days, the palace was secured, Artemian still confined to his chambers.

In a week, all of Highclere had declared for Arion.

Thousands crowded the streets to see the new king crowned. Lena watched from the entryway of Margot's townhome as he rode down the street, redolent in brocade and embroidery. All the fabrics and colors were a rich sapphire, gold, or cream. He wore no armor, just a gold circlet round his head, not a sun god but a man.

Lena waved to him as he passed.

<hr>

Two weeks into Arion's reign, the country lords convened at the palace, finally lured away from their demesnes. Most had come when the new king called. Some had to be coerced. But all came, one way or another.

Arion had specifically asked for her presence today, which was how Lena found herself standing in a ready stance one step back and three paces left of Arion in his throne.

She'd made herself available to the new king in the tumultuous days after the coup—it was only right to help sort out the mess she'd initiated. Lena took shifts guarding Artemian's apartments, she and Alix wiling away the hours as curious courtiers skirted past his locked door. She helped her mother assign rotations of knights and guards to lock down the palace as Arion's claim solidified. She coordinated with Alix and her gang of street children to suss out how common folk had taken the supposed sudden departure and poor health of Artemian.

She did all this and more, wanting to see with her own eyes that Arion kept his promises.

Though, if she was honest, it was also to escape the crowded townhome for a few hours. Her father Sir Warrek had arrived after the first week to show his support and see his lost daughter. He'd clasped her shoulders and drawn her into a fierce embrace, eyes watering. He said nothing of their last conversation all those months ago in Lindenfaire, then or any day after.

Between him and Margot, their retinues, three avians, a squire, and the squire's revolving line of hungry friends, the townhouse was fuller than Lena had ever seen it. Margot's cook was beside himself.

The lord and lady before Arion bowed low, though their backs were stiff and expressions displeased. More than a few liege lords had been skimming from the heavy tax collection, adding to the already heavy burden borne by the common folk. Lena thought of Sonja and Garett, Nina and Lorne, and felt no pity for the scolded nobles and their reduced holdings.

She caught Alix biting back a yawn from the corner of her eye, then she was the one fighting off a yawn.

Not for the first time, she wondered why Arion asked her there today specifically.

After another disgruntled set of nobles eventually saw reason and knelt before their new king, Arion looked over his shoulder. When his eyes found Lena, he winked.

"Lord Sanson Balderak," announced the crier.

Thud went Lena's heart.

Dressed in his usual all black, Balderak swept into the basilica like a raven king. Fine curls of black rippled along his cloaked shoulders, the black threads of his quilted coat gleamed, and his black eyes glittered sharply as he took in the scene awaiting him.

He came to stop before the dais, stance and expression untroubled, but his eyes went wide upon seeing her and Alix there.

They found themselves in just the opposite tableau they'd stood in almost a year ago. Lena couldn't help the vicious pleasure she felt then, looking down at him from behind the throne.

"Your Highness," Balderak said in that rich timber he had. It was a voice that'd seduced many court ladies and terrorized countless other women back in his demesne.

"Lord Balderak. I'm glad you could finally fulfill my summons."

Balderak smiled without warmth. "I've been busy tending my affairs. It seems you've been busy as well."

"There's been much to see to with my father's abdication," Arion agreed. A little smile teased the corners of his lips, as though he enjoyed playing with this spider cornered in his web.

"Abdication," Balderak repeated, laughing once without humor. "I'm sorry to hear the king's affliction is so strong. I wish him a hasty recovery."

"He is well taken care of."

When Arion said nothing else, Balderak's gaze flicked nervously to Lena as his feet shifted ever so slightly.

"I'm here to reassert my loyalty to the crown, then?" he said.

"You are more than welcome to," said Arion, "but first, I'd like to discuss a matter with you. As my father's affairs are now mine to tend to, and seeing as you've travelled all this way, I'd be remiss not to bring up last harvest."

Lena didn't know what Arion spoke of, but she enjoyed the anxious tick in Balderak's cheek, nevertheless.

"It wasn't as bad as we'd foreseen," Balderak said carefully. "Thank Matella for that."

"Indeed, the goddess smiled on your fields. Though, if I understand correctly, it was more than the goddess's favor that saw your harvest through last season. My father aided your demesne, did he not? Paid up-front for half of all crop harvests."

"Yes," Balderak said.

"I know it's a week's travel to your holdings, my lord. You've just made the journey yourself. So I'm curious as to why not a single sheaf of wheat has made it to Highclere?"

Balderak swallowed. "I..."

"I'm also curious, my lord, about your opinion on rubies."

"Rubies, Your Highness?"

"Yes. I hear you've purchased a hoard of them for your villa on the coast. Did you really encrust even the spoons?"

Balderak opened his mouth without saying anything.

Arion leaned forward, and the gathered crowd at Balderak's back seemed to lean forward too to meet him.

"Forgive me, my lord, it's been a long few weeks and I wanted to have my fun. I'll be clear now. You have committed fraud against the crown, and this isn't the first time. You've amassed a fortune in the name of your demesne but used almost none of it for your people. I'm ordering you stripped of your lands and title, effective immediately, for payments due."

"You can't do that! You need the south, you need *me*," Balderak sneered.

"My father needed your loyalty and was willing to buy it. But I don't need it and don't want it. Loyalty from a man like you isn't worth the price." Arion nodded to one of his knights, who drew alongside Balderak. "I'm also reopening the investigation into the claims made against you by Lady Maddalena Montcaer last summer. You are charged with the abuse, torture, and rape of forty-four women in your demesne. You will be held in Highclere as the matter is investigated and your demesne given to someone worthy of it."

Balderak's jaw went slack.

Lena couldn't quite believe it, either.

She watched as Balderak tried to throw off the guard who held him, bludgeoning the knight with the stump of his forearm, encased in a capped steel vambrace. His struggles only summoned more guards. He was finally taken, wriggling like a fish on a line, from the basilica for the lower cells by no less than four guards.

"I'm going to every day of that trial," Alix muttered evilly, watching the door close on Balderak with a feline grin.

The basilica settled into stunned silence, the hundreds of gathered knights, courtiers, and nobles looking on owlishly. The pockets of nobles who'd already been dealt with shifted uneasily, no doubt disturbed by the fate of one of their own.

Perhaps once Lena might've felt guilty over the dark pleasure she took in Balderak's demise and the nobles' discomfort. But that was before it'd been her receiving punishment, the same nobles watching on with their own kind of pleasure. It was before she'd learned the world was wider than the morals she'd been fed by poets and knight's codes.

Arion let the crowd stew in their shock for another uncomfortable moment before he stood from the throne and stepped to the edge of the dais.

"I implore you not to pity or mourn a man like Balderak. His actions are unconscionable and indefensible. His crimes are extensive, and those against his own people are egregious. But his aren't the only offenses committed against the people and the crown. Those of you feeling resentful for stripped lands or lost titles, be grateful for what you still have and remember that you serve at the behest of your people and your monarch."

And with that, Arion sat back down to receive the next noble.

•◆••

Afternoon sunlight streamed into the quiet basilica, Lena and Arion the only ones left. The court had dispersed quicker than normal, no one wanting to stay and see if Arion dealt any more sentences. Lena had sent Alix on home ahead of her, the girl nearly itching to get out of her formal clothes.

Lena stood beside the throne, waiting for Arion to speak. He hadn't asked her to stay behind today, but she could sense something on the tip of his tongue.

He sat now with elbows on his spread knees and head in his hands. It'd been a long morning, and though Lena relished Balderak's fall, the parade of court issues had ground her patience down. She'd served with him long enough to know that not every day was like this, but as the afternoon stretched, she wished she'd left with Alix.

Arion took a sharp breath and scrubbed his hands over his face. Plucking the crown from his head, he hung it from the arm of the throne.

"That's one more problem dealt with," she encouraged.

"Mm. Only a thousand to go." He slumped back, cheek landing on his fist. "All of this will be for nothing if we can't decide where to exile my father. Although," he laughed ruefully, "Finhöln is free now."

"Don't send him there," Lena said, killing Arion's tired smile, "don't do that to the townspeople of Longbourne again."

Arion gazed at her thoughtfully before nodding. "All right, somewhere else then."

"Thank you. Somewhere closer, perhaps." She knew the royal family had at least one villa on a set of islands south of Highclere and several more throughout Vagora. Any of those seemed suitable.

"Yes." Arion tipped his head, resting it on the chairback, his gaze turning fond. "What a queen you'd make, Lena." His voice went low, rumbly, a tone that would've curled her toes a year ago. "I could make you a queen."

"But you couldn't make me happy. Not truly." It'd taken her a long time to consider her own contentment in her decisions, and this would be the first true test of her resolve. Perhaps, if he wasn't a prince become king, they could've built something lasting. Perhaps, if she'd let herself love him completely, she could've found happiness with him. But none of these things were true and never would be.

Lines fanned around Arion's eyes as he smiled sadly. "It was worth a try anyway." He rested his head in his hand again, a long sigh escaping him. "This would all be easier to bear if I had someone I could trust beside me."

"You do," Lena said. "Not in a wife, not yet, but there are many glad to see you on the throne and will do what they must to support you."

"Yes. But it's not quite the same, is it? My father always said that was one of the privileges of becoming king, that he could finally marry my mother."

"Ordering a woman to wed you isn't a privilege, it's an abuse of your power," Lena said, not unkindly.

Arion looked up at her in surprise.

"You're not your father," she told him. Arion was better, a good man, but he had to learn that using his power to get what he wanted, even if he meant well, had consequences. It ruined what'd been between them once already.

"No," he sighed.

They lapsed into silence once more, and though Lena longed to start the walk back to the townhouse, she knew that angle to Arion's mouth.

Finally, he said what he'd been meaning to. "I do need people I can trust, at all levels throughout the kingdom. Balderak wasn't wrong when he said I need the south. His demesne is large and rich. The people deserve a good leader who will put them first. If you want it, that demesne is yours."

Lena's breath caught. The vision of it unfolded in her mind, the improvements she could make, the people she could help. She could bring Alix and her friends south, out of the city and poverty. She could make a difference and a name for herself.

Yet...

"Thank you, Arion, but no. I'm grateful, truly, but I don't think that's what I want." Just like marrying Arion, perhaps if things were different—but Lena wasn't the knight who'd knelt before this very dais to receive her spurs, nor the one who'd fought beside Arion at Aeriand and Hadria. She wasn't even truly a knight anymore; her name had been struck from the lists.

And she had a mate to consider, one who wouldn't thrive in the south, surrounded always by humans who'd never seen one of his kind before. Lena understood now how brutal it could be to be the only one and she wouldn't do that to him again.

She didn't know what the future held for her yet, but she did know it wasn't in the south.

Arion sighed and shook his head, obviously a little frustrated with her now.

"What is it that you want, then? You know I'd give you whatever you ask."

"You don't have to give me anything, Arion. I've made my demands and you've met them."

"Still," he said. "Ask me."

Lena considered a moment. *Well, if he really wants to...* "I want this war to end. Officially. Both avians should be healthy enough to fly—we need to send word to Hadria. End it."

Arion nodded. "I can have a draft written tonight."

"Good. I also want the street children in Cheapside to be seen to immediately. There are too many orphans of the war, too many children left to survive on their own."

Arion grinned wistfully. "I knew it'd be something like that. I'll see it done. Anything else?"

"Just to go home to my mate." She didn't mean to cause Arion's wince, but there was nothing left to say. Her duties were coming to an end here, and even if Arion found other ways to try keeping her close, Lena would return to Bel. Always.

———— ••◆•• ————

She found him in the back garden, lazing in a puddle of sunlight like an overgrown cat. Stretched out in one of the ironwork chairs her mother had installed beside a latticework table, Bel's wings sat slumped out to either side of him, almost glittering in the sun. A linen shirt draped loose and unlaced from his shoulders, the neck gaping low enough to spy the top of the bandages wound round his middle. Trous hung low on his hips, and his feet were bare, legs outstretched and crossed at the ankle.

He looked so peaceful, she almost didn't want to disturb him. Her need to touch him, though, to assure herself that he was mending was too strong. She approached slow and quiet, soaking in the sight of him as surely as he soaked in the sun on his upturned face.

Lena carded her fingers through his warm hair, leaning down to kiss his head. He leaned into her touch, rumbling happily as he rested his cheek on her breast.

She dropped her head to his, burying her face in his hair and just breathing him in. With a rustle of feathers, his wing curled around her, cocooning them together.

"I missed you," he murmured, nuzzling her throat.

She'd missed him, too. Although leaving the crowded townhouse offered a little respite from the noise, she's been reluctant to leave him.

Lena would never forget the sight of his wound, the different pinks of his organs gleaming inside an angry, oozing red mouth. She'd seen far worse wounds, had suffered her own stab to the gut, but this had been *Bel*. He'd terrified her, fainting from the blood loss in the basilica, and her fear had only worsened as he lay in bed for over two days without waking.

She'd seen him cleaned, stitched up, and bandaged; no infection set in, thank Matella, and he seemed to rest comfortably. None of it comforted her through those two long nights she sat at his bedside, willing him to wake up. When he'd finally opened his eyes on that third day, Lena cried for an hour in relief.

Now, Bel seemed content to sit and let her stroke his head as she told him of her day. He rumbled in approval when he heard Balderak's fate but was quiet listening to Arion's proposals.

"I declined," she clarified, not missing how his shoulders eased. "I think he's nearly ready. A signed treaty should be ready to go to Hadria in a few days."

"That'll make Ophir happy," Bel said. No doubt he was ready to be rid of the surly older avian. Taciturn at the best of times, Ophir had been downright cantankerous while forced to rest and allow his own several wounds to heal.

Lena hummed in agreement. Softly she whispered, "It's almost done."

His wing bases shuddered. "Don't go out tomorrow."

"I'll stay," she agreed. She'd given Arion enough of her time. Although Bel was back on his feet, he still needed her. He grew stronger every day, but something inside was still shaky. Lena suspected he'd scared himself with what he'd done, how far he'd given in to his rage. It was difficult to come back from that brink and impossible to return unchanged.

He hadn't left the townhouse grounds since waking, and Lena was grateful for it. Rumors flitted about Highclere that avians had been partly responsible for Arion's sudden ascension. While it was confirmed avians had brought a treaty to the city, Arion had remained quiet to questions about the avians and where they were. Most suspected they were held somewhere in the palace, secured like Artemian. Both Lena and Margot had agreed Bel and the others would be safer out of the palace, though Lena was grateful for the discreet guard Arion provided on the house.

Soon, though, he'd need to put on boots, lace his shirt, and step outside. The treaty had to be finalized, and Bel would need to see, approve, and sign it before delivery to Dartegn. They had this one last task; she had to hope he was ready.

But first, "I'm going to go see about dinner."

Bel grumbled but eventually let her go after tipping his head back for a kiss.

She didn't like the tired circles under his eyes or how his complexion still ran pale, even in the warm sun. The days were growing long and warm yet Bel was paler than he'd been at Finhöln in the depths of winter.

A hearty dinner was in order.

With a final kiss, Lena headed for the kitchen.

She stopped short just inside the stone threshold to find Margot looking at her, cup of coffee poised on her lips. The hearty sounds and smells of dinner simmering over the stove and fresh bread baking reminded Lena of the kitchen at Finhöln, where Pol spoiled all of them with jams and tarts. Margot's cook and his young assistant were far less interested in conversing while they cooked, and Lena suspected the cook didn't overly enjoy having the mistress of the house hover about the kitchen.

Margot nodded to the side, and Lena followed her to the sideboard, out of the way of dinner preparation.

When asked what was for dinner, Margot replied with a hearty meal of meat, roasted squash, and bread, contenting Lena. When asked about her day, Lena related her news from the court, already anticipating the way Margot's mouth scrunched with disapproval to hear she'd turned down both Arion's offer of marriage and appointment.

Margot held her tongue on it for as long as she could—

approximately a minute.

"You don't want to sleep on it? Both his offers are more than generous."

"No, mother."

"The south is very fine this time of year. You'd enjoy it after that winter up north."

"No."

"But just think of all the good you could do if you were queen." The comment was half-hearted, and Lena took it for what it was, Margot's last volley. She knew her mother couldn't live with herself if she'd thought she'd left something unsaid that could change Lena's mind.

"But I'd be doing myself no good." She smiled gently. "And besides, I already have a husband. If it consoles you at all, he *is* a prince—which technically makes me an avian princess."

Margot's eyes went wide with horror before her face broke in a rueful chuckle. "That'll take getting used to."

All of it would. For all that her parents had both served in campaigns against the avians, they'd been remarkably calm about having three of them in their home. Margot had agreed it made the most strategic sense to have them here, though she did seem to avoid being alone with any of them. Misunderstandings happened frequently and tempers flared now and again. Ophir and Warrek in particular didn't get on. But they bore it because this, all of it, was bigger than any of them.

Margot's gaze flicked over Lena's shoulder, watching Bel through the kitchen door. "Your father and I never could've imagined where your path would lead."

"Neither did I," Lena admitted.

Wistfulness suffused her mother's face, something Lena had never seen before.

"What the two of you have done...it's remarkable."

The praise speared through Lena, catching her unawares and unprepared. It left her ears ringing, not sure she'd heard right.

"Seeing you with him, I realized why all that training, all those things we did, were never quite right. We wanted you to walk our path rather than your own. But that's not what you were meant to do. You were right to make your own way."

A tear escaped Lena, and she swiped at it, horrified to be crying.

The sight made Margot grimace, and she shifted uncomfortably, taking another sip of her coffee to look away from Lena mopping her eyes.

Clearing her throat, Margot said, "That's what your father and I did, made our own way. We succeeded by making our own rules and taking our own chances. But I..." She drained the cup. "I became a mother because it's what people expected. Your father and I had been married for years, so successful together. The greatest love story of the age, they called it. Of course a child would come of that. An heir to our legacy."

Margot frowned at her empty cup, and Lena wondered what the coffee grounds told her.

"I regret that I...wasn't the mother I should've been."

The deep breath Margot sucked in warbled in her chest. That her mother may have been close to her own tears shocked Lena, and the little girl inside her, the one who'd always wanted these very words, hated it and wanted to make it go away. The woman she'd become clenched her teeth against the *it's all right* and *you did what you thought best* and *but it led me here* clamoring in her chest.

Lena didn't let herself say those things, didn't let Margot escape from her discomfort too soon. When she did speak, it was to say, "It's taken me a long time to realize that I have to meet no one's expectations or standards, just my own. I can't live someone else's life, only my own. So, I have to live it the way I want to live it."

47

The soft blades of the Grass Sea swayed in the afternoon breeze, making the copse of banners snap and shine in the sun. Three of the four sides to the main tent had been left open, letting the breeze through to rustle Bel's feathers and toss his hair.

King Arion and several select councilors and knights stood around a circular table, speaking of nothing in particular. Drinks had been poured but no one seemed to be indulging as attention kept flicking to the eastern sky. Bel's did, too.

The sky was almost painfully blue here, bright and boundless. And other than the warm summer sun, it was empty.

Relief and dread welled inside him every time he looked and saw nothing.

Lena's hand slipped into the crook of his elbow. When Bel looked down at his beautiful mate, she nodded at the outside. He went with her gratefully, the humming anticipation of the human court beginning to grate on his nerves like sand.

Out in the sun, the Grass Sea extended in every direction, barely a hill or small rise to break up the unending prairie. It'd been chosen for that very reason, that neither party could hide an ambush in such a landscape. The golden grasslands had long been a boundary between Vagora and avian country, the ground here soaked with the blood of many battles long past.

Movement drew his eye, and he watched Lena tuck an errant curl behind her ear. It took the breeze only a moment to free it, and Bel grinned at her disgruntled scowl. He twisted the curl around his finger before securing it behind her ear again.

Like the sun, Bel couldn't look directly at Lena for too long without being blinded by radiance. When she'd called him into the tent they shared that morning, he'd been stunned to find her with her bare back to him, needing help with the laces of her gown. It'd taken considerable discipline to tie her inside the dress when all he'd wanted to do was let it fall from her shoulders.

It was likely the slowest a gown had ever been laced, with Bel kissing every inch of exposed skin before hiding it away under silk brocade.

She'd shooed him away after that, and he indulged her. When Lena emerged to join him a while later, he'd adored the pleased little smile she wore even more than her dress. And he *adored* her dress.

Devastating. That's how she looked. Bel would always have a fondness for the gown she wore for their mating ceremony, but to see her buttoned and laced into a gown that had been made for her, every cut and contour complementing her shape and complexion, was delicious.

A light green to match her eyes, embroidery stitched with thread a shade lighter whorled in floral designs from shoulder to hem. The neckline, Bel's favorite part, dipped past her sternum, accentuating the soft curves of her breasts and strong lines of her clavicles. It flared at her waist, skirts falling in elegant folds around her long legs. Golden pins shaped like small suns had been clasped in her curls, and she'd strung a few little feathers through her rich brown hair.

Other humans had adorned themselves with fine metals and stones, but his mate needed none of it to glitter.

Lena rubbed his arm, concern touching her face. She'd been watchful of him since they'd made camp two days ago, awaiting his cousin. In truth, Bel was still nervous, though unsure quite why, but gazing down at all her loveliness soothed some of the worries.

"Have I told you how beautiful you are?"

"Yes," she said, blushing prettily. "And I've told you how handsome you are."

Bel preened, feathers fluffing. She threw him a mock scowl, ruined by her husky laugh. The sound had Bel thinking about the laces of her dress again.

He'd barely been alone with his mate since they started this journey from Highclere over two weeks ago. Arion's retinue was numerous and slow, their camp each night crowded. He and Lena often rode ahead or on a quieter, parallel path to escape the noise. This was nothing like their travels in the north, quiet nights around the fire under the stars.

But Bel bore the annoyances if only for the delight in seeing Lena's growing excitement as they neared the agreed place in the Grass Sea.

He wanted to feel what she did, an obvious bubbling, surreal excitement that *finally* this war would be over. Her smiles were fast and wide whenever the treaty or their destination came up, and Bel let her brightness shore up his courage.

He couldn't explain the small dread he carried with him, growing every day they neared the meeting place. He resented it, too, that what he should take pride in instead caused him to stay awake long into the night, holding his mate to him while his mind whirled with intangible worry.

Perhaps it was the anticipation of seeing his cousin again, of wanting something from him he wouldn't receive. Perhaps it was the fear that he wouldn't see Dar at all, that his cousin would refuse to meet with Arion.

Perhaps he feared that Dartegn would see how deeply Bel had fallen into his own rage, consumed by it almost beyond the point of recovery. Perhaps it was that Dartegn would be proud of him for the many things Bel had done to secure this treaty, things Bel wasn't proud of—that scared him, even.

Perhaps it was the casket of gleaming rosewood he'd kept careful track of, Maddok's wings laid out carefully inside.

Perhaps it was all of these or none.

Whatever the answer, Bel's chest went tight when he spotted a growing haze on the horizon.

Soon, the east was full of soaring avians, pinpricks of color that dotted the wide blue sky. They flew in a simple formation, gliding over the human camp in a wide arc before banking to the left. At their head, a black figure arrowed through the air, leading them in a gentle, spiraling descent.

Humans wandered out from the tent to watch the avian display, nervous excitement buzzing on the breeze. It clutched Bel's throat tight as he watched the avians swirl through the sky, Dartegn's features growing more discernable by the moment.

Lena squeezed his arm. "You're unhappy," she noted.

"Just nerves," he said, covering her hand with his.

Her lips pursed, unconvinced.

"There you are!" Alix came bounding from deeper in the camp, cheeks rosy and eyes bright as she looked up at the spectacle. "Now they're just showing off."

On purpose, of course. Of all the things Dartegn had learned while serving as king, how to make a dramatic entrance certainly seemed to be his favorite.

"And where have you been?" Lena peered around Bel to arch a brow at Alix. "And what happened to your hair?"

Alix was too savvy to reach up and check how the curls on one side of her head were pressed flat. Lena had worked diligently to get Alix scrubbed and brushed for the day, but already she'd gotten blades of grass stuck in her hair, lost her fine leather jacket, and shoved her embroidered sleeves up to her elbows.

Bel and Alix exchanged significant looks.

He'd stumbled on her kissing one of the serving girls a few nights ago and beat a hasty retreat. They hadn't spoken of it, only exchanged an apologetic look and threatening scowl, respectively, and Bel wasn't about to give Alix up now. Lena still had a hard time accepting that Alix was sixteen now and thoroughly enjoyed kissing.

"Look, it's Phae!" Alix squealed, shading her eyes and pointing at a tawny-winged avian warrior.

Phaedra and other warriors came to land a little ways away, securing the position before Dartegn and Cira gracefully alighted, seamlessly going from wings to legs, sky to ground. In another impressive show, the small flock arced and landed, keeping their formation, never stopping or losing stride.

The sight of it sparked pride in Bel, to see such a display of avian strength and elegance. With Dartegn and Cira at their head, the flock cut an impressive figure, walking through the tall grasses to meet the human camp.

"Time for introductions," Lena whispered, kissing his cheek.

Bel swallowed his nerves and strode forward, Lena at his side and Alix skipping ahead. Grass shifted and rustled as Arion and a few others followed them, but Bel's attention focused on Dartegn.

Despite the warm summer day, the avian king wore his usual black attire, dressed for the chill of higher altitudes. A gold belt was tied at his waist over a black leather coat, matching the gleaming gold of the chain of office strung about his shoulders. A crown of gold feathers circled his head and flared out like open wings at the sides.

Beside him, Cira nearly shone in a resplendent silvery-blue gown, shot through with silver threads. Little diamond chips had been sewn into the skirts to catch the light, and pearls decorated her neck and sleeves. Her white-blonde hair had been gathered artfully atop her head, woven between the tines of a shining crown of silver feathers.

A soft sling crossed Cira's chest, a little body wriggling inside the warm cocoon.

Bel's worries eased a little more at the sight of the tiny avian princess. Dar wasn't likely to do anything if he'd brought his mate and child.

Alix reached the avians first, hurling herself into Phaedra. The warrior broke ranks to catch her, laughing and swinging her about.

"Look at you, small human!" Phaedra said, measuring Alix against her chest with a hand. "You haven't grown at all!"

Alix made a rude gesture, making Lena groan.

Then there was nothing to distract Bel, he and Lena met the avian king and queen in the middle of the Grass Sea, the human king and his court behind them.

For a moment, the prairie was quiet save for the gentle wind making the grasses swish.

Bel swallowed on a dry throat—and held his breath when Dartegn stepped forward.

Bel stared into his cousin's dark eyes, searching for...what, he didn't quite know. Dar looked different somehow, the lines around his eyes not so deep, the angle of his mouth not so severe. He seemed...younger, almost.

Dar reached out a hand to clasp Bel's shoulder and pull him closer. He touched his forehead to Bel's in *ashar*, a familial show of affection and greeting.

The breath rushed from Bel's lungs, hollowing out his chest to fill instead with a sharp ache. The warm weight of Dar's hand branded Bel, cauterizing some of the hurts inside that still oozed and wept.

He took a shaky breath, filling his lungs and quelling the dread he'd had for today.

"They told me you were wounded," Dartegn said quietly, only for Bel.

"Yes. But I wouldn't miss this."

Dar nodded, bumping his forehead on Bel's. "I have something for you."

He stepped back to reach behind him. An attendant presented a velvet pouch, and Dar reached inside to pull out a circlet of gold.

Maddok's crown.

Holding it reverently with his fingertips, Dar turned it in the light, letting the sun catch in the smooth polished gold. It was a simple piece, nothing to the ostentation of Dar's, with its plain band and one set of open wings decorating the front—but it was the one Maddok had worn most, the one Dar had chosen to wear often in his reign, too.

Dartegn placed it on Bel's head.

The stiff metal was cool on his skin, the decorative wings pressing into his brow. The weight of it settled on Bel, and for once, it was a weight he wanted to bear. Not oppressive or demanding, it wrapped around him in a tight, comforting embrace.

It took a moment for his throat to work. "Thank you, cousin."

"You did well, Arubel," said Dartegn.

He stepped back to his mate, who was happy to show off their wriggling baby to Lena and Alix. Bel used the moment to collect himself, unused to this feeling of...pride. To inspire it in others and himself...

It was everything to the youth he'd been, the one desperate for Maddok's approval and the one shattered and broken after his death. He'd always be fractured, broken inside, but those scars were proof that he'd survived. Every gnarl and scab was who he'd been and who he would become. He couldn't change them, only accept them and the male they'd made him.

For the first time, Bel was grateful to have survived.

Lena rejoined him, admiring the crown, and then it was time to begin.

They beckoned Arion, and the human king strode forward confidently, that radiant smile nearly as bright as the sun. That warmth and knowing it was genuine almost made Bel like Arion. Almost.

Arion extended his hand. "King Dartegn. It's good to finally meet you off the battlefield."

Dar reached out to clasp it with his own. "King Arion. I'm glad to meet you off the mountain." He presented his mate and daughter, and Bel saw the wonder in Arion's eyes to behold an avian mother and child as he took and kissed her hand.

"She's beautiful," Arion said, making Cira smile in pleasure.

"Her name means *hope* in our language," Cira said in careful, accented high Vagoran. "That is what she is to us. Hope. For her, let us make this a peace that lasts."

Moved by the queen's words, Arion gestured for them to follow him to the camp, where the final treaty awaited signing to begin their new peace.

The human and avian kings walked alongside each other through the swaying grass, already discussing a few of the finer points of the treaty.

Bel and Lena followed behind, Alix chatting easily with Phaedra as the flock entered the human camp.

As Dartegn, Cira, Arion, and their councilors began to pore over the treaty, Bel was content to stand to the side and let the politicians quibble over the details. He'd already seen and approved the treaty Arion sent on with Ophir and Phaedra back to Hadria in spring. All the important tenets would remain, though there was still much to discuss—where Artemian would ultimately live out his exile, what would be done about the villages in the north, some very close to avian borders, what trade would be established, and how to help their people heal and ensure a war such as this never happened again. He was also eager for news of Aeriand and how the rebuilding went.

All of it was important but not likely to be decided or solved today. Bel was ready to play his part when the time came.

For now, he was more than content to stand beside his strong, beautiful mate.

Bel caught Lena's eye as they looked on at the peace being crafted between their people. She grinned up at him, her excitement glittering in her eyes.

He couldn't help himself—he curled a wing around her to pull her into his side. His head dipped to capture her lips behind his feathers.

Bel felt her surprised huff of a laugh on his lips and smiled, letting the sound soak through him to his very soul.

Standing beside Lena in a new peace, in a new world—it was *everything*.

EPILOGUE

The bubbling laughter of the cadets greeted Lena and Bel as they rode into Lindenfaire on a crisp autumn afternoon. The academy had already been strung with garlands in warm hues, preparations for the harvest festival. It'd always been a favorite of Lena's growing up, and she enjoyed returning to her father's land for it every autumn.

They shared a smile, dismounting near the steps of the manor house. Lena tugged her scarf over her head, balling the knit monstrosity into her saddlebag. It'd been a gift from Alix two years ago, *"To remember me by. I know you love mine so much."* Lena blinked against the prickling in her eyes thinking of her former squire.

She couldn't cry, not when Alix would be here herself tomorrow for the festival, bringing with her a fresh class of new cadets from the poorer neighborhoods of Highclere. It was a program her father Warrek had begun in earnest almost four years ago now; their first class of children had already graduated on to squire for many good knights or apprentice with tradesmen.

And they weren't the only new additions to Lindenfaire.

Lena's eye caught on a pair of avian fledglings winging along the blue rooves and jumping between the dormers. The boys flipped and dove, zigzagging through the garlands and making her heart jump into her throat.

Bel just chuckled. "Look." He pointed with his eyes at a growing group of girl cadets cheering them on.

Lena rolled her eyes. "Oh."

As part of the peace Arion and Dartegn negotiated, it was decided that staying so separate could never bring about a lasting peace—treaties had been brokered before between humans and avians, none of them spanning more than a few generations. This, they hoped, was the solution. Integrate the young ones, teach them how others lived.

Cira herself had come to deliver the first group of avian youths to Lindenfaire three years ago. She'd inspected Lindenfaire from top to bottom with a chubby, toddling Elia balanced on her hip, offering gentle suggestions and comments in that way she had. Warrek was hanging on her every word within an hour.

Several avian families stayed with their fledglings through the training, living on the grounds and working various jobs or teaching classes to the cadets. Lena and Bel had stayed on at Lindenfaire that first tenuous year, smoothing ruffled feathers and shoring up support, until Lena accepted her current post.

When the position of governor of the north had been created two years ago, Lena had happily accepted the opportunity. Vagora had a nominal authority over the northern townships at best after a year of negotiation between the crown and village representatives. They wouldn't accept a lord or lady but agreed to an appointed governorship, though Lena was still sometimes called Lady Northland.

She and Bel spent their winters and springs in the north, travelling between towns, offering aid and counsel when needed, securing the crown funds needed for projects, and keeping the southern trade routes open and safe.

They'd taken a home in the largest village on the Fish River, close to Nina and Lorne's Riverbend Inn. It was a modest affair compared to Lindenfaire, built by a man with more money than sense who'd since abandoned it and the north, but Lena loved it. The comfortable sitting room in the front, now full of plush chairs and cushions for Bel to read and nap in, the large washroom at the back with a copper tub, and the spacious bedroom on the second floor overlooking the river all made the home perfect to Lena. There were more rooms than they knew what to do with, but Lena liked having the additional space for when Alix or anyone else visited.

They spent the summer and part of autumn travelling—to Aeriand to see Dar, Cira, and growing Elia, to Highclere if needed by Arion, and of course here to Lindenfaire—yet when they returned north in the late autumn, it felt like coming home.

Ambassador delegations were swapped between Highclere and Aeriand, accustoming the different kinds to each other. Lena and Bel had both been approached about positions at either court, and one day, she hoped to take the offer. Right now, though, she was enjoying travelling with her mate—and having him and their home all to herself.

She looked forward to returning before the first snows came as well as the salmon run when they melted in spring.

The boys swooped and banked, making Lena chuckle at their antics. "I don't miss being a cadet."

"You mean you never made a fool of yourself trying to impress a boy?" Bel teased.

"Well," she drawled, "I did break a boy out of prison once. My mother was appalled."

She laughed and darted away when he went to nab her, but she let him catch her around the other side of Yvain. The warhorse huffed in that long-suffering way of his, unamused now by their banter.

Bel caught her around the waist and enfolded her in his wings, blocking the sight of him palming her backside from all the innocent eyes.

"He was *very* impressed," Bel rumbled, kissing her in little nips and pecks.

She'd be annoyed with him, kissing her in front of her father's house yet not kissing her *enough*, but she couldn't muster it. Not when she adored this playful side of her mate so much. Not when she lived for his smiles and his laughter and every new joy he got to experience.

In the first years of the peace, she and Bel had gone where they were most needed, but Lena had tried to find places along the way to delight him. They'd visited the Wailing Cliffs along the southern coast after a month in Highclere, where the trade winds buffeted the craggy rocks so fiercely, a person could sometimes lean over the edge and not fall. Bel loved it, catching the ferocious updraft in his wings and gliding on the currents. She'd spent the afternoon braiding grass and watching him whoop and dive and swirl—not unlike the avian boys did just then. She'd been impressed, too. Whenever they were called to Highclere, they made a point to visit so Bel could experience being airborne.

They'd visited the eastern sea, where Bel said mermaids had once lounged on the rocks. They didn't find mermaids but did see the long-legged birds Bel had been fascinated by. A handful of shells now decorated their mantel at home.

Lena's favorite was still the hot lakes of Visalia, actually not too far from Lindenfaire. Soaking in the thermal pools had eased years of tension from her shoulders—as had Bel's roaming hands. They'd made their own heat in the pool, indulging until their fingers and toes went white and wrinkly.

We should go again soon, Lena thought, before they had to return north again and beat the snows. She liked that idea very much as she tried to coax Bel into giving her the deeper kiss she wanted.

A chorus of giggles and snickers caught Lena's ears. Blushing, she pulled away to find another gaggle of cadets grinning and whispering behind their hands as they watched the headmaster's daughter get kissed on the manor steps.

Lena cleared her throat. "He hasn't spotted us yet, let's go in through the kitchens."

Bel just smirked. "You know he's going to have a list of candidates for you no matter what."

Lena was less worried about a list and more an actual gauntlet of possible squire candidates awaiting her in the great hall. Both Warrek and Margot had been pushing her to choose another squire, and if her father had his way, she'd be leaving with one after the harvest festival. Hells, so would Bel.

"*Alix was knighted almost two years ago,*" they said. "*It's time to take on another,*" they insisted. "*Your new position will attract many good candidates, no matter that you aren't technically a knight still,*" her mother said. "*Though of course we could fix that, get your name registered again. Arion would surely...*"

But Lena argued that no, she was still learning the nuances of her post and travelling too much to devote the time it took to training a squire properly and enjoying her time with Bel too much and and and...

And...she missed Alix. None of the squires paraded before her whenever her mother or father got the chance were quite right.

She'd take on another when she was ready. And after she'd seen Alix and heard all about her latest adventure and which court lady she'd seduced now.

Lena grabbed her reins and led them around to the stables, where two older cadets saw to Yvain and Ruan. Taking her hand and the lead, Bel strode for the wide kitchen door, thrown open to let in the afternoon sunshine.

Warm, delectable smells wafted to them even steps away, making Lena's stomach grumble and mouth water. Both knew exactly what sweet, buttery things awaited them inside.

Lena and Bel stepped into the expansive stone kitchen to find it full of young cadets.

It was an orderly place, every pot and drying sprig of herbs hung just where it belonged, the center chopping block clean of crumbs, and all the dishes stacked neatly in the army of cabinets lining the walls. The two enormous ovens always burned bright with delicious-smelling things, and that's where the cadets congregated, watching as Pol pulled out a fresh batch of sticky buns.

Pol couldn't hear the appreciative groans, but he smiled at the children gathered round him, wagging his finger and signing, *Wait.*

Lena watched in delight as the cadets signed back, *Yes, wait. Thank you, Master Pol.*

The dozen or so cadets, and Lena and Bel, watched raptly as Pol carefully placed the pan of sticky buns on a cooling rack. As they waited for the steam to clear, Pol led them in a popular rhyme, the children singing loudly and off-key as they signed the words along with Pol.

The sight was sweeter than the sticky buns. Pol cut each in half, revealing the warm cream center, and sent each cadet off with a half.

It left two whole buns for Lena and Bel, who he waved over after the cadets signed *thank you* and rushed from the kitchen before they could be caught eating before dinner.

Pol held his arms out for Bel, who was quick to embrace him. Bel touched his forehead to Pol's in *ashar* then hugged him tight in arms and wings. When Pol finally leaned back, he patted Bel's face, eyes gleaming with happy tears.

Just in time for dinner, as always, Pol signed.

And miss one of your meals? Never, Bel teased.

Pol turned to embrace Lena next, happiness radiating from his rosy cheeks.

It's good to have the two of you haunting my kitchen again.

One of the first places she and Bel had travelled in that first year of peace was Finhöln. It'd been surreal for Lena to trek up the mountains again, to pass through the town of Longbourne and up the switchbacking path to the crumbling castle. She couldn't imagine what it was like for Bel.

They'd found the portcullis raised as always and the bailey empty. It took them a while to work through the castle, Bel stopping to stare at all the familiar places and sights, a contemplative look etched across his face. Lena had stood beside him silently as they picked their way down to the kitchen, avoiding crumbling rafters and loose floorboards.

With almost everything gone, the castle seemed to finally be succumbing to its disrepair and the harsh northern winters.

But it wasn't entirely empty.

Pol had jumped nearly a foot when he saw them, even though Bel had tried to catch his eye and not surprise him. Bel and Pol had wept upon seeing each other again and stayed up long into the night speaking with their hands. When Lena had come down in the morning, she'd found them sound asleep at the table, one of Bel's wings curled around himself, the other draped over Pol's shoulders.

It'd taken a few days of convincing, but when Lena and Bel left Finhöln, they'd taken Pol with them. Though he'd never liked the man, Bel gave the same offer to Malthus, Pol's older brother and steward of Finhöln. Lena was relieved when the surly man declined, told his brother to take care, bid them farewell, and shut the door to his home in Longbourne.

It'd been difficult for Pol at first, who'd never been off the mountain. The journey south to Lindenfaire had been hard on him, overwhelming his senses. The first weeks at the academy had been so too, all the people rushing about. But once he'd found the kitchen, Pol thrived.

The children soon discovered that the way to get the best spoonful of stew or an extra roll was to learn his signing. Even Warrek had endeavored to learn, not to be left out of a good portion. He told Pol he could have whatever he asked, so long as he stayed on as cook forever.

Lena and Bel tucked into their sticky buns as Pol regaled them with the dramas of the academy. In such a short time, Pol had become invested in the cadets and their lives; he extolled their triumphs animatedly, hands a flurry of movement as he described their antics and adventures.

After a mug of Pol's special lavender tea, Lena decided it was time to find her father and face whatever he planned for their arrival. She kissed Bel's cheek and squeezed Pol's shoulder, leaving them to their silent chat.

She found Warrek in the great hall, herding a half-dozen older cadets into some kind of formation.

Oh no.

He saw her before she could creep up the stairs.

"Lena! There you are!" he boomed merrily, catching her up in a tight hug.

Warrek had never been effusive in his affection before, but after

Lena had returned from the wilderness and Hadria, she'd yet to meet her father without receiving an embrace.

She liked it, she just wasn't used to it, even years later.

"Come and meet some of our top students, all graduating soon with honors!"

<hr>

It was almost a half-hour before Lena could extricate herself, and in that time and her checking the rooms she and Bel took when they were here, she discovered she'd lost her mate.

Sent him along to get dinner ready, Pol told her. *He's always been useless in the kitchen.*

The sky glowed with waning light, struck through with pinks and lilacs in the coming dusk before Lena finally found him in the library.

He'd made himself comfortable in one of the plush wingback chairs her father so loved, a book open in his lap.

So much of his time at Finhöln had been tied up in books that Lena hadn't realized at first how much Bel enjoyed reading. Along with Pol, they'd packed up all his books and folios from his little library to bring with them to Lindenfaire. He hadn't lingered in the room that'd once been his, packing the books quickly but refusing to leave them behind.

He also enjoyed lounging in the sun, as he did now in the last shafts of sunlight streaming in from the window behind him. A corona of light outlined his golden head and cast him in warm hues, from his bronzed wings to the gold, healthy tone of his skin.

Sometimes she just looked at him, struck by how beautiful he was. *And he's mine.*

"I've read the same sentence three times already waiting for you to come in," he said without lifting his head.

She huffed a laugh, strolling into the library, ready when he reached out and tugged her into his lap.

Lena made herself comfortable against his wide, warm chest but was careful to angle her boots away from the fabric. Her father had forgiven the treason and avian husband—but ruining the wingback, never.

"What are you reading?"

Lena hummed happily seeing her own copy of a favorite set of fairy tales.

"I'd like to start my own library at home," he said, thumbing through the pages.

"That would be perfect." Bookshelves had been built into the walls of one of the back rooms, another ambition of the man who'd built their home. "We can take yours back with us."

He grinned at that. "It'll make a good start. I'll have Alix help me filch more from the archives in Highclere."

Lena bit her cheek, trying not to take the bait. The books and documents Bel had in mind were likely avian and therefore not Vagora's to keep—Arion would also probably hand over anything Bel wanted if he asked.

"You two are a prince and a knight of the realm. You don't steal."

His grin grew wider. She'd taken the bait.

"I'll even add to it," she said, tracing the vellum binding. "This is one of mine. One of my favorites."

"I thought it might be." He flipped through the pages until he found the beautifully illuminated frontispiece of a green dragon circling round a knight.

"I love Sir Yvain and the Green Knight."

"I know," he said fondly. He ran his finger over the shiny foil painted on the dragon's scales, a thoughtful look in his eyes. It was ruined by the mischievous grin he couldn't quite keep from the corners of his mouth. "Growing up, did you see yourself as Sir Yvain or the green dragon?"

"Sir Yvain." *Obviously.*

"But isn't that a little too obvious? You have more than a little dragon in you."

"If you want to be the Sir Yvain of the two of us, just say it."

They quibbled over who would be Yvain and who would be the green dragon for longer than strictly necessary. It reminded Lena of the early days of her attraction to Bel, when they'd sparred in the cold great hall of Finhöln, trading jabs and significant looks. He ribbed her to get a rise, and she enjoyed letting him circle her, stalwart against his attempts.

"We could both be Yvain."

"The story doesn't work with *two* knights."

Lena snorted. "Well, our story has no knights, so..."

"Now you're just fishing for compliments," Bel grumbled and pulled her higher up his chest. He set the book aside to wrap her up in both arms. "You're a knight through and through, Maddalena Montcaer Adiiron. When those ballads rhyme about all the goodness of knights, they're talking about you."

"Bel..." She squirmed in his lap, but he held her captive to his praise. "Goodness incarnate."

Her blush burned her cheeks and ears—he'd called her that many times before, usually when they both wore far fewer clothes.

"And you're *mine*," he said, nuzzling at her temple. "I love you, *c'vana*. My green dragon."

Her laugh turned into a moan as his *ashita* turned into kissing. He finally gave her the kiss she'd wanted earlier, deep and warm and engulfing. Like she could drown in him, in this life they were building, and never come up.

They were going to be late to dinner at this rate, but Lena didn't much care. She let her mate kiss her and praise her, blushing at the words even if he'd told her a thousand times before. She let him love her and adore her, every single part. And she let him make her happy.

But what was even more precious was that he let her do all this for him in return. He let her inside, let her see and touch the male he was underneath his quietness, his humor, his hurts. She saw his scars for what they were and kissed every one she found, even those Bel didn't see himself.

She loved him for all that he was and would be. Not a name, not a title, not a cause. Just Bel. Always.

Author's Note

You guys. I'm still in disbelief this book is done. Haven has taken me a long time to write; it's lived rent-free in my head and I'm thrilled to finally be sharing it with you now!

I wanted to thank everyone for being so patient with me on getting this book written and published. The pandemic hit us all hard, and it was so awesome watching many writers use their new free time to write write write. That wasn't me, unfortunately. My 2021 in particular was crappy, and I wrote absolutely nothing. But I set myself the goal of finally starting and hopefully finishing Haven—y'all had waited long enough and Bel and Lena needed their story told!

I hope you enjoyed where our noble lady knight and broody winged prince went and ended up. It was such a joy to return to these two and their world. The first chunk of the book was a bit hard to write, though. We've all been on a trip with people we love but after a while we want to smother them if they chew too loud one more time! I felt just as lost in that forest as they were, but once we started exploring the world, I really saw where they were going. And Chapter 10. Ohh man do I love Chapter 10. You may be able to tell, I never wanted the fluffy chapters to end!

I loved getting to explore the avian world, and it was so fun thinking about all the little twitches and flaps wings would make to show emotion! I hope you liked all the new avian characters as much as I loved writing them! Cira eluded me until right when it was time to introduce her. Then she fell into place. I loved writing her and Phaedra—it was awesome to have a bit of a girl group going!

Their world is at a new beginning, and I don't think I'll be leaving it entirely! Lena and Bel's story has been wrapped up, but there are definitely some possible plots rattling around in my noggin. This world isn't done with me, so I'm not done with it! Stay tuned!

If you enjoyed Haven, please consider leaving a review! Reviews and recs make the indie author world go round, they're so important!

Thank you for reading! –S. E.

Acknowledgements

I'd also like to take a moment to thank some of the people who made this book possible!

First and foremost is you, the reader. I've had so many people who loved Aerie reach out asking about the second book. It was the motivation I needed to finally get this book started.

A huge thank you to Jeanne and Mita, my amazing beta readers. I trust Jeanne inherently and she knows Lena and Bel almost better than I do. You're always right, Jeanne! And Mita, thank you so much for taking this on and providing such insightful, excellent suggestions! I so appreciate it!

Thank you to Leah, my awesome PA, who helped me go from hobbyist to big girl author with my own website and everything.

I'm also so grateful to my amazing ARC team! This was my first ARC group and everyone was so lovely. I loved getting to work with all of you.

And I have to mention too the amazing artists who have helped bring this duet to life. A huge thank you to Beth Gilbert, the stunningly talented artist who illustrated the covers. They're so gorgeous! I also want to thank Jeannine, Alex, Linda, Andrea, and more, you're all so amazing and I'm so grateful for the care you've taken with my book babies!

If you'd like to stay in touch, come on over to socials and say hi! I'm around on most platforms as se.wendel.author, and I'm most active on Instagram. Come check it out to find out about what I'm working on, get some reading recommendations, and get spammed with pictures of my cat. What's not to love?

You can also check out all my books, commissioned art, and book merch shop on my author website (www.sewendelauthor.com)! Lots of good stuff over there!

I've also started up a monthly newsletter. You can subscribe on my website to keep up with me and my news.

OTHER WORKS

A Time of War and Demons (House of the Rising Sun, Book 1), fantasy romance novel

Aerie (Broken Wings Duet, Book 1), fantasy romance novel
Haven (Broken Wings Duet, Book 2), fantasy romance novel

Stone Hearts (War of the Underhill, Book 0), historical monster/fantasy romance novella
Heartsong (War of the Underhill, Book 1), monster/paranormal romance novel, February 2026
Heartsworn (War of the Underhill, Book 2), monster/paranormal romance novel, October 2026

Halfling (Monstrous World, Book 1), monster/fantasy romance novel
Ironling (Monstrous World, Book 2), monster/fantasy romance novel
Sweetling (Monstrous World, Book 3), fae/fantasy romance novel
Faeling (Monstrous World, Book 4), monster/fae/fantasy romance novel
Changelings (Monstrous World, Book 5), monster/fantasy romance novella collection, Autumn 2025 + Spring 2026
Foundling (Monstrous World, Book 6), monster/fae/fantasy romance, Summer 2026

ABOUT THE AUTHOR

S.E. is a California native who grew up with animals; her ginger tabby is her current writing partner and lets her know when it's time to take a break (by laying on her keyboard). She graduated from the University of California, Davis with a master's in creative writing and uses all her available time to build worlds, characters, and their stories. She enjoys animal rescue shows, almost everything in Trader Joe's, and all the beautiful landscapes of California.